THE VERDANT CAGE

Jess Lourey writes about secrets. A bestselling author twice shortlisted for the Edgar Award and winner of the ITW Thriller, Minnesota Book and Anthony Awards, her work spans genres. From nail-biting mysteries to action and adventure, from young adult to book club fiction, Jess dives headfirst into it all. Her books have been translated into more than a dozen languages and enjoyed by over a million readers across the globe.

Jess lives in Minneapolis, MN, with a rotating batch of foster kittens (and the occasional puppy, but those goobers are a lot of work) and is a TEDx presenter who shares the vulnerable story of her journey to writing for all.

Visit **jesslourey.com** for updates, access to her newsletter and more information on her VIP reader group.

THE VERDANT CAGE

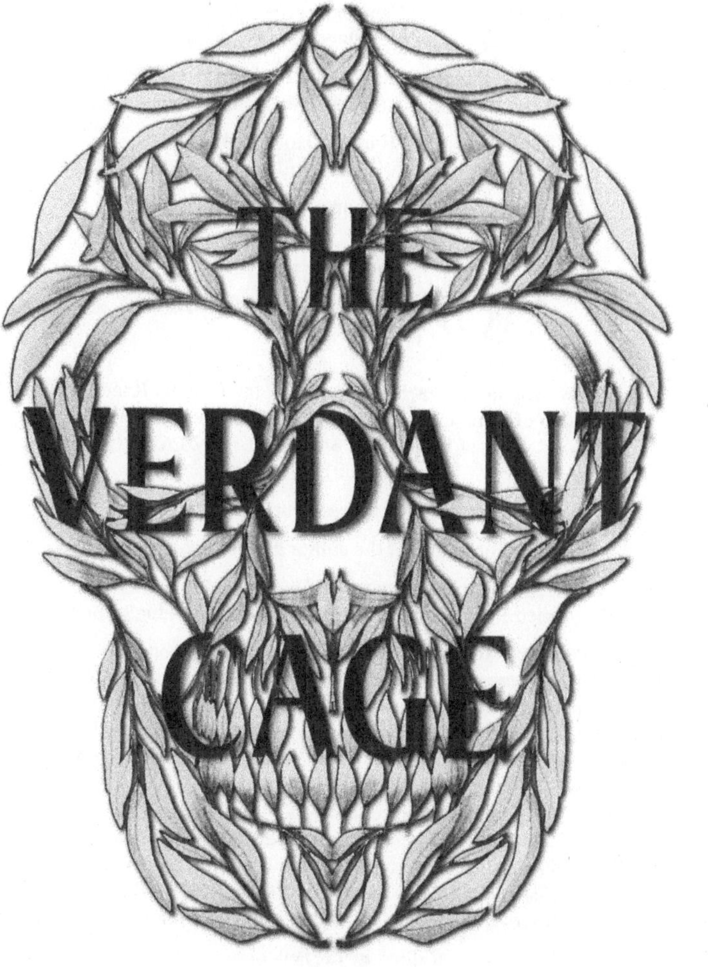

JESS LOUREY

PENGUIN MICHAEL JOSEPH

UK | USA | Canada | Ireland | Australia
India | New Zealand | South Africa

Penguin Michael Joseph is part of the Penguin Random House group of companies whose addresses can be found at global.penguinrandomhouse.com

Penguin Random House UK,
One Embassy Gardens, 8 Viaduct Gardens, London SW11 7BW

penguin.co.uk

Published by Penguin Michael Joseph, part of the Penguin Random House group of companies, in association with Mayhem Books,
part of Entangled Publishing LLC 2026
001

Copyright © Jess Lourey, 2026

The moral right of the author has been asserted

The Mayhem Books name and logo are trademarks of
Entangled Publishing LLC and are used here under licence

Penguin Random House values and supports copyright. Copyright fuels creativity, encourages diverse voices, promotes freedom of expression and supports a vibrant culture. Thank you for purchasing an authorized edition of this book and for respecting intellectual property laws by not reproducing, scanning or distributing any part of it by any means without permission. You are supporting authors and enabling Penguin Random House to continue to publish books for everyone. No part of this book may be used or reproduced in any manner for the purpose of training artificial intelligence technologies or systems. In accordance with Article 4(3) of the DSM Directive 2019/790, Penguin Random House expressly reserves this work from the text and data mining exception

Edited by Liz Pelletier
Original map illustration by Elizabeth Turner Stokes
Map images by KhWutthiphong/Shutterstock
Interior design by Britt Marczak
Interior images by KhWutthiphong/Shutterstock and kariiika/GettyImages

Printed and bound in Great Britain by Clays Ltd, Elcograf S.p.A.

The authorized representative in the EEA is Penguin Random House Ireland,
Morrison Chambers, 32 Nassau Street, Dublin D02 YH68

A CIP catalogue record for this book is available from the British Library

HARDBACK ISBN: 978-1-911-75300-1
TRADE PAPERBACK ISBN: 978-1-911-75301-8

Penguin Random House is committed to a sustainable future for our business, our readers and our planet. This book is made from Forest Stewardship Council® certified paper

ALSO BY JESS LOUREY

TRUE-CRIME-INSPIRED THRILLERS

Unspeakable Things
Bloodline
Litani
The Quarry Girls
The Crying Killer

REED AND STEINBECK THRILLERS

"Catch Her in a Lie" (Short Story)
The Taken Ones
The Reaping
The Laughing Dead

SALEM'S CIPHER THRILLERS

Salem's Cipher
Mercy's Chase
"The Adventure of the First Problem" (Short Story)

GOTHIC THRILLERS

The Blackthorn Women
Twice in a Blue Moon (Novella)

THE MURDER BY MONTH ROMCOM MYSTERIES

May Day
June Bug
Knee High by the Fourth of July
August Moon
September Mourn
October Fest
November Hunt
December Dread
January Thaw
February Fever
March of Crimes
April Fools
Monday Is Murder (Novella)
"Death by Potato Salad" (Short Story)

CHILDREN'S BOOKS

Leave My Book Alone! (Starring Claudette, a Dragon with Control Issues)

NONFICTION

Rewrite Your Life: Discover Your Truth Through the Healing Power of Fiction

Better than Gin: A Coloring Book for Writers

To Zoë and Xander, my fierce hearts

NOAH'S VALLEY

LIMESTONE CAVES

WESTERN POST

EDEN'S GATE

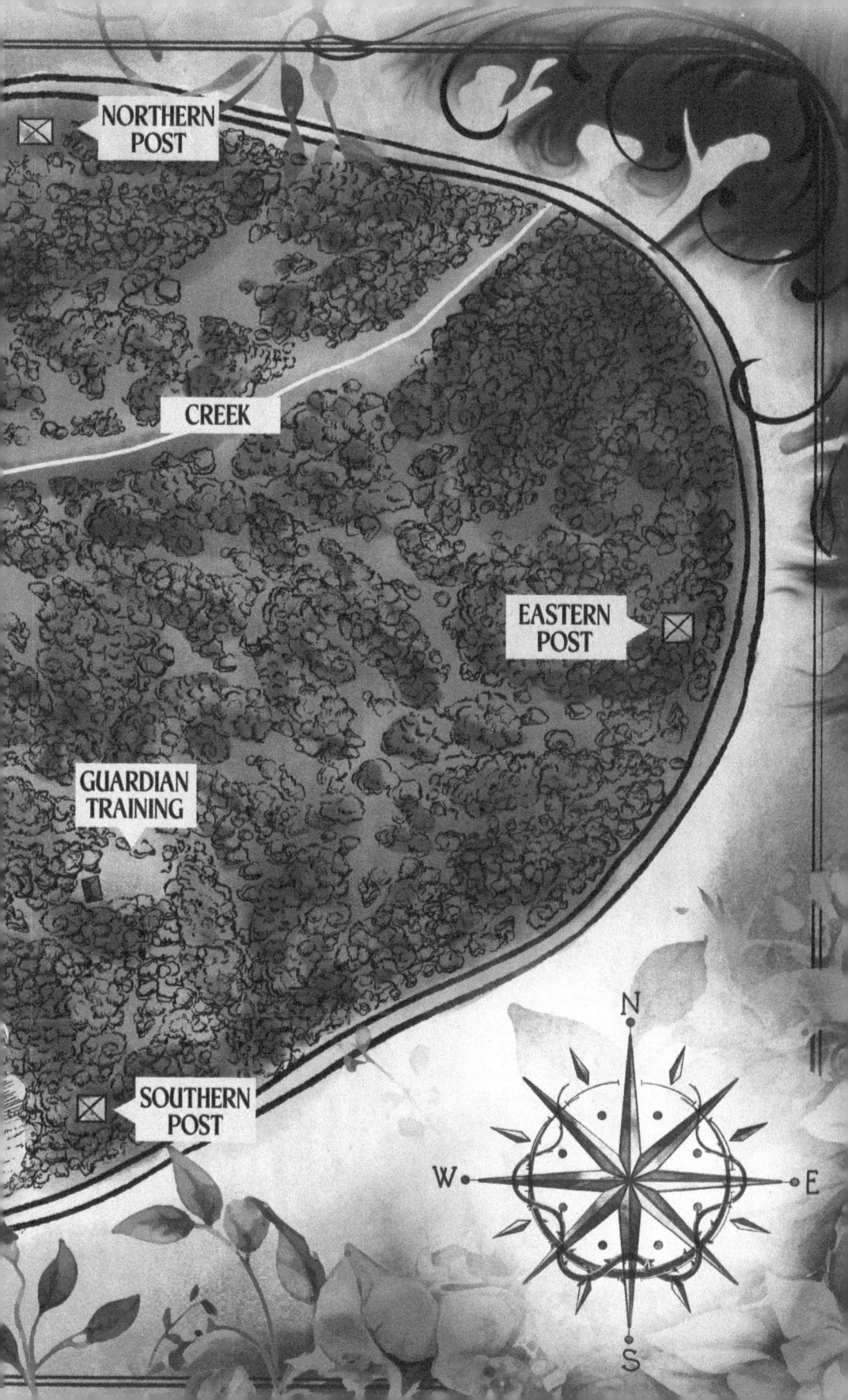

The Verdant Cage is an atmospheric dystopian thriller. As such, the story features scenes that might not be suitable for all readers, including violent and threatening situations, physical harm, death including death of family, and coercive power structures. Readers sensitive to these elements should take note before entering Noah's Valley.

Down in Noah's Valley

a children's lullaby

Peace in the Valley, under the skies,
We follow the rules here, nobody cries.
Out past the border, shadows do fall,
But here we're protected, safe in the Wall.

So sleep, my darling, don't you be scared,
The Wall made us whole, and our order repaired.

The monsters outside, great do they grow,
But inside the Valley, our candles still glow.
The beasts Beyond may yearn to tear us apart,
But you're safe in the Wall, you're safe in my heart.

So sleep, my darling, don't you be scared,
The Wall made us whole, and our order repaired.

We live by the Wall, Water, Soil, and Sun.
In Noah's Valley, each to a House yet one.
So sing me a story, dear, I'm down on my knees,
Praying to Heaven, bring me back, please.

So sleep, my darling, don't you be scared,
The Wall made us whole, love, and so we were spared.

1

Red signifies life.
Blossoms. Berries. Blood.

That's why everyone in the Valley will be wearing it today, almost four hundred bodies draped in crimson. They'll gather in the village square like a bounty waiting to be plucked, red and ripe and silent.

And all of them will be staring at me.

The thought makes me shudder.

I should get to the square myself, but I'm starving for a few minutes of peace before my whole life changes. I duck into the Apothecary greenhouse and breathe in the humid, dirt-scented air, gliding my fingers over the wild hops trellised against the wall. They're one of our more useful plants. Too bad they want to take over the world. Though it pains me, I grab my iron shears and snip off the graspers so the heart of the plant can thrive.

Sometimes you have to cut off a part to save the whole, I tell myself before moving on to the echinacea. I repot a shoot, trying to quiet my nerves. I wish I could stay here, postponing today's gathering forever. The blooming valerian looks as if it'd be willing to help me hatch an escape plan. *Thanks for the offer, Val.*

I'm startled when the back door swings open. My hand finds the tincture in my pocket, fingers curling around the little vial.

Thankfully, I don't think Jonas notices.

He's wearing red. Of course. We all are.

"Time," he says.

I nod and rinse my hands, stealing one last look at the rows of medicinal plants I've nurtured all my life—St. John's wort, black cohosh, wild bergamot, mint, the echinacea and hops. Seeing how they thrive, I allow myself a moment to imagine I might rise to today's occasion. I could walk into the crowd with my head held high, feeling proud and ready, couldn't I? I swallow a gummy lump as I pass by Jonas onto the cobblestones, shivering when the crisp breeze kisses my cheek.

"Nervous?" he asks, falling into step beside me.

I pinch the web of flesh between my pointer finger and thumb, a self-calming trick. "More like nauseous."

Jonas's smile falters.

Oh no. Nothing upsets my twin. If he's distressed now, it can only mean that every worry I've had about today is real. Dread pitches my stomach with such force that I have to lean against the nearest cottage for support. I press my forehead to the cool plaster as the scents of lavender and beeswax wash over me. Fresh candles? I notice the neat row of tapers cooling on the Candlemaker's windowsill. Each is the same height as the next, except for one that's a quarter-inch taller. I itch to shorten it. Cire must've been distracted, perhaps by another villager at his door.

Probably asking for blessing candles, I think. *Everyone wants extra protection these days.* My belly churns again.

"You should try not to vomit," Jonas suggests.

He and I have the same wavy brown hair. Duplicates of Mom's light-beige complexion. Two copies of our dad's broad nose, though neither of us inherited his heterochromatic eyes. My brother wears our shared features with an easy charm, though. He loves talking, laughing, people. Jonas is a jar of sunshine, whereas I'm more like...a well-made poultice. I don't begrudge him his carefree manner. In fact, I'm thankful for it, grateful he didn't end up a chronic worrier like me.

But then, Jonas didn't see what I saw twelve years ago.

"Solid advice," I say, straightening. The sound of the ornamental bells in my hair reminds me of a mosquito's whine. "Thanks a million."

My red gown tightens around me. I tug at the collar and take as deep a breath as the lacing allows. Forcing my mind to settle, I exhale and lift my eyes. All around, the unbroken white Wall soars to hold up a cloud-studded sky. I try to draw on it for strength, just as Gran taught me, but end up pinching the skin between my thumb and pointer finger again. It's a bad habit that annoys my mother all day and a night. She says it makes me look like I don't know what I'm doing.

"She's not here," Jonas says, reading my mind.

"Right."

My whole House should be walking with me, all of us strolling past the neatly swept stoops of Noah's Valley, gliding beneath the puffs of chimney smoke and golden autumn foliage, crossing the cobblestoned streets. But at the Council of Elders' request, the other Apothecaries gathered early at the village square. Mom's been there since lunchtime, along with our aunt and uncle, watching for signs of the Vex. That leaves Gran back at the cottage, skipping today's festivities for the only reason allowed—she's dying. Grief blooms in my chest.

I slide a hand into my pocket, touching the tiny medicine bottle to distract myself. It's a good thing the others aren't here, really. It would be difficult to leave the vial at Horace's cottage without at least one of them noticing.

"You ready to get moving?" Jonas asks, knocking the side of the Candlemaker's cottage and pulling me out of my reverie. He should be in the village center with the other Apothecaries, but he sneaked away so I wouldn't have to make this walk alone. Since their early attendance was technically a request, it isn't a rule broken. That'll be how Jonas sees it, at least.

"Not remotely," I respond.

"Good," he whoops and pulls me forward.

I laugh and nearly trip over the hem of my crimson gown. I'm usually sure-footed, but I've never worn a dress. With my hair done fancy and my beaded shoes slap-tapping against the cobblestones, I feel like a painted goat. I long for my simple Apothecary linens, the smell of crushed herbs, the steady, predictable rhythm of the mortar and pestle.

Normally, my morning begins with the bell. Three gongs. Outside, the village hums to life. The Cobblers' and Coopers' hammers sing as Bakers pull loaves from clay ovens (when we're lucky enough to have fresh bread). Farmers lead horses into the fields, Weavers tighten their looms, all of it thanks to the blessed Wall that encircles our community. For five generations it's kept us safe, and all that time we've lived in harmony because Noah's Valley runs like clockwork.

Usually.

Today, the gears are off.

At least I have a few more minutes with just Jonas and me, I think as he leads me to the village center. Of all the things I'll lose today, it's no longer living with my sibling that saddens me most.

"Is everything okay?" I ask him. "I mean, besides what's about to happen at the square. You seemed off back at the cottage just now."

His expression immediately shutters, that same ill ease returning. "I'm fine," he says.

Without slowing, I reach for his hand. I know he spent the morning with his friend. Maybe that's the problem. "Did you and Simon fight?"

"No, we got along fine." His expression grows pinched. "I saw something I wish I hadn't, that's all." He glances over at me. "In their vault."

My hand flies to my throat. Just when I thought I'd worried about everything worth worrying about. An Apothecary in the

Record Keeper basement is a major infraction. I glance around to make sure no one's overheard him, but of course they're all waiting for me in the village center. "Tell me you're only teasing and you didn't really go into the vault," I plead.

Something painful flits across his face. "Shoot, Rose," he says. "It seemed like good fun at the time."

I can hear the musicians warming up ahead. I need to know the extent of his violation lickety-split if I'm going to protect him from the fallout. "Today I'm allowed to ask for anything," I say, squeezing the medicine bottle in my pocket. "Your gift to me will be to tell me what you saw, and whatever it was better have been worth breaking the law."

He shrugs, almost to himself. "Rules that never yield belong to tinctures, not people, Rose."

"Jonas!" My blood pressure rises, heating my cheeks.

I know I'm a hypocrite for scolding him on this front, but I couldn't bear it if my twin was caught and whipped. We never used to have whippings in the Valley, but we never used to have the Vex or animal attacks, either. Those recent tragedies have cost us arable land, a precious commodity given our finite acreage. With that loss came new measures: food rationing, more frequent Harvests, the whipping posts, citizens seventy and older no longer receiving medical intervention.

The last one is why I smuggle the vial.

Jonas shakes his head as we turn onto Horace's street, the shortest path to the square. "Forget I said anything," he says. "I should've kept my mouth shut on today of all days."

"It's too late for that," I say firmly. "What'd you see?"

He grimaces. "If there's a creature more stubborn than you, I hope never to meet it." He side-eyes me for a moment, then groans. "Okay, Rosie. Like I said, it was in the Record Keeper vault." His eyebrows meet in worry. "I know I wasn't supposed to go down there, but I was dying to. I told Simon I wanted to see inside and that it was the least he could do for me today. You know, because I'm your brother." He tosses me a sad smile. "And I'm gonna miss you."

"Me too, Jackrabbit." I haven't used his childhood nickname in years, but if not today, when?

"Simon finally relented," he continues.

The Teacher cottage—Horace's—comes into view.

Jonas's voice grows pained, but he never slows his stride. "But I wish I'd listened to him and never gone in..."

My pulse quickens. "Get to the point, Jonas."

He glances around nervously again, even though absolutely every villager but Gran awaits us in the square. I allow myself to fall half a step behind him. In my pocket, I grip the vial.

"It was about our people," he says. He takes a deep breath. "Those of us inside the Wall."

I reach out my arm, stretching mid-stride, and plink the little miracle in the crack of my former Teacher's windowsill. Digitalis extract—a tincture distilled from foxglove—for elderly Horace's failing heart. Relief washes over me at a job discreetly done. It lasts only until I hear my brother's next words.

"We're not what you think, Rose."

I grab his arm, desperate to hear the rest, but of course he waited until the last possible moment. We've reached the square. String instruments swell at the crowd's first sight of me, drums joining in rhythm. I fight to breathe through the sudden, crushing weight on my chest as hundreds of eager, almost hungry faces turn toward us. Their clothing burns like fire against the emerald sprawl known as Eden's Gate, the section of the impassable Wall that serves as the backdrop for all our ceremonies.

I can smell the savory chicken pies cooking in the Bakers' outdoor oven, a rich gravy scent blending with the sweetness of apple bread. We'll feast today. I should be drooling—it's been mostly mealworm porridge and cricket flour biscuits for weeks—but nerves have frozen my gut.

Jonas hugs me quickly, anxiously, and whispers, "I'll tell you everything later." Then he slips into the milling crowd, leaving me to walk the final leg of my journey alone, as tradition demands. I want to race after him, ask him what he means, but when I realize the community's eyes are trained on me, a lifetime of conditioning kicks in.

I have a sacred duty, and it begins today.

I am to become a wife. A Guardian. A peg sliding into its perfectly assigned hole.

I try to swallow, but my mouth is too dry.

I glance up at the Wall to draw strength. Vines crisscross its stone surface, their leaves swaying in the autumn breeze, deep greens starting to purple at the edges. Nowhere is the Wall more beautiful than Eden's Gate, but something's off...

A chill runs down my spine as I realize what it is.

The Harvest basket is down.

It's propped against the Gate and looking for all the Soil in the Valley like the gaping mouth of a predator, not that I'd ever voice anything so disrespectful. But it shouldn't be down. Only two ceremonies call for the basket, and a wedding isn't one of them. Maybe it's down for servicing?

My gaze travels to the grand wooden stage in front of the Gate. It's where Gryphon and I will soon be married. The thought makes me dizzy, so I drag my eyes instead to the enormous stone chapel directly opposite. The two structures anchor our village square like sentinels.

Move, Rose, I tell myself. *The sooner you start, the sooner this is over.*

I don't make it ten feet before I'm distracted by a shadow hugging the chapel wall to my left. Baby hairs shoot up at the base of my neck, but whatever I think I see disappears in a blink. Gran's the only one with Council permission to stay home today. If someone truly is hiding back there, it's a whippable offense.

Who'd risk that?

I realize I've stopped moving, brow furrowed as I stare toward the chapel. The entire Valley is watching me. I want to unzip myself and step out of my skin. Thankfully, a village girl scurries forward, drawing everyone's attention.

She offers me a dozen breathtaking roses.

I've never seen my namesake up close before, and I'm momentarily enchanted by the riot of deep scarlet, each flower unfolding like layered velvet. Their scent is thick and heady, a swirl of honeyed spice and damp earth so captivating that I almost miss the row of needle-sharp thorns.

As I accept the bouquet, I see the child was not so lucky.

I recognize her as Agnes of the Beekeeper House, no more than six years old. A barbed thorn is embedded in her palm, blood beading its edges. She's trying to act like it doesn't bother her, perhaps hoping I won't notice, but my world has already narrowed to the two of us. I set the roses beside me so I can press on the edges of the puncture, forcing out a fresh stream of blood, and with it, the thorn's jagged tip. She whimpers but allows my ministrations, a proper child of the Valley.

Her blood, once flowing, is reluctant to stop, so I grab the only accessible cloth—a chunk of my ribboned hem, embroidered with Valley symbols over many late nights to ensure that my marriage is blessed with good luck and healthy children. Ah, well. Every Apothecary knows the urgent eclipses the eventual. I wrap the fabric around Agnes's wound. She hops up and shyly kisses my cheek before disappearing into the crowd. Mother will surely scold me for holding up the wedding ceremony, but I'm still an Apothecary, at least until I'm married.

I grab my bouquet and hurry forward just as the band switches to "The Groom's Ballad." This is the villagers' cue to part like water.

Revealing my betrothed.

Dressed in his wedding red, Gryphon Tzu is painfully handsome. Golden-brown skin, shining black hair, onyx-dark eyes above a strong nose, generous, soft-looking lips that make my cheeks blaze. My childhood best friend—until we fell out—is now my groom, assigned to me only after my original betrothed was honored with a Harvest.

Gryphon's cold stare makes it clear he's just as unhappy about the match as I am.

I tug a lock of hair over the plum-size birthmark above my right eye and hurry forward, trying to focus on all the reasons I have to be grateful. I am a citizen of Noah's Valley. One of the privileged few. As the world outside began to fall, our Founders gathered the best and brightest and built this paradise. They gave us limestone caves, freshwater springs, and dense forests. Planted crops, built insect farms and apiaries, and stocked creeks with trout and wild rice. They filled our barns with livestock and provided textbooks, medicines, and tools for their descendants.

They also built the Harvest basket that glides up our Wall at Eden's Gate, plus a handful of sustainable machines: a waterwheel for plumbing, solar-powered lights, geothermal heating, an icehouse to preserve meat. Our wise ancestors created the Houses we'd need to sustain our paradise, from the Engineers to the Carpenters to my own—for a few more minutes, at least—Apothecary House.

To honor our Founders, we live by their creed: mandatory attendance at ceremonies, chapel, and school; humane labor laws; arranged betrothals and House assignments; and once a month, we Harvest the one to preserve resources for the many.

I'm so very lucky to do my part.

That's what I'm reminding myself as I walk across the square toward Gryphon, where he waits in front of the stage, though the distance feels endless. When I reach the halfway point, "The Groom's Ballad" becomes "The Walk to the Wall," thunderous and demanding.

Get on with this, it prods me, the drums pounding in time with my heart.

There's no elegance as I hurry forward, but there is speed. I smooth my dress and feel something hard, like an acorn, in my pocket. Startled, I reach in, half expecting to find the vial of digitalis extract somehow still inside. Instead, I glance into the beady eyes of a tiny, wooden rabbit. It's a perfect replica of Lucky Bunny, a character from our favorite bedtime story. Lucky Bunny always got out of the worst scrapes, no matter what.

Jonas must have snuck me this on the walk here.

And just like that, I find my courage.

I tuck the toy back into my pocket, feeling such warmth that it's all I can do not to find my brother and bundle him into a hug in front of the crowd. He would've made a wonderful toymaker, if such a profession existed in the Valley. My eyes widen as I realize I've just thought heresy, and this time directly at Jonas!

I am *not* myself today.

The music is still ringing out as Aunt Florence and Uncle Richard appear at the end of the bridal path to stand beside Gryphon. Aunt Florence is blinking back happy tears, and my uncle's chest is so puffed up with pride that I worry he'll pop his burgundy vest's deer-bone buttons. The thought of no longer working alongside them hurts like a physical pain, but in honor of their obvious love for me, I decide to stop feeling like a thumb wearing a dress and stand tall.

You're a proper Valley bride, I tell myself. *Act like it.*

I adjust my posture and lengthen my stride, managing to keep my gaze unwavering, though I'm desperate to catch a glimpse of Jonas. He should be standing with my aunt and uncle. Come to think of it, where's Mom? She wouldn't miss this, no matter what duties called. She'd want to ensure I did everything perfectly. The two of them must be traveling through the crowd, as the Council requested, searching for signs of the Vex. We haven't seen symptoms in weeks—not since the Apothecaries quarantined the outbreak zone—but until we know the cause of the illness, we can't let our guard down.

The villagers staring at me all seem bright-eyed, no evidence of the bluish-gray pallor associated with the illness, though I spot a girl from the Waste Management House with a lacy rash near her left ear, and is that clubbing I see on the fingers of the Insect Farmer? I'll have to examine them both later.

No, I remind myself, *I'll tell Jonas to look at them.* The correction makes me numb inside, yet my feet keep moving. The drums are so noisy. Have they always been this deafening? Like a nail being driven into my skull. Suddenly, three beats louder than the rest startle me.

POUND POUND POUND

Then, to my great relief, the music stops.

The respite lasts a second before a scream pierces the air, sharp and shrill. The villagers to my right gasp and stagger back, like they're trying to peel away from something awful. I hurry toward the commotion, shedding nerves as my brain organizes for a potential emergency. Likely Mom and Jonas will reach the patient first, but are their medical kits appropriately stocked? I wish I'd been allowed to keep mine.

But instead of parting to reveal a collapsed villager, the crowd has drawn back from my brother, who stands alone, fifty yards away. My joy at locating him immediately morphs to horror as I spot the medical utility blade in his hands, his head swiveling in alarm.

Then my spine locks.

At his feet, sprawled upon the ground, lies our mother.

In an ever-widening pool of blood.

2

I drop the roses, their claret color mirroring the pool growing beneath my mother. I can't think, can barely breathe, but my body knows what to do. I leap forward, already deciding which supplies I'll call for—suturing, certainly, and antiseptic, and will there be time for a painkiller?—when a grip clamps down on my arm. I'm startled to see Tomris of the Guardian House holding me, her face implacable.

"Let me go! I'm an Apothecary," I yell. If this weren't an emergency, I wouldn't dare direct a Guardian, but there's no time for hesitation. I twist, trying to pull free, but it's no use. Tomris is a solid wall of muscle.

My gaze lurches back to Jonas. The bloodless silver blade trembles in his grip. Hand-forged, three-and-a-half inches long, the knife is one of our basic first aid supplies. He must have pulled it out to defend Mom. It falls from his hand as he drops to his knees to examine her for the source of bleeding—it's what I would do—but two Guardians yank him to his feet before he can touch her.

"Let him treat her!" I cry. I can't look away from the horror unfolding in front of me. Mom's chest, every part of her, is still. What was the last thing I said to her this morning? Something short-tempered, I'm sure, something about how I didn't mind that she wouldn't be walking with me to my wedding. I moan.

Augustus of the Plumber House stands just behind her body, his expression stark and unreadable. I thought he and Mom were friendly. Why isn't he doing anything? Why isn't anyone rushing to help?

I plead with Tomris again. "Let me go!"

There's an angry noise several feet to my left. I turn to see Gryphon, brow furrowed, also in the grip of fellow Guardians. He looks like he was trying to reach Jonas and my mother, but his comrades held him back.

"Quiet!"

The booming voice silences us all. Jarek Tzu, Gryphon's father and head of the Council, pushes through the crowd toward my mother. On him, Gryphon's strong nose appears beaklike, his night-colored eyes too deep-set. Still, Jarek has an undeniably commanding presence. Like a hawk among songbirds. Surely, he'll wake us all up from this nightmare. He's the face of the system, after all.

Jarek kneels when he reaches my mother, careful to avoid the blood, and places surprisingly gentle fingers against the side of her throat. He appears stricken as he stands, the three lines tattooed below his left eye stark against his sudden paleness. "She's gone."

My legs give out and I drop to the ground, the movement catching Tomris by surprise. Her hands loosen. I take advantage of that to scramble forward, reaching my mother's side before anyone can stop me.

It's true. Her pulse is still.

"No, no, no," I whisper, tasting ash. This can't be real. Her beautiful blue eyes stare half-open, the warmth already leaving them. Her chest is bloody, the darkest concentration in three distinct spots forming a rough triangle, exactly as if she'd been stabbed. *But Jonas's knife was clean. I saw it.* I drag my gaze to my brother, held fast by two Guardians.

His eyes are saucers. His mouth opens and closes.

"Jonas," I demand. "What happened?"

"Jonas Allgood has done something unspeakable!" Jarek roars, cutting off Jonas's answer. Then he turns to the crowd, his voice slicing clean through their wildfire exclamations. "He has committed murder!"

The word hits like a physical blow. *Murder.* I know it only from history class, a reference to a horrible act from the Before Times. There is no murder in the Valley.

"No!" I yell as Tomris and another Guardian begin dragging me away. "Jonas would never hurt our mother! He was trying to help her!" But the villagers are already buzzing, whispers echoing like a dark wind through the red-clad crowd.

"Jonas's knife!" I scream. "It was clean! He must have been trying to protect her."

A number of my fellow villagers glance toward the blade, which is now swimming in a pool of blood. Was I the only one who noticed the pristine metal before it dropped?

Jonas's face is a mask of anguish. "Rose, I didn't mean—"

"Stop your manipulation!" Jarek commands, cutting him off again. "The entire village just witnessed you standing over your thrice-stabbed mother, holding a knife. What can this be but murder? A most unnatural act, worthy of a most unprecedented consequence."

Eyes flit to Eden's Gate, the basket resting against it like a threat. The word "Harvest" slithers through the crowd, soft and low, passed from tongue to tongue. First as a question, then growing in conviction. *But that can't be.* The Harvest isn't a punishment. It's our greatest honor. I feel sick all over again. Jarek cocks his head as if to listen to the people, his expression lurching from grief to fury until he, too, looks at the basket leaning against Eden's Gate, his jaw muscle tightening.

Cold fear licks my spine. *They wouldn't. By the Wall...what is happening?*

Jarek taps his chin, a terrible mimicry of thoughtfulness as he addresses the crowd. "You think that to safeguard the whole, Jonas should act as this month's early Harvest?" His voice carries to the farthest corners of the square. "That could be a reasonable suggestion." He considers some more. "More than reasonable, in fact. An honor a killer hardly deserves."

Every cell in my body is screaming. I stare around in wild hope. These people know and love Jonas. He's one of the town clowns, a boy of good cheer, and he's an Apothecary. Of course he'd run to help an injured person. But to my horror, instead of speaking up, Valley citizens begin to turn their backs. One by one, they face away and kneel, every villager but those of the Priest House. They alone remain standing, eyes pinned on Jarek.

My bones turn to water. When everyone else is looking away—even Aunt Florence and Uncle Richard have their backs to us, their necks white with shock—Jarek nods curtly. "The village has spoken." He turns to my brother. "Your people have chosen to favor you despite your actions." He flicks his hand at his son. "Man the Harvest basket."

Whatever fight momentarily animated Gryphon has vanished. He moves woodenly, turning toward the Wall like a puppet on strings. Jarek strides to the stage, the place I was supposed to be exchanging vows with Gryphon at this very moment. He climbs onto it. Once he towers over us all, he signals a Guardian to lead Jonas to the basket and another to haul me before him.

My sweet brother stumbles toward his fate with his shoulders squared and chin lifted, a lamb dressed as a lion. Something is building in my throat, clawing to escape. I open my mouth, but no sound comes out.

"May the Wall protect us," Jarek declares, beaming down at me. There's something predatory in his eyes. "You look so much like your mother, you know," he says, as if he and I are alone rather than standing in front of the entire village, my mom freshly murdered, my brother about to ascend to the Heavens. "I'm so grateful you were selected for my House."

My twin. My sibling. He of the crooked smile and duck-fuzz hair, so friendly that he was elected May Day prince every school year from kindergarten on, and not a single boy could find it in himself to be jealous. My best friend—my only friend, really—and the kindest human I know.

He's about to be Harvested.

The worrying, the rule-following. It wasn't enough.

"No!" I croak. The awfulness of it scrapes my veins, turning everything orange and raw. "Jonas is my brother," I say to Jarek upon the stage. My voice cracks, but it carries. "We're Apothecaries."

Jarek knows this, of course he knows this, but I can't stop speaking even though my brain is slippery with terror. "We cannot be chosen for Harvest. My—" I start to say "my mother" and choke it down. "I'm sorry, but all Apothecaries are exempt. As much of an honor as it is, the needs of treating another potential outbreak require our exclusion. You can find a different way to punish Jonas, can't you?" I know my twin didn't kill our mother, but I'll say anything to keep his feet on the ground, even if that means invoking the very whipping posts I was recently keen to save him from. Once everyone's calmed down, we'll figure out what really happened.

Jarek tips his head and beaks out his lips, the picture of sympathy. "You should be grateful your community has shown Jonas such compassion. Murder surely overrides your House's Harvest exemption," he says. "And in any case, the Council has recently updated that directive. Our food shortage demands it."

An icy wave of powerlessness threatens to drown me. *But those were the rules. They can't be changed at the drop of a hat.*

Then something unexpected happens.

I feel a snap inside, and a burst of hot rage blooms in my chest.

I want to hurt Jarek. Obedient, quiet Rose wants to rip out his throat.

No. That's not me. With the exception of smuggling medicine

to the elderly, I always do what I'm told. I try to push down the fury, but it won't budge.

Jarek continues unaware. "Gryphon, guide Jonas to his ultimate sacrifice, won't you?"

Gryphon's exquisite face is a tight mask. His arms flex, and I have the wild hope that he'll refuse, that he'll reveal this as a cruel prank, a leftover from our childhood days, back when he and I used to be inseparable. But instead, he glides forward with the grace of a mountain lion. He takes Jonas from his handlers and begins to guide him toward the Wall.

They've almost reached the basket when Jonas breaks free of Gryphon's grasp. Jarek cries out in rage as my brother races toward me, slipping between the other Guardians.

"Rose," he whispers when he reaches my side. The whites of his eyes are visible all around his pupils. He smells of iron and fear as he embraces me, speaking close to my ear. "I didn't kill her. You'll find the truth in the Record Keeper cottage. Go to the vault. But protect yourself, Rose. Let no one see you there."

I sob and cling to him. Protect myself? All I've ever wanted was to keep him safe. Too soon, Gryphon wrenches him from me, and the hatred I had for Jarek finds a new home. I will never forgive Gryphon for leading my brother to his death.

"Remember, we're not what we seem!" Jonas cries.

The air feels liquid, everything around me moving too quickly and too slowly all at once. I rush forward, but strong arms circle my waist. If only I'd been better. More obedient. If I'd never snuck medication to the aged—

I look to the villagers for help. "This is not the law!" I yell.

Simon, who Jonas said allowed him into the vault this morning, is as white as whey. He melts into the crowd. His father, David, stares toward the cast on his newly broken foot, a tear trickling down his cheek.

Not one person will meet my eyes.

Desperate, I launch myself toward Eden's Gate, but new hands have latched onto me. They belong to Leonidas Khan, a Guardian and Gryphon's closest friend. I could sooner break free from the grave. Still, I twist and snarl, biting at his hands.

They don't loosen.

"Jackrabbit!" I wail. *Please, if there's any prayer left to say—*

Gryphon and Jonas reach the Harvest basket. For the first time in my memory, Guardians stand on either side of the welded metal cage with their swords at the ready.

"I love you!" I sob. I mean to send it as protection, as a plea, as a promise.

My twin steps into the basket. He wobbles, steadies himself. Then he tosses me a gruesome imitation of a smile, so wide and sad that it slices me in two.

I love you, too, he mouths.

He's still meeting my gaze when Gryphon whispers something in his ear. Jonas's eyes go wide, and then the basket is closed. Someone has brought Jarek the tablet that operates it. He jabs its screen, and the basket begins to hover up the Wall, lifting my cowlicked brother toward the sky.

From where no one has ever returned.

3

"Your hair is so beautiful," Artemisia Tzu tells me as she removes the ribbons and bells. Gryphon's mother is tall, muscled, her dark hair shorn close to her skull. Her expression is more thoughtful than kind. She continues. "It looks like you might have natural curls, though it's hard to know. I've never seen you wear it down. That lack of vanity will serve you well as a Guardian."

Noah's Valley requires balance in everything. Because my household had more members than Gryphon's on the morning of my wedding, I am required to move into his, adopting their trade, surname, and family as my own, leaving my former life behind.

My hair ribbons fall to the floor like shed skin. I suppose, in a way, they are.

"I *told* Jarek we should have announced the change to the Harvest rules before somebody had a chance to commit a terrible crime. It just happened so fast, what with your brother stabbing Henrietta."

Swish. Another ribbon glides to the floor. *Tinkle*, a merry bell.

Artemisia (*Misia, please*, she insisted, though I'd not said a word) and I are on the bottom level of the Tzus' two-story home. This floor is one large room, half of it occupied by a kitchen furnished with a plain oak table and six chairs, a wood stove, a sink, and cupboards. The opposite side contains a river rock fireplace with an unadorned pine mantel, two sturdy rocking chairs, and a sofa upholstered with heavy fabric gone gray with age. A single shelf holds the books of their trade; I see no other texts, no paintings or tapestries, no touch of warmth. The four walls are exposed wood, lacking even the lime whitewash most villagers use to brighten their interiors.

I sit in one of the kitchen chairs facing a full-length mirror, an item only the Tailor House should possess. Misia stands behind me. I do not look at my reflection because I know I'll see my brother's face staring back. A shudder grips me every few seconds.

Jonas.

"But I'm sure the bride would've liked to know about the rule change in advance. Your brother has ascended Eden's Gate to Heaven, but a surprise is a surprise, even when it's good news," she's saying. "No wonder you decided to postpone the wedding. We'll hold a small ceremony in a few days. Tack it right on with somebody else's."

Did I postpone the wedding? It felt more like I died.

As the basket holding Jonas glided up and away, my momentary fury gave way to a despair so profound, I was sure my heart would stop. My tongue didn't work, my legs wouldn't move. Jarek ordered my mother's immediate funeral, and her body was bundled into cloth and sent up the moment the empty basket that'd held Jonas returned.

Sojourner, the Head Priest, rushed over to embrace me after she was finished leading the brief funeral ceremony. She whispered nonsense words into my ear, surely meant to soothe. *What you inherit is not who you are. What you choose to carry—that's what makes you.*

I didn't move.

I don't know how much time passed, just that eventually the sound of whispers tunneled through my shock. Jarek and Misia materialized, blocking Eden's Gate from view. Jarek appeared offended, Misia annoyed. They angled their heads together, studying me like I was something they'd discovered on the bottom of their shoes. Finally, they seemed to reach some agreement, and Misia strode over and pinched the tender skin beneath my arm. It was enough to rouse me, enough for her to get me moving and lead me back here.

To Gryphon's house.

My new home.

How alone had Jonas felt as he glided toward the top of the Wall, staring down at the only home he'd ever known? How scared was he during his final moments? According to Valley doctrine, those chosen for Harvest are embraced by the Sun, their spirits released into eternal peace as a reward for their selflessness. Yet we sometimes hear screams when those Harvested reach the top, screams and hideous crunching noises, but not always.

Not always.

My brother is dead.

My chest constricts. Not my twin. I can't take that, can't survive if it's true, so I find my way back to the only two thoughts with the power to keep me afloat: finding out who really killed my mother, and making Jarek and Gryphon suffer like I have. I dig for that flash of fury I felt back at the Wall, vowing to dedicate every bit of life I have left to making them experience the raw agony I now feel. It goes against my training, this thirst for revenge, against who I thought I was, but connecting with it is all that keeps the darkness at bay.

The Tzus will know ruin like they've never felt, and it will come from inside their home.

A distant part of me wonders where Gryphon and Jarek went after they condemned Jonas to die. They didn't walk back with us. I remember only Misia, clutching the tablet in one arm and shepherding me with the other.

The sunforsaken piece of tech lies nearby, resting on the kitchen table. It's a flat, matte-black slab the size of an encyclopedia, though much thinner. Its surface is smooth, seamless, and it looks strangely heavy for its size, clearly built to endure. No visible buttons, just a faint grid of etchings near one edge. On impulse, I touch its face the same way I've seen Jarek—and the Record Keeper, back when their House was still responsible for the Harvests—do. It feels cool and slick beneath my fingers, but nothing happens.

"It's out of juice." Misia makes a tsking sound. "I'm afraid much of our Before Times technology is on its last legs. The tablet used to sunpower in an hour, or at least that's what the Record Keeper says. Now it can sometimes take days. Plus, it needs a charge after every couple uses."

That means nothing to me, except that in addition to operating the basket, the tablet decides who will be Harvested. It draws on census data from the Record Keeper to calculate births, deaths, food stores, family size, and projected crops, then runs a formula to pick the lucky citizen. An unexpected thought drops into my head. If the tablet dies completely, will there be no more scheduled Harvests? Could I destroy it, saving other families this suffering?

My brain immediately blanches at the heretical thought. Grief is tainting my mind. Harvests are our greatest honor. Without them, our population would have grown too large and many of those inside our Wall-limited paradise would have starved or had to resort to violence to stay alive.

Misia picks up the tablet and walks it over to a cupboard, as if to protect it from me. I realize she's not really that tall. It's the way she carries herself that makes her seem bigger, stronger.

She slides it into the kitchen cabinet and closes it with a *click*. "But you'll learn all the ins and outs of the tablet now that you're of the Guardian House," she continues. She says it like her family has always been the device's minder. "Of course your training can't begin until you're wed. But inside our home, you and Gryphon will share his room. Just like husband and wife."

I haven't spoken since I begged for Jonas to be spared. This, finally, jolts my tongue. I will not sleep next to the person who led my brother to the Harvest basket. "Do you think..." My throat is raw from screaming, my voice jagged. "Do you think I could have my own room until the wedding is official?"

Misia smiles, mistaking my concern for modesty. "Well, we only have the two bedrooms upstairs, and we can't send you back to your old cottage! How would that look? Besides, it's just a hiccup that you and Gryphon aren't yet married. We can look the other way, can't we? For the greater good?"

When I blink, my lids scrape my eyes. My brother's death is a *hiccup*?

"I won't sleep next to Gryphon." Now that I've spoken out once today, it's coming easier. What more do I have to lose? "Not now. Not ever."

Misia chuckles. It's a warm sound, even though her words erase me. "Don't be silly. You *will* share a bed with your betrothed. We can't miss an opportunity to create more little soldiers."

I was of the Apothecary House. I know how reproduction works, and I have no intention of becoming a broodmare. The Guardians and Farmers are the only ones with more than one cottage dedicated to their trade. They'll manage just fine without my blessed efforts.

"You must be exhausted." Misia taps the top of my head with the hairbrush, bringing my focus back into the room. "And it's too late to eat dinner. Why don't you give me that dress to clean and you can pop off to bed?"

I grab the front of my gown like it's a life raft. "I didn't bring any other clothes."

After a wedding ceremony, couples are supposed to parade through the village, blessing each villager before reaching the old House of the one leaving, so they can pick up their clothes. Then the pair walks to the new House, swears allegiance, and has the House tattoo inked on their bodies, the only permanent mark allowed inside the Wall. The Guardian symbol is three half-inch horizontal lines below the left eye. Gryphon and I never made that walk. Our faces are bare, my bags still at home. All I have is the red wedding gown on my back and the thin underclothes beneath it.

"I'll pick up your things tomorrow," Misia says brightly, holding out her hand. "No need to worry."

As if she means for me to undress in front of her. In the kitchen!

"Can you show me to my room, please?" I'm surprised by the steadiness of my voice. If she hopes to break me, she'll have to try harder. Today, grief coats me in its strange steel.

"I suppose you want to see where you're sleeping," Misia says after a moment, her eyes narrowed. "This way."

She begins up the wooden stairs. I glance at the cabinet once more before following her, surprised my heart still beats, that sorrow hasn't frozen it over. I've lost my mother and brother in one afternoon. My feelings for my mother are complicated. My grief for my twin is pure.

Forgive me for letting them take you.

A single, cold comfort penetrates my grief: my own transgression couldn't have condemned Jonas. If the Council knew I was sneaking medicine to the elderly, my name would've been called alongside his. The village really believes he murdered our mother.

The Tzus' top floor is laid out like my old home but smaller. Where the Apothecary cottage has four bedrooms, in the Tzu house there are only two, one on the left and one on the right. Misia opens the door to our left.

"This was Gryphon's room. Now it's yours. Yours and his."

I step inside. The bedroom is simple. A mattress wide enough for two, but with only one pillow. The bed is crisply made, which brings me the smallest comfort. Gryphon and I are both neat, at least. An end table. A dresser. A wardrobe. A desk.

I feel tears prickling.

Misia hasn't budged from the doorway. Her face makes clear that she wants the dress. Fine. I'll be happy to never see the crimson monstrosity again. It reminds me of what I've lost. I peel it off and hand it to her, hoping I remove the tiny wooden jackrabbit swiftly enough that she doesn't notice. My shift is thin, natural linen. I begin shaking, the toy rabbit hidden in my hand.

I can feel Misia appraising me, but I refuse to move until she's gone. I won't give her the satisfaction. *Let her stare.* A tear races down my cheek and lands, hot, on my foot. Another quickly follows, and then another.

Finally, Misia leaves, closing the door behind her.

I scurry to the bed and dive under the quilt. There'll be no rest tonight.

4

Despite my prediction, sleep creeps up, rolling over my body like a poisoned fog. When a soft *click* pulls me back to the waking world, it takes an unsettling moment to remember where I am. I blink, turning the solid black into shapes, and then, as my eyes adjust, to details.

Gryphon faces his wardrobe across the room. He's pulling his shirt over his head with a tug on the back collar. I'm in his house, in his bedroom, in his *bed*. My heart punches my chest with such force that I gasp.

Gryphon turns. I crush my eyes closed, pretending to sleep. He'll leave me alone if he thinks I'm out. *Right?* My head spins, a sickening swirl as I try to piece together the twisted path that led us here.

When we were children, Gryphon was my only friend outside the family. Following the rules was mandatory for every child in the Valley, but after my dad's death, it became my entire identity, to the point that no one else could stand me. By the time we reached third grade, everyone knew that if a teacher started asking a question, my hand would shoot up before the sentence was out of their mouth. If we were asked to skip dessert for a week because there weren't enough apples for everyone, I'd go without for *two*. When Salvatora of the Cobblers stole a cup from the chapel altar on a dare and Sojourner said it was our duty to turn in the thief, I was the one who tattled.

I wince in embarrassment. I don't fault them in their dislike of me, but Mom taught me that following the rules was necessary to keep my family safe. I had to be the best at it.

White-haired Marina—daughter of the Record Keeper House and sister to Simon—led the bullies against me in school. Gryphon was the only classmate who defied her. He was a natural leader.

More importantly, he was my first patient.

He often came to school covered in cuts and bruises from training. It took time and gentle persistence to earn his trust enough for him to let me tend his wounds. Unlike the other Guardians, Gryphon never set foot in the Apothecary House, so the quiet duty of mending his injuries fell solely to me. I came to look forward to the moment when he'd find me right before school started, a smile on his face even as a fresh sprain demanded binding on his wrist. How it overjoyed me to have someone to practice on!

That all changed on the day of our cohort's betrothal ceremony. By that time, I was thirteen, Gryphon fourteen, and thanks to all the quiet conversations we'd had as I rubbed salve on his latest abrasion or dabbed moss on a bruise, I'd developed a crush on him the size of a barn.

The betrothal ceremony was meant to be a celebration—the first time we'd hear the name of our future husband or wife. I hummed with excitement walking to school that day. I hoped to hear Gryphon's name joined with mine, naturally. I'd even gone so far as to imagine what it'd be like to kiss him one day. Still, I vowed to make the best of it no matter who I was matched with.

That resolve was tested when he snuck me a daisy right before the ceremony.

As couples were declared, some were better than others at disguising their feelings. Eero grinned when clever Meryl of the Entertainer House was announced as his match; less so Alarica of the Guardians when she was assigned to Ernest the Leatherworker.

I couldn't read Marina's expression when she was assigned to Jonas, though he appeared happy enough.

When it was down to only three of us and Nikola Bell of the Engineers was declared my fateful match, I pasted on my best smile despite the crushing disappointment. We'd already lost my dad by then, so I knew my place. My ridiculous grin lasted until my eyes met Gryphon's.

He'd been declared a Caster. A matchless spare.

He nodded, impassive, and strode out. I chased him, the daisy he'd given me still in hand, but he was too quick.

"Running after your boyfriend?" Marina taunted, snatching the flower and tossing it aside. Since her mother's Harvest, she'd grown sharp, all teeth. "Everyone knows you love Gryphon."

"I don't," I lied loudly, terrified the village would think me disloyal to my betrothed. My cheeks burned. "I love Nikola. Gryphon was only someone to practice on."

"Hear that, Gryphon?" Marina smiled ferociously.

I turned to see him behind me, raw pain flashing across his face before his expression hardened. He laughed, ugly and cold. "Consider the feeling mutual. I only ever liked your poultices." He walked away.

My heart splintered.

"He begged me to kiss him, you know," Marina purred. "I said no, of course. We must follow the rules." She patted my cheek, and then she, too, strode away.

Gryphon and I didn't talk much after that. He stopped bringing me flowers, stopped playing with me, barely even acknowledged I existed. My mother said it was only right for a friendship like ours to fade after the betrothals were announced. Whatever had existed between the two of us in childhood was left to shrivel in the sun.

What a cruel fate, then, that he and I are now bound together for eternity, currently sharing a bedroom.

He's been quiet for too long. I peer beneath my lashes and

am horrified to see that he's studying me. I'm so shocked that I instinctively pull back. Lucky Bunny falls out of my hand and drops to the floor.

Heart hammering, I watch to see what he'll do. I can't make out his expression in the dark, just that he's facing me, his head at an angle. Moonlight cuts across his broad chest and brutally powerful arms. Finally he reaches down and grabs the toy, which he holds up.

"Lucky Bunny?" he asks, something like delight in his voice.

Of all the emotions warring inside me, it's surprise that reaches the top. "You know the stories?"

His face has returned to the shadows. "You told them to me the first time you stitched me up." He sounds hoarse. "You don't remember?"

I hadn't, but at his words, the memory comes rushing back. I'd meant to distract him from the pain, and all I—a child—had in my arsenal was the fairy tales my gran told me, stories that'd brought me comfort when I needed it. I'm feeling a warmth toward Gryphon that I haven't experienced in years when suddenly, my brother's terrified face replaces it. I sit up, jutting out my hand. "Give it to me."

The blanket slides down, and I remember I'm only wearing my underclothes. I tug the cloth back up, but it's too late. Gryphon has seen my discomfort.

He makes an affronted noise, almost a growl. "Where are your night clothes?"

As if he doesn't know we didn't make the walk, and why. "At my house," I spit out.

He steps toward me, and I tense, heart clobbering against my ribs. I'm pulling my knees toward my chest, preparing to kick him in the stomach, when I realize he's not coming to me at all. He's striding to the door, picking his shirt up from the floor as he goes.

I yank the blanket up to my neck, wishing I could cut holes in it for my head and arms and wear it like a dress. Beyond the bedroom, I hear what sounds like an argument. Gryphon's voice. His mother's, low and savage.

Then silence.

The bedroom door slams open seconds later. I jump, still clutching the blanket.

"Your things will be fetched for you tomorrow," Gryphon says. "For tonight, wear this. I'm afraid I don't have anything cleaner to offer."

He tosses me his shirt, then strides to the wardrobe to pull out what looks like spare bedding. While his back is to me, I hurry to tug the shirt on beneath the blanket. It smells of the night, of pine trees, of Gryphon.

"Don't do me any more favors," I mutter, threading my arms through the sleeves.

He tenses but doesn't say a word as he lays a blanket and pillow on the floor.

5

Jonas.

I blink the sleep grit out of my eyes.

I'd been dreaming that he and I were playing in a field, weaving dandelion chains and chasing frogs when we were supposed to be gathering chamomile blossoms for Gran. He'd been laughing at something, laughing so hard his face sprang a leak. But then the laughter turned to tongue-swallowing fear as Jarek appeared, hoisted him over his shoulder, and marched him toward Eden's Gate.

I woke just as my brother was slammed into the Harvest basket.

I lie in Gryphon's bed, memory carving my mind with a dull blade as yesterday's horror returns in waves. Jonas, standing over my mother's body, gripping a bloodless knife. Tomris holding me back. Augustus the Plumber's odd expression. Did he see who murdered my mom? Did he do it himself?

Jonas must not know who the killer was or he'd certainly have said something. He'd simply been in the wrong place at the wrong time. Punished for trying to save his own mother, for doing what he'd trained his whole life for.

My blood ices as Jonas's final words return to me.

I didn't kill her. You'll find the truth in the Record Keeper cottage. Go to the vault.

What had he seen? How did it connect to our mother's death? And am I seriously considering sneaking into the Record Keeper vault to find out who the true killer is? With a pang of acceptance, I realize that I am. Without this final connection to Jonas, I'll drown in the rising tide of my grief. Plus, my mother deserves justice.

I peek over the side of the bed, making as little noise as possible. Thankfully, Gryphon's gone, his blanket folded and stacked neatly beneath his pillow. I don't like that I didn't hear him go.

I slide out of bed, feeling Gryphon's shirt brush against my skin. There was a time, not so long ago, when wearing his clothes would have made me feel close to him in a way I only allowed myself to dream about. Now the fabric is merely a reminder of all I've lost since yesterday.

I steel myself for the day and tiptoe into the hall and down the stairs (with far less grace than my betrothed, if the floorboards squeaking loudly beneath me are any indication).

"Look who finally decided to join us," Misia says, perched near the stove. Any pretense of a smile, of her and me being in this together, is gone. Whatever Gryphon said to her last night, she's clearly still upset by it. She takes in his undershirt, raising her eyebrows. "At least you got right to work."

My scalp tightens. *Eww*, I think. My mother never would have said that to Gryphon. Not for the first time, I wonder what it was like to grow up with Misia and Jarek for parents. I don't correct her, though. I need her trust if I'm to get into that vault and find my mother's killer.

"I didn't realize Apothecaries enjoyed such leisurely mornings," Misia continues. "Breakfast's gone. You'll have to wait for dinner to eat." She indicates the dirty dishes stacked on the table and the crusted porridge pot on the stove. "But you can clean up now."

"Sorry," I say reflexively, though her words sting. The Apothecary House works all hours, every day, which means we steal rest when we can. Only profound grief accounts for why I slept past sunrise.

My apology softens her shoulders. "Well, no need to grovel. Your laziness is being punished. Turns out there isn't another wedding to tack you onto until next week, and you can't begin training until you're officially a member of our House. A Guardian's instruction is sacred—that's one rule I refuse to bend. You'll cook and clean while you're waiting. You may also preview our texts, but don't get too comfortable. We're not Record Keepers, rotting away with our noses stuck in books." She tucks in her chin as if I've said a word in disagreement. "We're Guardians. We protect, we serve, and we *don't* cause trouble for the Valley. I'm led to believe you're better than your brother in that regard, at least."

"Understood." I manage to keep my voice submissive despite her jab. Does she know about Jonas's trip to the vault? It's not like it was his first infraction. The boy never met a curfew he could keep.

"May I visit the Apothecary cottage today?" I ask. "To get my things?"

"I told you I would," she says sharply.

If she does, I won't be able to slip over to the Seingalts' cottage to find out what Jonas saw. "It's a child's errand." I'm gambling on her ego. "Beneath a full Guardian, certainly."

Her nostrils flare as she studies me, and I do my best to appear innocent, grateful my reputation precedes me.

Years of walking the line pay off. "Fine," she says. "If you're quick. It's no good for anybody if you linger too long at your old home. You'll want to get used to us as soon as possible."

"Thank you." I have to fight the urge to curtsy, like we do in chapel.

Or worse, to lash out and kick her.

The thought startles me, sharp and unfamiliar, a leftover echo of the fury that broke loose yesterday at Eden's Gate. I need to get control of my grief, fast, before I do something I can't walk back from.

Misia glides to the front door, done with me. "You'll have the midday meal ready for us. We must return to patrol immediately after."

"You're working double shifts?"

Other than a few trades that deal with emergencies—Animal Farmers, Crop Farmers before a frost, the Apothecaries and Dentists—no citizen is meant to labor more than ten hours in a twenty-four-hour period without special dispensation.

She's strapping on her sword belt. It's constructed of the same leather as her trousers. "Of course we are," she says. Her gaze lands on me, her expression unsettling. "We're being hunted, Rose. You of all people should respect that, given what happened to your father."

I'm unequipped for the reminder. I've lost too much in one day to keep my dad's death contained in the mental compartment where it's meant to reside. For the first time in years, the memory crashes through my defenses.

6

I was five years old.

Gran was out training Jonas on a birth at the Crier cottage, Aunt Florence and Uncle Richard were dispensing inoculations, and Dad had gone out before dawn to deliver a body to the Elders for a funeral. We'd unexpectedly lost the Guardian in our care in the middle of the night. Only Mom and I were home, preparing a batch of painkilling tincture from white willow bark and wild lettuce, its pungent scent crimping the air.

Mom was in an odd mood that day, and I was somber, too, both of us affected by the loss of a patient. Her thick black hair was piled atop her head as she brewed up medicines and sang sad Valley songs. She barely startled when the door flew open.

"Hurry!" Eero of the Carpenter House screamed. He was a good friend to Jonas, but in that moment, he was nearly unrecognizable.

"What is it?" Mom asked, banking the fire and pulling on her cloak. I'd already strapped on my crossbody medical kit. By that time, I'd been assisting on field calls for months.

"It's Kirby," Eero choked out.

Dad?

The world turned inside out, sky becoming ground and air burning like water in my lungs. My father was the center of everything good, the shoulder I rested on when I was sad and the smile I ran to when I was proud. He couldn't be hurt. I'd seen him only hours before. He was bothered by the death of the Guardian, of course, but in peak physical health. I glanced to Mom in a panic, but she was already following Eero out the door. I tried not to think of the boy's bluish lips and fingernails or the pronounced white around his pupils. He was showing classic signs of shock. What did that mean for my dad?

Eero led us to a clearing at the edge of the woods. Bluebells, fresh and vivid—my mother's favorite—lined the path. We were closer to the Wall than I had ever been. Disrespectfully close, even. But that worry vanished as my brain caught up with the carnage before me.

At first, I thought I was staring at a heap of bloody clothes, that's how twisted Dad's body was. Mom gasped, then slapped her hands over her mouth. It was the only time I'd ever seen her freeze in a crisis, before or since. I dashed forward, my mind detaching from my soul so I could treat him. I told myself I wasn't looking at the man who taught me to dance standing on his feet and tied my hair into two low buns for school each morning. Who told me that I was going to be the best Apothecary the village had ever seen because I noticed things that other people missed.

He was only a patient who needed my help.

Yet I started trembling when I reached him.

What was left of him.

His face was so ravaged that I wouldn't have recognized him if not for the wooden turtle pendant he never removed, a gift from Jonas. His shirt front was sliced in several places, his intestines spilling onto the earth. The smell of human waste and congealed blood told me we were too late.

Still, I searched for a pulse before stumbling away.

"He's gone," I whispered.

"This is my fault," my mother wailed, startling me. She fell to her knees in front of my father's body, keening, burying her hands in the blood-soaked soil. She began sobbing, repeating a version of the same strange words.

I'm so sorry. It's all my fault. I shouldn't have stood out.

It made no sense. Whatever had happened to Dad was an accident, a freak animal attack. There were hundreds of acres of wilderness surrounding the Valley, and even the youngest among us knows not to wander too far into it. I studied the corpse, the pieces of my father lying in a bed of wildflowers at my feet, and I began floating away from myself as my mother continued to shriek her apologies to the sky.

Eventually, I heard leaves crunching. Footfalls sounded in the distance, but I paid them no mind. I didn't even care if whatever killed my father came back for me next. Mom seemed to, though. She gasped and scrambled toward me, as if remembering for the first time that I was there. I didn't fault her. No one knew how they'd react in the face of tragedy.

I, myself, felt nothing at all.

"Rose, you must be careful," she hissed, grabbing my face, saying those words to me for the first of what would be hundreds, thousands, of times. "Promise me, baby," she said fiercely, her hands slick with my father's blood. "Promise me you'll be good. That you'll follow every rule. Learn from this, Rosie. Don't draw attention to yourself. You and your brother's lives depend on it."

I'd meant to choke out a small assent between her sobs. To let her know I'd do whatever she asked. But the moment my mouth opened, so too did my heart, and I screamed instead.

That's when the Guardians appeared.

I don't remember who was in the party that searched the woods, or when we were told it was a wild mountain lion that'd mauled my father. I don't think I ever fully forgave Mom for surely being the reason he diverted into the forest that day—picking flowers, as he was always wont to do for her.

It was only later that night, in the cottage, as Gran handed me a steaming mug of honeyed mint tea, that I began to feel the horror of it descend past my head and into my body. I dropped the mug and ran to the sink to throw up everything I'd eaten.

The teachings at home changed that day.

Mom, who'd always instilled in Jonas and me a healthy respect for the Valley's systems and institutions, began to go at it with something like mania. *Learn the rules like your own name. Never talk back. Draw no attention to yourself.*

I came to believe that if I made one misstep, my family would suffer like my father had. It was on my shoulders to keep them safe, and the only way to do it was to follow the rules absolutely. That's when I started twisting the skin between my pointer finger and thumb, a reminder not to let heretical words escape my lips. From that day forward, I'd stayed completely in line—right up until I was told I couldn't care for my elderly patients.

I shake my head, returning to the now, to Misia's kitchen. I realize with a start that she's staring at me, expecting a response. What had she said to me?

We're being hunted, Rose. You of all people should respect that, given what happened to your father.

"I'm sorry, but I've never seen one of the predators." I shudder, and it isn't faked. "Though you're right, I've witnessed their handiwork."

The creature that got my father ate the body he'd been bringing to the Guardians, too. Years went by without another attack, to the point that we'd hoped those two deaths had been an anomaly. But eight months ago, two more Guardians were killed. One I saw, her bones shattered, skin hanging off her in sheets. The body of the second had been placed directly into the Harvest basket, covered, so I don't know what shape he'd been found in.

That's when the curfew was rolled out and the whipping posts built. I'm wondering why the restrictions weren't put in place at the time of the first animal attack—probably no one would have accepted them back then—when Misia lashes out at me.

"It must be nice to be so sheltered." Her words drip with sarcasm.

"Sorry," I say again.

I don't know why I keep apologizing, but it seems to calm her. The deep line between her brows disappears. She finishes cinching her belt and slides her sword into an attached sheath. With her lean, muscled frame, short hair, and the triple line tattoo branding her upper cheek, she's the picture of ferocity.

"No need to apologize. You haven't seen the beasts because we're doing our job," she says. "Pray we keep it up."

I think she's turning to leave when she glances at me, her eyes glittering with the same malice I witnessed in Jarek yesterday. "By the way," she says, "I was mistaken last night when I told Gryphon that your dress was wet and that's why you couldn't wear it to bed. *Sorry*," she says, mocking my string of apologies.

She glides a wicked-looking blade into each of her wrist braces and steps outside into the overcast day.

7

I find my wedding dress wadded up beneath a pile of dirty rags in the laundry lean-to. It occurs to me that while Misia Tzu may be twice my age, she has the disposition of a child. One who's dangerous and well-armed, but immature, nonetheless.

I grab my garment and shake it out, but it's no use. It stinks like mildew. I add this latest seed of anger to the growing pile before pulling on the wrinkled gown. When I step outside onto the village's cobblestone paths, I inhale deeply of the smoky air, noticing a sharp green edge to the scent. The Foresters must be burning recently cleared foliage.

My red dress stands out like a beacon in the misty, leaden day. Thankfully, those who work outdoors are already at their tasks: Farmers finishing their fall reaping, Guardians on patrol, Carpenters shoring up the Valley's aging structures.

I hurry toward my old home, my plan to change my clothes as quickly as possible before visiting the Record Keeper cottage. My hard-soled shoes echo on the cobblestones, just as they did yesterday. Through a window, I spot the Baker's daughter up to her elbows in flour. Before my conscious brain can counter the habit, I think to bring home a currant tart for Jonas, and an arrow of grief pierces my heart.

Only a handful of others join me on the narrow stone path

winding through our thatch-roofed village, and all of them quickly glance away. I don't think it's the dress or even the odor.

They know I'm Jonas's sister.

It hurts when they avoid eye contact, but then I remember I did the same to those who lost family to the Harvest before me. My own suffering is momentarily replaced by shame, hot in my belly. Moving forward, I'll be better. For now, all I can do is keep my head down and hurry to the Apothecary cottage.

...Where I stand, still as an oak, outside what used to be my door. *Do I walk in, or knock like a villager would?* I would've stood there until I really did sprout roots if I hadn't caught the sound of an argument inside. I recognize Gran's voice, stronger than it's been in a while, but the angry male one is unfamiliar.

I rip open the door, prepared to defend my gran.

Only to find Augustus, head of the Plumber House, standing above her. His face is the same blank mask he wore over my mother's body, and fear makes the ground tilt beneath me. Is he killing us off, one by one?

"Leave her alone!" I yell, lunging at him.

He sidesteps me easily. His beard is shot through with silver, his face weathered, but his arms and chest are corded with muscle from the carrying, pounding, and wrenching of his trade. "Watch yourself, girl," he says in a voice as rough as rock.

"Watch *your*self!" I respond, making fists of my hands. I have no idea how to fight, nor the consequences I'll face if I do, but I'm prepared to find out before I'll let someone hurt my gran.

Augustus snorts.

It's Gran who answers. "It's a misunderstanding, Rosie," she says in her reedy voice. She sits in her favorite rocking chair before the crackling fire. Her gray hair is braided over her shoulder, and she has ash-colored yarn and timeworn knitting needles in her lap. "I'm fine."

She seems to be speaking truth, but I can't get my blood pressure down. My eyes flick back to Augustus, who's still studying me.

"Are you in need of care?" I ask. Why else would he be here?

He snorts again. "Not any more than the next person." He nods to Gran. "We'll talk later," he says, and makes to leave, stopping alongside me. In a voice audible only to me, he whispers, "Do you take the path of your mother?"

Frost crawls through my veins. I wish I knew how to defend myself, now that we have a murderer loose in the Valley. When I don't respond, he expels a puff of air and leaves the cottage.

"Don't mind him, Rosie," Gran says, pulling my attention back to her. "He's just upset."

I'm trying to get my bearings. What just happened? "About what?"

"A bad deal that he made," Gran says. "We will forget he was here."

I want to protest, but I won't argue with her. Even if she weren't my elder, her fragile health means any stress could be dangerous. Gran's illness isn't treatable. It twists her bones and gnaws at her from the inside until she cannot keep down anything but broth.

"You've got some spirit in you today," I say instead.

I try to hold a smile, but it's too much. Instead, my eyes drink in everything I've always taken for granted. Gran's savory sage tea bubbling on the stove, the stick family Jonas painted when he was four still pinned to the wall because Uncle Richard loves it so much, medicine bottles so plentiful that our kitchen shelves bow beneath their weight. It's everything good, and none of it belongs to me anymore. Not even my gran, not according to Valley law.

"And you look like you slept standing up," Gran quips.

But a cough racks her, and I know from experience that she's putting on a brave face. How long had Augustus been here, and what did it cost her to talk with him? I rush to pour her a mug of tea, reaching for our—no, *their*—stash of honey to soothe her throat. But when I peek inside the pot, it's empty. There's been a shortage since the Vex evacuation forced the Beekeepers to close half their hives. I pour hot water into the container to dissolve the last of the crystallized sweetness, swish it around, and tip the honeyed water into Gran's cup.

I offer her the drink. "Are Aunt Florence and Uncle Richard making their rounds?"

"They are," Gran says. "Decided it's better to keep moving. It helps with the sorrow."

She's flirting with sacrilege. Joy and celebration are the only acceptable responses to a Harvest. She must be referring only to Mom's murder. I stare at the fire, feeling none of its warmth. I know her gaze is on me, but I can't think of what to say. Everything seems so settled. So final.

"Look at me, Rosie," she says softly.

I turn. She holds out her arms, and I sink into them as gently as possible, accepting my first loving touch since Jonas was stolen from me. But he was stolen from her, too, wasn't he? She'd lost her grandson and her daughter. Yet her grip on me is strong, and she smells like home. I'm suddenly overcome by sobs.

"I'm not originally from the Apothecary House, you know," she says minutes later, after my weeping has worked its way out.

I sniffle. I did *not* know. It's considered rude to ask. I'm pretty sure Gran's the one who taught me that to begin with. But if she's opened the door... "Which one did you leave?"

She'd been stroking my hair, but her hand goes still, resting on the back of my head. "Plumbing, if you can believe it. I've known Gus decades longer than you've been alive." I can hear the smile in her voice. "I can still fix a leaky pipe in the blink of an eye. Locate water in the sand. It'd be foolish to let a good talent go to waste, don't you think?"

A sharp jolt zips down my spine. If someone overheard her, she'd be whipped no matter how sick she is. I feel guilty for allowing the conversation to proceed—surely Gran's not in her right mind—but I'm unwilling to shut her down. Besides, I've followed nearly every rule all my life, and it still didn't protect my family.

"It was quite a shock to move here," she continues, "after I wed your grandfather. All the blood and mucus I had to deal with. For the first weeks, I was throwing up more than our patients." She chuckles softly. "There were so many new rules to learn, so many new procedures. I was terrified. There's no shame in that." She turns over her wrist, showing her tattoo to me. "I *earned* this."

I've seen her Rod of Asclepius, the Apothecary House symbol, so many times that I consider it a part of her. I trace the faded blue shape with my finger. It's a single snake wrapped around a staff. We're told it's the symbol of an ancient medicine god hailing from a far-off land. Healing. Wisdom. Sacrifice. That's what it means to me, and I'd always hoped to have one inked on my own wrist someday. Given the size of Nikola's household relative to my own, I was supposed to.

Gran begins stroking my hair again. Her touch feels so good, so safe. "Did you know Reatha of the Chemist House?" she asks, seemingly at random.

"Of course," I reply.

What happened to them was unprecedented.

The Chemist husband, Otto, a man with a great booming laugh, was honored with a Harvest last winter, leaving behind his wife, Reatha, and their kids, Albert and Marie. Albert was only three years younger than me. I knew him as quiet, maybe a little poky. He'd gotten his work done and often Marina's, too. He had a monumental crush on the Record Keeper daughter.

Then came his horrific accident.

He'd been scurrying up a tree, a wooden slingshot tucked into the back of his pants. He meant to shoot down apples for Marina like he often did, climbing high to get her the reddest, sweetest fruits in the Valley. But this time his foot slipped and he fell, cracking his spine.

Jonas and I were first on the scene. We were able to save his life, but not his mobility.

The Engineer House constructed Albert a wheelchair, and we all cut back on our requests of the Chemists. But Reatha must never have recovered because a month ago, she snuck into the Record Keeper cottage and stole our blessed tablet, loaded herself and the children into the basket, and self-Harvested. It's why the tablet is now kept by a Guardian House rather than the Record Keeper.

Reatha committed the worst crime we know. She stole from the Valley, deprived us of our vital Chemists. My own House relied on them to grow penicillin. Ever since, we've been without that life-changing medicine. I can never forgive her for that.

"Why do you bring up Reatha?" I bite out.

"She was friends with your mother," Gran says, cocking an eyebrow at my tone, a sliver of her old brightness returning to her voice.

Friends. Gran told me once that the word used to mean more to the adults of the Valley. Men and women across Houses spending time together in the evenings, taking walks, sharing stories. She said the villagers used to hold a dinner swap, where two Houses were randomly paired, with one cooking for everyone the first night and the other the next, so everyone got to know their neighbors. The village used to act like a family, she said.

I have only faint memories of that time.

"Your mother and I did you a disservice by holding on so tight, Rosie," Gran continues, shocking me with her admission. "We thought we were protecting you, and you're such a natural healer, so gifted, that it was easy to keep you busy. But we all need people. Life's too heavy to bear alone."

I'm too embarrassed to tell her that I have no friends because everyone thinks I'm a rule-worshipping snitch, not because she loved me too much. Most Noah's Valley teens bend a rule here or there, just as Jonas did, tasting curse words and pushing curfews. Not me. My rigidity has always stood out like a goat in chapel. If I'm being honest, a part of me was excited at the Council's recent advisory against mingling. It meant Jonas was home more.

But Gran has been speaking out against the system for too long. I'm about to warn her that she needs to be careful when the front door slams open.

8

I go weak with relief at the sight of Aunt Florence and Uncle Richard.

Florence looks so much like my mother, which means Uncle Richard was probably the one born to another House, just like Gran. I don't know which—I've never thought of him as anything but an Apothecary before. My hand finds my pocket and the wooden toy inside as I contemplate this new development in the family dynamic, wishing my brother was here to share it with.

"Rosie!" Uncle Richard holds his arms wide. He's a lantern-jawed man with a blob of a nose and a ready smile. He's also a ginger, and he always leaves a dusting of carrot-colored hair across his left cheek no matter how carefully he shaves.

I stand and run into his arms, starving for the love and affection of my family.

He squeezes me tight and kisses the top of my head. "Within the Wall," he says, offering the standard greeting in a choked voice.

Aunt Florence weaves her arms around us both. She smells spicy, like marigold salve. "It was an honor, of course," she murmurs, "for Jonas to be chosen."

I pull back. These are the words we're supposed to say, but do they need to be spoken here, inside the cottage? Gran's honesty has loosened my tongue. "He should *not* have been." I'm surprised by the heat in my chest.

"Rose." Uncle Richard glances toward the door. "Don't shake branches."

"The law says that Apothecaries are spared from Harvest in times of need, and with the Vex still unresolved, this qualifies." Now that I've started, I can't stop. "And who ever thought of using the Harvest as a punishment? We should have been allowed to decide the consequences together!"

Aunt Florence appears alarmed. She's the only member of our House who wears glasses. When she pushes them up her nose, their thick lenses magnify her eyes into two pools. "The law changed, Rosie." She blinks myopically. "It changed to protect us."

Uncle Richard reaches behind her to ensure the door is fully closed. "We must trust in the system," he says loudly. Then he lowers his voice, tossing a worried glance at Gran. "Has your grandmother been filling your head with stories? She hasn't been feeling well, you know. She isn't herself."

I pull away from them, heart thudding. I've never seen Uncle Richard or Aunt Florence behave this way. Paranoid. Scared. For a sickening moment, I wonder if they know I've been smuggling medicine to the aged. But how could they? I've been so careful. Still, my palms begin to sweat.

"I'm just here to get my things," I tell them uneasily. "A change of clothes. My suitcase."

"So Lillian hasn't told you any tales?" Uncle Richard exchanges a troubled glance with my aunt.

Gran appears to have fallen asleep.

"No," I say. "I just walked in."

It's a lie, but one that rests easy on my conscience. I turn to hurry up the stairs but pause. "Aunt Florence... Uncle Richard," I say, each word measured and careful. I'm moving into risky territory. "Why were Mom and Jonas not at the end of the wedding path waiting with the two of you?"

"Oh!" Aunt Florence says. "Just as Agnes was bringing you your flowers, we received word of a villager possibly displaying symptoms of the Vex."

The air changes, and I sense vital information is coming, information connected to who killed Mom. I nod, stiff enough to splinter. "All four of you received word?"

Uncle Richard scrunches up his face, obviously traveling back to the moment. "We were all waiting for you at the end of the bridal path—you looked so beautiful, Rosie, and that was so kind of you to tend to Agnes's hand. And then…" He trails off, perhaps trying to recall a face.

Aunt Florence completes his sentence. "Then she grabbed your mother and Jonas and led them away."

"She?" But my gut tells me I know.

"Marina Seingalt," Uncle Richard recalls. "The Record Keeper girl. But it turned out to be a false alarm."

9

Marina was the one who drew Mom and Jonas to the edge of the crowd, and according to Uncle Richard, she pulled them away unnecessarily. The patient they'd gone to see didn't have the Vex. But Marina couldn't possibly have been the one who killed my mother. While she'd taken great pleasure in bullying me, that was a far cry from stabbing someone. I still intend to ask her what made her think someone was in need of medical care.

I climb the stairs and enter the second-floor bedroom I used to share with Gran. It looks so childish now, with my A+ homework pinned above the headboard and a dried daisy chain hung over a bedpost. The girl who slept here had no idea how terrible her life was about to become. Sadness claws at my throat as I rip off my wedding dress. I'd like to burn it. Instead, I hang it near the window to air out. Our marriage garments are the only clothes we're allowed to sew ourselves, from stitch to seam. My labor can be traded for something my family needs.

My prior family, that is.

I walk to the pitcher and bowl I set out yesterday to wash up after Gryphon and I made the ceremonial walk. I use it to clean myself as best I can, wiping off grime and dried tears. Then I open my pre-packed suitcase. It contains a cloak, two shirts, two pairs of trousers, five sets of underclothes, one set of pajamas, my only other pair of shoes, and a small cache of the medicine I'm going to have to figure out how to keep sneaking to the elderly. I slip into clean underclothes and then my soft, buff-colored trousers and overshirt. I nearly cry when I trade my beaded shoes for soft goat's leather slippers.

My thoughts whirl as I dress. Marina, with her glossy blond hair and full lips leading my mother and twin to their deaths right before my wedding, either intentionally or not. Augustus here, in the Apothecary cottage. Gran, asking me about Reatha. Why, why, why? But there're no answers in this room. I brush my hair and wind it into two buns, then I fasten my cloak, snap my suitcase closed, and step into the hallway, remembering at the last second that Lucky Bunny is still in the pocket of my wedding dress. I'm turning to get him when a hushed conversation at the base of the stairs catches my attention.

I pause, my fingers grazing the wood of the railing. Aunt Florence's voice, sharp with worry, reaches me. "I can't believe he went through with it."

Uncle Richard exhales, a tight sound. "If he suspects we know..."

What comes after is too quiet for me to hear. I can't help but think of my aunt and uncle turning their backs on Jonas yesterday. I want to believe they're separate from that action, that pure hearts can abandon someone so completely and still remain decent. The two of them have always sided with the community; Jonas's Harvest was simply no exception. Good citizens of the Valley don't disrupt hard-packed soil. That's all it was.

Aunt Florence is speaking again, this time loud enough to reach me on the landing. "We can't hide for much long—"

I shift my weight, and the floorboard groans beneath me. Their voices stop. Then Uncle Richard says, "Rosie?"

I tiptoe back into my old bedroom, uncertain why I don't just answer him. What did I overhear? Those two are the straightest of arrows. They were likely whispering about a patient. In the room, I return to my wedding dress and rescue the precious wooden rabbit.

"Sorry I almost left you behind, Lucky Bunny," I whisper, kissing his nose. I tuck him into my pants pocket and, on impulse, dash into Jonas's room. I inhale the peppermint scent of him, touch the clothes he'll never wear again. It's too much. I close his door behind me and dart downstairs, my heart cast in lead. Aunt Florence and Uncle Richard are standing near the kitchen table, still talking, their voices low and gestures agitated. Gran is seated by the fire, where I left her. Her eyes are closed, but she clutches her mug of honeyed water.

"I'm going home now." I try to keep my voice light, though the word "home" is a slimy rock sliding down my throat. "See you all at chapel?"

Aunt Florence and Uncle Richard smile back, but it's strained. Gran's eyes remain shut. I realize she's humming a lullaby she used to sing to Jonas and me.

I begin humming it, too, unable to remember the words, and then I surprise myself with an announcement. "I'm going to leave through the lab," I say. "Grab a few things for the Tzu family."

10

The Apothecary lab with its attached greenhouse is my favorite place in the whole world. I relish the embrace of warmth and humidity, the way the scents of dirt and lavender automatically soothe me.

I stand at the threshold, my pulse thrumming in my ears.

This is the last time I'll be here. When I leave this cottage, I'll belong to the Guardian House in name, if not in heart. Never again will I be allowed in this space, never entrusted with the craft that's shaped every aspect of my existence.

I inhale deeply, steadying myself as I realize that I came here to say goodbye.

My mind catalogs the room, taking in every neatly arranged tool and precisely placed ingredient. The drawers of medicinal powders are closed, their contents safe. The bottles of distilled liquids lining the shelves are labeled and aligned, the mortar and pestle on the center worktable clean and ready for use. The rootlings in the next room that I speak to like friends thrive in their neat pots.

Something's wrong, though. I can feel it prickling across my scalp.

That's when I spot something my wedding jitters must have hidden from me yesterday: a nearly imperceptible dusting of black speckles scattered across the third shelf to my left. I step forward and drag my finger through it, bringing it to my nose to smell. *Charcoal.* The trail leads behind a row of tincture bottles. Strange. Mother—the only other person who regularly used this space—was meticulous about cross-contamination. I reach behind the bottles and feel...*a book?*

My breath catches as I pull out Mom's journal, far from its usual home on her workbench. I'm surprised she's left it this close to the greenhouse. She always lectured Jonas and me about how damaging humidity is to paper. My fingers skim the cover, tracing scuffs and scratches, before I remember I don't have time for sentimentality. I flip through the pages, scanning her precise handwriting, looking for any explanation as to why this book would be hidden away.

Most entries are exactly as I remember them—detailed notes on preparation methods, dosages, contraindications. But an error on the belladonna page makes me pause. She's listed it as safe for children in small doses. Nonsense. A few pages later is a note on foxglove—the very plant I turn into digitalis extract to treat Horace's weak heart—warning that it should never be used on a heart patient.

Deliberate inaccuracies.

Mother never made mistakes like this. My mind sharpens, dissecting. What had she been up to? A misdirection? If so, there must be a pattern to the falsehoods, a rhythm to their placement. But I can't work it out now. I'm away from the Tzu house on borrowed time already. I slip the journal into my suitcase, trying to ignore the guilt. It's not stealing if it was my mother's, after all, and no one else in this House understands plants and potions well enough to use it.

I'll give it back, I tell myself. *Once I clear Jonas's name and find Mom's killer.*

I take one last look at the room, confirming that everything remains precisely as it was before I entered. I'm about to slip through the rear door when a soft creak sounds from the other side of it.

My heartbeat double thumps.

Someone is shuffling around out there, and it's not my aunt or uncle. They're still back in the main room with Gran. And a villager would enter through the clinic. I scramble for a hiding place inside the greenhouse, pale daylight pressing through windows that line the walls from floor to ceiling. I dive beneath a table stacked with yarrow and goldenrod just in time, tucking myself away as a door opens across the lab.

I can't see the intruder from here, but every part of me is straining to listen. I hear the careful shuffle of footsteps, the faint sound of pots being moved, the telltale rustle of turned pages across the room.

Whoever it is, they're looking for something.

11

I exhale slowly.

I don't know what's happening, but if this person really is searching the lab, then I can't sit here waiting to be discovered.

With quiet, measured movements, I lift my suitcase and creep toward one of the retractable, ground-level windows that encircle the greenhouse. I open a pane slowly, wincing at the faint squeak of the glass. I shove my suitcase and myself outside and breathe a sigh of cool air and relief when I'm not followed.

Closing the window as silently as I can, I sneak away, hurrying to the Record Keeper cottage. Marina answers the door, bundling me into her arms as soon as she lays eyes on me. The affection is unsettling. She's only ever paid attention to mock me.

"How are you?" she asks, releasing me to look me up and down. Her blue eyes, startling against the pale cream of her skin, bore into me. "Do you know I was the last person to talk to your mother? I've been telling everyone how awful I feel! But a child of the Tanner House looked off-color to me, and I was so sure it was the Vex. I went to inform Henrietta and Jonas exactly as procedure dictates, and you know the rest."

Well. I guess that puts to rest the question of whether or not she killed my mother or knew who had. "Uncle Richard says it wasn't the Vex."

She shrugs dismissively. "Turned out the child suffers from allergies."

Anatol, then. Thirteen years old, allergic to stone fruits and pollen...neither of which would give him a sickly pallor. Had his stomach been upset? Before I can ask more, Marina tugs me into her cottage. I need to focus on getting inside the vault, so I force my Apothecary training to quiet. I'm sure my prior family will follow up on Anatol's condition.

I enter Marina's home. The interior looks like every other village house I've visited. The only difference is its size. This house is connected to the communal library, and beneath that lies one of only two cellars in the village. The Record Keeper basement is for preserving our history, the other for gatherings after chapel, just as the Founders intended.

While I've visited the library many times, I've never been to this side of the cottage, the living side, not even to set David's foot last week. We prefer to treat broken bones at the site of injury, but David had been hauled to the Apothecary cottage by a pair of stone-faced Guardians, his foot crushed in one of their animal traps, they'd said. He'd been in too much pain to speak. I requested he stay for observation after I set his bones, but the Guardians carried him home against my advice.

Marina guides me to the couch before dropping into a plush chair across from me. She leans forward expectantly, throwing me off an already shaky guard. "How are you? Tell me everything."

"I-I'm actually here to talk to you about Jonas. Is that all right?"

She nods, but she's staring off into the distance. That's when I realize: she's also lost Jonas. Now that he's gone, she's a Caster. Unless a wife in our cycle is Harvested or dies, Marina will never have her own wedding night. Out of instinct, I grab her hand. She flinches but doesn't pull away.

"He was telling me a story on the way to the wedding," I continue. "He said he saw something. He was about to tell me what, but then...then...you know. It's probably nothing, but I'd feel better if I made sure."

"What did he say he saw?" Marina asks absently.

"Something in the vault."

Suddenly, I have her full attention. "That can't be right. Only Record Keepers are allowed down there, and besides," she says, a spark returning to her eye, "Jonas wasn't even here yesterday. Simon was busy prepping new census forms. It's time for an update, what with all the weddings and Harvests."

My brow furrows. Jonas had been clear that he'd stopped by yesterday morning. I can't believe Marina would lie to my face like that. Actually...I can. "Is Simon around?" I glance toward the stairs leading to the second story.

"He isn't, but I'll tell him you called." She stands abruptly.

I rise, too, a polite reflex.

With a tight smile, she grabs my elbow and steers me toward the exit. I barely catch the handle of my suitcase as she hurries me along. I'm being dismissed, though I can't fathom why. Perhaps Marina can only muster up a few minutes of civility per day. I ought to thank her for spending them on me for once.

In the open doorway, she drops my arm and then her eyes. When she drags them back to my face, the dark blue of her irises swirls toward black. She lowers her voice and leans forward. "The records say it's possible to survive out there, you know."

I'm not sure I've heard her correctly. "What?" I ask, my body suddenly rooted in place.

Marina makes a show of looking around. We're alone. "It's in an older text, one you must be a Record Keeper to read. It speculates that some who are Harvested could potentially live on top of the Wall."

"For an hour or two." My tongue feels clumsy and swollen. "Maybe a day."

"No, I mean survive *forever*." She glances over my shoulder and up, presumably at the Wall. Then she touches my wrist, briefly. "I'm not supposed to tell, but…we were almost sisters."

I open and close my mouth, words failing me.

"Maybe Jonas is up there." A smile cuts across her face. "Waiting for you to help him get down." In one fluid movement, Marina shoves me into the crisp autumn air and slams the door in my face.

I stand there, reeling. I truly do not understand that girl. When my senses return, they ride on the back of a lullaby, the one Gran had been humming right before I stepped into the Apothecary lab to say goodbye. It's a song she put Jonas and me to sleep with when we were children, a tune everyone in the village knows. A verse comes back to me.

> We live by the Wall, Water, Soil, and Sun.
> In Noah's Valley, each to a House yet one.
> So sing me a story, dear, I'm down on my knees,
> Praying to Heaven, bring me back, please.

12

I throw my suitcase in the narrow gap between two cottages and race toward the square. I forget my sorrow, my resentment, my best intentions to return to the Tzu house as I fly toward Eden's Gate. Only those making the ultimate sacrifice and the honor guard accompanying them have earned the right to approach the Wall. I know the privilege is not mine to claim. Unfortunately, I'm out of my mind.

Jonas is alive!

Or, at least, he could be, if I get to him soon enough.

I'm not sure of my new plan. I don't have one. Before I spoke to Marina, I'd intended to find my mother's killer and make the Tzus hurt like I do. But now? Well, hope's a dangerous thing. Is it possible Jonas is alive up there, desperate to return?

I stop short before the Wall. I've reached an invisible boundary, my deepest-rooted beliefs holding me back. The cobblestones before me are notably darker. Hardly anyone has dared to step this near.

For Jonas, I must.

I take a tentative step forward, heart pounding.

I never imagined I'd see Eden's Gate up close.

It isn't smooth or perfect beneath the vines, like I'd always imagined. The stone is cracked and weathered, and the thick green tendrils clinging to it are barbed like wedding roses. A glistening sap coats each thorn, bringing to mind my antimicrobial sundews in the greenhouse. I take a moment to appreciate how the edges of green leaves give way to brilliant purple. My whole life, I've never seen such a lovely shade of violet. I tip my head back. The Wall stretches endlessly up, vanishing into the mist.

I take another few steps. I'm now close enough to see the soaring strip of silver panels that harnesses the holy Sun and lifts our Harvest basket to the sky. Both technologies are so advanced it boggles my mind, but it makes sense our Founders would invest in this, our most sacred ceremony.

A breeze flutters one of the violet-tinged vines to reveal a chunk of a panel missing. I search for it on the ground but don't see it. The panels must be decaying with age, like the tablet that operates them. But even with a piece missing, I can feel the Wall's power, soft fingers trailing across my skin, raising the hairs along my arms.

What would happen if I touched the Wall?

Or if I climbed those vines all the way to the top?

No one's ever tried, not that I know of. Not only is it forbidden, it's stupid. One of the first stories Valley children are told is about a boy named Jack who tried climbing the vines and got too high. The plant pulled away from the Wall, and Jack plummeted to his death.

Only a fool would attempt it.

The breeze kicks up again, even stronger this time, rustling the vines against each other. The shushing noise it makes sounds like a voice. My skin lifts away from my muscles. When the breeze becomes a gust, the vines dance. Their barbs scratch like nails against the Wall, leaving behind oily streaks and whispering what sounds like…my name? Something primal in me goes still, listening.

Rosieeeee…

"Jonas!" I scream. There must be a crack in the Wall! My brother somehow made it down the other side and is just across from me, calling for me from the Beyond. I must get to him. I dive forward, legs pumping. I'm reaching out—fingertips nearly brushing stone—when I'm thrown to the side by a great force. I land on my back, hard, and the wind is knocked out of me.

In a single, fluid motion, Gryphon reaches down, grabs me at the waist, and hoists me over his shoulder. Before I can react, we're moving. I thrash against him, wild with rage as he carries me away from the Wall. He pins my wrists at an angle. Since I can no longer strike, I lunge to bite. He immediately clamps his other hand on my head, holding it away from him firmly and effortlessly. I can't hurt him, but grief has stripped me of dignity, and so I keep snapping air like a wild thing until he drops me, hard and graceless, the requisite twenty feet from the Wall.

"You shouldn't be here," he says, his voice low, eyes gliding over me. "What were you thinking, coming that close?"

"I heard Jonas!" I cry.

His eyebrows shoot up, not with anger at my idiocy or pity for my delusions, but with surprise. He runs his hand across his face to hide the expression, but it's too late. Something explodes in my heart. "You know! You know that people can survive Beyond! How could you not tell me?"

Gryphon unsheathes the sword at his side and pretends to examine it. "It's unlikely."

"But possible?" I demand.

His jaw twitches. He studies me and then his blade. "I've heard it's possible," he finally says.

Marina had told the truth. I feel like I could float away. "Then I must save Jonas!"

I launch to my feet, but my legs are shaky. Gryphon leans over. I think he's going to offer me a hand. Instead, he places his pointer finger where my shoulder meets my arm, catching me off balance. He pushes me back with all the effort it would take him to flick on a light. I land back on my butt with an *oof*.

"You're weak," he says arrogantly. "You don't have the strength to go Beyond."

"I don't need it!"

"No," he says, matter-of-factly, "you need the tablet. And that's under Council protection."

I narrow my eyes, picturing the cabinet I saw Misia return it to.

As if he can read my thoughts, Gryphon laughs. "Don't even think about it. They keep a close eye on the tablet ever since what happened with the Chemists." The joviality falls from his eyes. "And I'd turn you in if I thought you were planning to steal it. Rules are made to be followed, Rose. It's my job to see that they are."

I'm still on the ground. I feel like he'd take me more seriously if I was standing, but I don't want to risk him pushing me down again. So I stay put, feeling as small as a raindrop in the river.

He squints into the misty, cloud-bloated sky. "Even if the tablet fell into your lap right now, it wouldn't have enough charge to work. It can take up to three days of direct sunlight between uses nowadays."

It's similar to what his mother said. I suspect it's true. Nevertheless, my anger's returning, building. Suddenly, I'm raring to punch Gryphon in the throat, just like I wanted to do to his mother earlier. "I can wait seventy-two hours."

He crosses his arms. "Rose," he says quietly, "a person would need bottomless luck and a lifetime of combat training to survive out there. Jonas might've had one, but he definitely didn't have the other." His voice hitches in a way that makes me want to cover my ears. "I'm sorry, Rose, but he's dead."

His eyes are so sad, so vulnerable, that I lower my gaze. It's been a long time since I looked at Gryphon and saw the boy who brings me daisies.

Gryphon returns to his patrol, certain that I'm done with foolishness for the day. His absence is a relief. It gives me time to parse out what I've learned.

A person would need bottomless luck and a lifetime of combat training to survive...

Marina had been tormenting me again. For the last time, I vow. The Rose she used as her own private plaything died alongside my mother. This Rose is angry, and she's tired of living small. My mother's quiet obedience after my father's death—always walking with her head down, never questioning the Council, never even raising her voice—didn't protect her *or* my brother, did it?

I pound the ground with my fist. Jonas shouldn't have been Harvested. Not on my wedding day. Not ever. He was young, healthy, and a good citizen up until the end.

Wasn't he?

Entering the Record Keeper vault was a rule broken, sure, but it shouldn't have been enough to get him Harvested. Besides, he was in the vault right before my wedding, and the Harvest basket was already lowered when we showed up. Someone had planned for a body to go in there all along.

I close my eyes. There'd been more. What were his last words?

We're not what we seem.

What could that mean? I sigh from the bottom of my soul. There's only one way to find out. I *will* get around Marina and into her basement on my next attempt. I have to, for Jonas, for my mom, and for all the villagers still at risk with a killer on the loose. The thought gives me a thin sense of purpose, enough that I'm able to get to my feet.

I'm brushing myself off when footsteps approach. "I'm going," I snap at Gryphon. "Just give me a moment."

But when I lift my gaze, I see it isn't him.

It's Leonidas Khan, his normally smug face as slack as a bag. He's twenty-five to Gryphon's eighteen, but the two grew up training together and have always been close. It needled me with jealousy when we were younger.

"There you are," he says in a strained voice. "You're to come immediately. There's been another animal attack."

13

Leonidas stalks ahead of me, shoulders rigid, every step pulled taut like he's bracing for impact. We soon round the corner to the border of the industrial district. Smoke still clings to the brick here, smelling of iron and burnt grain even though no one's worked here for months.

The industrial district is where the Vex began. It appeared first in the Potters' cottage, then spread like wildfire to the Wheelwrights, Coopers, and Blacksmiths. Two dozen villagers were struck within the first week. The illness started with the bluish-gray tinge followed by a cough and fever, progressing quickly to red, hot blisters that broke open on the skin. The exposed tissue was raw, sometimes oozing. Edema, stomach cramps, and vomiting marked the end. Six of our patients died. Their bodies were carried up the Wall.

On advice from my mother, the Council of Elders quarantined this area, abandoning the surrounding orchards, hives, cottages, and their single well. That last wasn't much of a loss; the water was orange-tinged and apparently always tasted of rust. Our community was gutted by the loss of food, though, plus the evacuated Houses being unable to work until temporary shelters were provided.

Still, it's for the best until we ascertain what exactly the Vex is and how it's transmitted. We found no bacteria in the well water, and the illness didn't respond to antibiotics. We left off hoping it was a virus now gone for good.

What would have drawn wild creatures to this abandoned area? And why had Leonidas summoned me, a girl no longer of the Apothecary House? I'm working up the courage to ask when we turn the final corner and come within twenty-five feet of the Wall.

My breath catches in horror.

There, at the edge of the cobbled path, the Council of Elders stand in a triangle—Jarek, of course, with Nero Carter of the Farmer House and Alexandra Yevele of the Masons. Their dark robes billow in the breeze, the intricate stitching at their hems catching what little light filters through the clouds.

A body lies between them.

This set of Elders should have stepped down weeks ago. Council terms rotate every five years, with new voices elected from the heads of Houses periodically. This is meant to prevent an individual amassing unsafe amounts of power. But that was before the Vex caused panic, and before the uptick of wild animals hunting in our farmlands. At some point, it was decided that this Council would stay on a bit longer—just until everything settles back to normal.

I hurry to the body they're gathered around. A teenage boy, supine, his face frozen skyward. The positioning is unnatural—limbs askew, torso twisted—but it's his color that captures my attention.

Or, rather, the absence of it.

His skin is cadaverous: waxen, parchment-thin, hanging off the contours of bone. The sclerae of his wide-open eyes, normally white, have clouded to a sickly gray, a telltale sign of hypoxia. His lips are drawn back, exposing teeth in a grimace that mimics a scream. His hands are the final horror, his fingers flexed into tight contractures, nails splintered and blood-dark, suggesting he'd been desperately clawing against something at the moment of his death.

My mouth pools with saliva, and I have to choke back a wave of bile as I place the victim's face at last.

Holy Wall, it's Peter.

Peter is—or was—prone to ear infections. Six years below me and Jonas in school, a lover of knock-knock jokes. His friends called him "Potter," a play on his name and trade. Before his death, his cheeks were still pink and rounded, having not yet taken on their adult shape.

I know this boy, and he died an agonizing death.

Something about the violence brings to mind my father's body, though the style of carnage is far different. Where my father was all wet and crimson, Peter's corpse appears to be sucked completely dry. In fact, I see no blood, and the dirt on the cobblestones is disturbed in long strokes behind him.

Peter didn't die here.

Something or someone dragged him here postmortem.

"He's dead?" Jarek asks.

I choke out a sound. "Yes."

"I-i-is that..." The head of the Mason House trails off, as if she cannot bring herself to say it.

"It's Peter Martinez," I confirm, slipping into Apothecary mode.

Nero and Alexandra stare at the poor boy, anguish draping their features. Jarek's lips thin to a blade. I crouch next to the body, centering myself before gently opening his shirt to search for his injury.

I gasp when I see it.

Three puncture wounds mar his chest, the same pattern that I believe marked my mother. There are no bite marks, no scratches, no blood. This wasn't an animal attack.

Before I can think better of it, I speak the thought that's pressing against the inside of my teeth. "We have a murderer in the Valley, and it's not my brother."

The words are barely out before the slap comes. My head snaps sideways, the taste of copper blooming on my tongue. Jarek's hand is still raised when I level my gaze to face him. His expression is as unreadable as ever.

"Calm yourself," he says, like I'm a child, like I'm hysterical, *like I'm wrong*. "This was an animal attack, just as Leonidas should have told you. You'll lecture anyone you encounter about the danger of exploring outside their assigned duties. In trying periods like these, everyone should spend as much time as possible inside their own homes, with their own families. Don't you agree?"

I look past him to the other Council members. They should be questioning this absurdity, demanding the truth. Nero glances away, and Alexandra stares at her shifting feet. Even Leonidas pretends not to hear.

They're asking—no, *ordering*—me to lie.

"This is your chance to prove your loyalty to your new family, Rose," Jarek croons. "Don't make me regret it."

That's when the final seam in me tears, the last fragile thread of trust I had in our leadership, in our system, and in everything I once so earnestly believed. I stare at Peter's body, my mind already cataloging evidence, forming theories, and plotting next steps. Because I'm certain now. It isn't some*thing* hunting us, as Misia tried to suggest, but some*one*.

And the Council is covering it up.

I make my way back to the Tzu house, remembering to get my suitcase from the alley where I threw it a lifetime ago when Marina told me Jonas might still be alive. I can hardly feel my feet against the path as I walk. My mind's a storm, thoughts colliding so fast I can't pin any of them down. My cheek still stings where

Jarek struck me. *Animal attack.* The words replay in my head, hollow and ridiculous.

I rub my arms, trying to shake off a chill that has nothing to do with the temperature. Around me, the village hums along as if everything hasn't changed. A Miller carries sacks of grain to the bakery. Girlish laughter escapes from a window. In the distance, the sharp crack of a Mason's chisel on stone echoes through the streets.

No one else sees the rot.

Too much violence in too short a time has me unravelling. My breath comes fast, keen. I force myself to walk, eyes locked on the Tzu cottage ahead. I need to get somewhere I can think.

I'm beyond grateful to find the cottage empty. I will not be preparing any midday meal for the family.

I hurry upstairs, craving answers.

And I think I know where to get them. After everything I've seen today—so much lawlessness it threatens to spill out the sides of my head—I'm convinced my mother knew something.

Something that got her killed.

It's a good thing I found her hidden journal.

14

I'm perched on the edge of Gryphon's bed.

When I open Mom's journal, the scent of pressed herbs leaps out at me. This time, I start on the first page. Each entry is meticulously written, every plant cataloged, every remedy described in detail. But it's the errors I'm here for, the deliberate inaccuracies only a trained eye would notice. I find the first on page seven. I run my finger along the line. *"Cutleaf toothwort grows in sandy, sun-drenched fields,"* it reads. But that's wrong. Cutleaf toothwort, with its peppery taste and ability to ease sore throats, grows in moist, shady woodlands. I've harvested it myself, felt its damp leaves beneath my fingers.

My brow furrows as I read the false line again, slower this time. That's when I notice it. In the word "cutleaf," the letters **e**, **t**, and **a** are faintly darker than the others, as if Mom had gone over them a second time. I stare at it, my heart fluttering. I flip to the next page, belladonna, the one where she'd written that it's safe for children. My heart thuds. The **o** in belladonna is ever so slightly emphasized. Not enough to pick it out unless you're looking for it, but a pattern nonetheless. I hurry to the foxglove page, where I'd already spotted another mistake, and am gratified to see that both the **x** and **v** stand out almost imperceptibly from their peers.

It's a while until I find the next certain error. *"Goldenrod blooms in early spring,*" the entry states. That's wrong. Goldenrod—miraculous in its ability to fight infection and inflammation—blooms in late summer, its yellow plumes bright against the fading green. My pulse quickens as I see a faint distinction in the **r**.

I flip to another page, the edges of this one brittle. It's been turned to often.

"*Horehound is used to induce sleep,*" it reads.

My lips press together. Horehound is an appetite stimulant, a remedy for coughs and congestion. It sharpens the senses, wakes the body—the opposite of inducing sleep. My eyes narrow as I trace the words, and there it is, subtle but deliberate: the **h**. Next comes a page that says basil should never be planted next to tomatoes, which even a layperson would recognize is a lie. The **s** and the **i** are marked.

I scribble down what I have so far: ETAOXVRHSI. Then, switching the order: ISTHROVXAE. Then another: TROXSAHIVE. None of those options make sense. It feels like I'm on the edge of something, a secret my mother is whispering from the grave, but no matter how my brain spins, I can't decipher it.

Suddenly, three letters jump out.

V-E-X.

My heart thumps. Had my mother discovered a cure? If so, why keep it a secret? I pinch the soft web of skin next to my thumb, then stop, remembering how much she hated when I did that. I have HAROTIS left. With that I can make ROAST or SHORT or dozens of smaller words, and there's even more possibilities if the V, E, X can be reused. None of them makes sense combined with VEX, though, not that I can see. I keep scouring the journal for more letters but am unsure what else is meant to be a clue, if anything.

Did my mother deliberately leave a message, or am I chasing falling leaves?

I'm suddenly overcome by an exhaustion so pure—abject grief

and confusion and fear distilled into a potent tranquilizer—that my head dips. I will rest my eyes, just for a few minutes, and then get back to the journal. I shove it beneath Gryphon's mattress and curl up on the edge of his bed.

"Here."

The rough word jars me awake. I blink, panicking momentarily at the darkness. "Gryphon?"

His shadowy figure stands over me, holding out a bowl. Outside the window, night has fallen. I must've slept for hours. I shoot up so quickly that my head spins.

"I told my mother you weren't feeling well," Gryphon says, his face unreadable. "She was angry you weren't available to cook for us today, so be ready to deal with that next time you see her."

I rub my face. It isn't just the hour making me light-headed. I haven't eaten all day. That's when I smell what he's offering me. "Is that soup?"

He sets it on the end table, placing a spoon beside it and removing the plate he's set over the bowl to keep it warm. A delicious puff of steam curls into the air between us. "The butcher offered it to me for helping move some heavy boxes," he says gruffly. "It's little more than broth and vegetables, but he said it's well-seasoned, at least."

"I'm not that hungry," I say, refusing to thank the boy who led my brother to his death.

He's quiet for a moment, then inclines his head, the gesture almost tender. "It's hard to take care of everyone else," he says, "if you don't take care of yourself."

A dangerous softness tugs at my ribs. I drown it in anger before it can take root. "I said I'm not hungry," I snap. Naturally my traitorous stomach chooses that moment to grumble like a goat locked out of the barn. I cross my hands over my belly to muffle the embarrassing sound.

"Suit yourself," Gryphon says. Is that laughter I hear in his voice? He turns toward the door. "I recommend you don't come down until tomorrow, if you can help it," he is saying. "Both my parents are in a mood." He stops with his hand on the doorknob. I think he's going to say more, but then he steps out into the hall and shuts the door behind him.

I wait all of five seconds before I scarf down the soup.

15

Belly fuller than it's been in a while, I considered digging back into Mom's journal, but it doesn't feel safe with all three Tzus just beneath me. Any one of them could barge into the room without warning. Plus, my eyes are still heavy. I've witnessed the physical symptoms of grief many times over. I could fight it, or I could take the advice I would give my patients and rest.

I fall back asleep and am awakened the next morning by Misia Tzu leaning over me, face inches from my own. "You don't look sick."

I cough feebly into my hand, and she gives me a long, calculating stare. "Fine. You can stop by the Apothecary for medicine, but I need you to run errands today—take clothes to the Tailor House to be mended, ask the Engineers to send someone to look at the washroom light. And you'll have the midday meal ready for all of us, *unlike yesterday*. Keep us waiting at your peril." She makes a disgusted noise. "Can't have you sitting around all day while the rest of us work. It's going to be a full-time job keeping you busy until the wedding, isn't it?"

I shake my head, unsure what to say. I certainly don't need to be minded. Then again, if Jarek and Misia have something to hide around here, maybe I do.

She studies me for another second before turning on her heel, leaving me alone in the room. If Gryphon slept here last night, I'd been too tired to notice. In any case, he's gone now. I sit up, pushing aside the thick curtain of grief that threatens to smother me. I can breathe, but just barely. I have to keep moving or it'll suffocate me.

The weak light filtering through the window tells me we have another cloudy day on our hands. I dress quickly and head downstairs, where I'm told again that there's no breakfast because I've slept past sunrise. The kitchen is filthy. At least Misia doesn't tell me to clean it. I accept the pile of clothing she shoves into my arms and hurry to the Tailor cottage, trying to plan the shape of my day. If I rush to the Engineer, I'll have all sorts of time with Gran. Maybe she can help me decode what I've found in Mom's journal so far. Then, I tell myself, I *will* sneak into the vault.

I'm between chores, plotting my cellar break-in, when peripheral movement catches my attention. A flicker across the square, behind the chapel. My baby hairs stand on end, just as they did when I spotted the shadow before my mother's killing. I charge forward on instinct. I don't know what I expect—a murderer clutching a knife?—but then the shadow moves away from me, and I feel a burst of adrenaline. Someone was there!

To follow them risks a whipping or worse, the Tzus confining me to their home indefinitely if I fail to return in time for lunch, but my body bolts in pursuit before my brain can stop it. Heart in my throat, I race toward the retreating shape, not sure what I'll do if I catch it. It seems to be hugging the shadows, racing through the inner ring of cottages, weaving through alleyways all the while, always just out of sight. The clouds in the sky distort it, warping it, turning it into something bizarre and inhuman.

Still I follow, running by the empty Chemist cottage, its shingle swaying in the breeze, its dark windows two bleak eyes staring at nothing. Trying to ignore the burning in my thighs, I wonder for the first time what's inside the empty home. Do the books of their trade collect dust on the shelf, or have their texts gone to the Record Keeper? Will people be taken from existing

Houses to form a new Chemist one? Why didn't I question these things before? And more importantly, what else have I missed in my lifetime of near-perfect obedience to the rules?

I will my legs to move faster, narrowing the distance between myself and the periodic whirring sound I'm following, the noise helping guide me through the maze-like streets. We're almost at the edge of the village. If whoever it is reaches the forest before me, I'm sure to lose them. I must catch up.

I'm nearing my physical limit when I get my first stroke of luck: my target has missed a shortcut, favoring the main road for a change. *Gotcha.* I skid to a halt, pivoting to dash through the narrow alleyway that funnels wastewater out of town. I run with one foot on either side of the aqueduct, the movement awkward. A few seconds later, I burst into the open, scanning the area before plunging between the next row of buildings. The main road curves up ahead, turning to the north and offering the shortest route between village and forest. I'm gambling that the shadow will be charging into the woods, and from this position I'll be able to see them when they cross the prairie separating town from forest.

I'm catching my ragged breath, muscles tensed and about to take off, when a crack rings out from the woods. I recognize the sound—a branch falling from a tree—but reel back anyway. At the same time, the edge of the nearest cottage's roof explodes. I instinctively drop to the ground, my face stinging. My birthmark is porcupined with tiny splinters. When I swipe at them with the cloth of my tunic, the fabric comes away bloody. Glancing up, I see what looks like a smooth rock embedded in the wall. Its impact must have released the shards of wood.

It's not the first artifact from Beyond to fall into the Valley. Occasionally, a sharp rain that reeks of sulfur crosses overhead, or an eerie scrabbling is heard on the other side of the Wall, or there's a boom followed by the ground quaking beneath our feet. One time, a chunk of sky-metal, rough and blackened, fell with a clatter that echoed through every home. That's what this looks to be.

I glance toward the forest just in time to see the shape I've been following slip into the trees, offering me my clearest glimpse of it yet. Except...it can't be. The thing in front of me glides forward with a grace that is entirely inhuman. It disappears into the woods, quick and fluid, as if moving without taking any steps at all.

What in the Wall?

I'm suddenly too terrified to follow. My hand travels to my pocket, seeking the wooden rabbit. When I wrap my hand around him, a memory surfaces from my childhood, a moment I haven't recalled in years. It was the first field visit Jonas attended with me; we went to stitch up a Fisher who'd cut herself cleaning river trout. Dad had recently died, and Mom had declared us shorthanded without him, so Jonas—who'd always preferred woodworking to blood—was officially kicked out of the nest.

"Do you think someone from our House will be Harvested soon?" he'd asked on the way.

We were seven at the time. I'd been mentally running through the supplies we'd need, making sure my kit contained them all. Sterilized thread made from sheep intestines. Precious needles passed down from our ancestors, the first Apothecaries. Honey, which was available back then, to dress the sutures.

"What?" I asked absentmindedly.

"A Harvest," Jonas said, his voice high. "Do you think our family will be honored soon?"

We'd witnessed a difficult Harvest the week before. The person selected had been old—Grandmother Bea of the second Farmer House—and very dear to the Valley. She had wailed her way through the ceremony, detained by Guardians and screaming blasphemies, even though there were children present. It'd been shocking. Unlike any Valley citizen, but especially her. Raising our voices in anger is frowned upon. She remained so defiant that she had to be sedated to be placed in the basket, the first time that had ever happened, as far as I knew.

Gran was the Apothecary tasked with administering the sedative.

Afterward, I'd asked Mom how Missus Huerta got to be so old without knowing what an honor it is to be Harvested.

"She was sick in the head, darling."

I couldn't let Jonas get sick, too. "We have to trust the system," I blurted. "No matter what happens."

"Of course, I'm so sorry," he responded in a rush.

I immediately regretted the shortness of my answer. "I'm the one who should apologize," I said. "I'm just worried about Meeman."

It was true. The Fisher's son had been as pale as a frog belly when he'd charged in and told us how much blood his mother was losing. I'd been surprised Mom had sent Jonas and me to tend to it.

"Meeman will be fine," Jonas said proudly, the fear he'd expressed seconds earlier pushed aside to comfort me. "You'll stitch her up real good. You're the best Apothecary in the village."

That wasn't true. I had so much yet to learn. Still, it was nice for Jonas to say. "You're so good with people, Jackrabbit. You'll find your strength, too."

He proved it that day. We came upon Meeman seated in the cleaning room, grasping her injured hand with a towel so drenched in blood it was impossible to tell what color it used to be. The room reeked of fish guts and iron, and if there was ever a smell to turn the stomach, that was it. I strode over and gently asked her to remove the towel. Her cut ran from one side of her hand to the other, her metacarpal bones a shock of white against the red gore.

I worried Jonas might pass out at the sight of it, but I had to focus on my patient. I administered a painkilling draught.

"That should take effect quickly, Missus Meeman, and relieve your pain enough for my sister to work," said my twin. "Warm water, please," he gently ordered her children, who were crowded in the corner, weeping.

I cleaned the wound and began the painstaking process of sewing Meeman's palm closed, stitching from the inside out. Whether she'd have full use of her hand again depended on how clean and meticulous I was. It was with pride that I was perfectly able to realign the fish tattoo on the inside of her wrist, and I was pleased to discover that I couldn't have asked for a better assistant than Jonas, who fed me thread as I needed it, kept my work surface sterile, and murmured soothing words to the Fisher that were well beyond his seven years.

He did such a good job that I had him dress the wound once it was closed. His honey-calendula application and bandaging were impeccable.

"Keep it clean and dry," he told Meeman, "and let us know if it starts feeling hot or tight. We'll come back to check it every day for the next week. Count on it."

Despite her injury, Meeman, a lovely woman with watery brown eyes and close-cropped, cloud-colored hair, actually smiled.

We helped the children to clean up the mess, and then I slipped them each a lavender lozenge wrapped in a bit of cloth. It was medicine and should've been reserved for the sick, but I justified it by telling myself that not every illness was visible to the eye.

Once outside, I drew deeply of the fresh air, wondering how long until the briny scent of the Fisher cottage left my hair. "You did wonderful in there, Jonas." And because it was true, and because I was so proud of him, I finished with a terrible lie: "And don't worry for another second about a Harvest. You'll never be chosen. You're too important to the Valley, and our Founders above know it."

How foolish I'd been.

The memory spurs me forward, sprinting into the woods after the gliding monstrosity despite my abject fear. I lied to Jonas, gave him a false sense of security and failed to uphold it. The least I can do is clear his name.

16

The last sounds of civilization—faraway bursts of laughter, the bone-jarring clank of metal striking metal—vanish as I plunge into the dark forest. Soon, I hear nothing but my ragged breathing and the crunch of leaves underfoot, my every step stirring up the scent of dying things. The temperature has dropped. I paint the air with my breath.

Whatever I'm following has gone quiet. Motionless. Are they watching me?

"Hello?" My voice is tentative. "Can you show yourself?"

There's no response. I rotate in place. The woods have closed around me, each massive tree appearing exactly like the next. There's no path forward or back, no one to call to for help. My throat closes in on itself, and the air turns as thick as porridge. I recognize the signs of panic but am powerless to fight it. My mind is beginning to choke when a great rustling ahead frightens me back to myself.

I've only seen a handful of animals in real life—the birds and beasts the Farmers raise, of course. From them we get eggs, milk, quills, heavy labor, and—when they grow too old for anything else—meat. I've seen river trout and the occasional wild turkey, rabbit, or squirrel that wanders out of the forest. I love the songbirds that flit overhead. But that's it. We learned about other animals from before the Wall in school: cats and dogs and unbelievable monsters like the elephant, an enormous horse-like creature with a tube for a nose. Or the shark, which resembled a giant trout with a tall fin and rows of razor-sharp teeth. Even something called a platypus that was so ludicrous-looking, I'm positive it was a joke.

But I've never seen or heard of a beast that *floats*.

I think back to the Guardian whose body I'd witnessed eight months earlier, her bones shattered, skin hanging off her in sheets. And every time I blink, I see Peter's corpse, sucked dry, flesh loose and wrinkled. Despite my earlier confidence that Peter's "animal attack" was a lie, I'm suddenly worried. What do the Guardians know that they haven't told us? Why wasn't Gryphon surprised to hear it's possible to survive Beyond—and did that mean something could breach the Wall from the other side?

I shake that last thought from my mind. *Our Wall is impenetrable.* Security was so important to the Founders that they didn't even install an exit. There's no need to scare myself. I take a deep breath and locate the tallest tree. Setting it as an anchor, I begin a course I hope will take me home.

It's a good thing, I decide, that we're not allowed to enter the forest. It feels awful here. Dangerous. I try to pick up my pace, and a branch snakes the edge of my shirt. I swipe at it, heart beating so loud it sounds like it's following me. Suddenly, I hear a rumbling, and my blood turns to jelly. Was it a growl? I spin in every direction.

Nothing.

Yet, how foolish I've been not to carry so much as a stick to defend myself. I search desperately until I locate a loose branch nearly as tall as I am. I wipe off leaves and sidewinding insects, not sure how I'll use it. To boop a flesh-eating monster on the nose? I laugh shakily, telling myself I imagined the noise.

Marching onward, I push through a wall of underbrush until, at last, a lightness ahead suggests a change in the terrain. Is it the village? *Please be the village.*

I practically sprint toward the light, throwing my arm up to shield my face as I burst through the trees.

Where I'm stopped cold by shock.

"Albert?" I ask. Or think I do. I'm pretty sure I'm dreaming because it looks like the son of the Chemist House is sitting in front of me in his wheelchair, hovering just above the ground. Behind him are enormous caves that show evidence of being quarried for some of the village structures. Is he living out here?

He flashes a buck-toothed grin and drops his chair the short distance onto the earth. "In the flesh."

"It's not possible," I say. Even if the fourteen-year-old hadn't self-Harvested with his mother and sister, the chair the Engineers made him was rudimentary technology. And yet here he is, alive, inside the Wall, sitting in a wheelchair that was just floating. Two impossibilities, but my mind clings to the strangest one.

Dumbfounded, I point at the chair and ask, "How?"

Albert's whole demeanor changes as he sits up proudly, patting the wheelchair's armrest. "It's not hard to make something hover! Assuming you have the chair, you just take some wood and screws, a thick cloth, and..." His breath hitches, and he clamps his mouth shut.

I know guilt when I see it. I focus in on the chair. Its joints are fitted with near-perfect precision, the carved patterns in the wheels hinting at repurposed materials. The base of the chair, an elevated platform between the wheels, is dark canvas. *Impressive.* But it must be power hungry, and few technologies inside the Wall can generate that. Except...

My eyes go round as saucers. "You didn't!" I gasp, but of course, he did. "Holy Wall, Albert, you stole a solar panel!"

His cheeks bloom red. "It's not like that, I swear," he pleads. "Someone gave it to me."

I cross my arms, inviting him to elaborate.

"I can't tell you who." He winces. "Just...trust me?"

"I do not!" I scoff. "Why would I?"

"Albert!" a familiar voice calls from behind him.

Reatha emerges from the caves, visible annoyance at Albert shifting sharply to shock when she spots me. I can't say I'm any less jolted to see her. She looks as I remember her: dark brown coils in plaits, eyes slightly tipped up at the edges, and deep-set lines like parentheses encasing her lush nose and mouth.

When Albert's little sister, Marie, follows, her hair in two cheerful puffs, I grab a nearby tree for support. I'd thought all three were long dead.

Something like resignation flows over Reatha's face. "Rose," she says. "How are you?"

I discovered the phrase "cat's got your tongue" in a dusty novel I once checked out from the library. At the time, its origin perplexed me. I thought maybe housecats used to eat human body parts. I think I understand it now. I cannot form a single word, my tongue pinned in place.

"It's shocking to see us, isn't it?" Reatha says as Marie steps in front of her, draping her mother's arms around her shoulders like a cloak. The girl's eight, if I'm remembering correctly, with a habit of eating herself to bellyache at ceremonial meals. She smiles shyly, her dimples accenting an overbite identical to Albert's.

"You're all dead," I sputter. It's a ridiculous thing to say, given the circumstances. "You self-Harvested last month."

Reatha smiles without showing her teeth. "Why don't you come inside? I can answer your questions over tea." She shoots Albert another annoyed look before turning to go back inside the cave she just walked out of.

I follow her, thinking of my mother's corpse, and the Potter boy, drained and discarded, both killed by someone acting outside the system. Someone who moves too gracefully for human step, who I chased into the woods not ten minutes from here. It dawns on me then...

Albert.

17

The Chemists' cavern is three times the size of the average Valley cottage, its smell damp and mineral, its walls showing the deep gouges of past limestone mining. Reatha and Marie walk a well-worn path to what looks like a dead end at the rear.

Then they disappear.

Heart thudding, I hurry to catch up and see that they've stepped behind an outcropping and through a concealed door. On the other side is a home as nice as any in the village, except for its lack of windows. The living room holds a couch and two chairs. The kitchen is attached, though it currently looks more like a laboratory than a place for cooking. Its stone-carved countertop is strewn with glass beakers, small burners, and technology I can't identify. Open-faced cabinets holding plates and pottery are carved directly into the limestone, as are the bookshelves lining every wall.

I guess I know what happened to the Chemists' texts.

A table in the far corner is covered with metal, wires, and machinery the likes of which I've never seen. Two door-sized openings appear to its right, both hung with gray blankets. Likely the bedrooms. If I had to guess, the bathroom is outside.

Reatha bustles to the kitchen, calling out, "Is mint tea all right for you?"

I nod, tensing as Albert enters the room, rolling his wheelchair as normal. But I can't get the image of it hovering out of my mind. "How long did it take to modify?" I ask, trying to remain calm as suspicion roils hot in my gut. Was he the shadow I saw behind the chapel before Jonas was Harvested?

He gives a quick shrug. "Only a couple days, once I got the parts."

I inhale, about to say something to Albert that I'll regret, when my father calls out to me from a memory. *In medicine as in mysteries*, he admonishes me, *one must never draw conclusions from insufficient facts.* My heart softens. It's been so long since I've heard Dad's voice. And he's right: no one's guilt is a foregone conclusion. Accusing Albert now would only sour the milk, and I don't even know what I'd be accusing him of. Lurking at my wedding? He certainly didn't zip in, stab my mother, and zip out unnoticed. His wheelchair might be able to hover, but it isn't invisible.

"Your chair is wonderful," I tell him honestly. "I know villagers who would benefit from it." Like Gran, who can no longer walk far, or Sandor of the Fermenter House, who had both legs amputated at the knee after a terrible accident. At least, Sandor *would* have loved to have a chair like that, if he hadn't been Harvested.

"It's the easiest of the things I've created," he says sullenly. "A child's science project from the Before Times, scaled up for size."

"Albie's a genius at building things," Reatha says proudly, handing me a warm rag and pointing at her head. It takes me a moment to realize she's referring to the blood on my face from the wood splinters that rained down on me back in the village. I had completely forgotten.

I clean myself up as she returns to the kitchen to pour hot water into mugs. "Aren't you, darling?" she says, continuing to praise her son. "He made me a solar-powered centrifuge from one of our charging panels and a micro-scale from salvaged metal springs and counterweights from a broken clock." She smiles softly. "It makes sense he's so gifted. Albie's dad was a brilliant Engineer before he joined the Chemist House. Some of our talents are passed along in our blood, are they not?"

Albert ignores her. He's staring at me. Warily, I think.

"You wish to build machines, then?" I raise an eyebrow, feeling Reatha's attention sharpen on me. "The Council listens to new ideas if you did want to pursue Engineering," I say, when Albert doesn't respond. "There's a petition process, isn't there? The village could really use a talent like yours."

"When was the last time you heard of anybody allowed to do something other than what they were born or married to?" Albert rubs the back of his hand angrily across his broad nose.

I accept a mug of steaming tea from Reatha. It's fragrant with a scent I haven't smelled this strongly in months. "You have honey?"

"We have a hive out back. I developed a process to graft it from the ones that had to be abandoned." She pauses, clearing her throat. "Due to the animal attacks."

I take a sip. It's so sweet my teeth hurt.

"You'll want to know what we're doing here," she continues. "I'll keep it simple." She seems to be avoiding looking at Albert or Marie. "Jarek asked something from me that I was not willing to give. For my children's safety, we were gone by morning."

I set down my tea, hard. "So you went into hiding? Instead of pleading your case before the Record Keeper, you made us think you self-Harvested and left your community in mourning?" Even if I could understand committing a crime as severe as abandoning my duty, I can't fathom the effort of faking a Harvest and then making a home in the caves.

Unless she was running from something more dangerous than I can imagine.

"David wouldn't have listened to me," she says.

"He has to!" It's true. It's written into our charter. The Record Keeper House must keep track of our laws and adjust them when fairness demands.

Reatha's eyes glisten. "Does he? If Jarek convinces him otherwise? If Jarek convinces the *whole village* that we're guilty of some crime and ought to be sent up the Wall?"

I swallow. She knows about Jonas. Well, that confirms it. Albert came to spy on my wedding ceremony, probably sneaking into town to catch a glimpse of his beloved Marina. He knew the streets would be empty, after all. I felt bad for the kid even before his accident, always trailing Marina, doing her dirty work in exchange for bread crumbs of affection. Whereas I tried to avoid her completely, he sought her approval like roots wanted rain.

Rather than answer Reatha's question, I ask one of my own. "So you know my brother was Harvested two days ago. You also know my mother was murdered?" I try to look at all three of them at once. "And Peter Martinez was killed just yesterday?" My voice cracks on the last word, and I realize I'm stretched thin from the violence.

Reatha drops into the nearest chair. "Albie told me of your brother and mother. I'm so, so very sorry, Rose. I didn't know about Peter."

She's either an excellent dissembler or telling the truth. Marie, too. She appears ready to weep at the news. Albert, however, only goes to the sink to wash his hands. I cannot see his face, nor do I know how to interpret his behavior.

I rub my arms, trying to return to my body. The cave is surprisingly clean and cozy, the faint sulfuric smell of cold rock the only indication we're surrounded by limestone.

"This place has been here forever," Reatha says, watching me. She's still ashen as she spreads her arms to indicate the space. The Chemist House symbol is visible on the inside of her left wrist: a perfect circle with another half circle on its top and a cross on its bottom. "A group of us have been outfitting it for years. We used to meet up here."

"Who?" I ask.

She shakes her head. "It doesn't matter. They're gone, and Albie, Marie, and I live here now."

My head's spinning with everything I've learned. I focus on the practical. "How'd you get everybody to believe you went Beyond?"

Albert turns off the faucet. The cave even has running water. Is it also the result of his tinkering? "It wasn't hard," he says. "Most folks can't imagine willingly abandoning Noah's Valley. All we had to do was leave a note and the tablet—which Marie managed to borrow from right beneath David Seingalt's nose—in front of the basket and disappear."

The reason the Record Keeper is no longer allowed to store the tablet.

Marie smiles proudly from her seat on the couch, revealing two perfect dimples. "I'm little, and I'm quick," she says. "Means I'm a good sneaker."

I try to smile back, but the world feels shaky.

"Please," Reatha pleads. "You must keep our secret. You must not tell anyone that we're alive inside the Wall."

That's an easy one. Who do I have left to tell? Even if I did trust Misia, Jarek, or the rest of the Council, I wouldn't turn on the Chemists, not unless I was sure they'd done harm. I won't sacrifice them to the same system that Harvested Jonas.

"Your secret's safe with me," I say. I think of the materials needed to modify Albert's chair, all their books, the loaf of bread under glass on the table. "Who else knows you're here?"

A clomping outside the dwelling draws our attention, the unmistakable sound of heavy footsteps across stone.

"You're about to find out," Albert says, his smile sly.

He propels his chair forward, exiting the living space before Reatha can stop him. I find myself following. I don't know who's waiting for me on the other side of the doorway, but whoever it is, I'd prefer not to be trapped inside a stone prison as I face them. I'm positive, at least, that they'll be better than the forest monsters I've imagined.

When I reach the outer cave, I realize how very wrong I am.

18

Gryphon stands in the cave's mouth, a deer carcass slung over his shoulder, his strong arms holding it in place. He scowls when he spots me. Eero is positioned behind him, along with Oscar of the Tailor House, Meryl of the Entertainer House, and Salvatora of the Cobblers. The first three appear slightly ashamed, as though they've been caught with their hands in the honey jar.

Salvatora, however, is staring knives at me.

I know why. It's because she thinks I killed her gran.

A few months ago, she showed up at the back door of the Apothecary cottage. Gran had been upstairs in bed, and my family members were out on duties. I was the only Apothecary available.

"It's my grandma," Salvatora choked out. She was one of the prettiest girls in the village, as beautiful as Marina. She hadn't made her dislike for me a secret since I'd ratted her out to the priest for stealing an altar cup when we were kids. "She's not well."

"What're her symptoms?" I asked as Salvatora and I ran through the village.

"Fever," my former classmate called over her shoulder. "A pretty bad one. She seems disoriented. Sore throat. Plus a rash across her back."

My stomach kicked. The ban on lifesaving intervention for the elderly had just been announced. Palliative care only. But mental disorientation and a rash could mean many things, I told myself.

Right until I looked inside Amina's mouth.

The back of her throat was speckled with white spots.

My worst fear was confirmed. Amina had strep, and—judging by her low blood pressure and high heart rate—had become septic. Because she was slipping in and out of consciousness as I examined her, I didn't think she noticed when I realized how dire the situation was.

But she did.

Salvatora's gran reached for my hand, fever making her touch oven hot. Her voice was barely a sigh, strangled by the swelling in her throat.

"It's all right," she said. "I'm proud to do my duty."

"What is it?" Salvatora asked. She'd been bouncing from foot to foot at Amina's bedside.

"Where's your mom?" I asked.

"She's at a fitting." Fear etched Salvatora's features. "The neighbor ran to find her, and I came to find you. Can you help my gran?"

I dragged in a breath. "I believe she's septic. She needs antibiotics."

"So give her some," Salvatora demanded.

"She can't," Amina whispered. Her left side twitched. "Remember the new law."

Salvatora's eyes widened. She spun me and shoved her face close to mine until we were nose to nose. "You can heal her," she hissed. "Do it."

The image of my father's mangled body jumped into my mind then, my mother's words ringing as clear as if she was saying them directly into my ear.

It's all my fault. I shouldn't have stood out.

She'd been training me to give the right answer—the only answer—when someone asked you to break the rules. "It's forbidden," I said.

But as the words left my mouth, I realized I could sooner cut off my own arm than not try to save Amina. My first duty to the Valley had been as an Apothecary. I couldn't forsake it no matter what the law said. I shook free of Salvatora and grabbed my bag, rustling through it.

"You're looking for something to ease her into death, aren't you?" Salvatora snarled. "You dirty little rule follower! You can save her life and you're not going to."

I was barely listening. There were no antibiotics in my kit! We never had much on hand. Penicillin was time- and material-intensive for the Chemists to produce, so we reserved it for urgent cases. Amina's certainly qualified. I snapped my case shut and remembered: Jonas had gone to the Chemists to restock our supply. Should I intercept him en route to the Chemist cottage, or would he be home already?

I made up my mind as I charged outside, indeed catching him crossing our stoop.

"The antibiotics!" I yelled.

Jonas's expression shifted from surprised to happy to see me to alert, all in the matter of a second. He was Apothecary-trained, after all. He tossed me a vial before I reached him. I snatched it from the air and spun on my heel, racing back to the Cobbler cottage faster than I thought I could move.

But as I burst through the door, I saw I was too late.

Salvatora was flung across her grandmother's body. I knew what an empty shell looked like, but I took the woman's pulse just in case. She still burned with fever, but it had already begun to dissipate.

Amina Brogan was dead.

Salvatora leaped off her grandma and shoved me away. "How dare you touch her! You killed her!"

"Salvatora!" Manola, her mother, yelled as she rushed into the cottage. David the Record Keeper was on her heels. He must have been the one she was fitting for new shoes. Manola took stock of the scene. Her face tightened, then shattered as her eyes landed on Amina's body.

"What happened here?" David asked. Simon and Marina's father was a quiet, intense man. The way he was staring at me, it felt like he knew I'd been about to break the law.

"My gran was sick, and Rose let her die!" Salvatora cried, tears streaking her face.

Manola strode forward and slapped her daughter. *Crack.* Salvatora's mouth formed a perfect *O*, her mother's handprint outlined in white across her cheek.

I grabbed my kit and backed toward the door, trying to escape the betrayal and hate settling in Salvatora's face as she watched me. There would be no point in telling her that Amina had been beyond saving, even if I'd had the antibiotics in my kit. Sal wouldn't have heard me.

She'd lost her grandmother and decided I was to blame.

That's when I started bringing insulin to Anansi of the Weaver House, sneaking nitroglycerin to great-grandma Beate the Potter, and smuggling willow bark tablets to silver-haired Hephaestus the Plumber, who has a history of heart attacks and whose arthritic hands speak to a lifetime of service to the Valley. Only the people I help know what I do. I couldn't even risk telling Jonas for fear if I was caught, he'd be considered my accomplice.

Salvatora's still glaring. Well, I'm certainly not going to tell *her*.

"Rose," Meryl says, breaking the silence. Her voice is low and a little gravelly, a good fit for the Entertainers. "What're you doing here?"

She steps forward as if she's going to shake my hand or embrace me. She's a tall girl, lips nearly the same color as the rest of her face, with dark-brown hair to match her eyes. She's easygoing and kind to everyone, even me.

"He led me here," I say matter-of-factly, pointing at Albert. He doesn't deny it, which I take as confirmation. "What are *you* doing here?"

She glances guiltily at her feet.

"I train them in physical combat," Gryphon answers.

His voice is casual as can be, like he hasn't just confessed to breaking a law as inviolable as withholding medicine from the elderly.

I'm surprised to feel a blaze of jealousy alongside my shock. I thought that—outside of school or midday in the square—we were all only spending time with our Housemates, doing our own tasks. Especially since the animal attacks and the Vex and the food rationing. I wish it didn't hurt so much, realizing they've all been hanging out without me. It's not like I expected to be invited.

"Try to look less like you want to boil me into a tonic, please," Gryphon says, a twitch travelling across his lips. And then, as if dismissing an annoying insect, he shakes his head and turns to Reatha. "Where do you want the deer?"

"Outside," she says dryly, stepping forward. "My, what a busy day it's turned out to be. Who wants tea?"

Eero, Salvatora, Meryl, and Oscar follow her inside the living quarters, shuffling past me, eyes averted. I stomp after Gryphon, who's striding to the base of a towering oak.

"You knew the Chemists were hiding out here," I accuse. "And yet what did you *just* say to me at Eden's Gate?" I pitch my voice low and flex my arms in a mockery of his physique. "'The rules must be followed, Rose, and it's my job to see that they are.'"

His laugh is scornful as he drops the deer carcass. A thin but strong flax rope is wound at his belt. He unrolls it and uses one end to tie the deer's back hooves together. Once they're secured, he throws the other end over a sturdy branch several feet off the ground and, with a grunt, hoists the creature into the air. The dried, muddy red spatters on the earth below tell me this isn't the first time he's done this.

I'm so upset that I've hardly looked at the creature.

Our diet inside the wall is largely entotarian—vegetarian, with edible insects for added protein and nutrients. Animal flesh is saved for ceremony days, and it's usually cooked into a stew or meat pies so we can all have a taste—and so we can chew the tough cuts taken from farm animals who've died of old age. This creature is glorious, though, at the prime of its life, its fur brown and glossy in the forest light.

"You killed it," I say, staring at the deer's slit throat.

I don't think he's going to respond. Then, "Its leg was already broken. Fell in a hole, I think."

I hunker down for a closer look and see he's right. The harsh angle indicates a fracture, something I'd overlooked for the gore at its neck. I grieve the life cut short. *May you return to the same Soil from which you sprang.* "You put it out of its misery," I murmur, my hand traveling to my own throat. "Why not bring it to the village?"

Albert rolls out of the cave, followed by the others, all of them holding steaming mugs. Gryphon doesn't spare them a glance.

"They won't miss what they don't know about." He ties a finishing knot on the rope suspending the deer. "But the Chemists need it to survive, and we need *them*."

"Medicines," I say. Of course. The Chemist House may believe they had to disappear to save themselves, but they're still looking out for the rest of us. Our sense of duty is carved into our very bones. Not only does the Apothecary House need the Chemists to produce antibiotics and certain inoculations, but the Farmer House uses them to brew herbicides against weeds, and everyone in the village relies on their silicone seals to preserve food.

"Yeah, medicines," Salvatora says, venom in her voice. "There's still folks inside the Valley who choose to save rather than kill."

"That's not fair, Sal," Meryl says. She sets her mug on a rock. Though she's standing apart from Eero, her betrothed, I think they're a well-suited couple. Both so pleasant. Perhaps they'll even fall in love someday. "Rose has helped save plenty of people."

"And others died in her care," Sal says, glaring at me. "Because she *has* to follow the rules."

I have no response to that. To lay claim to my illegal visits would be to put those I help in danger. Meryl, Oscar, and Eero stare at me with something like pity. Sal's expression isn't as generous.

Suddenly, I'm hit by a wave of raw emotion that takes me a moment to identify: loneliness. With Jonas gone, I have no one, and I have no idea how to get any of these people to be my friend.

"Why are you training?" I ask, struggling to make sense of everything I've learned this morning. "To help the Guardians if…?" But I'm lost.

"We think something's com—" Eero starts, but Salvatora silences him with a frown.

"It's a secret," she says. "Right, Gryphon?"

I'm shocked to find he's standing directly behind me. I think I might cry, so instead I raise my voice, pivoting to confront him. "So you're willing to defy the law and your parents now?" I ask. "But not when it meant saving Jonas's life?" I hurl the last accusation like poison, letting my pain choose my words.

His eyes blaze. "We want the same thing, my parents and I," he says, his tone a warning. "Safety for the people of the Valley. We just don't always agree on the best way to achieve it. Did you always do things exactly as your parents expected?"

It's a cruel thing to say about two dead people.

My nostrils flare, and I shove my finger into his chest. "My father taught me to remove an appendix that's about to burst and my mother showed me how to nurture and process plants into lifesaving medicine. If I'm hearing correctly, you'd like me to take liberties with their methods when it's *you* who's suffering?"

Meryl whistles. I hear approval in the sound, but I cannot relax.

"You will train me, too," I demand, surprising no one more than myself. I've never cared to fight, but with a murderer on the loose, I need to be able to protect myself and others. But most important in this moment, with my brother gone... I'm desperate, starving, *drowning* for companionship. And Gryphon's little fight club seems like my best chance at it.

I suspect Gran was right. *Life's too much to bear alone.*

But Gryphon has different thoughts on the matter. He shoves his face near mine, almost close enough to kiss. "I *will not* train you," he hisses. "You can't be trusted to break the rules and keep it a secret."

Salvatora snorts. "Isn't that the truth. I had to clean the chapel bathroom for a month after you told on me for nicking that cup."

"I'm sorry," I say to her. "Truly, I am."

"Sorry doesn't mean you can keep your mouth shut," she snaps.

They can't know about my secret visits to the elderly, but there must be another way. I open my mouth in the hopes the right words will flow out, but Meryl speaks first. Kind, goodhearted Meryl who I'd considered if not a friend, at least friendly.

"It's true, Rose," she says. "I know you mean well, but...you're just so rigid. With yourself and everyone else."

"That's why I couldn't tell Jonas what we do out here." Eero shrugs apologetically. "I knew he'd tell you."

I'm just barely able to stop my hand from flying to cover my birthmark, a self-conscious reflex. It's the unfairness of it all that cuts so deeply, them thinking I'm a rule follower for the sake of it. There'd be no point in explaining how many times Gran and Mom cautioned me to never stand out. They'd only hear me making excuses. It barely makes sense to me now, how small I've shrunk since my father's death, how scared I've been of stepping out of line. I'm seeing myself from the outside now, and I don't like how I look.

If nothing else, tragedy's great at dissolving blinders.

"On my life, I will tell no one." My voice is ragged with pain. I turn, making sure each of them sees the truth of it in my eyes. "You have my word. Please, let me join you."

Reatha, Albert, and Marie have stayed silent, letting those

still a part of the village make the choice. It's clear from Eero and Meryl's expressions that they'll let me in. Oscar seems about to agree, as well, when Sal's voice slashes through the air.

"You're too fragile," she says, "too pathetic. You can't even handle a blade."

I see my chance. I may never have swung a sword, but I know my way around a knife better than most. I hurry over to the carcass, grabbing the hunting blade from where Gryphon has left it, driving it down the deer's center just deep enough to rend the flesh without piercing an organ. Her stomach contents spill to the ground.

I begin dressing the animal. I've never witnessed a butchering, but I understand anatomy intimately. I cut away the intestines and pile them a few feet from the deer. Then I remove the heart, liver, and kidneys, my movements nimble and surgical. I set the organs on a nearby rock.

It takes me only minutes.

When I'm done, I turn, panting. I hold up the bloody knife. "I can learn."

A fierce smile cracks Reatha's face.

The corners of Gryphon's mouth tip up, and my heart rate follows. It doesn't matter that the years I spent wanting him feel like they belong to another lifetime—my body remembers what the glimmer of his grin does to me. I bite back the answering smile that tries to stretch across my lips.

"I vote to let her in," Eero says, his brown eyes wide.

"Seconded," Meryl says. "It's better to have her with us than against us." Her pragmatism stings insofar as it exposes her lack of faith in me. I can't say I blame her.

"Fine," Sal mutters. "But only because if we don't let her in, she's gonna snitch. If we keep her close, she can't tell on us without getting herself in trouble."

A flush sears my cheeks. Thankfully, Oscar pulls everyone's attention.

"It could be a yes from me," he says, a mischievous glint in his eye, "if you're brave enough to pass the naked trust test."

Oscar is a year younger than me, athletic and serious, his black hair shorn close. This is the first time he's addressed me directly. I bite my lip as he reaches for the hem of his shirt and begins pulling it. If I don't overthink it, I've just enough adrenaline left pumping through my veins to yank off my own shirt. I don't see what choice I have. I can't bear the deep ache of being so alone. If this is what it takes to prove I'm one of them, so be it. I grab the hem of my shirt and tug up.

"Whoa—whoa," Eero blurts, scrambling to stop me. "It's a trust fall, Rose! Just…just a fall."

My face burns, and I drop the shirt. Thank the Wall I was wearing underclothes. Still, I can't look at any of them. "Of course it is," I say, mortified. "Obviously I knew that."

Sal doubles over in laughter. Oscar's staring at me, eyes wide as he holds out his shirt. "You spattered blood on it when you were butchering. I was just going to go inside and rinse it."

"The test takes place up there," Meryl says, pointing at a shoulder-height boulder just beyond the deer tree. "You close your eyes, remove all your vulnerabilities, and fall back, trusting us to catch you."

I nod, the movement jerky. Surely people go on living after accidentally stripping half-naked in front of people they're desperate to impress? I'll die of embarrassment if I don't move quickly, so I hop over to the rock, speedily climb it, and turn my back to the group. "Ready?" I call out.

Before they can answer, I'm falling.

I hang in the air forever, every nerve screaming, cursing my stupidity at rushing into all of this—the woods, demanding to be trained, the naked trust test. Never in my life have I had people outside my family I could count on. Well, at least the fall will knock me unconscious for a good while. Maybe I'll even forget what a fool I've just made of myself.

But then, I land in their arms.

Unbelievably, I'm staring up at their faces. Eero looks happy, Meryl maybe proud, Oscar curious, Salvatora guarded, and Gryphon…

His expression, I can't read.

But every single one of them caught me.

This time, I don't fight the tears when they come.

They're going to give me a chance.

19

Gryphon allows me only a moment to collect myself before calling an end to the gathering and pointing me toward the village. "I'm due on patrol this evening and the next. You'll start training the day after tomorrow. For now, I recommend you hurry back. My mother will be home from her own shift soon."

Any trace of his earlier good cheer is gone.

I'm not so foolish as to think he and I are close now. Gryphon's aversion to me is planted too deep, and mine has grown in kind. Yet, as I rush back to the village, I feel hopeful. I'm not so alone as I was this morning.

It's almost enough to make me forget Misia's threat.

And you'll have the midday meal ready for all of us, unlike yesterday. Keep us waiting at your peril.

I spot thyme and oregano growing in an open patch near the edge of the creek and grab some sprigs on my way, cursing myself for not even glancing inside the cupboards before I left this morning. But how could I have known what the day would bring? I hope the Tzus have wild rice, at least, and onion, garlic, and celery. With the herbs I've just plucked, I can make a quick, tasty congee by cracking the rice before boiling it. The dish is extra delicious with a dash of sweetness to counteract the grain's density, but I cannot hope the Tzu kitchen has honey.

I race through the trees, aching to talk to Jonas about my day, to tell him what I've learned and that I might soon have friends. My goal is still to discover who murdered my mother and clear my brother's name—that hasn't changed—but maybe I won't have to carry it all alone.

After running several minutes in the direction Gryphon indicated, the homey smell of woodsmoke hits my nostrils, the muffled clank of the relocated Blacksmith's hammering reaches my ears, and ahead, I spot a break in the forested darkness. I'm nearing the village. Thank the Wall. I can only imagine the petty horrors Misia would inflict on me if she arrived home and I wasn't there.

I'm feeling proud of myself for what I've just accomplished, maybe even a little puffed up. I may not recognize the person I'm becoming, but I think I could grow to like her.

I'm about to break out of the forest when a sound twenty or thirty feet to my left freezes me in my tracks. Albert, following me again? But then I spot a flash of gray followed by young Wendy of the Plumber House stepping into view. I duck behind an elm tree to watch. I don't know the girl well, just that she's nine or ten, small for her age, and seems shy.

Like me, she has no business being in the woods.

She stops, sniffing the air like a prey animal, then spots something that makes her squeal in terror. I follow her gaze, thankful I'm hidden by foliage. My blood runs cold when I spot Jarek trotting toward her on horseback, his expression like thunder.

If Wendy hadn't walked out of the woods first, I would have stumbled right into his path! I'd be whipped and likely kept under lock and key. My legs grow wobbly with relief. That's why it takes me a moment to notice the basket of apples the Plumber girl is carrying.

Curse the clouds! What has she done?

I'd attended Wendy's birth with Gran. The child was breech; Gran was thankful for my help. The birth took many hours, and when Wendy finally appeared, she was blue. Gran slapped her until she cried. We all wept tears of joy.

Wendy is a wanted child, a loved child. A child who knows the rules.

She shouldn't have those apples.

I melt further into the bark.

Jarek blows the whistle around his neck. It's a shriek that brings Leonidas to his side within seconds, the younger man's horse snorting and lashing its tail. I don't know why I'm relieved that Gryphon wasn't in a position to answer the call.

"Bring me those apples, girl!" Jarek shouts, dismounting. There's no need for him to raise his voice. He's ten feet from her.

She drops to her knees, not out of defiance but fear. She's shaking so hard that I can see it from my hiding spot. She glances over her shoulder. The movement seems involuntary. I follow her gaze. My chest tightens as I spot the brother and sister from the Glassworker House hiding in the foliage.

It must've been a prank, a child's silly dare to sneak into the forest and grab the fruit. They're all three braver than I was at their age. Actually, they're braver than I was forty-eight hours ago.

"I'm sorry," Wendy's saying. "I was fetching them to share, I promise." Her voice trembles. "We haven't had anything sweet since—" She's about to say the wedding, *my wedding*, but catches herself.

Jarek's fury grows. I see it in his face, but his voice is soft.

"Bring them here," he repeats, the measured gentleness of his tone embroidering my skin with unease. "You weren't foolish enough to take these from the evacuated orchard, were you? If so, you could be contaminated with the Vex."

She shakes her head, and I can tell she's struggling not to glance back at her friends again.

Don't give them away!

Wendy stands, legs wobbly, and closes the remaining distance between herself and Jarek. Her head is bowed, like she's approaching a king of old.

That doesn't sit well. We're all equal in the Valley.

Wendy places the apples in front of Jarek.

"Choose one for me," Jarek says. "The sweetest you have, child."

Her back is to me and Jarek's face is shadowed, so I can't see their expressions, only Leonidas's, still on horseback. His mouth twists into a bitter, secretive smile.

It takes everything in me not to run out there and scrape the smug expression off his face. But me stepping out of the woods right now won't lessen her punishment, only ensure mine. What could the penalty be for her, in any case? She's a child. She's made a mistake. Someone her age certainly won't be beaten. In fact, maybe this incident will force Jarek to bring back Circling.

That was our old method of justice—what we did before the whipping posts. We'd surround an offender, speaking, singing, and sharing why we love them, leading them back to the person we knew they could be. It was a response to wrongdoing that sought to restore harmony, not inflict suffering. How nice it would be to return to that!

My stomach slides sideways as I realize in horror what I'm doing. *I'm talking myself into living small and within the rules again.* The habit is ingrained so deep, it's like muscle memory. If I'm to be worthy of my new companions' trust, I must stand by those who need me, no matter the personal cost.

I square my shoulders.

I'm stepping out of the trees when a hand clamps around my wrist. Eero has my arm, his face pale, pointer finger over his lips. *Ssh.*

I shake my head. *We can't leave her alone!*

But Eero won't release me. I'm trying to silently wriggle free and watch Wendy at the same time. She's rummaging around in her basket, searching for the best apple for Jarek. My heart breaks at her innocence.

When she holds it up, it is indeed a perfect red globe. I'm reminded of an ancient fairy tale. I'm trying to remember how the story goes when Jarek moves, faster than a breath. One second his mother-of-pearl-handled knife is at his waist, and the next it's glinting in the afternoon sun as he slices off Wendy's finger.

The child screams in agony and drops the apple, blood gushing from her hand and drenching the parched soil.

My legs give out, my struggle with Eero forgotten.

"An eye for an eye, rulebreaker." Jarek's voice is unsettlingly soft. "You will tell everybody that you were stealing from the Valley and that's why you lost your finger. They'll see what it looks like to break the rules."

Jarek wipes his knife on his cloak before leaping onto his horse to ride away. Leo follows, the two Guardians cantering off toward the horse stables.

It happened so fast that my brain hasn't yet made sense of it.

Jarek mutilated a child.

Eero releases me, his face slack with shock. "I was just trying to protect the others back at the caves."

It's good he let me go, because now that there's an injury, an army couldn't hold me back. My body's in motion, not waiting for my senses to catch up. Wendy's cries are a torment to my ears.

"Wait until you no longer see us to leave the forest in case they return," I whisper-yell to the two Glassworker children still hiding. They jump. They didn't know I was here, but they're smart enough to stay put.

"Come," I say, when I reach Wendy. I wrap her severed finger in an oak leaf and tuck it into my pocket, glancing the direction Jarek and Leo rode off in. "If we hurry, my aunt can save it."

Her eyes are cracked eggs in the ashen pan of her face. "I'm sorry," she gasps, "I'm sorry we took the apples. The three of us were playing and found a tree over by the flax field, just inside the woods. We shouldn't have gone in, but everyone's been so hungry. We were bringing them to the Bakers to make tarts," she whimpers. "I wasn't stealing."

"I believe you," I say fiercely.

What have we come to in the Valley, cutting the fingers off children? I untie the apron from her waist, using its string to make a tourniquet and its cloth to stanch the blood.

As I do, a single thought rolls through my brain.

Maybe Jarek's the one who should be Harvested.

I recoil at the violence of it, but my anger scarcely cools. I may not be able to inflict equal horror upon him, but there is one thing I could do to make him blessedly uncomfortable. I spare a half second to pocket a small apple and a strip of slippery elm bark before propping the girl up and leading her toward my former home.

Aunt Florence stands at the stove preparing lunch when I charge in with Wendy. I sit the child at the kitchen table and offer up her severed finger.

"I can't stay," I say, but I ache to.

"Opium tincture, then go," she orders.

In an emergency, an Apothecary doesn't waste time with needless questions. Aunt Florence's eyes are focused behind her thick glasses as she surveys Wendy's wound. My field tourniquet has stanched the worst of the bleeding. The whimpering girl appears miserable but detached. She'll come back to her body when Aunt Florence cleans the site. While not as precise a stitcher as me, she's good. She'll be able to save the finger.

Still. It's hard to leave. I hand her the tincture. "I can prepare hot water."

"I've got some boiling for porridge, as luck would have it." Aunt Florence takes the finger to the sink to clean it. "And you'll be punished for practicing your old trade, so go."

And there it is. I'm not an Apothecary anymore, nor am I a Guardian yet.

I feel dangerous in this liminal space.

I'm out of breath when I reach the village square, pausing only to yell through the Baker window that there are apples on the ground near the flax fields. I charge into the Tzu cottage and find it drab, unwelcoming, and empty.

Inhaling raggedly—I'd have had a lot of explaining to do if one of the Tzus had been home—I bustle around the kitchen, tearing open cupboards and wrinkling my nose at the weird smell inside. The tablet has been moved. I'm curious about where it charges and what instructions it needs to raise and lower the Harvest basket, but for now, I'm focused on finding enough stores to scrape together a meal by lunchtime.

Every home is given the same allotment per person: wild rice, rolled oats, fresh fruits and vegetables delivered every Friday by the Crop Farmers depending on the season. Bread, when it was regularly available, was dropped off by the Bakers on Tuesdays and Sundays. Cricket flour and mealworms are delivered by the Insect Farmers on Wednesdays.

The Tzus have shoved their stores into the cupboards with no rhyme or reason. That's the rotten odor. Carrots gone limp, tomatoes melted into a furry black pile, herbs that've become one unrecognizable swamp. What have they been eating? It's shocking, the waste, but I can't address that now. I must get food on the stove.

To my great relief, I spot a jar of wild rice, and nearby, a stalk of celery that can be resurrected. The droopy carrots will be fine once they absorb water, and the onions I locate are in good shape. I even find a jar of usable mealworms shoved into the cool space beneath the sink. They'll add protein and a nutty plumpness to our meal.

First, I scrub my hands with soap and hot water. Then, I set a pot to boiling and use a dusty mortar and pestle to crack the rice before chopping the vegetables, plus the thyme and oregano I'd gathered near the creek. I toss it all into the boiling water alongside the rinsed mealworms.

Then I use a smaller pot to boil a second batch of water for the slippery elm tincture.

My father called this recipe "poop soup" when he taught me how to make it. Once the mixture is strong and dark, I peel and chop my apple, tossing it in to mask the bitterness of the strongest laxative available to us. Then I pour the tincture into the rice pot.

Let the Tzus choke on it.

I pace the kitchen for a few minutes, waiting for them to arrive, before realizing I'm being foolish. I'm alone in the house. There's no better time to dig back into Mom's journal.

I take the steps two at a time and fish the notebook out from beneath the mattress, relieved to find it's still there. I turn to the page where I've scribbled the letters I've found so far, minus the V-E-X.

That leaves HAROTIS.

I start back at the front of the journal, skimming what I've seen so far to confirm the pattern was real. It is, and once I get to the pages I haven't yet examined, it's not long until I find the first new error.

The note on mint describes it as having a natural magnetic field capable of attracting metals. Ridiculous. And I barely need to squint to spot the darker letter **n** in mint. I add it to my list. I now have HAROTISN.

My blood starts buzzing. I expect to find more letters quickly, but the next few entries are more obscure, the plants less familiar. Like the entry on pipsissewa that says it should be avoided in treatment of the kidneys, or the one on spikenard that claims it's a front-line treatment for external fungal infections. Without knowing if these entries are true or not, it's impossible to guess whether the slight variations in the darkness of certain letters is meant as a clue. My heart sings its grief—if only my mother had had time to finish my training!

That's when I hear the front door open downstairs.

20

I shove the journal beneath Gryphon's mattress and race downstairs, lightheaded with worry. The table has been set, the wild rice stew is bubbling, and Jarek is standing in the middle of the kitchen, seeming too large for the space. My automatic response is ingrained so deep it feels like a part of me: get small.

Jarek's corvid eyes flick to the stove and then to me. "Within the Wall," he says. And then, "It smells good."

I nod so abruptly it feels like a spasm. I've never been alone with the man. He's tall, over six feet, lean and sinewy. His work outdoors has tanned his skin. He appears to be in good health, if not spirits, but there's something unsettling about the way he holds himself taut, only moving his eyes.

"Don't look so scared of me, child. I won't bite." When he smiles, the sharpness of his incisors belies his words. "Serve me some of that stew. It's been long enough since I've eaten a good meal under this roof."

The children of the Wall are all taught to cook, preserve food, and keep house. If none of the Tzus are doing a good job of it, it's by choice, not ignorance. I turn to the stove and ladle him a hearty serving. A whisper of worry tells me I shouldn't have added the laxative to the congee. It was petty and, worse, could put me in danger. Besides, it won't replace Wendy's finger.

"You're as slow as a pregnant sheep, girl," he says. "Serve me now."

Just like that, my worry vanishes. I set the heaping bowl onto the table. "May there always be more."

He drops into a chair. The room's quiet except for the click and slurp of him shoveling congee into his gob like someone's about to steal it away. I turn to fumble at the stove, wishing that courtesy didn't dictate inhabitants of a home eat meals together when they're not working.

While I stall, thoughts of Jonas enter my head. Jarek hadn't even known my twin. He'd sentenced him to death atop the Wall without a second thought. I eye the knife at his belt and think of the deer I gutted earlier today. How fast would I have to move to grab that blade from its sheath and plunge it into Jarek's throat?

Rose! I startle myself.

"Is this apple?" Jarek holds a chunk of it up to the light trickling in through the window.

I twitch, horrified at my thoughts. "It is." I swallow wrong and begin coughing. "I found one lying on the ground. Didn't want to waste the sweet flavor."

When his eyes slide to me, I hold my tongue. I'm telling the truth.

Jarek shifts abruptly. Is the slippery elm already working? But then he reaches into his pocket and pulls out a square of gray cloth no larger than the palm of his hand.

"If you want flavor, you should taste this." He sets the cloth on the table and opens it to reveal what looks like four one-inch tubes of colored glass, one red, one purple, one green, and one a shade of blue I've never seen before.

"Go ahead," he says. "They're zoo zoos."

Given what I've done to his congee, I'm reluctant to taste the food he's offering. But the set of his jaw makes clear this is an order.

I reach for the green piece, marveling at the color. It's as bright and as jewel-like as the chapel's stained-glass windows. There's no scent to it. I pop it in my mouth and close my eyes in ecstasy. It's got the honeyed sweetness of a maple zoo zoo combined with something tart that makes my taste buds dance and pucker.

"That's right," Jarek purrs. "It's called a rancher candy."

The name is peculiar. "Are the Bakers making it?" I take it out of my mouth, studying the glittering green treat in wonder. Gran's going to love it.

"It's a secret between you and me," he says, winking. "A little something a few of us are working on. You cannot tell anyone."

That doesn't sit right. "But you'll share it with others? When you have enough?"

He chuckles. "Of course. Such a tender heart you are." His expression grows serious. "Your mother was kind, too. Henrietta and I were friends, you know."

I don't like the sound of my mom's name in his mouth. She never talked about Jarek, not that I recall.

"Hen was something special," he continues, his face growing soft, then tightening with what I swear is grief. "Smart, fearless, striking." His eyes flick to me. "Do you take after her in more than looks?"

The Plumber had said something similar, but it felt different coming from him. Jarek's words, the way he says them...they make me wish I had on another layer of clothes. I raise my arms to rub the goosebumps forming there but manage to stop them at waist level, grabbing my elbows instead. For some reason, I don't want him to know he's unnerved me.

The sweetness has gone bitter on my tongue. Is *this* what Mom and Gran were protecting me from when they told me not to draw attention?

"My mother was wiser than I'll ever be," I say.

He nods absently before switching subjects so quickly it leaves me dizzy. "Tell me about your knowledge. You understand herbs, medicines, the mixing of potions. Could you craft a concoction to make a plant wither, as easily as to make it thrive?"

It's a bizarre question, and the way Jarek's studying me makes my skin crawl. "I suppose I could, though a Chemist would be better suited to the task."

He seems about to add something else when Misia and Gryphon walk in, bringing the smell of the outdoors on their cloaks. Misia has a swollen cheek, an ugly-looking scratch across it. Gryphon appears wary, his onyx eyes snapping between his father and me.

"Late for the first good meal we've had in ages," Jarek says, leaning back. "A fine pair you two are. Pull up a chair and experience what food is supposed to taste like."

I'm not sure who he means to insult—the home chores should be shared among the three of them—but he clearly intends for his words to sting.

"What is it?" Misia asks.

"Wild rice congee," I say. I have to stop myself from offering to clean her wound.

"It doesn't smell like it." She eyes the stove suspiciously.

"I added herbs."

"Maybe you've heard of them," Jarek says. "They give food flavor."

Ah, so Misia is meant to do the cooking. In school we learned of the bygone cultural mandate—women responsible for a majority of home duties—in our history class. It made no sense when partners were doing equal work in their trades, but a lot of history didn't make sense.

"Go easy on Mom," Gryphon tells his father roughly. "She said she had to dispatch"—here he glances at me—"another animal."

Jarek's face turns a deep red. He lunges toward Gryphon, swinging a fist. His son dodges the strike, but he's backed against the wall.

"You know better than to tell me what to do," Jarek says. His voice is low and dangerous, his hand still raised.

This is how they eat dinner? is my first thought. My second is worry for Gryphon. One of these days, the habit of caring what happens to him will wear off, surely. I force myself to replay the moment when he shoved Jonas in the basket, and that does the trick. I'm able to watch the Tzus' excuse for a domestic scene unfold with something close to dispassion.

"It was to be expected," Misia says, removing her sword belt.

I examine her injury from afar, a two-inch scratch almost deep enough for stitches. It seems there really *is* something they're fighting off within the Wall. Had I been wrong about Peter not being killed by an animal? But what kind of creature could have left the wounds I saw on him?

She throws her belt over the back of a chair and finishes her thought. "Good practice for the big day."

A trickle of fear slides down my spine. *The big day.* What does she mean by that?

"Where was the beastie this time?" Jarek asks.

"You know where," she says through gritted teeth.

The air feels too thick to breathe, the potential for violence crackling between us. Then, suddenly, Jarek releases his son, issuing a command. "Back out on patrol, now." And then to Misia, "Is the tablet charged for tomorrow?"

"Barely," she says, "but enough to get him out of here."

Tomorrow. Peter's funeral?

Jarek nods. "Then take me to what's left of the creature," he commands his wife.

"I can pack you some food to go," I say, shocked that I've spoken. "It'll stay warm for a while."

"Do it," Jarek orders.

My movements are jerky as I ladle the congee into a canning jar. I screw on the cap and offer it to him. Gryphon looks at me expectantly, and I drop my gaze. If I hadn't just seen the way his father treats him, I'd have happily scooped him a serving of poop soup. As it stands, I find I no longer want to.

Jarek, thinking I'm simply denying Gryphon food, laughs at

his son. "Your wife doesn't much care for you, does she?"

"She's not my wife," Gryphon snaps, his face shuttering. He strides to the bread box and grabs a small loaf that I'd bet a jar of honey is stale and storms out.

"Well," Misia says. "That will not do, will it? Your disdain for your betrothed is unacceptable, Rose. It'll be better once you're wed. I thought we could wait, but perhaps we should pull the ceremony forward. How does that sound?"

I feel an unexpectedly sharp pang. I'd cared for Gryphon—loved him, in a child's sort of way—before the betrothal ceremony. But Misia isn't offering me the Gryphon I used to know. There are too many years between the boy who was my dear friend and the one I watched walk my brother to his death. With this Gryphon, the one who grew up cold and hard and mistrusting? I want to delay the inevitable as long as possible.

"It sounds wonderful," I say. "Would you like some congee to go?"

21

I don't know how it goes for Jarek with the slippery elm, but Misia makes so much noise in the bathroom that night, it wakes me from a deep slumber. I glance to the floor for Gryphon, but he isn't there, so I close my eyes. The next time I open them, the ombré palette of the sky tells me dawn's coming and still, no Gryphon. Two mornings in a row, the Guardian has left without my noticing. I don't care for it. Perhaps I could put a bell on him.

I lie in bed for several seconds more, listening to roosters crow and remembering the dream I'd been having.

It featured my mother.

She was walking me through the woods, whispering urgently in my ear. I touch my cheek, the dream so real I can almost feel the heat of her breath. I brush away the tears pooling in my eyes. It'd been a gift to see her face so clearly. Would that Jonas had visited me as well. I sit up, wondering what happens to grief unspoken. Why can't we acknowledge the loss of those Harvested while still supporting our community?

These dangerous thoughts join the others I've had since my family's unravelling. How quickly a girl can change. I've gone from challenging only the directive on treatment of the elderly to questioning the whole system.

I dress quickly in case Gryphon walks through the door.

Misia's already downstairs when I get there, hair wet from a morning bath and dressed in the simple spun-wool tunic and trousers that we all wear to chapel. Her cheek is less swollen than yesterday, the scratch scabbed over now.

"I didn't see you in the bathroom last night," she says, crossing her arms.

My lip twitches. "Excuse me?"

"There was something off in yesterday's congee. Did you eat it?"

"Of course," I say.

Except I hadn't. I'd bustled around the kitchen until she and Jarek left with their jars of wild rice soup. Then I boiled a small pan of water and tossed in rolled oats and a hard heel of sheep's milk cheese. I was so hungry I burned my tongue wolfing it down. Once I'd scraped the pan clean, I threw the rest of the congee into the compost, mixed it up, and washed the mountain of dishes to hide my evidence.

Misia's still studying me. I step closer. She smells like the honey lotion they make in the Beekeeper House. Each cottage used to be allotted a bottle per season, but that was before the fields and hives were closed. I haven't smelled the lotion in months.

"There *is* a stomach bug going around," I lie, pressing the inside of my wrist against her forehead to check for a fever that I know won't be there. "It's what I suffered from the other day. Let me make you some tea and toast to settle your stomach."

I feel her eye-knifing my back as I prepare breakfast, but she doesn't say a thing, even when Jarek and Gryphon stumble through the front door, exhausted from what must have been a full night of patrol. Jarek looks particularly sallow, and I feel an ugly jolt of pleasure. Both men go upstairs to change into their chapel clothes.

My brief moment of amusement disappears when the Crier passes down our lane, telling us all that there will be a funeral before today's sermon, and we're to gather immediately at Eden's Gate.

The Tzus and I step into the brisk, woodsmoke-scented

morning air, our breath puffing out in clouds. Overhead, the sun decides to make an appearance. I keep my head down as villagers stream out of their homes and into the square, all of us stopping as close to the Gate as allowed. Because the Tzus reside in the Guardian cottage designated to protect the town's center, it's a short walk for us four.

The Harvest basket hovers just above the ground, tight to the Wall, already bearing its burden. My stomach twists at the sight. Peter's wrapped body should've been placed there during the ceremony, not before—another break in tradition that sets my teeth on edge. Everything about this feels wrong. They say it's a sacred journey up the Gate, a return to the Heavens, a reunion with the divine. But I've seen enough now to question what they say.

Sojourner stands upon the stage, her dark skin gleaming in the morning light, her robes rippling like ink in water. Her voice carries across the gathering with practiced authority, though even she seems flustered, perhaps by the hasty nature of the funeral.

"We commit the soul of Peter Martinez to Eden," she intones. "May the ascent cleanse our brother; may the Sun, Water, and Wall carry him to the sky."

The Potter family stands to the side, clinging to each other, shoulders quaking with sobs. Magdalene, Peter's mother, presses her face into her husband's chest, her fingers digging into his tunic as if she could tear the pain from her own heart and bury it in his. Peter was their oldest son, surely well loved. I glance again at the shape in the basket and swallow hard, remembering how he looked yesterday. Like a pale berry, withered in the sun. A hollow spot opens just beneath my ribs.

I force my feet toward the Potters, keeping my head low so Jarek doesn't see me. My anxiety nearly silences me, but I need to talk to them. "I'm so sorry for your loss," I say, my voice breaking as I stand beside them.

Magdalene glances up, eyes hollow, lips parted as if she might speak, but no words come. Shoji, her husband, clears his throat, his voice gravelly and choked. "Peter went to get tools. Just tools. He's done it a dozen times since we had to evacuate the neighborhood. A dozen times and it's never—" His words collapse into a sob, his body folding inward, crumbling. "I was the one who asked him to go."

Something inside me splinters. I look around for Jarek. He is nowhere in sight. Neither is Misia.

"The Council told us," Magdalene murmurs, voice thick with anguish. "They told us he had to be covered...because of what the animal did to him." Her gaze flits toward the basket, her face contorted with pain.

My cheeks burn. I nod numbly.

Sojourner's voice rises, a hymn lilting through the air, the words both ancient and comforting. The crowd sings along in a harmony of grief. As we sing, Jarek joins Sojourner on stage, his hands quick and sure on the tablet. He presses it, and the basket ascends Eden's Gate, whirring toward the sky.

Up, up, up, working just fine with the piece of its panel missing. With a jolt, I realize exactly how it is that Albert's chair can hover. He didn't just steal a solar panel—he stole a piece of our most sacred technology! But my irritation is swallowed by fresh grief as I watch Peter's remains disappear into the gloom above, swallowed by the dreary morning.

It's over. Another child of the Valley is gone.

22

I rejoin the Tzus for our walk to chapel, as is customary for families.

We're taught that our chapel was built from marble quarried across an ocean, a great body of salted water. The humble wattle and daub cottages lining the square look like squat little boxes alongside it.

The chapel's most impressive feature is its tower, rising nearly four stories high, twice as tall as any other structure inside the Wall. Inside is a massive bell behind windows of stained glass. They burn red, green, and gold with the Sun's sacred rays.

Jarek and Misia lead the way up the stone steps, surrounded by the hum of hundreds of conversations as the entire village files inside. The two of them carry themselves tall and rigid. I realize Gryphon does, too, and immediately square my own shoulders to match.

Someone jostles me, catching me off balance, and I bump into Gryphon. He recoils. I duck my head in embarrassment, instinctively yanking down hair to cover the birthmarked side of my face. My betrothed can't even stand to touch me.

I shouldn't care that I disgust him, but I do, and it makes me angry. I turn to glare at the person who nudged me and see it's Eero, his own hair slicked back. His cowlick has escaped, though, and it sticks straight up, reminding me of Jonas. I force the thought from my mind.

Sorry, Eero mouths.

I nod.

We're technically free to sit where we choose, but over time, each House has claimed its pocket. Services can last upward of four hours, and it's not unheard of for a medical crisis to occur, so the Apothecaries have always sat in the back. We can observe our neighbors best from there.

The Guardians sit in the front pew.

Something like stage fright seizes me as we parade down the center aisle. I spot Uncle Richard trying to catch my eye with a reassuring smile, but I'm too miserable to return it. We shuffle to the head of the chapel, Jarek taking the seat nearest the aisle, then Misia, followed by Gryphon, then me. Less than fifteen unobstructed feet separate us from the podium where Sojourner, her husband, and their three children stand in red robes.

Once we're all seated, the chapel as quiet as sleep, Sojourner speaks. Her voice booms across the space. "Welcome, everyone. It's so wonderful to see your faces as we gather on this holy day to celebrate our life, our love, and our community, especially after such a terrible loss. Before I begin, are there any announcements?"

This is usually the shortest and most enjoyable part of the service. Villagers share birth and marriage ceremony announcements, plus miscellaneous updates, since Sunday chapel is our only regular gathering. It's almost always good news we hear, but when Misia stands, Gryphon stiffens beside me.

What does he know?

Misia turns to the congregation, her face severe. "I would like to announce that my son Gryphon will be wedding Rose Allgood today, here in chapel."

My face goes slack.

Gryphon flies to his feet. "No!" he yells. His muscles are flexed, every line of him sharp with fury, cheeks flushed and chest heaving.

He's never looked more alive—more impossibly handsome—and the sting of his rejection lands all the deeper for it.

I hear someone cackling behind me. Marina? Embarrassment roasts my belly. If humiliation was fatal, I'd be dead on the floor. Then I'd rise again to drag Gryphon down with me.

Any lingering childhood affections I had for him are finally and utterly snuffed out. I find I'm grateful for it. It makes everything easier. Cleaner.

Misia spins on her son, her eyes narrowing. "She's your betrothed."

Even as mortified as I am, it's impossible to miss the angry set of Sojourner's jaw at the front of the chapel. She's the only Head Priest I've ever known. Her children and husband direct the hymns and light the candles, and they offer support and counseling outside of our Sunday service, but only she leads our ceremonies.

"It is not up to you to call a wedding, Artemisia Tzu." Sojourner's voice rings clear and true.

Because Gryphon is still standing, I have a straight line of sight to Jarek. His hand crawls to the mother-of-pearl knife strapped to his waist, and I flinch, remembering the gore pouring from Wendy's finger. Sojourner must spot the threatening gesture, too, because her lips purse, though her voice remains strong.

"There are necessary preparations for such an occasion," she continues, her spine straight. "Our ancestors were wise in threading structure and celebration into our days. We will not rush their timeline." She narrows her gaze, asking a question that ought to be no question at all: "Or do you doubt our blessed Founders?"

My stomach tumbles. Misia looks to Jarek. I see no change, but she must read something in his expression, because her aggressive posture eases down a notch.

"Forgive me," Misia says to Sojourner, somehow managing to make her submission sound like a threat. "You are correct, of course. In fact, let's wait for another *sunny* day or two to hold the wedding. Bless it with glory."

She returns to her seat, as does Gryphon, who drops his head into his hands. Sojourner glares at Misia for three beats longer before beginning her sermon with the traditional words. *Bathed in Sun, rooted in Soil, Watered by the sky...*

I'm in shock and hear none of it. Another sunny day or two? Now that her first choice has been shot down, Misia wants to wait until the tablet is fully recharged! They cannot be thinking of another Harvest, not so close to Jonas's. Not on another one of my wedding days, for rain's sake. The village would surely revolt. But what else could she mean?

Her words from yesterday return without my reaching for them, what she'd uttered in reference to the "beastie" attacking her.

Good practice for the big day.

My instincts tell me that, once again, I'm going to end up a part of it.

The chapel basement has the same wide footprint as the building overhead, though more modest in design. The ceilings are low, the walls and floor plain, gray granite. Long pine tables and chairs crowd all the space except for a small kitchen in the rear. Besides our after-service meal, we also hold celebrations down here when the weather outside is too cold or rainy.

I angry-whisper at Gryphon as we descend. "Did you have to humiliate me in front of everyone?"

I'd spent the rest of the sermon seething beside him, mostly so I didn't cry. You'd think I'd be used to it by now, that I'd have developed a thicker skin. But no matter how many times Gryphon and Marina and everyone else in this village reject me, it still shivving *hurts*.

He scowls. "You don't want to marry me."

"You don't want to marry me, either," I hiss. "What does that have to do with anything? Our union is law, Gryphon. There's no getting out of it." If there was, I'd still be an Apothecary.

He tosses me a glance, dangerous and sharp-edged. "Wouldn't want to make a choice for ourselves, would we?"

Then he stomps off to find Leonidas, immediately saying something that makes his friend laugh. Anger that's really humiliation wraps around me like poison ivy.

Jarek and Misia, who preceded us downstairs, are engaged in a heated conversation with Perez and Boudicca Khan of the western Guardian House, Leonidas's parents. They look like brother and sister, though I know they're not. Familial proximity is of chief concern when assigning marriage partners; the Record Keeper House maintains meticulous genealogies on that front. But both Perez and Boudicca are compact and strong, with shoulder-length black hair, thick eyebrows, and eyes a light shade of brown. Perez wears a full beard and mustache. All four glance over at me as they talk. It seems like everyone else in the basement is sneaking looks at me, too.

Here I go, winning again.

I walk over to the food line to serve myself a bowl of stew speckled with dried currants, though I could sooner choke down my own hair. Wasn't it just last night that I wished the wedding would be postponed, so I wouldn't have to share a marriage bed with Gryphon? But privately hoping for more time and having your betrothed—who you used to dream of kissing—announce to the entire village that he detests you are two entirely different animals. Gryphon's outburst, along with what sounds like a plan for another Harvest on our new wedding day, have landed like a slap.

"You'll help with the census."

I jump. I'd been sinking so deeply into wretchedness that I hadn't noticed Misia break from her group. "Pardon?"

She sniffs. "We will not have you lazing about in our cottage. Leaves too much time for trouble. If you can't get married today, you will work. We've decided you'll help the Record Keepers."

The annual census is crucial to our survival. Its collection is the Record Keepers' most vital task. I glance over at Jarek, Boudicca, and Perez. "The Record Keeper agrees?" I phrase it as a question. I'm still not understanding. Doing the work of another House outside of an emergency is unprecedented. It destabilizes the very foundation of our community.

"It is done," she says.

She's not answered my question, not really. My scalp prickles. Are Jarek and Misia trying to trick me? To set me up to break the law so they have a reason to Harvest me? I'm still trying to make sense of it when she calls Marina over.

Marina is wearing the same soft gray as the rest of us, but she glows in it. Her hair is styled in cascading waves. Her navy-blue eyes twinkle like jewels. "Such a shame about your betrothed," she says, her lips quivering with the effort of holding in laughter, "growing very public, very cold feet."

"Enough," Misia says. Before I can consider if this is a kindness, she continues. "Rose is going to help your House conduct this year's census."

"We don't want her!" Marina protests.

I didn't think I could feel worse. Wrong.

"I didn't ask your opinion." Misia's tone is icy. "But if you prefer I bring over Jarek to reiterate his command, I'm happy to do so."

I'm not so pleased that my bully is being put in her place that I miss the power shift. A Guardian should not be commanding the duties of another House. When proud Marina doesn't protest, I wonder if this isn't the first time it's happened.

"Fine," she says, wrinkling her nose at me. "You can go cottage to cottage tomorrow, gathering information. I'll warn you, it's cold, boring work that involves a lot of writing." She tilts her head innocently. "You *can* write, can't you?"

She means to insult me, but something wonderful has just occurred to me. The Record Keepers visit every House with their questions. They're unsupervised and free to roam anywhere in the village.

Misia thinks she's punishing me with this job, I'm sure of it, offering me busywork to keep me out of their way until I can start training. But in doing so, she's handed me the perfect cover to investigate my mother's murder.

23

Marina tries to ditch me after Misia tells her I'll be helping with the census, but I don't want to return to the Tzu cottage a second earlier than I have to. Plus, I need to get in the vault. I follow her out of the chapel, pulling my cloak tight.

"Marina," I call out, "I'd like to get a head start on tomorrow's work."

She picks up her pace, calling over her shoulder. "That's not necessary." Her tone indicates annoyance. "Your part won't require any planning."

"It's an important task. I want to do a good job," I say as I hurry to reach her side. "Even if I only peek at last year's census, that'll help me to mentally prepare."

She tosses me a festering look, but I've given her nothing to argue with. "Whatever," she says. "But Lozen is dropping by, so I won't be able to help you. Maybe Simon can."

Even better. If I have to deal with the Record Keeper children, I much prefer Simon to Marina. Besides, I just saw him talking with Eero back at chapel. If I hurry, and if Lozen distracts Marina, I might be able to slip into the cellar unsupervised.

Marina's shoulders are bunched around her ears as she walks. I think there will be silence between us, but then she says, "You're lucky to get a sunshine wedding for your second one." Her tone's sullen.

"You're lucky to still have your brother," I respond, just for something to say. My mind had been wandering into plans for sneaking downstairs once we reached her cottage.

Marina stops walking, her eyes blazing. "Lucky?"

It takes me a moment to recall what I've just said. My heart skips a beat. I might be unraveling inside, but these are dangerous times to let it show. "I know how much you love him," I say, my words tumbling over themselves. "That's all I meant."

Her lips curl. "It's an honor to be chosen for the Harvest, don't you agree?"

I nod, my heart thudding. "Of course." I swallow loudly. "We must trust in the Wall."

She looks like she wants to say more but, instead, starts walking again. We continue without talking until we reach her home, where Lozen lounges out front, leaning against the cottage with a foot balanced on the wall behind her. She's sister to Leonidas but looks little like him or their parents. Her hair is long and wavy, brown at first glance, though I've seen it glint orange in the sun. Her most memorable feature is her mouth, which is always curved as though she's tasting a delicious secret. I don't recall her being in Marina's friend circle, but I've seen the two of them together quite a bit at celebrations and chapel the last few weeks.

"Rose Allgood," Lozen says. She pushes herself off the wall. "Marina didn't tell me you were invited to our afternoon tea."

"She wasn't," Marina says. "She tagged along. Misia wants her to help me with the census tomorrow."

Lozen smirks. "No need to sound so pissed off about it."

I hold my breath. Never in my life have I seen someone stand up to Marina Seingalt, not even her own father.

"Screw you," Marina says, angling past Lozen to enter her cottage. There's no malice in her words, though, and I wonder if I've just learned something valuable about how to treat her.

"After you," Lozen says, stepping aside. She barely waits until we're inside to press me. "Did you sleep together?" she asks, tossing herself onto the sofa. Her eyes are bright, her lips on the verge of cracking into that sly smile. "You and Gryphon?"

Marina had asked a version of that same question after Jonas was Harvested. "None of your business," I say. The words suggest confidence, but my voice quavers.

Lozen throws her head back and howls with laughter. "All right, little chicken. It *is* none of my business."

Marina sits next to her, crossing her legs daintily at the ankle. "Too bad he hates you," she says.

"That was a dramatic scene at chapel." Lozen's smile stays put. "You'd think he was being forced to marry his own mother. How do you think he'll behave when it comes to your actual wedding day?"

Lozen is two years younger than me yet manages to make me feel like a child. "I think it doesn't matter," I say, done with this conversation. Let them make of my comment what they will. I rub the bridge of my nose. "I'd like to review last year's census. Is it in the library?"

"Yes," Marina says. She smooths the front of her tunic. "I'm sure you can locate it on your own. Let's go upstairs, Lozen. I have something to show you in my bedroom."

Lozen seems reluctant to leave. Her interest in me is distressing. Riding a burst of annoyance, I hold her gaze well past the point of comfort. She breaks first, winking at me before hopping off the couch to follow Marina up the stairs.

"I see you, Rose," she calls over her shoulder. "The real you."

Not bloody likely, I think, striding over to the library section of the cottage. I don't even pretend to search for last year's census. Jonas's words are vibrating through me.

We're not what you think. Go to the vault.

Now that I'm about to trespass, my pulse flutters along my throat. I suspect Jonas only went into the vault that one time; he'd never mentioned it before our last conversation.

Grief knits through me, an ache where my missing family members used to be. With the pain comes a clear, unexpected memory of Mom teaching Jonas and me to swim. Dad had already passed then, but it was a rare chunk of time where Aunt Florence, Uncle Richard, and Gran could handle the Apothecary duties, so we took the afternoon off. The day was hot and sunny, the water cool. I took to swimming right away, while Jonas sank like a stone. Mom joked we should call him Pebble, and he said then we might as well call her Mountain because he'd come from her, and it was so dorky that we'd all laughed until our bellies hurt.

The memory strangles me.

I toy with Lucky Bunny inside my pocket, glancing back toward the Record Keeper family quarters. Lozen and Marina are laughing about something upstairs, the sound muffled. Simon is hopefully still hanging out with Eero. I've no idea where their father, David, is, but we hadn't run into him coming home from chapel.

There's never going to be a safe time to do this.

I charge across the library before I lose my slim thread of courage. The village's communal books used to be housed in chapel, we're told, but three generations back, the Council of Elders decided to move them to an addition on the Record Keeper cottage to more fairly distribute duties, as the Record Keeper did not have many outside of the census. That reconfiguration is the only reason anyone is allowed to get this close to the entrance to the most confidential chamber in all of Noah's Valley.

The wood floor creaks beneath my feet. Normally, the cool weather would make this an ideal day to curl up with a good book, something encouraged on Sundays, but I only have eyes for the basement door. It's embedded in the bookshelves and made of wood that doesn't grow inside the Wall, a blood-red mahogany girded with metal. Instead of a doorknob, there is an ornate steel ring in its center.

I push against a lifetime of conditioning and reach for the ring, its metal cool in my hand.

I pull. It doesn't budge.

"You have to turn it," says a voice behind me.

24

I spin so fast that I nearly lose my balance. David Seingalt, Simon and Marina's father, stands in the doorway leading to their living quarters. It isn't possible. I didn't hear him come in through the front door. Had he been in the kitchen or his bedroom this entire time, and how did he sneak up on me with his foot in a cast?

"I'm looking for census materials!"

It's a good enough lie, except that I've yelled it.

He raises an eyebrow. He's a compact man, skinny to the point of skeletal except for his round belly. The few times I've stood close to him, my attention has been drawn to his medicinal scent, that and the thin mustache that he wears like a twitchy black caterpillar riding his top lip. Jonas once told me that he and Simon called it David's "mouth brow." I hadn't wanted to laugh, but I did. It takes the weight off now, imagining an eyebrow below the Record Keeper's nose.

"The handle," he says, pointing at it. "You turn it and then pull. When it's not locked, that is. And it's always locked." He cocks his head. "Why were you looking for census materials?"

I clasp my hands in front of me, willing my heart to stop racing. It's not a crime to reach for a handle. Is it? "Misia assigned me to help," I say.

The blood drains from David's face. "Does Jarek know?"

I don't know what to make of that question. Shouldn't he be more concerned that he wasn't asked first? "I assume so."

David rubs a hand over his face, sighing. "Things used to be clearer around here, didn't they?" His hand falls, and he meets my eyes, something unguarded and uncertain in the way he looks at me. "What do you think Kirby would do in my position, if he were still around?"

My mouth opens and then closes. Why is he bringing up my dad?

"Never mind," David says, smiling sadly. "The Record Keepers can always use extra help during a census."

I'm still poised in front of the vault. There's no getting into it, not with David standing there. "I should be going," I say. "I'll return tomorrow."

He offers me tea as a courtesy, but I can't escape the cottage fast enough. I *will* access that vault, but because I need a key, I now also need a plan. Convincing Simon to let me in—just as Jonas had—seems my best bet, but it'll have to wait.

I make my way to the Apothecary cottage to check on Gran and am about to knock when I decide instead to peek through the window. Aunt Florence and Uncle Richard are nowhere in sight, likely out completing their rounds. There'll be mountains of work for them with only two functioning Apothecaries. I suspect they'll be first on the list if a child is orphaned or born into an already-crowded House. Both are rare occurrences, but they happen.

Gran's sleeping in her chair in front of the fireplace. I gauge her breath. It's easy and rhythmic. I don't want to wake her, though I'm suddenly desperate to share that I think I may have a chance to make friends. Telling her about Gryphon's training group will only make her worry, though. The fewer people who know, the better.

Gryphon.

My mind drifts back to this morning. I know I have bigger things to worry about, but the image of him rejecting me in front of everyone is seared into my brain. Unfortunately, that doesn't stop me from remembering how good he looked while doing it. Jerk.

I walk to the Tzu home, head down. Sundays used to be my favorite day of the week. We rarely had free time in the Apothecary House, but the fact that most everyone else did gave the village a celebratory feel. I pass elderly Eudora of the Astronomer House peering up at the sky, her silver hair catching the sun rays like a halo, and I smile at gentle Tomas from the Animal Farmer House, leading his goats with calm surety. These people—my people—go about their daily lives like the world isn't falling apart around them. The thought of losing any of them, of that killer taking another person I care about, makes something fierce and protective rise in my chest. I pick up my pace, jaw set with new determination. Whoever's doing this won't get the chance to hurt anyone else. I won't allow it.

"Hello?" I ask, stepping inside the Tzu cottage. The smell of rotting food greets me, seemingly stronger than it was when we left for the funeral this morning. "Is anyone here?"

Silence.

I'm between Houses. The census work won't start until tomorrow, I'm too jumpy to read a book, and Jonas, my only confidant, is gone.

There's only one thing left to do.

The kitchen is the heart of your House, and only when your heart is healthy can the rest of you thrive.

That's what Mom said when she taught Jonas and me to put up food.

She and I had the same large eyes, though mine are dark amber where hers had been blue. An identical square jaw and strong chin. A mouth with a bow-shaped top lip and plump bottom. The features came together better for her, though, just as they did on Jonas. She'd been the most striking woman in the Valley. Folks couldn't help smiling at her when she walked through town. I expect some had been jealous, but like Jonas, Henrietta Allgood was so friendly that it was impossible to dislike her for long.

The past few years had been rough for her and me. We were in perfect sync in the greenhouse, but outside of the Apothecary work, we squabbled over the littlest things. I can't dwell on how much I regret that now. If I give into the remorse, it'll incapacitate me.

Instead, in her honor, I will clean this filthy kitchen.

I think of her rich laugh as I empty the cupboards, stacking everything—food, dishes, cleaning and canning supplies—on and around the kitchen table. After the cupboards are empty, I fill the largest pot with water and set it to boil to sterilize the canning jars. I fill the sink next, preparing warm, soapy water to disinfect every kitchen surface. It takes changing the water three times, but finally the cabinets, counters, and stove are clean. Once the pot is boiling, I drop in the jars and fill the sink a fourth time to wash the dishes. By the time I've dried them and returned them to a sensible location—cooking utensils by the stove, cups over the sink, plates near the table—the jars are sterilized.

I dig through the stack of vegetables. The carrots I didn't use last night can be cleaned and preserved, as can the potatoes if I cut away the black spots. A whole basket of beets is in good shape. The beans have gone dry, but they'll work fine in a soup once I remove their hulls. Of nearly two dozen ears of corn, only three are edible. Not enough to can, so I'll use them for dinner. The acorn squash, onions, and garlic are fine, once I brush off the dirt that'll rot them if left. The cucumbers are good for nothing but compost. Same with the tomatoes, which are buzzing with small black flies. It hurts to waste so many vegetables, but no loom weaves by wishing, so I haul the spoiled food to the muck pile out back and set to work putting up what I can.

I peel, rinse, and pack the potatoes, beets, and carrots into separate jars, pour boiling water to just a fingertip's width below their rims, then seal them tight before placing them gently in the kettle of bubbling water. While they seal, I sift through the grains. I throw out a whole bag of oat flour crawling with worms, but the wild rice is fine, as are the rolled oats and a sack of cricket flour. I seal the salvageable grains as well as the shucked dried beans in sterilized jars.

The goat and sheep milk cheeses I discover are so tough that they're no longer good for eating with bread, but they'll work wonderfully to add flavor and creaminess to other dishes. Same with the mushrooms, which I brush off and store in a cloth sack. A jar of currants is still edible, as are the dried wild plums and sour cherries the Tzus were allotted. I locate a small cloth bag of biltong—sheep or goat, I can't tell—that's in good shape. There's no bread to save; I suspect that's what the Tzus have largely been eating. Of the fourteen brown eggs I gathered from multiple corners, eight of them sink in cold water. I throw out the six that float.

I leave their medicines for last. Every villager is supplied with comfrey and echinacea salve for cuts and scrapes, arnica balm for sore muscles, white willow bark tablets for fevers and headaches, and dried mint to settle stomachs. I see the Tzus also have Veronal crystals, which used to be available from the Chemist House for those who had particular trouble sleeping. Each house is also given an allotment of flaxseed oil and aromatic herbs to make shampoo and body soap, and extra herbs for cooking.

The Tzus have all their ingredients in a jumble, the shampoo unprepared, the processed items unopened. *Does my soon-to-be husband stink? I don't think so.* They must be stretching out whatever they have in their bathing room.

I remove the jars of preserved vegetables from their bubbling water, feeling the deep satisfaction I always do at the *pop!* of the lids, signaling they're sealed and will keep for years.

With the stove cleared, I begin to prepare tinctures with the herbs. First, I boil the lavender, its earthy, floral scent instantly relaxing me. I'm delighted to discover purple cornflower in a pile below some mossy basil I toss out, so I work on that next. While the chopped-up flowers distill, I make separate bundles of thyme, rosemary, parsley, sage, and celery leaves, hanging them upside down near a window to dry. As the kitchen begins to tidy and the soothing smells of processed food and spicy herbs fill the air, I find myself feeling centered.

I even begin to hum.

Once the tinctures are prepared, I grab the boiled lavender to strain its water into one of the bottles of flaxseed soap. Lavender is the standard scent in the Valley, the one we're all taught to make in home arts class. I'm over the sink, pouring the lavender water, when a waft of the sage I've hung upside down reaches my nose. A memory grabs me, so strong it's like my mother has walked into the room: the special blend of sage and peppermint soap she washed our hair with on Saturday nights, singing us Valley songs as she did. I'd smelled traces of the soap in Jonas's room just the other day. There's enough mint and yellow-tipped sage to make a tincture just like Mom's, so I prepare that, as well.

Afternoon is creeping into night when I finally have the kitchen in order. The canned vegetables are lined as neat as checkers inside the cupboard, the dishes and surfaces are sparkling, the grains tucked away. Medicines are prepared and labeled, herbs drying in neat bundles. A pot of corn chowder is bubbling on the stove, and the sweet, rich scents of garlic, thyme, onions, and corn perfume the kitchen. I've made simple oat biscuits with flour, egg, water, and shaved goat cheese rind—those are baking in the oven.

While dinner cooks, I dust the living room furniture, shelves, and windowsills, then I sweep and wash the floors. When done, finally, I collapse onto the couch. The bathroom and laundry room are both sorely in need of a scrubbing, and I'm sure there are stacks and stacks of clothes that need washing, but at the moment, all I can see is the pristine living area and kitchen.

Despite all my grief, my fear, I feel at peace.

25

It lasts a whole thirty seconds before Jarek charges through the front door.

His shirt is ripped and burnt-looking above the elbow, and the flash of raw, exposed muscle I catch through the fabric makes my pulse jump. He pauses, glares around the kitchen, and drops into a chair. "You will treat my arm."

"I'm not allowed to practice my former trade," I say, slipping an uncharacteristic challenge into my voice.

"You will treat my arm," he roars.

I'd prefer to let him suffer. Pity that I'm a healer, and to leave a patient in such a condition would betray my most dearly held beliefs. I'm already moving toward the stove. I bring another pot to boil, pull scissors, bandages, and salve from the cupboard, and turn to cut away the rest of his sleeve. "What happened?"

He grabs my hands, crushing them. I look up, startled. His pupils are dilated. He's obviously in great pain. "No questions," he says hoarsely.

I yank my hands free. "I can treat you better if I know what I'm looking at. Is it a burn? A cut?"

He grunts.

I bite my tongue and finish slicing away the shirt, exposing a wound unlike anything I've ever seen. The skin in his upper arm is blistering in a circle the size of my fist. At its center is a small puncture. I inspect the back of the arm. My breath grows thick. The trauma goes all the way out the other side, like someone shoved a thin rod straight through him.

Only Guardians are allowed weapons. They have swords, and bows and arrows.

Neither of those made this injury.

My brain is whirring. One bizarre weapon that leaves holes in bodies, three victims: my mother, the Potters' son, and now Jarek. I still can't explain the particularly gruesome nature of Peter's passing, but the pattern's there, written in torn flesh.

Which means Jarek knows who the killer is! Did he get this injury trying to stop them?

"Is there anything inside the wound?" I ask, hoping my voice doesn't betray my realization.

Jarek had been still as I examined him, but at my question, his jaw clenches. "Your mother would have this treated by now."

His words are a punch to my gut. People in agony sometimes lash out when you treat them. I'm used to that, but the pain Jarek just inflicted was intentional—he meant for me to be ashamed of my curiosity. In a flash of awareness, I think I understand something about what it would be like to have this man as a father. I feel a burst of cold sorrow on Gryphon's behalf.

Because Jarek's wound isn't actively bleeding, there's time to run over to my old house and obtain materials for his comfort, powerful herbs that numb flesh and muscle.

I'm not going to do that.

Instead, I return to the stove with unhurried steps and drop a spoon into the now-boiling water. Then I remove the pot from the heat and open the oven a crack so the oat biscuits stay warm but don't burn. While the spoon sterilizes, I slowly, thoroughly, wash my hands. Continuing my leisurely pace, I use tongs to remove the molten instrument, setting it on a towel next to Jarek.

I *could* tell him what I'm about to do will hurt.

Instead, I walk over and jab my pointer finger as far into the hole as I can to make sure there's nothing inside. He makes an involuntary cry before biting short the noise. I almost smile. As expected, I don't encounter anything except the suctioning murk of rent flesh. I retract my finger and use the tongs to pick up the spoon. The metal is still unbearably hot.

I maintain eye contact as I insert the spoon's searing handle into Jarek's wound, not flinching at the smell of freshly cooked meat. If the wound wasn't entirely cauterized before, it is now.

This is for Wendy's finger.

Jarek's eyes blaze on mine and his mouth twists, but he doesn't cry out this time, even as sweat beads across his forehead.

Tapping the nub of spoon that has emerged from the back of his arm, I say, "It's as clean as I can get it." I yank out the spoon, speaking matter-of-factly. "But I can't stitch you. A wound this deep needs to heal from the inside out. I'll pack it with comfrey salve and dress it. You'll need to apply more salve and change the dressing every other day. If you don't keep it clean, you might lose use of that arm."

Jarek nods curtly.

I sterilize and bandage his wound. When I'm done, he wobbles to his feet, using the table to steady himself. Lightheadedness is a perfectly natural reaction in his condition, but I sense he'd hate for me to see it.

"Feeling feeble?" I ask, enjoying myself. "You'll want to give it a moment."

He frowns. "I don't have a moment. Misia and Gryphon will be here soon." He nods toward the pot of chowder. "You'll serve us when they return."

Of course, is what I should say. *As you wish.*

It would be the polite thing. The perfect example of the harmonious words that we're encouraged to always choose. I'm about to utter them sarcastically when instead, I surprise myself with a realization so sudden, so powerful, that I gasp as it lands.

"You've gone outside the Wall."

It's many pieces coming together as one: Seeing up close this strange wound made by no weapon of Noah's Valley. Gryphon suggesting there might be a way to make it in the Beyond. The green sweet Jarek had me taste. The ornate mirror in the Tzu home. I've been so busy enacting petty revenge that I've missed the obvious: the Guardians are somehow exploring outside the Wall.

"Heresy," Jarek says, his tone sharp. "Our Founders ensured the only way out of the Valley was over Eden's Gate."

Despite his injury, he's fully capable of hurting me if I don't walk back my words. I don't care about the danger he presents, though. There's only one thing that matters to me.

If our Guardians can survive Beyond, Jonas might still be alive, too.

Marina said some of those who were Harvested survived. I'd been confident she was messing with me, but then Gryphon conceded it was possible before breaking my heart by letting me know Jonas would have never stood a chance. But if the Guardians are going outside and returning, that's no longer true!

I lunge toward the door, but even injured, Jarek is too fast, too strong.

I haven't made it a foot before his good arm wraps around my waist like iron. His other hand, the one attached to the arm I just fixed, is clamped to my neck, striking a nerve that paralyzes the right side of my body. The left side twists and claws, but I can't land any strikes.

"There, there, little piglet," Jarek coos into my hair.

In a surge of anger, I manage to swing my left arm around to his bandaged wound and twist the skin just above the puncture.

Jarek grunts and drops me.

Gryphon walks in just then, a cloth-wrapped bundle tucked under one arm. His face goes to stone as he takes in the scene. Me in a pile on the floor, heaving with adrenaline, my hair loosening from its two buns. His father, hands clenched into fists, towering over me.

Jarek glares at Gryphon. "Don't look at me like that, boy," he growls. "If you don't want her, I certainly don't."

It takes me a beat to realize what this would look like to someone who'd just walked in. My cheeks burn. I note with pleasure the blood seeping through Jarek's bandage.

"Do...not...speak of her that way," Gryphon snarls.

Jarek's eyebrows shoot up. "You care now? You humiliated her in front of the entire village in chapel this morning."

I hate that Jarek has made a fair point. Gryphon's gaze jerks to me. Fury rages inside him, but for once, it's not directed at me. "Apologize," he orders his father.

My mouth drops open.

Jarek laughs. It sounds like river ice cracking underfoot. "First you shoot me, and now you tell me how to behave?"

I stifle a gasp, suspecting Jarek has just divulged something important, even if I don't quite understand his meaning. I zero in on the wrapped cloth Gryphon carries. The way he's holding it, I can tell it has some heft. The weapon used to make the hole in Jarek's arm? And perhaps the Potter boy and my mother, as well? But that makes no sense. Gryphon may be no friend of mine, but he's not a murderer.

"Dock it in the charging station," Jarek says, nodding at the object. "I need to speak to the Engineer about its capacity." Then his whole demeanor changes. He swivels to face me where I still kneel on the floor, drawing his heels together and bending at the waist in a quick, smart bow. "So sorry if I hurt your feelings," he says, his voice gone buttery the same way it did right before he chopped off Wendy's finger. "We can't all be the loving gentleman your husband-to-be is."

I stare from Jarek to Gryphon, trying to understand the game.

Jarek strides from the cottage before I can.

26

With his father out of sight, the most terrible shadow of loneliness crosses Gryphon's face. I look away, sensing that any words of comfort would only make him feel worse, which I suddenly have no interest in doing. In any case, I have my own reeling emotions to contend with. Was I wrong about Jarek going Beyond? From the interaction I just witnessed, it seems he was wounded using a weapon the Engineer House created, not one from outside the Wall. Perhaps hope and desperation have clouded my judgment, forming connections where there are none.

"What's in the blanket?" I ask, getting to my feet. I make a show of turning away to retie my buns so Gryphon has a chance to collect himself.

"A weapon," he says.

"What kind?"

Gryphon is quiet long enough that I turn. He's standing exactly where his father left him, eyes on the blanket he holds.

"Gryphon?"

He blinks as if waking up. His eyebrows gather in annoyance as he recalls, I assume, how much he despises me. "It's new. For protection."

He hasn't answered my question, but he has raised a new one. "From what, exactly?"

"You don't want to know," he says, striding toward the rear of the house. He bumps me as he passes. I think it's an accident, but it ignites a fire in me. I'm fed up with his attitude. I'm fed up with *everything*. I storm after him.

"Oh, but I *do* want to know," I say archly. "What sort of animal are you hunting?"

Gryphon opens the back door and steps into the brittle fall air. The bleating of sheep carries from the barnyard on the other side of the village as I follow him out. He tucks the bundle under his arm, steps onto a ladder nailed to the rear of the cottage, and begins to climb. "We must be prepared for any danger inside the Wall, and for any threats trying to get in," he calls over his shoulder.

He's not getting off that easily. "Okay, and what exactly *is* outside the Wall?" Gryphon's already halfway up and doesn't answer. "I have a right to the information," I call out, hoisting myself up behind him.

He reaches the top of the ladder and hops onto the roof and out of sight. I race to follow. When I'm on firm footing again, I continue. "You said there's a chance Jonas is alive. I deserve to know what he's up against!"

"Jonas is dead, and you're a fool to think otherwise."

The pressure inside me snaps. One second I'm upright, the next I'm lunging, every cell screaming to make him hurt the way he's hurt me. I slam into him low, driving my shoulder into his knees. He staggers with a grunt, the bundle cradled tight in one arm as he pitches forward. His free hand snaps back, catches the collar of my shirt. We spin, a chaotic blur of limbs and momentum, until he hits the roof hard on his back.

I land sprawled across his chest, breath knocked from both of us, his grip still tangled in my collar, the weapon clenched in his other hand.

"Careful!" he barks.

"No!" I shout, "Not until you explain yourself!" I can hear years' worth of rejection and hurt in my tone, but I don't care how pathetic I sound. I'm tired of not knowing. "Why do you hate me, Gryphon? What did I ever do to make you loathe me this much?"

He rolls me off him and stands, setting his bundle on a ledge. "I don't hate you," he mutters.

I jump to my feet and grab his arm, forcing him to face me. "You sure act like it! You basically ignore me, even when it's just the two of us, and on the rare occasions that you deign to acknowledge me, you treat me like my existence is a personal attack. Not to mention how you're so disgusted by the prospect of our marriage that you humiliated me in front of the entire village!" I'm practically yelling now and have to force my voice back down, lest our neighbors overhear our first premarital spat.

"The idea of spending the rest of my life with someone who doesn't even want to share a bed with me isn't my dream, either, Gryphon." I realize that's not entirely fair to say—in fact, I appreciate that he hasn't pushed for that intimacy, bare minimum as that ought to be—but hurt isn't always logical. I take a calming breath, but my grip on his arm remains firm. "It's clear how you feel about me. You've felt it for years, and I'm tired of not knowing why. So can you please just explain it to me?"

He's studying me now, really staring at my face.

Still, he doesn't speak.

I sigh and drop his arm. "You don't have to lie about it. I've known for years that you're in love with Marina. She told me the truth after the betrothal ceremony. I was just giving you the chance to confirm it."

His eyes flash. "What?"

I hold myself against the cold. "That's why you hate me, isn't it? You loved her, and I guess I—" I swallow, surprised by my own candor. "I guess I was too attached to you, and it was obvious, so you abandoned our friendship. And now that Jonas is dead and I'm the only thing keeping you from marrying her, you hate me even more..." I let my voice trail off, processing the admission I just made not only to him, but myself.

"You got too attached?" He sounds dangerous.

"I didn't mean to," I admit, willing my voice to remain steady, "and I'm sorry for putting that on you. You were my best friend, and you wanted Marina." My voice catches in my throat. *Why am I telling him this?* I guess with all the recent tragedy, I'm no longer willing to bottle up old wounds.

"You wish I'd wanted you instead?" His expression is inscrutable.

"Yeah," I say, shocked into honesty. "I guess I did."

"Allow me to make up for it," he says, his voice husky.

His jaw muscle twitches. I think he's going to say something cruel, but instead he wraps a strong arm around my waist, pulls me close, and presses his lips to mine. My body reacts instinctively, curving to his shape. Already on my tiptoes, I think he might lift me off the ground, but for how he's kissing me, I might as well be floating. For all the many times I've seen Gryphon's frown—the expression he seems to reserve especially for me—I never imagined his mouth could be so soft...and so electric.

His kiss carries the weight of all the words we've left unspoken. I've been choking on them for years, but now I taste their honey sweetness, their languid heat.

Then he releases me.

I stumble back. He's watching my mouth, breath heavy.

Then he steps away, toward a waist-high glass cube at the center of the rooftop. What is it, and how long has it been up here? Is there one on top of every Guardian cottage? And more importantly, did Gryphon Tzu just kiss me?

"Come here," he says, having already recovered from the moment.

I shake my head. I don't think I'll ever be able to move again.

"Please." There's something tender in his voice.

It's enough to get my legs moving. I walk over, gently touching my swollen lips. A bundle of emotions throbs in my chest, and now isn't the time to detangle them.

"Look," he says, unlocking and then opening the top of the cube. The Harvest tablet is resting inside. He touches its screen with his finger, and it flashes to life before going black again.

"It needs to charge after Peter's funeral," he says. "A couple of days of sun, and a person could use it to ascend the Wall." He avoids looking at me.

"But you said I'm a fool if I think Jonas—"

"I'm just saying it's possible," Gryphon interrupts, his voice gruff.

"The Guardians have been taking the Harvest basket Beyond?"

He shakes his head. "We have not." A dark cloud crosses his face. "At least not that I've been told. But my father is getting strange items from...somewhere."

Gryphon stares into the distance, his profile carved by the moon's own hand. Understanding dawns on me. "You whispered to Jonas before you pushed him out," I say, forcing myself to remember that awful scene. "What did you tell him?"

Gryphon rubs his hand across his eyes. He doesn't answer.

"Did you tell him how to survive?" I'm shaking.

Gryphon nods once, the motion tight. "I told him to look for a way down the other side and water and shelter if he reached it. That's all."

We're told that those honored with a Harvest leave the basket and ascend directly to the Heavens. What does it mean for them if survival is possible? Could a human hope to crawl down the other side of the Wall? My voice wobbles. "Are there dangers? Atop the Wall, and in the Beyond?"

"Almost certainly. The exact nature of the ills that sent our holy Founders behind this Wall have been lost to time, but the ongoing threats from Beyond are thoroughly imparted on the children of my House." He turns to face me, eyes black in the shadows. "That's why I think Jonas can't be alive. I'm sorry. I shouldn't have given either of you false hope."

My brain's buzzing. "Then why are you telling me any of this now?"

His face hardens. "I tell it to everyone who's training. If we're caught, we'll be Harvested. We need to know the basics of survival Beyond, at least as best as we can guess."

"You're training us for death, then?"

His frown deepens. "My father has plans he's keeping from me. All I know for sure is that he thinks this new weapon will make the Guardians invincible. That it can stop whatever's picking us off inside the Wall." He glances at me, his expression fierce. "I disagree. So I train anyone brave enough to ask. We must be able to protect each other."

My head's spinning. There are too many threads to track. "You know Jonas didn't kill my mother, that he's no murderer. Peter's death after Jonas's Harvest proves it."

Gryphon's face shutters. "All I know is that there's a danger inside the Wall. That doesn't mean your brother was innocent."

Just like that, I remember why I dislike Gryphon. I'm a traitor for kissing him.

His next words, spoken so softly I can barely hear them, catch me off guard. "But my father is right about one thing. He knows what you're capable of. You're the best Apothecary the Valley has seen. He wants you in our House for whatever it is he's planning."

He states this as fact, not praise. I can't unpack it, though, as a new horror has dawned. "Is that why Nikola was Harvested? So I'd be made a Guardian?"

"I don't know." Gryphon's jaw is rigid.

I'm stunned, without words. And my heart aches for the boy possibly put to death for the crime of being betrothed to me, childhood paste-eater though he was.

Gryphon studies me for a moment and then makes an impatient sound. He returns his attention to the bundle he brought up, removing the object it holds. I finally see the tool that cut a hole through Jarek's muscle. Like the wound it made, the weapon is completely unfamiliar. Its handle is four inches long and constructed of smooth, silver-colored metal. A longer glass tube is fused to the silver. A small loop is connected to the vee where glass meets metal; a switch rests inside. The end of the tube is scorched.

The revulsion I feel for it is primal.

"My father believes this will be key to our defense," he says. "He let me fire it today."

I'm still staggering from everything I've learned. Yet my curiosity gets the best of me. "What does it do?"

"I think you know firsthand," he says. "It shoots projectiles that tear through any surface." A dark satisfaction lights his eyes. "I saw my father's bandage, and the blood on it. Remarkable amount, given that the bleeding had nearly stopped the last I'd seen him."

I feel a surge of shame—I'm a trained healer, after all, and I'd deliberately hurt Jarek—but I extinguish it quickly. No explanation or apology is required when it's self-defense. "He said you were the one who gave him the original injury."

Some light leaves Gryphon's eyes. "It was an accident. My fault entirely."

"Are there more of these, or only one?"

His expression closes. "More. They're stored in the weapons barn over by our training grounds."

I consider this. "How loud is it?" I ask.

"What?"

"When you use it. How loud is it?"

He sucks on his teeth. "Really loud. And it recoils when you fire it."

The drums of the wedding march were cacophonous, but hadn't I heard those three strange beats before the screaming began? The music could have disguised the sound of Jarek's new weapon. But had it killed the Potters' son? No, Jarek could have bled from his wound for hours and never reached the shriveled state in which the young boy's corpse was discovered.

I'm racing through the implications of everything I've learned. "You'll still train me?"

Gryphon stares at the moon, all sharp lines and golden skin, Apollo in shadow. "That's what you'd choose?" he asks.

I don't hesitate. "It is."

He sighs deeply, eyes finding mine. "Then it's lucky you've been assigned to the census. If that's not enough cover, my parents will be working double shifts for the foreseeable future. You should be free in the evenings."

I nod. Given what I've just learned, it's more important than ever that I learn to fight.

The first time I heard there might be survival atop the Wall—when Marina whispered it, and later when Gryphon confirmed—I dismissed it. Marina lies as easily as breathing, and Gryphon had sounded like he was repeating stories he barely understood. But if he's telling his trainees, if he told Jonas…then it must be real.

And if it's real, then Jonas isn't gone. He's waiting. He's fighting. I cannot let him face that alone. The moment Gryphon confessed that he gave Jonas hope, I knew what I had to do. I'm going up the Wall as soon as the tablet has the power to take me.

That means there isn't much time to find the murderer.

27

I'm woken by cries.

At first, I think they're from my nightmares—I'd been dreaming of Jonas huddled atop the Wall, weeping—but then I see Gryphon tossing on the floor, battling something in his sleep. I watch him, thinking of all the reasons I shouldn't comfort him. I tell myself that I want to see him suffer, but it's not true anymore.

Not after that kiss.

I touch my lips, remembering the first time I gave Gryphon stitches. I was five and he was six. He'd been playing rough with Leo and cracked his head against a rock. By then, I'd gotten my first crossbody medical kit so I could respond to emergencies, but I'd never practiced suturing on a real person. I remember being terrified. Seven stitches later, though, Gryphon was almost as good as new.

The next morning he started walking me to school, bringing me a daisy every day they were in season. He kept it up even after my father died, when I became convinced that rigid adherence to the rules was the only way to keep my family safe. When Marina and the others started taunting me, he'd still walked me to and from school and sat by me most days during lunch, right up until the betrothal ceremony.

I wish I could make sense of him, of how he must have felt that day. Sure, he didn't know how I felt about him back then, so he couldn't have known just how deep his abandonment would cut. Still, on behalf of that sad, lonely little girl, I deserve an apology.

But so does he.

Before I can change my mind, I slide out of bed, feet silent against the cold floor. Even in sleep, Gryphon's jaw is clenched. His hand twitches, reaching for a weapon that isn't there.

My heart kicks at the sight of him like this—vulnerable, tormented. He confessed at training and then atop the roof that he is defying his father, a man whose love and respect he so clearly craves. It must be torture to have your loyalties pulled in opposite directions.

I drop down beside him, carefully lifting his head onto my lap. His eyes fly open, wild and alight before recognition softens his features.

I smooth his hair back, my fingers gliding over the dark and silky strands. He tenses again, eyes fluttering shut, then open, then closed again.

I sing softly, and the fight leaves him. It's a tune Dad used to sing to Jonas and me when the world was simpler. Different from Gran's favorite, "Down in Noah's Valley," its melody is sweet and haunting.

> Blacks and bays, dapples and grays,
> Coach and six little horses.
> Hush-a-bye, don't you cry...

My fingers trace slow circles on Gryphon's temple, coaxing the tension away.

His eyes open again. His hand closes around my wrist, and my heart stumbles. His gaze is pleading. "I don't need you," he rasps. "I don't need anyone."

He's not fully awake. I don't move, don't even breathe, waiting until his grip loosens, his hand falling away, fingers brushing my thigh as they slide to the floor. A shiver races through me. *I'm repaying a friendship debt*, I tell myself, my heart thudding against my ribs. *Nothing more.*

My fingers resume their slow, rhythmic strokes, moving over his forehead, smoothing the lines etched by worry and pain. His breathing evens out, his head sinking deeper into my lap. My hands glide over his temples, massaging away the knots coiled there.

His breath shudders, his lips parting slightly, and my eyes are drawn to the curve of his mouth, soft and full. I imagine the faint whisper of his breath against my skin. My pulse is pounding.

I knead his jaw gently, easing the tightness there next. His body softens, melting into my touch. He's asleep. *Really* asleep this time. He's beautiful like this. Peaceful. I let myself linger a moment longer. Then slowly, carefully, I ease his head off my lap, lowering it onto the folded blanket. He stirs, brows drawing together like he feels my absence, but his eyes remain closed. I stand, my knees stiff, my legs trembling. I watch him for another heartbeat, then force myself to turn away.

I'm crawling into bed when his voice halts me.

"Thank you," he whispers.

I crawl under the quilt without answering as a truth slices through me: my future husband may not hate me.

The knowledge is cruel.

It comes just as I'm about to leave Noah's Valley behind.

28

I wake when it's still dark out.

I'm almost relieved to see that Gryphon's already gone. My cheeks warm as I remember our kiss, and the moment of closeness we'd shared after. Best leave those thoughts to the night. I dress quickly and step into the upstairs hallway.

The soft snoring I hear from Jarek and Misia's bedroom tells me one or both are asleep. I pad downstairs to the bathroom to wash myself and comb and bind my hair into its practical buns. Now that the kitchen and living room are clean, the state of the bathroom is almost too much to bear. If I didn't have the census to begin today, I might have at it. As it stands, I plan to make breakfast to keep the Tzu parents happy and then hurry to the Record Keeper cottage. If I finish my census tasks early—and I will finish them early—I can disappear into the forest for training.

The tablet should be charged in a sunny day or two. If little Marie was able to steal it, then so can I, though I imagine the Tzus keep a much closer eye on it than the Record Keeper had. The brightening but still gloomy sky suggests it'll be another sunless day, so in the meantime, I need to sneak inside the vault—the more that I think about it, the more certain I am that's the reason Jonas was targeted—and acquire as many fighting skills as I can to survive outside the Valley. I have no delusions that a couple of days of practice will save me from the horrors Beyond, but doing *something* keeps me from sliding into panic at the mere thought of it.

I clutch Lucky Bunny inside my pocket, pressing his edges into my palm just a bit tighter than is comfortable. "We're going to have a big day, aren't we, little one?" I murmur.

The solidness of him, like a tough little nut, comforts me as I make my way to the kitchen, and while I'd planned to reheat last night's chowder, I find it's already been eaten. *Lend me your patience, Lucky Bunny.* I take deep breaths as I mix rolled oats with a handful of flaxseed and red currants, enough for the whole household. I'm grateful for this moment of grounding before Misia comes down the stairs.

"You're going to spoil us with your cooking," she says, her tone neutral. The severity of her close-cropped hair highlights a new black eye opposite her injured cheek.

"What happened?" I ask.

"Training accident," she says, tapping the edges of her bruised flesh. It's the same thing Gryphon used to say when he showed up to school with injuries. She nods at the stovetop. "What are you making today?"

"Rolled oats. I'd like to add some beet sugar, but I don't see any. Do you know where your allotment went?"

"Gryphon, probably," she says, a rare burst of warmth in her voice as she speaks of her son. "He's got a real sweet tooth. I'll pick up some more tomorrow."

I've only been here a few days, but it's long enough to know the Tzus—and possibly more Guardians—don't follow the same rules as the rest of us. Still, I'm shocked she says it so brazenly. Sugar has already been distributed for the month. There shouldn't be more for two more weeks.

"What are your duties for the day?" I ask as I reach for the teapot. It's a standard morning greeting, but I'm genuinely curious.

She sits at the table, a soft, unguarded smile flickering across her face when I hand her a hot cup of chicory tea. The morning drink will focus her thoughts and aid her digestion.

"We have an outpost on the north side," she says, inhaling deeply the bitter aroma. "I'm on watch."

"I'll bake corn cakes to send with you," I say.

"You'll make a good wife."

I look to see if she's mocking me, but she seems sincere. Husbands and wives share homemaking duties equally in the Valley. If I were to truly be a good spouse, I'd require the others to pull their own weight. For the first time, I consider how lonely Misia must be.

The oats begin bubbling over, pulling me from my thoughts. I leap toward the stove, knocking a spoon off the counter by accident.

"Clumsy girl," she murmurs.

"I'll grab another," I say brightly, filling her dish. The specks of red currant look like blood clots in the porridge. Any appetite I'd woken with is suddenly gone.

Misia studies me for a second too long before digging into her meal.

The morning passes quickly. If not for Jonas's absence, I might even have enjoyed the census work. Walking outdoors, popping into workshops to survey villagers as they practice their trades, talking to people I've only ever greeted in passing…it's all a pleasure. Cottage by cottage, I log the members of my community, all the while keeping an eye out for clues about the two recent murders. But the only thing I notice is how tired many of us appear and how bare the kitchen cupboards are.

Once I've completed the day's work at record speed, I slip into the forest.

Reatha the Chemist has fresh spring water and honey-drenched cricket cakes waiting when I arrive. Meryl, Sal, Eero, and Gryphon are already there. There's a jolt in my belly at the sight of my betrothed, his shirtsleeves rolled up to his elbows, exposing his forearms as he demonstrates something to Sal. I haven't seen him since last night and begin to spiral. Is he disgusted by the memory? It's possible no one—including my soon-to-be partner—wants me here.

Did they all talk about me before I arrived? My stomach cramps, and I consider turning around. Then Eero walks over to clap me on the back, and Meryl flashes me a smile, and suddenly my worry melts away. *You can do this, Rosie.* I smile. My inner voice sounded like Jonas that time.

"Circle up," Gryphon commands.

I snap to attention. The others follow suit, fanning out around him. Albert's nowhere to be seen, but Marie seems happy to watch on the sidelines, fresh curls bouncing as she listens to Gryphon explain what we're to learn this evening.

"We'll start with hand to hand, and if the newbie doesn't hold us back too much," he says, glancing my way for the first time since I arrived, "we'll move to the staff."

His words should embarrass me, but there's something new in his tone, something welcoming. He's teasing me as he would the others. His regular coldness isn't gone, exactly, but eased up. It makes me feel like there are bubbles under my skin.

I pop them. In the cold light of day, I realize I cannot allow myself to let my guard down around Gryphon, one great kiss be damned. Besides being the one who walked Jonas to the basket, he's the son of the man responsible for manipulating and lying to the Valley. Maybe he wishes it weren't so, but I can't afford to fall for someone so tangled in the very roots I need to tear out. I break our locked gaze.

"Let's pick up where we left off last week," he says, frowning, "with wrist and throat locks."

I can't believe it when I see my hand rise. "What should we imagine we're fighting?"

Sal punches my arm, and not too lightly. "Shut up and listen."

Meryl rubs Sal's back. "It's a reasonable question, isn't it?" She looks to Gryphon for support, but his eyes are still narrowed on Sal. "You taught us that our pivot points change based on the size of the opponent, after all."

Gryphon runs his hand back and forth across his scalp. He's agitated. Have I already spent the very limited goodwill between us?

"Come here," he directs me.

What does he plan to do? My stomach twists as I step into the circle. I'm too nervous to look at the others. Is this some kind of hazing, like the trust fall but worse? I stand in front of Gryphon. His breaths are quick and tight, but his hands are loose at his sides. I stare at them because I'm afraid to look at his face. They're strong hands, ribboned with scars; his nails are short and clean. The day is still overcast but surprisingly warm, and his shirt is open at the collar. My gaze travels across his bare neck, over his lips, up to his strong nose, and finally, lands on his onyx eyes.

Then I'm on my back.

Stunned, I gasp for air. An upside-down Sal is smiling at me, her cheeks round with merriment.

Next to her, Eero gives me an encouraging nod. "Been there," he says. "You're gonna want to get up."

I could sooner grow claws and burrow into the earth.

"First lesson for you," Gryphon says, standing over me, blocking the light, "is to always watch your opponent's eyes, no matter their size or shape. The eyes always tell."

"Ifff," I say.

He leans forward, offering me his hand. "What's that now?"

Still gasping for breath, I reach for his hand. "Ifff...my opponent is—"

Quick like magic, he's flipped me onto my stomach, my cheek planted in the dirt, the little breath I'd managed to gather gone out of me.

"You did it again," Gryphon says.

Eero nods sadly. "You really did," he says, kneeling as he aims his pointer and middle fingers at his eyes. "You were looking at his hands rather than his peepers."

I nod, a hot little fire building inside me. I roll onto my back and stare up at Gryphon. His smile is arch as he offers me his hand yet again. My eyes flick to it, baiting him.

Quick like a wasp, he strikes for my wrist, but I'm expecting it this time. I let him grab it, but rather than try to stand, I pull him toward me. He's caught off balance. I sweep my leg around, hooking him behind his ankle, placing unexpected pressure on his Achilles tendon—one of the weakest points in the leg. He begins to buckle. I launch myself off the ground, planning to shove him over while his stability is compromised.

But he has years of training on me.

We meet in the middle.

He uses my upward momentum to stabilize himself, grabbing me around the waist and pivoting his weight to the left leg. He holds me off the ground, tight to him, our faces inches apart, our breath dancing. I keep my eyes locked on his, defiant, and feel his body pressed against me. It's like being held by a tree. A warm, confusing tree.

"Whoo-hoo!" Eero says, clapping.

Gryphon releases me. I stand on my own two legs, which are surprisingly shaky. He still hasn't looked away, so I don't, either. His expression is one I've never seen before, at least directed at me. Surprised delight? Before I can decide, his eyes take the slightest tack to the left and I hop to the right, avoiding the hand he thrusts out. A lifetime of studying patients' every move, anticipating their weaknesses, their needs, and their flailing limbs, has paid off.

To my everlasting surprise, I throw my head back and laugh. I feel strong, and I feel *good*.

"Did she learn that one quick enough for you, Gryph?" Eero teases.

My laughter melts as I realize I have no idea how Gryphon is going to react. I nearly bested him in front of his trainees. He might be outraged. His father certainly would be. But to my relief, I see that he's grinning. It's full and generous and flies straight to my heart. For the second time this week, I consider that the boy he used to be, the friend of my childhood, might be standing before me.

"Yeah," Gryphon says, chuckling. "That's quick enough for me."

I risk a glance at the others. Little Marie is open-mouthed, Eero mirroring her, and Oscar is shaking his head with a smirk. Meryl looks like she wants to hug me. Sal's the only one who appears unimpressed. The reflex to make myself small again is automatic; it takes all my will to shove it down.

"Pair up," Gryphon says, his smile gone as he returns to business. "Eero and Rose, Oscar and Meryl. Sal, you're with me. Everyone watch us demonstrate before trying it on your own. Here's how to use wrist locks to contain someone."

Gryphon is placing his fingers on Sal's trigger points and explaining the results. I'm thrilled to discover my medical training lends me a hand in this exercise, too. I bring Eero to the ground quickly and repeatedly. He gets in a few good locks on me, though.

"Sun and Soil, Rose, you're pretty good at this," he says as he rubs his elbow where he's just landed on it. We're both filthy and soon to be covered in bruises, but I don't know if I've ever felt more alive. "You sure you don't practice in secret?"

I offer him a hand up. "Oddly enough, Apothecary training helps a lot."

Eero grins, displaying his easygoing nature. It's clear why he and Jonas were—no, *are*—friends. They're both even-tempered and big-hearted. But Eero's a few years below us. In fact, wasn't he in the same class as...

"It's odd that Albert's not around," I say, trying to sound casual. "But I guess I don't know him well. Were you two ever friends?"

Eero's thick, dark brows knit together. "Not really. Why?"

Because I think I saw him lurking behind the chapel the morning my mother was killed. "No reason," I say, pasting on a strained smile. "Just making conversation." I reach into my pocket and give Lucky Bunny a squeeze.

Across the training ground, Sal gets a well-placed clamp on Gryphon, and he drops to his knees. He lets her help him up and congratulates her, offering tips on how to refine her movements. As much as I want to guard my heart, it does something strange to me to witness how generous he is with his knowledge. I can't imagine Gryphon's parents being anything but furious to be bested by a mere villager. Where did he learn this grace?

As if hearing my thoughts, he looks over, his eyes holding mine in a way that feels like physical touch. I turn away, my cheeks flushed.

"You know," Eero says, glancing between Gryphon and me, "if the two of you played like you were in love instead of, say, announcing to the entire village how much you hate each other in chapel, Misia and Jarek might give you both more freedom."

He's not wrong, but my stomach flips as I imagine broaching the subject.

Hey, Gryphon, want to build off that random angry kiss last night and act like we're not allergic to each other? Maybe hold hands and smile into one another's eyes occasionally?

"Switch partners," Gryphon says before I can respond to Eero.

My breath hitches. Are he and I going to spar again? My skin starts humming.

"Oscar, you're with Eero. Meryl, you move to Rose."

I tell myself the falling sensation I feel is relief.

Meryl stands in front of me, a serene smile on her pale face. "So, you gonna kick my butt, too?" she asks in her raspy voice. Her expression is open, not a stitch of judgment in it.

"I'm having a good day," I admit. "Beginner's luck."

"Maybe you can share some of it with me?" She smiles, then makes like she's going to adjust her shirt but instead loops her arm around my neck and drops me to the ground. The impact rattles my teeth. We wrestle for several more rounds. I'm asking her to show me how she managed a wrist lock that blindsided me when I notice Gryphon leave the circle, striding into the cave. He emerges a moment later holding a stack of straight, polished branches, each as tall as him and half as wide around as my wrist.

"Who wants a weapon?"

Eero whoops in joy.

29

I'm all ears as Gryphon reviews basic moves using what he calls the bo staff. We stand in a circle, him at the center. It seems the others have trained with this weapon before, but it's all new to me. Still, it becomes immediately clear how a tool that allows you to strike from a distance is beneficial in combat. We're told to treat it as an extension of our arm or leg, only deadlier.

Something crucial when fighting non-human creatures.

"Like what?" I ask. I can't let it drop. Gryphon told me he's training the others so they're able to protect themselves. I don't know if he shared specifics, but if he knows who *or what* is hunting us inside the Wall, he needs to spill.

Gryphon's jaw twitches in a gesture I've come to suspect means that I've annoyed him. "Dangerous animals," he says. "Beasts."

"*What* beasts? Mountain lions?" We're told our ancestors drove them to extinction generations ago, but then I think of my father, mutilated by a creature no one ever found. "I've never seen any."

"Maybe you were too busy being Little Miss Perfect to notice," Sal says darkly.

Her words shoot an arrow directly at my heart. I thought we'd all been getting along. "I'm not perfect."

Meryl puts her hand on Sal's arm, but the Cobbler girl shakes her off. "Coulda fooled us. Always turned your schoolwork in early. Never missed a sermon. Accepted Nikola as your first betrothed as if you'd been given the moon, even though we all know you wanted someone else." She shoots Gryphon a glance, and I swallow my gasp before she locks her angry eyes back on me. "Let my grandmother die." She uses her foot to flip a staff into her hand, tosses it to me, and then grabs another. "We saw you, those of us who didn't fit inside the system."

"Didn't fit in?" I ask, bewildered. No one was more of an outsider than me. "Everyone knows you've always had a close friend in Meryl. That your betrothed, Simon, will be an excellent addition to the Cobbler House."

Sal shakes her head. "Simon is awful. I'd never pick him."

"Salvatora," Meryl says. Her voice is firm. "That's not Rose's fault and you know it."

"But it's people like her who make it possible!" Sal yells. She pitches her voice into a singsong and swivels her head mockingly, uttering the morning pledge that every student says at the start of the school day, but that I always said the loudest. "Protect the system and it shields us all, follow the rules so we never fall." She spits onto the ground. "Meanwhile, I no longer have a gran, I'm stuck with a fiancé I'll never love and required to do a job I hate, all because we're trapped in rotten Noah's Valley."

Trapped? There might be danger in here, but there's far worse out there. We'd be dead without the Wall! What I wouldn't give to have Jonas safely back inside with the rest of us. I open my mouth to argue, but before I can say a word, Sal's on me. She swings the bo staff for my shins and gets a good thwack in. I jump back, biting my tongue to keep from crying out. I find my stance quickly, but not in time to block her shoulder strike.

I look to Gryphon for help.

He's holding the others back. He means for Sal and me to fight this out.

Some teacher. I duck and pivot just in time to dodge her swing for my head. She's coming for blood. I shove my staff between her ankles and pull to the left, forcing her legs to fight each other for balance. She drops to the ground.

I turn, offering her a hand. "I'm sorry."

I'm surprised to feel wetness on my face. Am I crying? Her strikes left an awful, stinging ache, but it's more than that. Sal's hurting in a way that can't be healed, and she believes I've helped cause it.

Rather than accept my hand, she leaps to her feet and shoves the butt of her staff into my stomach. I grunt and double over.

"Sorry?" she says. "The laws you uphold make my life meaningless, and you're *sorry*?"

She swings again. My staff flies up to block it. The crack of wood meeting wood echoes through the trees. My arms vibrate with the force.

"Yes," I say. We're both panting from the fight. "I had no idea."

I try to sweep her legs out from under her, but she jumps, imitating a game we used to play as children. Her feet come down at the same time as her weapon, narrowly missing my ear.

"Those of you who aren't waking up are keeping the rest of us in the dark," Sal spits. "The old rules don't work anymore, and maybe they never did, but because of ignorant kiss-asses like you, we're going to live and die in here like trapped sheep."

Suddenly, my anger scorches to life, the heat of it like pleasure and pain dancing through my veins. It messes with my eyes, turning everything overbright. I'm coming at her, swinging my staff. "Yeah, I followed the rules. What else was I supposed to do? I'm just one person." Sal falls backward, and I leap on top of her, my weapon poised. "I didn't know there was anything else *to* do. *I didn't know.*"

Her staff swings around, hurtling toward my throat with startling speed. I lift my own to block it in a move I know could break her wrist, but it's that or feel my trachea crushed.

Iron hands stop our weapons just before they connect.

It's Gryphon. I gawk at him, my breath heaving.

Oscar, Meryl, Eero, and Marie are staring at us, slack jawed.

"Enough," he says.

I hate the pity in his expression. Pity for the both of us, it appears.

"You should've paid attention," Sal mutters. She still sounds angry, but also a little scared.

I stare around the circle at the faces of people my age who for weeks if not months have been jeopardizing their safety to train here. It feels unfair, but I know Sal's right. I should have paid attention much, much earlier than I did.

"I'm sorry," I say, meeting each of their gazes in turn, just like I did when I vowed to keep their secret safe. "I've been a coward." I won't explain why I behaved as I did. There was a point when the Harvests started ramping up where I should have spoken out, but instead I kept my mouth shut and followed the herd. "Sal's right. I've kept my head in the sand."

"Aw, Rose, you're not gonna tell her?" Eero asks.

We all turn to look at him. He's wincing, like it pains him to speak.

"Tell her what?" I ask.

He glances quickly at Sal, then back at the ground. "Jonas made me swear not to share, but you're being so stubborn right now."

I want to shake him. "Share what?" I ask.

He points at Sal. "Share that you've been treating people like her gran. That you're willing to risk being whipped to care for our elderly, even though it's illegal." He drops his hand. "Jonas and I saw you sneaking into the back door of the Forester cottage to treat Matthias's infected wound when his family had already been told to prepare for his funeral. Jonas said you were doing the same for all the elderly and made me promise never to spill, but you should at least tell Sal, so she knows you didn't just let her gran die."

Sal's chest is rising and falling. She steps closer to me. "You tried everything to save Amina?"

I don't know who to look at. I feel so exposed. Jonas had known about my visits? I'm desperate to take the out that Eero provided me, but I won't. It's time to own up to my mistakes.

"No, Salvatora," I say, "I didn't. I'm so sorry, but I won't lie to you. I hesitated before going for antibiotics." I feel bare beneath the truth of it, but I keep going. "But that day changed me. Your grief and the injustice of it all woke something inside of me. There are villagers alive today who wouldn't be if not for the lesson your gran taught me. That's Amina's legacy."

"She was too far gone, but you tried anyways." Sal breathes hard, as if the words cost her. "You did, even knowing the price you might have to pay…and I accused you of killing her."

My heart aches. "You'd just lost your gran."

She raises her hands, and I flinch, but the next thing I know, I'm in her embrace. "I'm sorry," she says simply. "I was wrong."

She's surprisingly strong, nearly squeezing the breath out of me. "You were right about me telling on you to the Priest," I say into her thick, wavy hair.

"Yeah, I know." She laughs, letting go and stepping back. "You were such a brown noser."

"But one who took care of so many people inside the village," Eero says. "And she wouldn't be here right now with us, training, if she was that same suck-up from before. That counts, too. Not just what we did then, but who we are now."

He reminds me so much of Jonas in that moment. My throat's too tight for words, so I only nod, accepting the insult along with the praise.

I can do better. I will do better.

Eero's face drops as if he's just thought of something. "Dang, though. There is one more thing."

My breath catches. I don't believe I can bear any more. "What?"

He glances down, appearing sorrowful. "It's like this..." he says, clearly reluctant to spit it out.

I'm in a panic. But when the Carpenter lifts his head, there's a glint in his eye. He's grinning. "The last one in is a rotten egg!"

And then he whoops, his pretend sad expression wiped clean, and rushes off into the woods. Oscar throws back his head and matches Eero's cry before running after him. And then—to my surprise—Gryphon follows. I guess training is over for the day.

"Last one in what?" I ask, feeling dense.

"You'll see!" Meryl grabs my hand and Salvatora's and pulls us into the trees.

We soon reach the creek. Eero and Oscar are already horsing around in the water when we arrive.

Jonas would love this, I can't help but think.

"The trick is not to think about it before jumping in," Meryl says. She's tugging her tunic over her head, leaving on just her underclothes. "Because the water is ice-cold."

Eero cannonballs into the clear creek. I gasp when a spray of water hits me. It's been cool all day, perfect weather for physical training. It's chilly for swimming, though. I stand on the shore watching Meryl and Eero splash each other, with even Sal getting in on the play. Oscar pops up ten feet down the bank, climbing onto a rock twice as tall as him. A mini waterfall has turned it into a natural slide. He rides it down, disappears underwater, then pops up downstream, shooting a plume of water out of his mouth.

"Feels great on sore muscles," Gryphon says. He's standing next to me, his arm almost touching mine. The way he carries himself, he reminds me of the statues in our history books, and a sudden need to put distance between us is what finally pushes me to strip off my overshirt and pants and take the leap.

The water is so cold it steals my breath. I drop down to the creek bed, digging my toes into the sandy bottom. The temperature makes my heart race, but it also leeches the soreness from my muscles, just as Gryphon promised. I stay down as long as I can bear and then push toward the surface. Everyone cheers as I come up. I hear a sound like music and realize it's me, laughing. That makes me laugh even harder. I twirl in the water, delighted to find that my body is acclimating to the temperature. I'm able to stay in several more minutes, watching the others splash and swim, before heading toward the bank. Gryphon is just ahead of me. When he steps out, I see blood coursing from the back of his calf. He must have scraped his leg on a rock.

"You need to clean that," I say, watching the crimson blood mix with the water. "Let me."

I search the shore for sphagnum moss and find a nearby patch. It's a natural antibiotic that'll also slow the bleeding. I grab a chunk, pressing it against Gryphon's leg. I don't notice I'm shivering until I feel the warmth of his hand on my shoulder.

"I can hold it," he says. As he reaches down, his fingertips brush against mine. He jerks back.

I feel my heartbeat. Are my cheeks as flushed as Gryphon's?

Eero appears next to us, dripping water, his teeth chattering. "Aww, it's just like the old days," he says, grinning at Gryphon. "Rose taking care of you when you showed up at school all roughed up by your dad."

I swallow. I always suspected Gryphon's injuries weren't just from training—why else would he refuse treatment at the Apothecary cottage? But now that I've spent time inside the Tzu house, there's no denying it. I look at Gryphon, aching to console him, but he's already checked out. His dark eyes have all but grayed over.

"We should all get back to our houses. It's late." He grabs his shirt, pants, and shoes and stomps back toward the cave.

I want to follow him, to say something that might matter, but I feel locked in place.

"Nice going, Eero," Sal says, glaring at him.

I can't help but agree. At least the boy has the good sense to look guilty as we pull on our tunics and trousers, shivering in our wetness.

I'm surprised when Oscar speaks. "Gryphon risks everything to train us."

"Why?" I ask, giving shape to the question that's been bothering me since I stumbled on their secret session. I know why Gryphon *said* he does it, but what do they believe? "And why do you all risk the same to learn?"

The four of them exchange glances.

"The Guardian House has too much power." It's Meryl who speaks for the group, her Entertainer's voice lending gravitas to her words. "They have for a while. They tell us they're doing it to keep us safe, that it's a natural extension of their regular duties. And at first, I think it was. But now they're calling Harvests without input from the Record Keeper. We can all see that. They confine us to our homes, keep us so busy working we barely have time to question them, let alone do anything about it." She shakes her head. "Gryphon agrees they've gone too far, though I doubt he'd admit it. The closest he can come is helping us."

"I was the first," Sal says. "My dad was Harvested for standing up to Jarek, and Gryphon was the one who walked him to the basket."

A shiver runs through me, raw and familiar. I know what it is to watch the people you love get taken, and to be left behind with the ruin.

"I think it killed Gryphon to do it. He knows his father's up to something, that we're all vulnerable inside the Wall as long as Jarek is running the show. Training us is how he makes peace with his role in that." She grins fiercely. "He approached me the night after my da's death, said fighting is all he knew how to do, but he was willing to share it. I said if I'm learning to defend myself, Meryl is, too."

"And I had to invite my husband," tomboy Meryl jokes, punching Eero in the arm.

He smiles goofily. "I brought Oscar on accident, when he caught me sneaking out to train."

"Hey, I wouldn't have ratted you out!" Oscar says.

By the way Eero laughs, I understand this is something they've joked about many times. Because they're friends, and they're brave. I'm feeling the warmth of it when Meryl's face grows serious again. "We know that a handful of us training the bo staff isn't going to be enough to make any change. There's got to be something bigger."

"Hush!" Sal says.

"Hush yourself." Meryl narrows her brown eyes, using a rare, firm voice with Salvatora. "Rose is putting herself in the same danger as the rest of us by being out here. She deserves to know."

Sal squares her jaw but doesn't disagree, so Meryl keeps talking. "We're going to stop Jarek," she says, holding my gaze. "He's the one heading all the new laws, the Harvests. It's supposed to be the Record Keeper, but David Seingalt is weak. This system's not going to change unless we do something about it. To start, we want to remove Jarek from the Council."

"How?" is my first question. My second is, "Does Gryphon know?"

"No, he can't." Eero grimaces. "And we're not sure how yet, but we've got some ideas. We're not the only ones, you know. There's others who've noticed the Valley isn't working right, some who're willing to risk their own necks for it. Especially since Jonas was framed."

The wave of emotion threatens to knock me over. "You don't think he did it?"

Meryl bundles me in her arms. "Of course we don't, Rose! We know Jarek is responsible somehow. He disposes of anyone who gets in his way."

"That's enough!" Sal interjects, her voice raised. "We've already shared too much."

Meryl releases me, and I feel unsettlingly light on my own. We bustle back to the caves. I braid my hair on the way to disguise its wetness, wishing that I'd considered that before jumping all the way in.

The angle of the sun tells me that we've lost track of time.

"Gryphon just left," Albert says, emerging from the cave upon our return. Was he inside this whole time? Even with his increased mobility, there aren't many places in the Valley a supposedly dead kid could spend the day. He wheels his chair closer to me the old-fashioned way, his tone pure sulk. "You're training here regularly now?"

"Mind your own business, Albert," Sal snaps.

I wonder what her issue is with him, but I can't disagree. The new evidence linking the Guardians to the seeming murder weapon has cooled my suspicion of Albert slightly, but I still don't trust him.

Eero stretches. "You're going to be sore tonight after the sparring, Rose, even with the creek dip."

"Count on it," Oscar says. "And it'll just get worse over the next few hours. My first day of training? I couldn't lift my arms above my waist. Good thing I only had hemming to do."

Everyone smiles. Everyone but Albert, who's watching me.

30

I notice the lights on in the Tzu house as I approach. I expected Gryphon to reach the cottage first, so it doesn't occur to me to be alarmed until I open the door and discover Sojourner sitting at the kitchen table. Next to her are Jarek, Misia, and my betrothed.

My stomach goes liquid.

"Where were you?" Jarek cuts each word into a neat cube.

"I already told you," Gryphon interrupts, his eyes warning me. "We wanted to be alone. I came back before Rose so no one would guess we were..."

Jarek swivels to face his son. He's swollen with anger. I don't want to know what he'd do if Sojourner wasn't here. "I asked *her*."

My heart is beating so hard it hurts.

"Misia called for me to drop by," Sojourner says, standing. She strides over and puts her hands on my shoulders, eyes searching mine. From behind, it must look like she's being overly solicitous, something her House is famous for. Up close, I can tell she's buying me time to collect myself. "She asked me to offer pre-matrimonial counseling. There's concern the two of you haven't yet found a way to connect. It's not unheard of for betrothed couples to need extra support in that area, but if you two are sneaking off together..."

She leaves it hanging in the air, as Gryphon had. I think of

Eero's earlier suggestion of playacting like we are in love, about how it might take the heat off with the Tzus. Before I can lose my courage, I rush toward Gryphon. He leaps to his feet, hands poised, like he expects me to attack. Instead, I lace my fingers behind his neck and tip my chin so I can stare into his obsidian eyes.

His expression slips, leaving his face momentarily raw. Is it because he was a Caster for so long? I feel a rush of guilt for manipulating him but see no other path forward. I lean my head against his chest—his heart is slamming, probably out of fear I'll get us caught—and peer through my lashes at Jarek and Misia.

"I'm sorry I worried you all," I say. "I've cared deeply for Gryphon since I was a girl."

The last bit is true, anyhow. They don't need to know that I stopped.

Jarek snorts. "You could've fooled me."

"Rose has always been reserved," Sojourner says, a note of admonition in her voice. "It's no surprise to me that we didn't know of her true feelings. Gryphon, do you feel the same?"

I want to see his response, but I also can't bring myself to look. Instead, I bury my face into his shirt. He smells of river and pine.

"I wouldn't have gone off with her if I didn't," he says. The words rumble like rocks inside his chest.

"We should've waited until we were married," I add. Our virtue is important when we're young, and we're supposed to protect it until we're officially wed, but if we're with our betrothed, most villagers look the other way. I know I'm telling them what they want to hear. It's so personal, though, that I have to step away from Gryphon.

I feel oddly unbalanced without his warmth.

"Maybe we should just marry you right now," Jarek says coldly.

"We will not!" Misia snaps. "You know David proposed this Friday. He agreed to a big celebration."

This surprises me, as does the slight keen in her voice. Why would the Record Keeper be involved in the timing of my wedding, and why would he want it to be an attention-drawing event? I need to ask that man some questions when I pick up my census materials tomorrow.

Jarek grunts. "Fine. Have your pageantry. I know how you crave that fluff."

"Have you forgotten that I'm a Guardian?" Misia's words practically ice over in the air, her deadly arms flexing where they rest against the table. "And soon, we'll have another. Gryphon, you'll bring Rose to tour the training grounds for second shift tomorrow, after she completes her census work. Will that satisfy you, dear husband? To get your little prize pig closer to her duty at last?"

Jarek stands without acknowledging Misia's jab. "Gryphon, come," he commands. "We've got work to do."

I risk a glance at Gryphon. He looks like he wants to say something to me. His eyes cut to his father, then drop. Jarek strides to the door, reaching for his weapons resting nearby. He straps his sword at his waist and his throwing knives at his ankles and wrists.

Gryphon follows suit.

31

"Wake up."

I'm torn from deep sleep. It's disorienting. Lucky Bunny is pressed so tightly in my hand that he's left indents in my palm. I'm sleeping in Gryphon's bed. He's standing over me.

"What were you doing down there earlier?" he demands.

He sounds somewhere between confused and upset. I sit up and scoot back until I'm pressed against the wall. Goosebumps prickle where the backs of my arms meet cool plaster. "What do you mean?"

"Hanging off me," he says. He strides over to the wardrobe and pulls out his bedding with such force that it sends feathers flying. Papers, too, but he shoves those quickly back in. "You were *pretending* to care for me, correct? If I may be so bold, could I recommend you spend some private time practicing? You had the element of surprise on your side tonight, but your performance was otherwise lackluster."

I lean forward, my heart thudding, suddenly seriously annoyed. Hadn't *he* been the one to lie to his parents that we were off messing around in the first place? I can't get a read on him, and I'm tired of it. "Why'd you kiss me the other night, Gryphon?"

I don't think he's going to speak. And he doesn't, for a while.

Then, "You were all I used to think about, Rose," he says, raw honesty in his voice.

The shock of his words yanks a strangled sound from my throat—embarrassingly close to a honk. I blink rapidly, wondering what in the Wall he's talking about.

He drags in a breath. "I was ashamed to come to school with cuts and bruises, but you treated them like they weren't my fault. You cleaned me up, and then you'd ask me about myself." His back is still to me, his strong hand splayed out on the wardrobe. "Do you remember? You wanted to know what my favorite food was, if I liked the color blue, if I preferred reading over playing marbles."

I blush. "I was a lonely kid."

"No," he says, shaking his head. His voice goes soft, and he sighs. "You were thoughtful and clever and a gifted healer. And you were selfless, Rose. Watching you made me better, when I could have easily grown up to be just like my father."

I slide off the bed and stand on legs made of glass. "You're nothing like him, Gryphon." It's important to me that he knows that. As much as I don't think I'll ever be free of the image of him putting my brother in that basket…I don't want my old friend to torment himself, either.

He continues speaking as if he didn't hear me. "Then you were betrothed to Nikola." He pauses. "And I had no right to you. Not in the way I wanted. It became easier to be angry at you."

My heart kicks up. *What is he saying?*

"It took everything in me to avoid you those first few months after the ceremony, but eventually I made it a habit. I came to accept my fate. Yours and Nikola's, too." Gryphon takes a breath before continuing, and the wait is almost painful for me. "But what you said on the roof…" He trails off, as if scared of where the thought might lead.

Instinctively, I reach toward him but pull my hand back. I feel like I'm vibrating, more emotion than human. Of course we couldn't have been *together*, but why have we sacrificed our friendship for the past four years rather than simply talk about our hurt?

He turns, staring at my mouth with an intensity that gives me goosebumps. But instead of crushing my lips to his, his eyes return to mine. "That's why I objected in chapel yesterday." His eyes are blazing. "I don't want you to be forced to marry me, Rose. When you came to me tonight, it *wasn't* lackluster. For a moment, I believed you might feel about me the same way I feel about you. I'm sorry for embarrassing you, and I'm forever sorry for being a part of Jonas's Harvest."

I nod, tears pricking my eyes, because I think he's telling the truth. "I believe you," I say, but what I mean is, *as much as I can forgive you, I do*. But it's too late. As soon as the tablet is charged, I must leave him behind forever.

32

I assume I'll have better luck levitating basketless up the Wall than I will sleeping after that conversation, but the day catches up to me before long. When I wake, my first thought is that someone has tied me to the bed and beaten me with a stick.

I groan, my hand going to my face. Oscar hadn't exaggerated about how sore I'd be. That's when I spot the green-and-purple bruises blooming across my wrist from practice yesterday. I'll have to make sure to keep my sleeves pulled low.

But then I notice something else, something wonderful: bright, yellow sunlight streaming in through the window!

I pop up. If it holds, that'll be a full day of charging for the tablet. If tomorrow is also sunny against the Astronomer's predictions, I'll be able to steal the tablet and ride the basket to Jonas. If I were him, I'd be staying close to Eden's Gate, either at the top of the Wall or just on the other side, if I were able to climb down.

Hang on, Jackrabbit.

I'm about to drag myself out of bed but see that, for the first time since I moved into the Tzu cottage, Gryphon is still sleeping on the floor beside me. I study him, my heart banging in my chest. His blanket is tangled around his legs. Did he have nightmares that I didn't hear? A beam of sunlight caresses his face, following the curve of his eyes, the arch of his nose. His bare chest rises and falls easily, one hand sprawled across it.

He appears so innocent in sleep, just an arm's length away from me. Without even thinking, I reach for his face. I don't believe I mean to touch him, but I'll never know, because he circles my wrist before I come close.

One yank, and I land with the elegance of a turtle, sprawled across the warm expanse of Gryphon's chest. "What're you doing?" I demand.

"What were *you* doing?" His eyes are clear, his mouth curved in a smile.

"You had a bug on your face," I lie.

He cocks an eyebrow. "And you were going to save me?"

I yank my hand back and stand slowly, groaning as I do.

"Sore?" he asks, rolling to his side to face me, resting his elbow on the floor.

"Nope." I don't know why I keep lying. I smooth the front of my pajamas. "I'm going to make breakfast." I grab my day clothes from where they're draped over the end of the bed. I can either dress here or go all the way down to the bathroom, which means possibly walking past Jarek in my pj's. "Turn around."

"We all swam in the creek yesterday," he says matter-of-factly. "You can't think that your wet underclothes left much to the imagination."

"Stop!" I cover my ears.

He's making a strange noise, and it takes me a moment to realize he's chuckling. "For an Apothecary, you sure are shy about the human body," he says.

"You sound like your mother." I can feel myself scowling.

"There are worse things. Sounding like my father, for example." He hops to his feet and walks to his dresser. He selects a clean tunic to put on, his back to me. Despite my own shyness, I can't tear my eyes away from the ripple of muscle beneath skin as he raises his arms overhead. It's when he begins to fold up his makeshift bed that I decide I'm being silly. I face the opposite wall and begin to remove my pajamas.

"Rose, stop!" he yelps.

I turn.

Gryphon appears pained, his expression a complete one-eighty from the teasing he'd just displayed. "Rose," he says, studying me. "Do you even know what you want?"

"Excuse me?" I glance around the room. I have no idea what he's talking about, but it feels like an insult.

He drags a hand down his face, sighing. "You were an Apothecary because you were born to it. You're amazing at it, don't get me wrong, but you never would have discovered that if not for a luck of birth. You were going to marry Nikola because you were assigned to him." His voice lowers. "Now me for the same reason. And you're about to change in front of me right now because I joked that you were too shy not to do it. Do you ever stop to ask what *you* care about?"

The question's pointedness is unnerving. I scramble for a truth I believe in. "I used to care for you, when we were children."

"Why?"

I think of the secret hopes and dreams and plans and fears we shared, the way he listened to me and brought out the best in me. "Because you were so easy to be with. I felt...whole when we were together."

"But you never told me." His tone is not unkind.

I throw up my hands, exasperated. "You're the one who stopped talking to *me*."

He tips his head in concession. *Fair enough*, I know he means. I should quit while I'm ahead, but old programming dies hard. "And I had no choice in the rest. It's how the Valley works."

He shakes his head. "But did you get upset? Rail against it?"

I think of the pledge on instinct, trailing off in my mind. *Protect the system and it shields us all, follow the rules so...* I've been stuffing down my true feelings for a while. With Jonas gone, forced to live in this house with people I can't trust, I haven't got the strength to keep the lid on it any longer.

"Losing my dad devastated me," I admit, holding his gaze. "I wish I'd questioned things then, but I didn't. I thought following the rules would keep the rest of my family safe." My voice cracks at how wrong I was. "But not anymore, Gryphon. I'm done going quietly. I'm ready to fight for what I believe in." My chest feels tight, and I'm breathing heavy. I don't understand why I'm so worked up. He isn't trying to hurt me.

He studies me quietly, a terribly sad expression on his beautiful face. "As your husband, I will stand by your side, even if you didn't choose me." And then he brushes past me, the scent of pine lingering in the air. "Make sure you eat today," he says as he passes. "You work too hard and skip far too many meals."

Then he closes the door behind himself.

It takes all my will not to run after him and confess that I'm going to look for Jonas. While it's nice to imagine that Gryphon might help me escape, he'd more likely try to talk me out of it. I couldn't fault him if he did, but the only thing more unthinkable than going after my twin is *not* going, wondering every day if I'd let him die a slow and painful death.

It's several moments before I collect myself, drawing in deep breaths as I stare at the wardrobe. I'm reminded of the papers Gryphon stuffed so quickly back into it last night. It's none of my business what they were, but curiosity is a better companion than fear. I hurry to the cupboard. Reach under the blankets and pillow. Pull out a sheaf of papers.

Charcoal drawings. Good ones, of trees and the Wall and farm animals. And a handful are of a girl who looks like me, except the sun is always shining on her.

My heart tugs, and I sigh. Life was easier a few days ago, when I had nothing but an enemy to leave behind.

33

When I reach the kitchen, I find only Jarek.

"Within the Wall," I intone, tipping my head in a gesture of respect I hope will get us off on the right foot today. "Will Misia and Gryphon be joining us for breakfast?" I walk to the wood stove to light it.

"You didn't ask your betrothed while you were in his arms this morning?" Jarek asks, but his voice lacks its usual bite. He looks even more exhausted today than the night before.

I glance at his wounded arm, covered to the elbow by his shirt. No visible signs of blood poisoning or undue swelling. I put a pan of water on the warming stove and drop rolled oats into it, followed by a sprinkle of lavender. I wish I had black walnuts to give it character. We should receive a fresh delivery of fruit and vegetables soon, the little that's left this time of year, but until then, it's going to be porridge for our morning meal.

"What are your duties for the day?" I ask.

"Same as usual," he says. "Check the perimeter for breaches. Guardian training. Gryphon will give you a preview this afternoon."

That's right: my betrothed is taking me to watch their training. It'll be difficult to find time for the vault today, but I can't give up on getting in, especially now that I'm resolved to go look for Jonas.

I don't think I've gone more than a few waking moments without thinking about him since the Harvest. There's always some joke I want to crack, some new discovery to share with him. Except now, instead of imagining his end and wondering if it was quick, I want to know if he's cold. If he's wounded. If he still has hope.

I'm no fool, not when it comes to life and death. I know my twin might already be gone, but by going to the top of the Wall, I can at least look for evidence of his fate myself. I survived seeing my father's body. As terrible as it was, there was a peace to it, a finality.

"You look like Henrietta when you cook."

I freeze, holding a wooden spoon just above the bubbling pot, its fragrant steam enclosing my face. I'd forgotten Jarek was there. "You've seen my mother cook?"

"Once, when I was young." His voice sounds far away. "Fourteen or fifteen. I was upset about something. Skipped training and found myself drawn to the Apothecary cottage by the most beautiful singing. Your mother was the only one home, preparing the evening meal. She sounded like an angel, Henrietta did. Looked like one, too."

He begins crooning "Down in Noah's Valley," the lullaby my gran was humming the other day. Jarek's baritone is surprisingly soulful. "So sleep, my darling, don't you be scared, the Wall made us whole, and our order repaired."

I risk a peek at him. His expression is relaxed. It's the first time all week he hasn't resembled a bird of prey. Could this man really have helped orchestrate my mother's murder, as Meryl and the others believe? He'd looked genuinely stricken in the moment.

Jarek rubs his hand across his short hair, like he's scrubbing away the memory. "I've never heard a sweeter voice. It's a shame she wasn't born to the Minstrels. I was in love with her. Did you know that?"

He isn't asking like he expects an answer, which is good because I'm speechless. He must be very, *very* tired to admit all of this to me. And as much as I hate the idea of Jarek mooning after my mother, I feel an unexpected gratitude. What a beautiful moment to have shared. It's how Mom would want to be remembered.

"In love with who?" Misia asks, coming down the stairs.

Fear zips down my spine. For all the emergencies that show up at the Apothecary house, we're a calm family. The Tzus behave like they're always one cross word away from a fistfight.

"Why you, of course," Jarek says, his words preternaturally smooth.

Just then, the porridge boils over, splattering the counter. I quickly move it to the sink, realizing this is the second time in two days I've nearly burned breakfast. As I wipe away the mess, I feel Misia weighing whether to believe her husband. Fortunately, Gryphon enters from the back of the house, breaking the tension. But then confusion takes over as he strolls to me, his hand sliding around my lower back. He leans over and kisses my forehead before staring into my eyes. I shiver and instinctively look away from the intimate gaze.

Misia stares at us suspiciously. That's when I realize what Gryphon's doing. He's pretending, just like I did last night. I bounce on my toes, stretch a bit, and land a clumsy peck on his cheek, accidentally making a weird smacking noise. I'm embarrassed to discover that he was right: I'm not great at this. It's not like I've ever kissed someone before. Well, until the roof. Yet Gryphon opens his onyx eyes slowly after my cheek attack, as if waking from a dream. The black glass is on fire. His mouth curves.

I try to slip out after serving the Tzus, lying that I promised the Record Keeper I'd show up early. Gryphon stops me, though, a raised eyebrow telling me all I need to know: he's not going to let me leave without breakfast. I huff, crashing into a chair to swallow some porridge. The Tzus' bickering makes eating difficult, but it would be a lie to say that a small part of me isn't touched by Gryphon's concern. It is usually me doing the caring.

I rinse my dish and head outside. On the doorstep, the sun lands like a smile on my face. I hope the tablet on the roof is soaking up every bit of it. When I reach the library door, I enter without knocking. It might be connected to the Record Keeper cottage, but it's still a public space.

Simon stands just inside, shoving a book onto the shelf. "Rose!"

He's wearing short pants, his knobby knees exposed. He didn't get Marina's facial symmetry, but neither did he inherit her mean streak. He appears both happy to see me and a little guilty.

"Hey." I twist the web of skin near my thumb. I've been waiting to get him alone since Jonas was Harvested. If I come on too strong, though, and straight out ask him what my brother saw in the vault that morning, will he clam up?

"What're you reading?" I ask innocently, tucking a loose strand of hair behind my ear.

"Something boring." He stuffs his hands into his pockets. "A book about solar energy."

"May I see?" I'm surprised at my own brazenness. We're taught it's impolite to ask someone what they're reading. It invades the privacy of their mind. Plus, many villagers don't read at all outside of school, and drawing attention to that would single them out.

It's just the right question for Simon, though. His face lights up. He reaches for the book he replaced. Its title is *Solar Power on a Budget*. It strikes me as a text more for the Engineer House, but I suppose that as a Record Keeper, it's important he have a surface-level understanding of many subjects. I allow him to show me some diagrams, explaining concepts I'm sure Albert would understand but fly well over my head, but I soon grow impatient with the niceties. The weight of not listening to Jonas the last time I saw him alive has become unbearable, and I don't know when someone else might interrupt us.

"Simon, please tell me what you and Jonas saw in the vault the morning he was Harvested. I miss him so much. Knowing what happened in his final hours would really help."

His face falls. He glances toward the living quarters. "Wish I could, but Marina would kill me."

My pulse rockets. He's accidentally confirmed that not only *had* Jonas seen something, but that it'd been something of value—something Marina knows about. "Why would Marina care?"

Simon shakes his head. "The contents of the vault are something only the Record Keepers should know. We swear it in our oath. I never should've let Jonas down there. I just wanted to show off."

"What oath? To whom?" We might work alongside our Houses growing up, but none of us are officially sworn into our professions until after marriage. Obviously, he and Salvatora remain unattached.

Simon twists his hands nervously. "I can't tell you." He shudders, dropping his voice. "It'd harm the villagers to learn it."

This is news to me. "If Jonas saw it, I need to know," I say firmly. "You don't have to be the one who shows me. Just point me in the right direction."

Simon shakes his head. "The cellar is locked."

I already know this. "Where's the key?"

He shakes his head again, more vehemently this time.

"Simon," I speak slowly, "I'm not going to let this go. I'd rather hear it from you, but if you don't want to talk, I'll find another way."

"Fine," he says, miserably. "I'll tell you, but only so you don't put yourself at risk, Rose. It's the least I can do for him." His voice cracks on the last word, and I know he's talking about my brother. The boy's grief is so palpable, so akin to my own, that I can't help but reach out and take his hand. "We've got the entire history of the Valley down there," he begins.

"Of course." I nod.

He glances around nervously and then lowers his voice. "What you don't know is that there's another room behind the standard scrolls. My dad discovered it about nine months ago, says the door just slid open one day. It's fulla stuff I've never seen before! Sweets like you wouldn't believe, food in metal jars, tools, weapons. The Founders must've stashed it, though I couldn't say for what."

His face is flushed with excitement, but I'm horrified. I think I tasted that sweet, the green rancher zoo zoo Jarek gave me. Was that also where he'd gotten the weapon charging on his roof? Sounds like it. But while what Simon has told me is shocking, I can't see how it would be enough to get Jonas Harvested. Some unexpected supplies from before the Wall? No, Jonas must have stumbled on something else—*we're not what we seem*—and I aim to see it for myself. I'm about to probe further when Marina appears.

"You're late." Her platinum hair is confined to four elegant braids twisted into a thick rope down her back. "You were supposed to be here before sunrise."

I don't think that's true. "I had to make breakfast for my family," I say, gagging internally at the word. But I must rebuild her faith in my obedience after my slip of the tongue on our walk back from chapel.

"How lovely." She stares down her nose at me, seeming unusually out of sorts. "Here's your census list. You should be able to reach fifteen houses by the end of the day."

"What?" I feel my chin draw in. "Impossible. I was told it would be eleven. I'm only one person, and I'm supposed to observe Guardian training later."

Plus, I need to break into your vault and sneak out to the caves.

She sneers. "But you're so good at everything you put your mind to, aren't you, Rose?"

That's so ridiculous, it doesn't deserve a response. I reach for the census materials, but she holds tight to them.

"I'd love to have you and Gryphon over for dinner this week," she says. "Maybe after the wedding."

"Don't hold your breath," I mutter.

Her face contorts like she tastes something sour. This time, I pull hard, yanking the papers out of her hand.

Then I step back into the sunshine.

34

"Hello?" I greet the child standing in front of the Plumber cottage, her back to me. "Are your parents home?"

When she turns, I see it's Wendy, the girl whose finger Jarek amputated.

"Oh," I say, eyes travelling to the site of her injury.

She blinks, and a shy smile spreads across her freckled face. She's got brown eyes, like most villagers, but hers are slightly tipped upward at the edges, giving her an impish appearance. She holds up the heavily bandaged hand. "Your aunt thinks it'll work fine again. She says it's thanks to your quick response."

A weight lifts off my chest. "I'm so happy to hear that." Without touching her, I examine her face for signs of fever, her exposed wrist for the telltale red streaks of infection. She appears to be in perfect health. "Does it hurt very badly?"

"Only if I bonk it on things." Her smile disappears, head hanging. "It's nothing compared to the shame of being a thief."

My throat burns. She's too young to think of herself like this. "You didn't steal, Wendy." I crouch until we're the same height, forcing her to look at me. "Finding food to bring to the village isn't a crime."

Her eyes swell with tears. "But I wasn't supposed to be in the woods."

I set my jaw, heart aching for how worthless Jarek has made the girl feel. "Playing somewhere you aren't supposed to is different than stealing. And we're only forbidden from going into the forest for our own protection." But I don't believe that, not now that I've visited the woods myself. It wouldn't serve Wendy to hear the truth, though. I stroke her hair and give her braid a little tug. "You didn't deserve that. Jarek shouldn't have done it."

"You're speaking against your House," she says quietly.

My stomach lurches. When had it started coming so naturally? Despite myself, Mom's words still ring in my ears. *Don't stand out.*

"Wendy!" Augustus steps out of the cottage. I haven't seen him since I believed he was threatening Gran.

"Within the Wall," I say, holding up a hand in greeting. "I'm helping the Record Keepers conduct the census. May I borrow some of your time?"

"I'm busy," he says. The wrinkles around his eyes and mouth suggest he's no stranger to a smile, though I can't recall the last time I saw it. He and Mom had begun walking the village together the past few months, Augustus always looking serious. He wipes his hands on his heavy work apron. "But you saved my girl's finger. I owe you for it."

I'm shocked. "There's no payment required for helping one another."

He glances both ways down the lane. His is the last cottage I'm visiting today. The streets are empty, villagers tucked away at work.

"Used to be that way," he says. "Why don't you come inside?"

A cold thrill grips my spine. The families I visited yesterday were friendly. They adhered to custom, offering me tea and a seat at their table, and they answered all my questions to the best of their ability. The Plumber's comment about how things *used to be* is the first time I've smelled the spark of rebellion that drives Meryl, Sal, Eero, and Oscar. Have I misread Augustus this entire time?

I follow him inside. Except for the toolkit near the door, the length of piping stacked against a wall, and the rows of plumbing and library books on the shelves, it looks like every other cottage in the Valley. Kitchen, dining space, and family room on the open main floor, stairs leading up to the bedrooms, door leading out the back to the laundry and bathroom. It does lack the dampness that many of our homes have acquired over time, that faint tinge of mildew in the walls. *Well, I suppose they've never had a leaky pipe.* I don't see anyone else home.

"Can I pour you some tea?"

"No, thank you." I learned the hard way that I should turn down most drink offers. I ended up nearly swimming to the final houses yesterday.

"I'll help myself to a cup," he says. "You let me know if you change your mind."

"All right. Thank you."

He's wearing his work grays, but I notice his pants and tunic have more pockets than mine. What a useful addition. I wonder if he sewed them on himself or put in a special requisition with the Tailor House.

He brings the bubbling kettle to the table.

"My gran used to be of the Plumber House," I blurt out. The room tilts for a moment. Was that too bold for testing the waters?

Augustus stops mid-pour. "Indeed. She was my own father's sister."

"Do you remember her? When she lived here?"

He chuckles, and the beautiful lines on his face deepen. I find myself relaxing around him for the first time. "I'm not that old, child. Your gran left at seventeen to marry your grandfather." His eyes grow serious. "She told you she used to be a Plumber?"

I nod. I still can't believe I said it out loud for anyone to hear. I tug the census materials out of my bag. My shirt catches on the edge of the cloth, revealing bruises all up my forearm.

He slams the tea kettle on the table, his voice a low growl. "Jarek did that?"

I tug down my sleeve. "No," I say quickly.

He studies me, head tilted. "Then they're combat bruises," he says. "And yet you're conducting a census rather than training with your new House."

I keep my eyes averted, worried they'll give away the truth. When I finally peek back at him, his expression is thoughtful, like he's making up his mind about something. He finishes pouring the tea, then returns the kettle to the stove and walks to the front door with the mug. Wendy's sitting on the stoop. "Let me know if you see anyone on their way might need our services," he says, offering her the tea. "This'll keep you warm."

My pulse does a two-step. I think he's just asked his daughter to keep watch.

Wendy accepts the mug gratefully. He closes the door and takes a seat, pushing his chair away so he can cross his legs at the ankle. I sit across from him. His posture is relaxed, his words anything but. "We haven't much time," he says. "When you visited other cottages, how long were you inside asking your questions?"

"Twenty minutes or so in each." I loop the bag off my shoulder and set it on the table. "I need to know—"

He holds up a weathered hand. "I know what you need to know. I'm fifty-eight and my name's Augustus Auger. I live here with my father, Hephaestus, who's seventy-six and who you've kept alive with willow bark tablets since his most recent heart attack."

My stomach leaps into my throat.

He makes a clicking sound, blowing past the statement that could end my life if the wrong person overheard it. "I know you think we don't know, and I'm content to keep it that way. I live with my wife, Coco, forty-nine, my brother, Alphonse, fifty-four, and his wife, Kate, who's fifty-six. They have a fifteen-year-old son named Edward who's at school at the moment. Coco and I have two girls, Wendy, outside, who's nine, and eight-year-old Lydia.

Lydia's also at school, but I'll be outside the Wall before I'll allow her sister to go back before that hand is healed. No one's calling Wendy a thief."

He smacks the table. The crack makes me jump.

"Coco and Alphonse are out performing the regular tasks of our House. Mending leaks. Checking water pressure. Unclogging drains. Kate's been on loan to the Carters for a few weeks now, setting up some quick and dirty irrigation for the new fields. Me too, usually, but I stayed back today with Wendy. Hephaestus is likely upstairs napping. None of us plan to die, marry, or get pregnant anytime soon. You've got all that?"

I review everything I've feverishly written. I nod.

And then he utters the words sure to get me Harvested: "Good. So you're part of that group being trained to fight?"

35

I make a thin squeak.

He nods. "That's what I thought." He leans forward, drumming his fingers. "That gives us fifteen minutes or so to talk about what's important. We're not losing arable land to any creature known to the Valley."

The charcoal of my pencil snaps. "Pardon?"

"What I'm about to say doesn't leave this room," he says, each word weighted, heavy as stones. "Not unless you want us both riding the basket up Eden's Gate as soon as that tablet is charged."

A shiver runs through me, cold and quick. I nod, my tongue thick in my mouth.

He glances toward the front of the house, the muscles in his neck straining as he listens. Only when quiet answers does he speak again, softer than before. "The Council's been saying it's wild animals hunting us in the fields and near the hives just east of the Gate."

I nod again. It hadn't taken long for fear to spread, thick and quiet as smoke, after those areas were closed off. Hunger followed.

"But there's no animals out there." Augustus's voice drops again, now so low I have to strain to hear him. "No scat, no tracks, not a single print. No living creature has risked the abandoned area since the last rainfall, at least."

My breath catches, and I bite my lip to stifle the sound. I suspected the Council was lying when I saw Peter's body, but no animals at all? "Jarek said—"

"I know what he said." Augustus's response is harsh and quick. He runs his hands through silver-shot hair, his fingers trembling just enough to make my pulse race. "I went out there myself, Rose. I saw it with my own eyes. There's no animal sign. Not a rabbit, not a deer, not even a damn fox."

I picture the now-abandoned swath of farmland beside the Wall where two Guardians lost their lives eight months prior. I shudder, and Augustus nods.

"If I didn't know better," he says, "I'd say the animals are as scared of that place as we are." He seems to want to say more but grimaces instead. He shouldn't have gone to investigate. We both know it. The rules are clear. Only the Guardians are allowed in the closed fields.

I open my mouth, but the words stick, tangle. "What's out there, then?"

For a moment, I think he won't answer. His gaze drifts past me, toward the door. Finally, he speaks. "Something terrible. And Jarek wants it that way. You see who he's been Harvesting, don't you? The people who push back against the new rules or who might be able to tell us something about what's really going on."

Exactly what Meryl and the others have been saying. *He disposes of anyone who gets in his way.*

"Your mother crossed Jarek, and she and your brother were taken as a lesson to the rest of us," Augustus says, his voice heavy.

I sit up straight. "Did you see? Did you see what happened to my mother? You were very close to her."

His face falls. "I didn't. She was standing, and then she wasn't, leaving your brother there holding that knife." His forehead grows heavy. "But I know Jarek has something to do with it. He has an agenda we cannot see. I don't imagine your gran or my father will be allowed to stay much longer."

The enormity of it overwhelms me. "You must tell the Record Keeper."

Augustus adjusts his chair with a screech. "I don't trust David. He's not strong enough to stand up to Jarek. And if you tell anyone I said that, I'll swear you're lying." He looks me in the eyes. "And they'd probably Harvest me anyway."

He's placed an incredible amount of trust in me. More than I probably deserve, given my history. I nod and pinch the webbing near my thumb, sewing what I've just learned with what Gryphon said about his father wanting me in their house.

"There's more," Augustus says.

My eyes fly to his face.

"I think Jarek's hoarding food, distributing extra to the people in his favor. The Guardian Houses I've entered to work on their plumbing seem to have more on their counters than the rest of us."

"You're right," I say. "I've seen it for myself."

My new friends were spot-on: Jarek is a danger to us all. He's destroying the paradise and peace we've built in Noah's Valley.

"I'm only telling you the truth of this because of what you've done for Wendy and Hephaestus," Augustus says gruffly. "And because I trusted your mother. She was a good and honest woman. You should know what you're getting into, and I've got a piece of advice to accompany that." He leans forward, pressing down on the table with his pointer finger. "When you've got nothing else, search for anger. It's an excellent companion, at least for the short term. Doesn't need to eat or sleep or shit." He leans back abruptly, holding up his hands. "And that's my debt repaid."

"May the Wall always protect you," I say. Our sincerest expression of gratitude has never felt more fitting.

Something in his face softens, a crack in the stone. "Please be careful, Rose. This Council doesn't like questions. They like answers even less. And please, don't go to the closed-off area of the Wall. Whatever the truth may be, there's a reason the animals avoid it."

I nod, my throat tight, and pack up my census materials.

Augustus seems about to say more, but he's interrupted by Wendy's strangled cry.

Augustus is up before I can speak. I follow him out the door, the sunlight temporarily blinding me. I blink and see Lino Chihuly of the Glassworker House running past. He clutches the limp body of his son to his chest. Without thinking, I sprint after them, the soles of my shoes pounding dry earth, Augustus cursing behind me.

The path leading to the Apothecary cottage is winding, and villagers step aside as Lino barrels through. "Please," he keeps saying, "please, please, please," in a rhythm that matches his desperate footfalls.

I know before we reach the clinic. I know from the blisters at the boy's nose and mouth, visible when I catch up to his father. I know from the stillness of the boy's dangling hand. I know because I've seen this before.

The Vex is back.

36

Uncle Richard is hunched over a mortar and pestle when we burst in, grinding some concoction. His eyes widen as he takes in the scene, then narrow with dreadful recognition. He sweeps his work aside with one motion, clearing space on the table.

"Lay him here," he commands.

Lino lays his son down with such gentleness that it leaves a hollow ache in my chest. The boy's blond curls are damp with sweat, his freckled face slack. There's a slight spatter of something black at the corners of his mouth, across the blisters. The same stain I saw months ago, when the first victims of the Vex began to die.

Uncle Richard leans in, listening for breath, feeling for a pulse. I already know he won't find them.

His shoulders sag as he steps back from the table. "I'm sorry. He's gone."

There's a silence then, vast and cruel. The Glassworker collapses into a chair, cradling his son's hand like he can still warm it with love, making a sound I'll never forget—a raw, animal keening that seems to come from outside his body.

"He was fine this morning," Lino chokes out.

I step closer to Finn, my eyes tracing the boy's form. That's when I notice his shirtsleeve has a faint, still-drying splotch at the wrists, like it's been dipped in an orange liquid.

Or water with a high metallic content.

Water only available in the forbidden part of town.

Uncle Richard sees it, too. "He visited your old workshop in the quarantine zone?"

"Absolutely not," Lino swears.

"Is anyone else ill in your household?" I ask. "Even a tickle in the throat, a low fever?"

Lino shakes his head.

I was just in that area myself to examine Peter's body, and I feel fine. A thought lands heavy, one so terrible I have a hard time believing it: free of hosts for so many weeks, any virus should be non-viable. Antibiotics failed to treat its prior victims, ruling out bacterial infection. And if it isn't either of those...*then the Vex isn't an illness at all.*

"Uncle," I begin, but he shakes his head, warning me to silence.

Outside, the village bell begins to toll—a warning. Someone has already alerted the Guardians. They'll be here soon, and if they find me near medicinal herbs...

"Rose," Uncle Richard whispers urgently. "You need to leave. Now."

I want to argue, but he's right. I back toward the door, unable to tear my eyes from Finn's face. He looks so vulnerable with that terrible stillness and the blisters on his face. I remember him laughing just last week, running through the marketplace with a kite made of oiled parchment and thin wooden dowels that Jonas had helped him make.

That's when I remember something else: Finn, in the woods hiding with his sister as Wendy was caught with the apples. What had she said to me as I hurried her back, guiding her with one arm and holding her severed finger with the other?

The three of us were playing and found a tree over by the flax field, just inside the woods. We shouldn't have gone in, but everyone's been so hungry.

She might be able to give me more answers. I race out of the cottage, desperate to locate her. If what I now suspect is true, then Jarek is terrorizing us beyond our wildest dreams, but I need confirmation. Fortunately, I find the girl right where we left her, standing in front of the Plumber cottage, fists clenched at her sides. Her cheeks are red and wet. She looks like she hasn't blinked since Finn was carried past her.

I kneel, gently. "Wendy. You're friends with Finn and his sister, aren't you?"

She nods. A hiccup. "We played in the woods. Before…"

Before her punishment. "Please, Wendy." I put my hand on her arm. "Where else did you play?"

Her eyes grow wide, but she shakes her head rather than answer.

"I already know Finn went into the quarantine zone," I say. "You're not in trouble, but I need to know if anyone else was with him."

"It was only Finn!" she says, clapping her hand over her mouth in horror at the confession.

"It's all right." I squeeze her arm. "He's beyond punishment. Where did he go? To his cottage, maybe, to gather a favorite book?"

She shakes her head. "He went to the well. Only to the well, but *a lot*. He said that was the only water that tasted good to him." She makes a face. "I think it tastes like rust, but Finn grew up on it. He made it like a game, racing in and out unseen."

"Tell no one what you've told me," I command, "and please stay where it's safe." Then I sweep her into a hug and race to the quarantine zone to confirm what I already fear to be the truth.

I hurry down the cobblestone streets, ducking behind the Leatherworkers' drying racks when a Guardian patrol passes. I think through what I know, trying to fit the awful pieces together.

According to Simon, nine months ago his father discovered a room off the vault full of weapons and supplies. Shortly after that, the Guardians were killed, supposedly by a wild animal, though now I doubt that story completely.

Jarek—who has made himself head of all five Guardian Houses—declared the farmland near the Wall unsafe, and soon after, the rations began. Whipping posts were constructed next, a curfew enacted. All under the guise of "keeping us safe."

Four months later, the Vex appeared. It had all the hallmarks of a virus, so on my mother's advice, the Council ordered a quarantine of that section of the village—opposite the area that had been closed off due to supposed animal attacks. That cost us even more resources. People grew hungry and restless.

Some initially spoke out against Jarek and the Council. According to Augustus's and Meryl's suspicions, those people were Harvested. If they were correct, what used to be an honor that allowed members of the Valley to care for their community even in death was now a weapon that Jarek controlled. Then, a month ago, Reatha—apparently a close friend of my mother's—pretended to self-Harvest the Chemists.

Sometime in there, my mother started coding a message in her journal, which I'd found hidden in a trail of charcoal. And only a few days ago, she was murdered in plain sight, possibly with a weapon from the secret room the Record Keeper discovered.

My brother was framed and Harvested, his punishment almost certainly pre-planned given that the basket had already been lowered from its perch among the Heavens. The day after, Peter of the Potter House was discovered in the evacuated industrial zone, far from the site of the other two animal attacks. The state of his body was disturbing, and he appeared to have been dragged from the original site of his death.

We *are* being hunted, though not by any animal I've heard of. Augustus confirmed as much.

And Jarek knows it. Does he command the killer, or is he simply hiding in its shadow? And more important to my current mission, why is he poisoning us?

For that's what I now believe the Vex to be: poison.

I stop to catch my breath and sanity, near a section of the Wall covered in purpling vines so thick they almost obscure the ancient stones. This is very near where Peter's body was found. Around me are a cluster of empty homes: the Wheelwrights, the Leatherworkers, the Potters, the Glassworkers, the Coopers, and the Blacksmiths. The cottages stand eerie, like empty skeletons.

But I'm not here for them. I've come to see the well.

A cluster of children's footprints surround it. It's rained several times since the quarantine, so these must belong to Finn, a boy who'd simply craved the taste of his favorite water.

Water that's certainly toxic.

I duck into the abandoned Glassworker cottage and find a small bottle. Hoping my theory is correct, that I'm only in danger if I drink the water, I walk to the well and scoop out a bit, stoppering the bottle.

I pop the sample into my satchel and am turning to leave when I notice a second set of footprints around the backside of the well, these adult-sized but peculiar. One is a regular footprint, but the other drags, as if the walker was wearing something unwieldy on their foot...like a cast.

David.

Was he here chasing the same terrible hunch? I add that to my growing list of questions for the Record Keeper. If David suspects—like I do—that Jarek's been poisoning us in addition to colluding with a killer, maybe he can help me uncover why. And maybe this time, he'll stop looking away and *finally* take a stand.

That's what I'm thinking when a shadow slices across my path.

37

Gryphon strides toward me, his Guardian uniform impeccable as always, his face dark with anger. His hand rests on the hilt of his sword. "What in the Wall are you doing here?" he demands.

"A child is dead," I say. "Another victim of the Vex. Or so it appears." For all I know, Gryphon is in on his father's grand plan, as much as it sickens me to think it. He *did* know about his father's strange weapon and presumably the resource hoarding, too.

His expression shifts minutely—surprise, followed by concern. "You shouldn't be here," he says, softer now but no less insistent. "It's not safe."

"I need to—"

"You need to do as you're told," he interrupts, stepping closer. Too close. I can smell the leather of his uniform, the metal polish on his sword. "You can't wander in forbidden areas, Rose. You'll be punished."

His bossiness ignites my temper. "Since when is my safety your concern, Guardian? Your duty is to your father, not to me."

Something flickers across his face—hurt, probably—before his expression hardens again. I grimace, realizing my words came out harsher than intended, but Gryphon needs to learn he can't order me around forever.

"Let's go," he says, reaching for me. "We'll get something to eat on the way to the training grounds. Remember your orders for the day."

I pull away. I've got to talk to David and get this water sample to Reatha and do the thing that feels most important of all: find out what my mother knew. V-E-X, she'd hidden in her journal, and now I have an idea why. Maybe that inkling can help me decode the rest.

"Not until I stop by the Apothecary cottage," I counter. "I have to check something."

"Rose—"

You catch more flies with honey, Gran has always said. "Just for a minute. Please."

"Fine," he relents, his voice gruff. "But I'm coming with you."

We walk in tense silence, and I can't help but wonder about Gryphon's sudden overprotectiveness. We were friends once, of course, but this feels different. *He's keeping something from me.* I'm sure of it. Well, he can join the rest on that front. This whole village is a spitting nest of secrets, I'm discovering.

"Wait here," I tell Gryphon outside the Apothecary cottage.

He follows me through the back door anyway. I make an exasperated noise. At least Uncle Richard is gone, likely summoned by the Council of Elders to explain Finn's death. Good. I don't need him questioning what I'm about to do.

"What are you looking for?" Gryphon asks as I move purposefully toward the storage closet.

I ignore him, pulling open the heavy wooden door to reveal shelves stacked with herbs, tinctures, and medicinal supplies. My mother's dedicated shelf is untouched. I ignore the dried roots and glass jars to slide open her drawer.

Charcoal.

Packets of it. More than any normal Apothecary would need.

"I knew it," I whisper.

"What?" Gryphon asks, suddenly too close behind me.

I turn to face him, my voice low and steady despite the fury building inside me. "The Vex is no virus, Gryphon. It's a poison. My mother knew. She prepared these packets in case of another 'outbreak.'" I take a deep breath. "*That's* why she was killed."

His face pales. "Rose, you can't just accuse—"

"The Record Keeper knows it, too, I suspect. I saw his footprints around the well." I put my hands on my hips, eyes narrowing. "What is your father up to?"

Gryphon grips my shoulders, and I'm acutely aware of the size of his hands. "Lower your voice," he hisses. "This isn't safe to discuss."

"So you *do* know something!" I challenge, searching his gaze.

For a moment, I see conflict in his eyes. Then he releases me, and I feel too light where his hands used to be. "We need to go to the training grounds," he says, voice carefully neutral. "My mother is waiting."

He's not going to answer me. I know without asking that he won't accept any further detours, either, not until we've done our Guardian duty. Fine. Tonight, I'll try again to crack my mother's code. Whatever the truth is about the Vex, about her death, about this village with its stone Wall and ancient secrets, I'm going to find it. Even if it kills me.

Which—given what I've learned today—seems increasingly likely.

True to his word, Gryphon has us stop by the Bakers' after I drop off the day's completed census materials at the Record Keeper cottage. He charms yesterday's rolls off the Bakers' youngest daughter. I'm surprised to see how friendly he can be with others. We're eating and walking, the warm sun shining down on us, when a question surprises my lips. "Do you think your parents care for each other?"

His brow creases. "Why do you ask?"

Because I suspect Jarek was responsible for my mother's murder, and his loving her would complicate that.

"Something your father said this morning." I wonder if I should even repeat it, but I've gone too far to back out. "That he was in love with my mom when they were teenagers."

Gryphon's expression is pained but not surprised. "Through here," he says, directing me down an alley I've somehow never walked before. The Guardian training ground is out of the way, and few of us ever have reason to visit. I'm excited to see somewhere new in the Valley.

I think Gryphon's ignoring my question and decide I won't press the issue, but then, "My mother loved my father. My father loved your mother. He never hid it. In fact, shortly after your dad died, he petitioned to end his marriage to my mother so he could wed Henrietta."

My jaw drops. "End their marriage?" I'd never heard of such a thing.

"Yeah." He sounds as disgusted as I feel.

Imagining Gryphon ending our betrothal to wed someone else elicits a sharp and sudden pang of empathy on Misia's behalf. And I don't even *like* my fiancé. Much.

I think about my mother being courted by Jarek. Could two people be more opposite in temperament? As far as I know, he never visited, except for the one incident he'd confessed to this morning. The moment Mom was killed, I believed I'd seen raw grief on Jarek's face, but he'd immediately covered it. Of course, I've since learned he is a man who hides a lot. He could have been pretending to be sad to throw off any suspicion about his involvement.

Yet it'd seemed real. "The Record Keeper denied his request?" I ask.

Gryphon spreads his hands. "Didn't have to. He asked your

mom and she said she was content to remain a Caster for the rest of her life. I overheard my parents fighting about it."

I feel a surge of fierce pride. My mother *had* stood up to Jarek. Maybe, and it's agony to think it, he'd been so offended by her rejection that he'd arranged her death and Jonas's setup. The thought roils my gut. But no, I think, quickly dismissing the prospect. It sounds like my mother rejected Jarek over a decade ago. Her recent murder wouldn't be related to that, right?

"Why did your father ban us from watching you train?" That restriction had come with the curfew.

Gryphon shrugs. We've left the village and are now hoofing it through the fields, the golden wheat surrounding us shorn as close as a haircut. "You don't want to watch the Blacksmiths ply their trade, do you? Or the Plumbers plumb?"

"But I *could*," I say. "If they were doing it in front of me. Say they came to my cottage to fix something, or I went to the Blacksmith to request a tool made."

He shoots me a bemused glance. "You're that eager to watch the Guardians exercise? Have our midday demonstrations not satisfied your appetite?"

My blush mortifies me, but it seems to delight him. Before I can think of a comeback, we step onto a narrow path at the farmland's end and are forced to proceed single file into the woods. We're hiking for several minutes when I hear an unfamiliar sound, like a drumbeat, right before we break into a clearing.

A huge barn stands straight ahead, whatever's making the noise just beyond it. But Gryphon wants us to look inside the building first.

"My father's toys." He pulls open the double doors.

It takes a moment for my eyes to adjust. When they do, I don't know what to make of what I see. It looks like a regular barn at first: stalls—likely to quarter the Guardians' patrol horses during training, though they spend the night at the larger stable our Animal Farmers maintain—a hayloft, shelves for tack.

But the back wall is a veritable armory.

Some instruments are familiar, like swords, bo staffs, and bow and arrows, but most are alien. Iterations of the weapon Gryphon accidentally wounded his father with. Pairs of metal bracelets. What looks like large watering cans. And on the ground, several baskets of round, bumpy objects.

I shudder at the potential for violence Jarek has accumulated. Much of it must've come from that secret room below the Record Keeper cottage, because I've never seen weapons like this in Noah's Valley.

Before I can speak, Gryphon slams the door shut. He's holding himself so still he looks like he'll break. "The Record Keeper found the weapons in the vault. He shared them with my father, who is tasking the Engineer House with building more. Explosives, mostly, seem to be Dad's primary interest, but that's the one thing the Engineer House is unable to recreate. They require materials we don't have inside the Wall, as desperate as my father is to obtain them."

He looks at me like I'm supposed to know what this means. When I have nothing, he shakes his head. "Shall we go to the training field, then?"

He takes off around the barn.

I follow, horrified at what I've seen.

38

I know there are five Guardian homes. Thanks to the census, I've also learned the village currently has forty-three Guardians—over ten percent of our population—though I wasn't allowed to enter their cottages. Twenty-eight of them are in front of me now, marching in lockstep in an open field, swords strapped to their sides, eyes braced forward as Misia commands them from a viewing platform ten feet above the ground. Seeing so many Guardians clad in full battle gear is overwhelming, particularly when I think about the control Jarek exerts over them.

Gryphon leads me up a ladder to a second viewing platform, a mirror of Misia's. The field between us is enormous, an oval shape surrounded by thick trees.

Misia acknowledges our presence but doesn't stop the practice.

"What are they doing?" I whisper to Gryphon. My quiet is unnecessary. They can't possibly hear me above the pounding of their feet.

"Marching. It's Jarek's latest order." His distaste is unmistakable.

"You think it's a waste of time?"

Gryphon raises a shoulder. "He wants obedience. Uniformity. I prefer we know how to fight well."

"So you skip out when they practice marching?"

Before Gryphon can respond, a piercing whistle shrieks

through the air, followed by a flash of light. I slap my hands over my ears as an explosion rocks the ground with such force that it bucks me off my feet. I land, hard, on the wooden platform. The sound is powerful this close, but I can see from the way it shivers only the nearest branches that it's contained to the training ground.

Gryphon offers me a hand. I take it, shaking my head to clear the echoes. My heart is galloping. "What *was* that?"

He indicates the training field. The Guardians have lost any pretense of orderly marching. They're grappling with one another, fighting with speed and force. Misia watches, her face shining. When she blows her whistle, they stop as if frozen. When she blows again, they begin where they left off, fists and feet flying, teeth flashing.

"They're going to kill each other," I say.

"They're not." Gryphon jerks his head toward two men who hold blades at each other's throats. I expect to see blood, but just at the killing edge, they both sheath their weapons and begin fighting barehanded instead. "It's part of our training. Knowing when to pull back, when to go for the jugular." He glowers. "The training has grown brutal. Far more so than we're used to."

My ears are still ringing. "What was the noise and light?" I doubt Jarek would waste irreplaceable explosives in training, but it didn't feel like Valley tech, either.

"A flash bang. The Record Keeper read about them once, mentioned it to my father. Jarek loved the idea so much that he had them made. He says we don't know a person's true strength until they're under pressure. He uses the sound and commotion to simulate fighting under unexpected conditions."

Apothecaries must learn to perform under stress, too, but we certainly don't make a habit of inviting it. "How can you stand it?"

Gryphon's whole body grows rigid. "I can't. I told my father as much when he first introduced this style of training. I've not been allowed to return since, not until today." He makes a pale imitation of a smile. "It would seem my father doesn't trust me to do anything but perimeter patrol on the distant side of the Valley. It's a snipe hunt."

"A what?"

"Snipe hunt." He sounds bitter. "It's a term from Before. Means an exercise in pointlessness. Snipes aren't real. Neither is a threat inside the Wall, at least outside of the area where the bodies have been found. I should know. I've walked every inch of this place a hundred times over."

"No threats in here," I correct, "except for the creature that killed my dad." It's a silly thing to get defensive about, but I don't appreciate him implying that the beast that mauled my father wasn't a real danger.

Gryphon looks away. "Except for that."

I study the soldiers—for that's what they remind me of, a military force like I've only read about in history books. Their faces I know, but I've never seen them act like this. Precise. Unthinking. Violent. And if the way they're following Misia's every command is any indication, Jarek has gotten the mindless subordination he's asked for.

"I want to go," I say.

Gryphon tips his head. "Seen enough?"

"Enough spectacle," I say. "I'm ready to practice honest fighting."

The fierce gratitude in his gaze must knock the sense out of me, because despite everything, I find my hand reaching for his as we start down.

39

Eero, Sal, and Meryl are waiting near our training spot, Sal and Eero sitting next to each other and Meryl perched on the naked trust rock. Marie and Reatha are nowhere to be seen, but Albert sits in the mouth of the cave, his chair firmly on the ground. It must take a great deal of energy to hover, so I understand why he saves the feature for difficult terrain. His expression is sullen, and he looks like he hasn't slept or bathed in days. The dark brown skin under his eyes is sunken, but the way no one else spares him a glance tells me this appearance isn't unusual.

Perhaps he feels guilty for the tech he stole.

I take a second to fantasize that I might steal it back—use Albert's panel to charge the tablet faster and chase Jonas up the Wall. Too bad I wouldn't know the first thing about connecting it. I shake my head.

"Albert, can you run some tests on this water sample?" I ask, digging the bottle out of my bag.

For as much as I mistrust Albert, he's still a trained Chemist. As long as I don't tell him where I got the water, he should do fine.

"What am I testing it for?"

His sharp tone catches me off guard. "Anything that isn't water."

"What? That could take days."

Like he's got something more important on his schedule? He lives in a cave. "Please do it as quickly as you can."

He glares at me before taking the bottle inside.

"Where's Oscar?" Gryphon asks the others.

"Working on the wedding gown for your highness," Sal says, rolling her eyes at me. "It's supposed to be quite the showstopper."

"What?" I ask.

"Oh," Meryl says, her face flooding with sympathy from atop her perch. "You didn't know. Misia ordered Oscar to collect your first wedding dress and turn it into a gown 'worthy of a queen.'"

"What?" I say again. It's apparently become the only word I know. Our survival inside the Wall depends on equality, harmony. Putting me forward in finery will undermine village solidarity, with me as the target. Is that what Misia's after?

"What will you be wearing, Gryphon?" Eero's tone is teasing.

Gryphon lunges for him, moving with catlike grace. They wrestle for a few moments until Eero starts laughing too hard to continue. Gryphon shakes his head, but he's smiling.

"Today, we're going to learn to get out of chokeholds," he tells the group.

He pairs us off, having Eero sit out because we're an uneven number without Oscar. Gryphon guides me to the center of the circle to demonstrate. He maintains eye contact, which should make me feel awkward but instead allows me to relax just enough to take in what he's saying.

"If your opponent is gripping your neck with one hand, like this," he says, "swing your dominant arm up and around, bringing it down on the crook of their elbow with all the power you have. Joints are weak."

I do as he says. His hand releases.

"If they've got you by two hands..." He looks to me for permission. I nod, and he places both around my neck. My heart rate spikes, body instinctively alerting me that I've allowed myself to become unsafe. But the alarm disappears almost immediately, replaced by an unexpected certainty: Gryphon won't hurt me, at least not like this. I'm hungry for his next instruction, motivated like I've never been to learn how to fight.

"Interlace your fingers in front of your chest," he's saying, "and shove them straight up toward the sky, directly between their ar—"

The moment his words clear my subconscious, I'm in action. I catch him by surprise, yelling as I split Gryphon's hold—something he'd encouraged yesterday, but I'd been too shy to try until now. I think he was right, though... It *did* make me feel powerful.

Gryphon blinks, and we break into two copies of the same smile. His nearness, the intimacy of our shared emotion, quicken my pulse.

"And if they've got you pinned?" I ask, feeling bold.

A flicker of surprise softens his face, and he guides me backward to the rock, pressing me against cool stone. Sal and Meryl's gazes snap together—*are you seeing this?*—as Gryphon raises his forearm to hover in front of my neck. That blocks my view of the girls, but not Eero's shit-eating grin. With willpower I didn't know a human could possess, I force myself not to blush.

"Your forehead is surprisingly strong," he calls over his shoulder, tapping his own. "It can do a lot of damage, especially when your opponent has you pinned. Proximity gives you power. Drive your forehead into their face, remembering not to signal the move."

"What if you're shorter than them?" Meryl asks.

"All the better if your forehead hits at nose level." He rests his hand on the back of my head and softly guides it forward and down. The top front of my skull perfectly meets the bridge of his nose, his lips nearly grazing the center of my forehead.

Albert glides out of the cave then, stopping a meter away from Gryphon and me. I take the respite, tearing my eyes from my betrothed, but Gryphon seems not to notice him. "Meryl and Sal, you two practice all three releases with each other. Eero, I'll get to you in a minute."

He returns his attention to me. When our eyes lock, a full-body jolt courses through me. He's so breathtaking, so confident in his strength and knowledge that for a second, I consider what our future would look like if I did nothing but let my choices be made for me: Marry Gryphon. Train. Have babies. Let a murderer walk free and allow Jarek to gain more and more power in the Valley.

I know it's impossible. Ignorance is a fur-lined cage you can't return to. Not once the door's been opened. But still...

I accept his hands around my neck again. Like yesterday, my anatomy training helps me remember where—and understand why—to direct force in my moves. After an hour of repetition, I've learned to reliably break free from all the basic locks Gryphon tries to put me in. I even get in a good headbutt to his cheek before he can dance away.

"Oh oh," Eero calls out from where he watches on the rock. "Marina won't like your pretty face bruised like that, Gryphon."

The comment makes me miss my footing. I take a jab to the shoulder, and needles shoot down my hand. I pivot, barely avoiding the uppercut that frequently follows one of Gryphon's punches.

"Shut up," he mutters to Eero, never taking his eyes off me.

I know Eero was just teasing. Except, was he? Had there really been something between Gryphon and Marina? My childhood insecurities, nurtured in the fertile soil of years of taunts and rejections, seek the surface.

Albert is near enough that his sharpened words land in my ear. "Yeah, Eero. Shut it."

I'm so shocked by the ferocity in his young voice that I turn to look at him.

"Pay attention, Rose," Gryphon barks, "or you're going to get hurt out there." The anger that simmers below Gryphon's surface is suddenly at a boil. Eero's teasing, my carelessness. I don't know what sets him off, but his face tells me he's considering aiming his frustration at me.

"Eat dirt," I say, refusing to be his target.

I step away from him. I need a second to sort through the bloom of jealousy I just felt. Everyone knows Albert's a duck for Marina, so it's no surprise he wouldn't want to imagine Gryphon and her together. But Eero hadn't teased Albert. *He'd teased Gryphon.* That, plus the depth of the younger boy's reaction, makes me think there might really be something between Marina and my betrothed. I'm ashamed I began to let myself fall for him. I don't know what his endgame is, but it doesn't matter. His caring for Marina will make leaving to rescue Jonas that much easier.

"Are you done with your break?" Gryphon sounds deeply annoyed.

And with that, he's flipped my switch. I'm back in it, swinging at him with a dramatic right hook. It would be impossible not to see it coming, which is why I'm able to sneak my real move, an uppercut, past his initial defenses. It's only his years of training that keep my fist from striking true. Rather than burying it in his chin, I land a solid hit on the arm he raised to block me.

He stumbles slightly, rights himself.

Irritation flits across his features. His shoulders and then his arms make all the micromovements—almost a shudder—that signal he's flexing to rain terror upon his opponent: me. I find myself matching him move for move, rolling onto the balls of my feet, a taste like metal on my tongue. I sense he's about to spring when, to my great disappointment, he goes still, restraining himself with visible effort.

So that's the trick to upsetting him. Get in a strike while he's dreaming of Marina.

"Break." His voice rings deeper than I've ever heard it.

Adrenaline surges through me. I'm dying to make some crack about him forgetting to watch my eyes, but Meryl has me by one arm and Sal the other, and they're dragging me toward the creek.

"That was fun," Sal says dryly, shoving me toward the water. "Why don't you go cool off?"

"Why don't you mind yourself?" I snap.

The walk has allowed me to calm myself enough that I'm no longer boiling, but I'm still on edge. Neither Eero's wisecrack nor Gryphon's reaction should have set me off that much. It's got to be the accumulated grief of the past few days leaking out.

Meryl clucks her tongue. "Out of line, Rose."

"You think?" Sal says. She addresses me, pointing at the silvery creek. "Cold water helps you to get back to yourself." She tosses me a wicked look. "A slap to the face works, too. But only if you prefer."

I scowl but kneel and splash the crystal water across my cheeks. It's so cold that I suck in air. My hands are going numb, but I don't stop splashing because Sal's right: the water makes the prickly feeling fade. When I'm in control of my senses again, I drop onto my butt at the creek's edge. "Sorry, Sal. I don't know what came over me back there."

Salvatora plops down next to me, but it's Meryl who responds. "The Guardians call it battle anger. We've all felt it. You can be practicing fine for a couple hours, then someone gets a hit in just right, and out of the blue, you're ten feet tall and made of fire."

"It's even worse if they say something mean," Sal continues as Meryl takes a seat on her other side. "And it's probably more intense when you're fighting your *husband*."

I glance at her to see if she's serious, but her mouth is tilted in a rare smile. That burns off the last of my...what had Meryl called it? Battle anger. Now I just feel tired. And thirsty. I lean forward to take a long pull of the creek water. "He's not my husband."

"Same difference."

"No, it's not." I dry my hands on my pants. "You don't understand. There are difficulties to this particular betrothal." Most couples-to-be don't have a long history of animosity *or* a bride who plans to run away before the wedding ceremony, so when Sal jumps to her feet, I'm caught completely off guard.

"Get over yourself, Rose," she mutters, stalking off.

My mouth hangs open. I don't know what I've said to upset her. I glance at Meryl and realize I'm waiting for her to comfort me like she always does when Sal's too harsh. She's just shredding a brown leaf, though, and not meeting my gaze.

"You don't know about us, do you?" she finally sighs.

I tilt my head, scrambling to make sense of what's happening.

"Me and Sal?" Meryl holds up what's left of the leaf, a skeleton stripped of its flesh. "We love each other."

I'm about to say that of course they do, they're best friends and everyone knows it, but then I understand. We're cautioned not to fall for anyone but our betrothed, but even I know that's not always how emotions work. Case in point: me with Gryphon. "I'm sorry."

Meryl's holding herself utterly still. "It's the way of the Valley, isn't it? Our partners are chosen for us based on our House size, age, and bloodline. Not much room for love, especially for a couple who could never bear a child."

Meryl tosses what's left of her leaf into the water. We watch it float downstream, light as a spider on the creek's surface. "She and I want something different," she says. "Something better."

Something better. I roll the words around in my head. Before Jonas was Harvested, I was too busy working and staying in line to even consider such a thing. *A better community than the one I was born to... What would that even look like?*

What I wouldn't give for my father's guidance right now. I'd been so young when he was killed, but I remember him as steady and supportive. An optimist, even in the hard times.

"Do you trust Gryphon?" I ask Meryl. The question suddenly feels important.

"Trust him?" She appears to weigh her words. "He's loyal to his family, but he loves the Valley, too. He's in a tough spot, and it makes him seem like two different people some days. He tries to do his best by both groups, but I think he'll have to choose soon. Us or them." She hops to her feet, wiping leaves off her trousers before offering me her hand. "We have to stop being grateful for crumbs and start fighting for freedom, Rose."

I let her help me up. "I'm ashamed to say I thought we had it. Freedom. Happiness."

She shakes her head, soft brown eyes overcast with a wisdom beyond her years. "You can't have either without choice, not really." Then she lightly punches my arm. "But I don't think you should feel ashamed. We all wake up at different times and for different reasons. What matters is what we do after we hear the call."

40

Reatha stands outside the cave when we return. She's moving with a particular tightness, hand placed against the side of her back in a way that suggests her kidneys are bothering her.

"Are you well?" I ask.

She flashes a smile. "A kidney infection is all. It's likely to go away on its own."

My eyebrows knit together. That's not a treatment plan. "The Apothecary cottage will have a bearberry tonic for you. Perhaps I could bring it to our next training session?"

She nods, accepting my assistance. "Thank you. If your mother were here, she'd already have given me some pipsissewa. That's what always worked the quickest, though she said the plant is fussy to grow."

I've never worked with pipsissewa before and am trying to remember where I've even heard the name when a page in my mother's journal flashes in my mind.

Pipsissewa should be avoided in treatment of the kidneys, she'd written.

And hadn't the **p** stood out slightly darker? I didn't know enough to include it back then. Reatha has stepped over to help Marie, who's just appeared, bind her hair. It allows me to squeeze my eyes tightly shut, envisioning my current list of letters:

I see V, E, X, in my mind's eye. *Vex.*

Below it O, A, R, I, S, H, T, and N.

And if I add P?

O, A, R, I, S, H, T, N, P.

No.

P, O, A, R, I, S, H, T, N.

Hmm.

P, O... I, S...N.

Poison. Of course! A wave of satisfaction courses through me as my suspicions are confirmed. I smile grimly. *I got that one, Mom.*

That leaves A, R, H, T. Hart? *No, that's not it.*

But if I reuse the E...

Reatha.

Looks like I brought my sample right to the source.

41

"Reatha, could I have a word?" I'm astonished at the steadiness in my voice.

"Of course," she says brightly, finishing up with Marie. She watches until the others have disappeared into the woods, our training done for the day. I expect her to invite me into the cave, but she stays outside, sending Marie in to get started on their dinner.

I rub my arms against the late afternoon briskness, not sure what to ask. *Are you poisoning the people of Noah's Valley? Oh, and by the way, did you also happen to murder my mother and Peter, because only a fool would think the deaths aren't connected?* Finally, *are you using your fourteen-year-old son to do your dirty work?* I doubt the last one because she's always *seemed* like a doting parent, but I won't discount my conviction that it was his shadow I saw that day, either.

She catches me off guard. "Is this about the water?"

"Albert told you," I all but confirm.

She nods so sharply, her braids jump. "He wasn't your best bet. My boy's a brilliant tinkerer, but he's never been much for chemistry." Before I can gather my thoughts to respond, she purses her lips. "You remember the meetings I mentioned the first time you visited here?"

I nod, unsure where she's going with this. "Yes. You used to hold them here, but you wouldn't say who with. Only that they're gone now."

"That was partially true. Two of them are." She inhales loudly through her nose. "Marc, Salvatora's dad. And Henrietta."

I stand up straighter. *Mom?* "What were the meetings about?"

"I'm forbidden to tell you."

I can't hide my annoyance. "Then why say anything at all?"

To my surprise, she doesn't appear upset that I've raised my voice. If anything, she looks proud. "Claim that spirit, Rose," she says. "You're going to need it."

"All right," I say, a fire sparking my gut. "I'll claim it right now. I know you've created a poison to use against the villagers." Her composure slips for a fraction of a second, and I'm imbued with fresh confidence.

"I suspect you may have killed to cover up your crimes," I continue, the pieces coming together as I speak. "My mother, Peter, and those Guardians eight months ago. All of them must've caught you in the act." I'm guessing with that last part. By the Wall, I'm guessing with all of it. But if Mom suspected her, then I do, too.

Reatha jerks back. "You don't know what you're talking about!" Her cheeks are blazing. "I had *nothing* to do with those deaths, Rose Allgood." She takes a calming breath, which my body involuntarily mirrors. "I didn't create the poison, either, but I did *recreate* it...at Jarek Tzu's command. At the time, I had no idea what he intended to use it for."

I inhale sharply. "Recreated it?" My hand finds Lucky Bunny in my pocket at the same time Reatha's eyes seek the Heavens.

She whispers her next words. "Forgive me, Hen. She needs to know." Reatha holds herself. "Jarek discovered a cache of Before Times items somewhere inside the Wall."

The secret room in the Record Keeper vault, the horror that keeps on giving.

"It included a bottle marked 'herbicide,'" Reatha continues. "Jarek brought it to me to replicate, said he needed more to protect the

Valley. He gathered it was something the Founders considered crucial to our continued survival. I followed his orders at first, fearing what he'd do to my children if I didn't. But then, a month ago, I stopped."

My blood feels thick. "Why?"

Her eyes slide away. "Your mother figured out what the herbicide was causing."

"The Vex," I say.

Reatha's eyes widen, and she nods. "The Vex."

"Why would Jarek poison his own people?" I ask.

Reatha shakes her head. "I don't know, and neither did your mother. Possibly to weaken us, or to stir up panic and give himself an excuse to consolidate power."

"But *why*?" I repeat. "We have all the tools for paradise inside the Wall. Why would someone use them to destroy rather than build?"

She holds her hands out, palms up. "Only Jarek knows. He's the source of our evil."

Frustration crashes over me. "Why didn't you stand up to him, then?"

Her grimace deepens. "We tried, those of us who met here. But by the time we realized Jarek and Misia were no longer following the rules of the Valley, it was too late. They took away our freedom so slowly at first that it hadn't occurred to us to fight back; now they wield too much power, coming after our families if they see us as a threat."

"So you fled to the caves," I say softly. "You hide out here."

"We hide and we hope."

"For what?"

"Rebellion. Led by your generation." Her mouth ribbons to a thin line. "There was a time when we believed our community was only as strong as its weakest member. When we took care of each other. We can find our way back to that, with the help of those of you who train."

"You drop your problems on our shoulders without even telling us what we're up against!" I can't contain my reaction, my voice rising at the unfairness of it. "Meanwhile, you're hiding out in a cave. *Your* family is safe." It's an unkind thing to say, but I can't help myself. She's feeding my anger without providing an outlet.

She reels back as if I've struck her. "Something big is coming. You have no idea."

I throw up my hands. "So tell me!"

"Mom?" Marie peeks out from the cave, her brown eyes wide with fear.

I've upset her. "I'm sorry," I say, before returning my focus to Reatha, preparing to convince her of something—*anything*—and, if that doesn't work, to make her feel ashamed for what she's allowed to happen. A warmth inside my hand startles me back to myself. It's Marie, lacing her fingers through mine.

Her buck-toothed smile is tentative. "I saw you fight today. You're so quick and strong."

I try to return her smile. "Thank you. I like it." I inhale a trembling breath. "The combat, that is."

"Gryphon said he'd teach me. When I'm older. Do you think he will?"

She looks so hopeful. "If he said he would, he'd be a terrible person not to."

Marie wrinkles her nose. "That's not an answer."

My laugh surprises me, releasing some of my steam. "You're right." I crouch down so she can look me in the eye. "Here's what I think. If Gryphon promised he'd teach you, then he will. It's important to him that we all know how to defend ourselves."

She nods happily. "That's what he said, too. Rose?"

"Yeah?"

"Do you think you could bring me a potato roll from the Bakers next time you come? I'm mostly okay living out here. I hardly even miss my friends." She squirms in a way that makes me instantly not believe her. "But I dream about those rolls sometimes."

My eyes flick to Reatha, already knowing what I'll find there. Her face shines with a mother's regret. I turn back to Marie. "You bet. Next time the Baker makes potato rolls, I'll bring one for you."

42

I carry Marie's grateful smile with me as I make my way back to the Tzu cottage, clutching it like a lifeline against my crumbling worldview. So many things I should have already known. *Spoken out against.*

The whipping posts. The rolling Harvests. The curfew.

But those are recent changes. Meryl made me see there are problems baked into our system. The law requiring we marry into Houses based not on love, but on numbers. Need another worker? Here you go. Have too many? Shift one somewhere else. Want to keep your skills after you join a new House? So sorry, you must stick to the furrow you were assigned to plow. I've seen how destructive these rules are up close and personal during the census, caught a glimpse of tiny cracks that I wouldn't have noticed before Jonas's Harvest.

Didn't I witness Sylvan, son of the Forester House, standing outside the Potters, watching with something like love as Toshiko worked the wheel? Maybe caught a glint of despair in the face of the Ropemaker daughter when she told me how she loved to write stories but understood she couldn't have pen and paper beyond what was necessary for schoolwork? If I'm honest, even my own brother had been ill-suited for the duties of our House. Jonas was learning, and he was so good with people that he'd have done fine, but his real talent was in toymaking, and hadn't I experienced the unfairness of it all firsthand when I was lifted from the Apothecary House into the Guardians, expected to relinquish a lifetime of training?

The blind rigidity has always been there, but I chose to see it as a fixed reality rather than a problem with a solution. After all, I was lucky enough to be born into the perfect House for me. Others, like Sal and Meryl, had a front-row seat to the rottenness of a system that stifles us all.

I'm walking down a cobblestone path, nearing the Tzu cottage, and close enough to imagine I can smell the wild rice I left covered and simmering on the stove. It'll be creamy by now. I smooth my hair, my tunic, my trousers. Jarek and Misia shouldn't be home, only Gryphon, but given what happened last night, I want to be prepared in case they've returned early. If they're inside, I'll swear I got lost doing the census. Or maybe I'll say Gryphon and I ran off again. I shiver at the thought.

I glance around. The Tzu house is a ten-second walk around the corner. The lane is empty, most everyone gathered around their dinner tables by now. Assured I'm alone, I lend a swish to my hips as I close the distance between myself and the Tzu cottage, imitating a walk I've seen other women of the Valley perform. Eero was right that the more I'm able to act like I'm in love, the better, so I try to think wifely thoughts, but in this moment I can't imagine what they'd be.

"What do you think, Lucky Bunny?" I whisper to the toy in my pocket. "Between this ridiculousness and my cooking, I should be able to keep Jarek and Misia off my case for a few more days, right?"

"Rose."

I jump. It's Gryphon. He's been waiting outside his front door, hidden in shadow. *Sun and Water, what a nightmare.* He just saw me practice flirting!

"I had something in my eye," I babble. "And in my shoe. That's why I was walking that way. I was also—"

I don't get a chance to finish my sentence, because he steps forward, his gaze so lovestruck that I think I must be dreaming. He holds out his arms, and I glide into them. I stare up into his eyes, astonished.

I can't believe walking like that worked!

He opens the front door with his free hand and dances me into the warmth of the Tzu cottage, mouth inches from mine. I can't look away from his obsidian eyes, the yearning in them.

Is he going to kiss me again? My brain's twirling.

He leans over, his mouth moving closer to mine. It passes my lips, and I feel an ache of something lost. But then his breath is hot in my ear.

"You were at Oscar's trying on your dress," he purrs.

Someone clears their throat.

I straighten myself. Glance around the Tzu kitchen.

And feel the blood drain from my face.

43

"We've been waiting on you," Misia says.

She's seated at the dining table, as sharp as a chess piece with her close-cropped hair. Behind her, standing by the stove and wearing oven mitts, is the raw-boned middle daughter of the Bakers, Irma, the one who makes Jonas's favorite currant tarts. Two large planks of wood and several more chairs have been brought in to create a table big enough to accommodate the dinner party. The Tzus—Jarek, Misia, and Gryphon. The Khans—Perez, Boudicca, Lozen, and Leonidas, but not Leo's wife, Hedda, or their four sons. Then David Seingalt and his children, Marina and Simon.

Oscar.

Gran.

I think I'm falling. I reach for something solid and find Gryphon. I cling to him. The smell of roasting meat is overpowering in the crowded space, the scent greasy and aggressive.

"Your aunt and uncle couldn't make it to our dinner," Misia says, her voice syrupy with faux disappointment. "An illness in the Plumber House they had to tend to."

My eyes fly to Jarek. Had he gotten word of the heresy Augustus shared with me? Had his Guardians hurt the Plumber family? But the man's face gives away nothing.

"The youngest was sent home from school with what might be the flu," Gran says. She appears surprisingly alert, her voice clear, shaded with the perfect tinge of regret. "Must be the start of the season."

Oscar keeps glancing urgently down at his arm and back up at me, moving only his eyes. It's like they're trying to escape his head. *Why is he here?* The Seingalts and the Khans are friendly with the Tzus. Irma, impossibly, appears to be cooking for us, like a servant of yore. And Gran is clearly here as a reminder of the power Jarek and Misia hold over me. But Oscar?

You were at Oscar's trying on your dress.

That's when I realize it's not his arm he's looking at. It's his shirt. *Clothes.* I finally understand. "It was so kind of you to invite me to your home this afternoon to see the progress you'd made on my wedding dress, Oscar."

His head droops in relief.

Misia's lip curls. "We were concerned when you didn't arrive with your Tailor."

Oscar tugs surreptitiously at his collar.

Another leap. "I was changing out of the dress. No reason for both of us to keep you waiting."

Jarek appears bored with the exchange. "I'm hungry."

"I think it's done," Irma says, turning to peek inside the oven, "but I can't be sure."

"It'll be done enough," Jarek mutters. He reaches for a basket of fresh bread—bread that wasn't here when I left this morning—and pulls out a potato roll. He squishes it into a ball and shoves the whole thing in his mouth. I feel sick to my stomach, imagining how Marie would have savored it. I lose the thought quickly, though, as every nerve in my body calls out that I'm in danger.

I just don't know what kind.

"It was so nice of the Tzus to invite us all over," Gran says to no one in particular. Her cheeks are pale and shiny. I hope they didn't make her walk here. "It's been so long since I've enjoyed dinner at another's House."

Irma pulls a large pan out of the oven. She struggles to lift it.

Gryphon goes to help her, leaving me standing near the door. When I spot the monstrosity he brings to the table, I wish I still had him to lean on. It's an enormous pink mound of meat, larger than a newborn lamb. I've never seen flesh that size cooked whole, only flecks of it swimming in stew or pie, or strips cut and dried.

"What is that?" I blurt out.

Jarek smiles. "It smells wonderful, doesn't it? It's a wild pig harvested from the woods."

Gryphon maneuvers the roasting pan to the center of the table, setting it between bowls of steaming corn, baked plums, whipped potatoes, and a pot of garlic butter. It's a feast, but the idea of keeping it to ourselves while the village slowly starves sours my appetite.

"A pig?" I know from our books that they were large, tube-shaped animals with stubby legs and snouts for noses. The male, called a pigboar, had razor-sharp tusks. I'd never seen them inside the Wall, and this huge meat lump? It could be any creature. There's no head, no legs. Just roasted flesh in the shape of a giant loaf of bread.

Gryphon shakes his head at me, once, quickly, his meaning clear.

Don't eat it.

My belly burbles uneasily.

"Sit," Misia commands me. "Irma has been kind enough to cook us dinner. You disrespect her by standing."

That would be true if this was Irma's home, but it's not, which means we disrespect her by not offering her food *we've* cooked. I catch Irma staring at the table with open hunger. It's mealtime across the village, and she's surely worked a full day, just like the rest of us. Why is she being forced to labor for someone else's meal, preparing food she can't eat?

"Please, Irma," I say, ignoring Misia's glare as I claim the open seat beside my grandmother. "Will you sit next to me? I want to hear about your schoolwork while we eat."

"She's done, aren't you, girl?" Misia says. "Thank you for your help. We can take it from here."

Irma nods and removes her apron, curtsying to Gryphon's mother like we're in chapel. She throws a final, longing glance at the table and disappears out the door.

Jarek removes the knife from his belt, stroking its mother-of-pearl handle. Without cleaning it, he slices off a hunk of the meat. "Who wants some?"

The Seingalts and Khans eagerly lift their plates.

"This will do me just fine," Gran says cheerily, indicating the pot nearest to her. It holds the simple wild rice porridge I'd left slow cooking all day. Her hand is shaking, but Jarek doesn't seem to notice.

"Nonsense," he says. "Smell this meat. Isn't it glorious?"

The odor is rich and cloying, unlike anything I've experienced before. The pink, glistening color of it clutches my guts. Even without Gryphon's warning, I doubt that I'd have tasted it.

"At my age, there's only so much the stomach will tolerate," Gran says.

"Let me help you," I tell her. I scoop her some porridge and a portion of stuffed plums, since I know she adores them. We finished the last of our summer fruit at the Apothecary House weeks ago. "Gryphon? Oscar?"

I take their plates and fill them with food from my end of the table, avoiding the slippery meat. Oscar stares at it longingly, but he doesn't object. Misia looks like she wants to force us to taste it, but Jarek is talking, commanding all the attention in the room.

"Let's have some pruno, as well. Misia, pour us drinks."

"Hear! Hear!" David calls, holding out his glass.

Jarek's wife stands, filling our cups from a pitcher. Other than Gryphon bringing the meat to the table, only women have served the meal. That goes down sideways. I smell the brownish liquor she pours me and wrinkle my nose. I've never tried pruno, a drink normally reserved for village feasts. It smells like fruit gone bad, and those who drink it become silly or morose. But what've I got to lose? I take a sip. The flavor's sharp on my tongue but not as bad as I'd expected. I take a second swallow and decide I prefer water.

Jarek drains his glass and holds it out to Misia for an immediate refill. "Our training is going well, wouldn't you agree, Perez? Boudicca?"

Boudicca has a great, shiny lump of meat at the end of her fork, poised just outside her mouth. That's when I realize what it reminds me of, both in sight and smell: the burnt flesh of Jarek's wound. The bite of baked plum I'd just taken rushes back up, but I swallow it down.

"We've never been stronger," Perez answers for them. His wife pops the pink bite into her mouth, smiling and nodding as she chews.

"That's great," Marina says, sounding as bored as humanly possible. She looks particularly lovely tonight, her hair bound in intricate braids that cleverly join into a rope trailing over her shoulder. Her dark blue eyes shine like river water and are equally cold. I notice she's also avoiding the meat, cutting it into small pieces and moving them around her plate. "But can we talk about something that includes all of us?" she continues. "Like Friday's party?"

David's mouth tightens. "Quiet," he says. Marina is unmarried, still a girl. She shouldn't be wresting control of the conversation from an elder.

Marina turns her attention to me, ignoring the man to talk about him. "You should thank my father. He's the one who decided your wedding would be this Friday, and that for auspiciousness, it must be held in the evening."

I hear a rare jealousy in her voice, though I don't think she's glanced at Gryphon once since he and I entered. I hope it's a sign that whatever existed between them is over now, at least from her end of things. It's an unfair thought. I'm leaving, after all. The kind thing to do would be to wish for happiness between him and Marina, but I can't do it.

"He insists no other day will do," she continues. "His research says it must be a big celebration, as well. Our House is vital to everything inside this Wall."

While she talks, Simon impersonates his father, adopting his posture and prim, disapproving look so perfectly that I struggle to contain my amusement. Lozen and Leonidas don't even try, laughing aloud at the Seingalt father.

"Quiet, I said!" David barks.

But Jarek hardly seems to notice. "None of this would be possible without the Record Keepers," he says magnanimously. "Neither the skill we've obtained, nor Friday's joyous celebration. Your knowledge," he says, raising a glass to them, "is our power."

Marina smiles at me across the table. "And I've got the key."

She glides her thumb below a white ribbon at her neck and lifts. We don't have many locks in the Valley, which means I haven't seen many keys, but I do recognize the style of this one from a book. It's a warded key made of gray metal, the length of my pointer finger and half as thick. One end has an arched design that reminds me of the chapel's stained-glass windows. The other is constructed of lines of metal as intricate as a maze.

It can only be one thing: the key to the Record Keeper vault. Simon must have told her I'd asked about it. *That little snitch.* I try to catch his eyes, but he looks away.

The meal continues. The Guardians, all but Gryphon, do most of the talking. Their voices grow rowdier the more they drink, until no one else can be heard above them. We're forced to listen to crude jokes I only half understand, boring stories about their training, and gossip about the people of the Valley that finally draws Marina into the conversation.

My food congeals on my plate. The two swallows of pruno have given me heartburn. The room feels hot and crowded. Worst of all is that Gran's fading. She should be in bed by now. I'm deciding that I don't mind at all that we stopped doing dinner swaps in the Valley when I realize there's a pause in the chatter and everyone's staring at me.

My breath hitches. I glance around the table. Marina and Leo appear to be gloating, happy that I've fallen out of sync with the group. Oscar looks worried. Lozen's trying not to laugh.

"Did I not speak clearly?" Misia asks. She means to embarrass me, but the fact of the matter is that she's slurring her words. She's drunk at least four glasses of pruno.

"I'm sorry," I say. "I wasn't listening."

Misia's eyes narrow. "I asked what your favorite part of your new wedding dress is."

"It's not complete." It takes all my effort not to look to Oscar.

"Surely it's *nearly* finished, though," Marina murmurs. "The wedding is just around the corner."

"Unless you lied to us, Oscar," Misia says, "about your ability to finish it in time."

The room is suddenly, inexplicably pulsing with anger. Misia stands, an unsheathed dagger appearing in her hand. I jump up, dashing to insert myself between her and Oscar. Gryphon is on his feet nearly as quickly.

"The beadwork!" I interject. "I love the beadwork. It's much prettier than my own."

Misia is panting now. She's so close that I can smell meat and sour drink on her breath. Out of the corner of my eye, I see Gryphon inching closer.

"Oscar is doing a beautiful job," I say softly. Light glints off the knife in her hand. "He'll have it done in plenty of time."

Misia blinks. Her eyes regain focus. It's like she returns to the room, turning to take a long draw of her drink before dropping back into her chair. The breath empties from my lungs. When Gryphon stands next to me, I see his hand is on his own blade.

"Now, where were we?" Jarek asks, as if that whole scene hadn't just happened.

"You were talking about the Apothecary House when we all realized Rose wasn't listening." Marina's eyes shimmer with malice. "You were saying that you'd like them to have a special seat of honor Friday."

"Ah yes. Lillian, what do you think of that?"

We all turn our attention to Gran, who's slumped over in her chair with her chin tucked into her chest.

"Gran!" I hurry to her, but Gryphon gets there first. He gently touches her neck and then leans his ear close to her head.

"She's sleeping," he says. He addresses his father. "You shouldn't have ordered her attendance tonight."

I feel like I've been punched. He *ordered* her here? As if my gran was a Guardian in training?

Jarek raises a brow in warning. "I don't believe I heard you. Care to repeat yourself?"

Gryphon shakes his head. "I do not. What I care to do is help Lillian get home." We all watch as he gently lifts Gran into his arms.

"Put her down," Jarek growls, "so she can apologize for falling asleep at the table and rejoin our conversation."

I've never seen Gryphon openly defy his father. He goes still for a moment. I'm waiting for him to cower, to do his duty by Jarek as he always has. Instead, he walks Gran directly to me.

"Would you like to wish her good night?"

I'm still in shock, so it takes me a second to catch on to the incredible kindness he's offering—the chance to check Gran's pulse and breathing before he brings her home. He must understand I won't have a moment of rest until I do. I blink furiously, refusing to cry. I kiss Gran's cheek. Her breathing is regular. I touch her neck, noting with relief that her pulse is weak but normal.

"Thank you," I say, for his ears alone.

Watching him carry her out the door, I'm humbled by a sudden realization.

Jonas couldn't possibly have slipped free of Gryphon before his Harvest like I'd thought. My brother has always been thin—a healer, not a fighter. Gryphon has repeatedly established in village demonstrations that he's one of the strongest Guardians in the Valley.

He had intentionally released my twin so we could say goodbye.

44

I say I'm not feeling well and go straight up to bed. The last thing I want to do is spend another second with this crowd. I feel guilty for abandoning Oscar, but not enough to stay. I'll make it up to him somehow.

As soon as I reach Gryphon's bedroom, I dig out Mom's journal, for comfort more than anything. It's exactly where I left it, buried beneath the mattress. I settle onto the floor, leaning against the bed, and light a candle. With my free hand, I roll Lucky Bunny between my fingers.

Reatha suspects something big is coming, and Misia and Jarek have as good as confessed to it being this Friday, same as my wedding. Is it tied to the herbicide he used to poison the industrial district? And another thing that's been bugging me—why there? I shudder to imagine the casualties if he'd selected a well people actually *liked* to drink from.

A fat, hot tear splashes onto the journal's worn leather, and I realize I'm crying. My mother figured out the Vex was a poison long ago enough to code the information into her notes and prepare those packets of charcoal. So why hadn't she said anything to me?

Perhaps she wanted to test her theory before revealing the truth. That would make sense. She'd want to be certain before accusing Jarek. Did she have any guesses as to why he did it?

I sniff. If she did, they might be in her journal.

I open it at the beginning, searching for a missed clue, anything out of place that I might have overlooked. My mind wanders as I scour the text. For all her suspicions, my mother still followed the old rules, the unwritten ones that tell us to keep quiet about things that make folks uncomfortable. She raised me to skate on the surface, sticking to pleasantries. It was that village-wide denial that allowed all this unhappiness and inequality to fester and grow.

The candle burns down as I turn pages, reading and rereading.

I uncover no new information, try as I might. Finally, when my eyes grow too heavy to read, I close the journal, my fingers trailing across the leather. I slip it back under the mattress and blow out the candle moments before it's bound to go out on its own. I lay across the bed, working at the puzzle of what we're up against until sleep takes me.

I'm awoken sometime later by a rustling from below. "Gryphon?" I ask.

I hear an intake of breath near the floor and figure that's the only response I'll get from him, but after several beats, he whispers, "Yeah?"

I hesitate. But then, picturing him gently carrying Gran home this evening, I decide to take a leap of faith. "Jonas saw something in the Record Keeper vault the morning he was Harvested. He was trying to tell me about it, but I was too..."

"Too busy being forced to marry me?" He sounds weary. Not just "woken up" weary, either. Exhausted.

"Something like that," I say, because it's close enough. He doesn't need to know the specifics, that I'd nearly vomited. I peer over the edge of the bed. "He...didn't get a chance to tell me what he saw down there, but whatever it was, I think it affects us all."

Gryphon props himself on an elbow. It's nearly a full moon tonight, so I can see the look of rapt attention he's giving me. "Like what?" he asks.

I sit up, pulling the blanket around me. "I don't know, but what Jarek said about the Record Keepers' knowledge at dinner tonight makes me wonder if they're connected." I don't tell Gryphon what Reatha has told me—don't mention the poison, either. I still don't know if I can trust him fully.

"Have you asked to look inside the vault?"

I can't tell if he's mocking me. "Of course I have. Marina denied Jonas was even there that day. Simon at least confirmed Jonas saw something he shouldn't have, but he wouldn't take me down, either. The cellar door is locked. I assume that's the key Marina's wearing."

He lies back down, crossing his hands behind his head.

I lean forward. "Do you know what your mom and dad have planned?"

Gryphon shakes his head, his voice sounding like two rocks scraping together. "My father doesn't share his plans with me." He's quiet for a moment. "If he means to hurt others, will you fight him?"

"Of course," I say, without hesitation.

Silence spools between us. I can smell the pine scent of him, hear his steady breathing. I think I'm prepared for anything he'll say next, when he murmurs, "I won't allow it."

I snort. "It's not up to you."

"We shall see." He stares up at the ceiling. "What were your parents like? At home, I mean."

The change of subject catches me off guard, but the clean sorrow it brings is almost a relief. I recline on the bed, subconsciously mirroring Gryphon's position. "Dad was a book nerd like Jonas. They spent a lot of time reading by the fire. And he loved bugs—our neighbors would call on him when there was a spider to be caught and released." I suspect he came from the Insect Farmer House, but of course we never talked about that. "And Mom? She was something special, as you know. A genius with plants and potions, and a caregiver with the gentlest touch."

"Like you." His voice is thoughtful.

"I suppose." I wonder why my skin feels hot. "Only better, I think. Better with people, at least."

A bright memory appears behind my eyes. It makes me smile.

"Dad planned a party for her once," I say. "She'd had a difficult week. A respiratory virus was sweeping through the Valley, and Mom was the only one who could soothe the sick babies. She was averaging two or three hours of sleep per night, so Dad decided we'd let her know what she meant to us. And not just those of us in the Apothecary House, but villagers, too." I adjust my position on the bed. "He baked her favorite lavender cakes, invited everyone who was free, and had us hide in the living room. When Mom walked through the door, we all jumped out and said, 'Surprise!' Except for Jonas. We were only five, and he had a speech impediment back then. He yelled, 'Per-pise!'"

I'm tracing the seam of the bedsheet, recalling my twin as a little boy and trying to hold my heart together with hope and spit, when I remember something shocking. *Jarek had been there.* At the party. I thought he'd never visited, not other than the time he mentioned. But I'd been wrong.

"Do you think our parents were ever friends?" I ask.

Gryphon blows air out his nose. "You know my father loved your mother. He didn't try to hide it."

Except *I* didn't know. Not until yesterday, when he told me. "He was at my mom's surprise party." Something else occurs to me: my father's death was a few days later.

"Sounds about right," Gryphon says.

We're quiet for some time. "What was wrong with that meat tonight?" I ask next, hoping to continue one of our longest conversations since childhood.

"Didn't recognize it." He clears his throat. "It didn't look like any creature I know inside the Wall."

"And you *would* know," I say, repeating what he told me at Guardian training, "because you've walked every inch of the Valley a hundred times over on your snipe hunts." My stomach plummets as it finally dawns on me what he had really been saying. What I'd refused to hear but can no longer deny. I sit up slowly, my pulse galloping through my veins.

"Yep," he says, his own mind clearly wandering. "I would."

"And there are no large, dangerous creatures inside the Wall," I say.

His response comes more slowly this time, the word drawn out. "Riiiggghhhhtttt."

"Except for the one that killed my father."

No response. Time stands still.

"Gryphon?" Still nothing, though my heart is pounding so loud it's difficult to hear anything above it. My voice is small when it finally comes out. "Did Jarek kill my dad?"

I'm watching him, so I see when he stops breathing. An emptiness crawls beneath my skin.

"I don't know," Gryphon answers, but he's lying to us both. "My father can be short-fused, but I don't want to believe he's a killer."

I think of my own, kind dad. Healing everyone, hurting no one. Then Jarek, moody and angry, hateful toward his wife and son. How could darkness be more powerful than light?

"Rose?" he says softly.

"What?" I'm swiping at my eyes.

"I won't let him hurt you."

Is he trying to distract me? From the likelihood that his dad *murdered* mine? "Too late."

I no longer feel like talking, but I need something only Gryphon can provide. My goal is to stop Jarek and bring my brother back, but I'm no fool. If I manage to make it up the Wall, I know my odds of returning are close to zero.

I swallow my emotions, keeping my voice calm. "But you can promise me something. Will you take care of Gran if anything happens to me? You were so kind to her tonight, so...will you make sure no one hurts her?"

His response is strained. "It's my duty as a Guardian."

I chew and swallow the pain of leaving her behind. "But do you promise?"

A pause. Then, "I promise."

"Thank you, Gryphon."

"Nothing's going to happen to you *or* her as long as I'm alive, Rose. I swear it." I hear him turning over. "Now try and get some sleep."

It's a long while before I do.

45

The next day is cloudy, to my disappointment. I prepare breakfast as Gryphon cleans up from the previous night's gathering. We work in a tired silence. When my morning chores are complete, I hurry to the Record Keeper cottage, entering through the library just as I have previously.

I find myself alone with the books this time. I check the mahogany door leading to the vault, even knowing it'll be locked. I'm considering simply knocking Marina unconscious and taking the key next time I see her when I hear a snuffling coming from the living quarters. It sounds like weeping.

"Hello?" I say tentatively. The sound stops, but no one responds. If it's Marina, I really don't care that she's crying. *Unless she's injured.* As much as I despise her, I can't leave a wounded villager unattended. "Is everything okay?"

I'm answered with a crash coming from the Seingalts' kitchen. I rush toward it.

David is kneeling on the floor, trying to stack things in his arms. I drop to help him before seeing what they are: brightly colored packages from Beyond. Metal cylinders with labels for Chicken Noodle Soup, Baked Beans, and something called Water Chestnuts. *This is food!*

David's eyes are red-rimmed, his thin mustache glistening

with moisture. Had he been the one crying?

"Please," he says. "Don't tell. I can explain."

"I already know about the secret room you found in the basement." Disgust twists my mouth. "And the Before Times bounty inside it."

"I get it," he says, noting my expression. He stands, picking up the cylinders and stacking them in the open cupboard they must have fallen out of. "I despise myself, too. It happens so slowly, you don't even notice it at first. Inch by inch, you become comfortable getting a little bit more than everyone else. After a while, your brain does a neat trick and tells you that you've earned it, even though you're not doing anything different or better than everyone else around you." He shrugs. "Once you convince yourself it's your due, you'll fight to keep it."

My mouth feels dry. "People are going hungry in the Valley."

David nods, facing the cupboard, and continues stacking. The colors of the containers are shocking to me. The red and white of the soup, golden edging on the beans, the vivid blue of something called SPAM. When they're all stacked back inside the cabinet, he closes it and turns to me.

"I wasn't always like this," he says. "Weak, I mean." He shoots me a sad smile. "When Joanne was alive, we balanced each other out. Everything was better then."

He's flirting with heresy by suggesting her Harvest was anything less than an honor, but I'm far past caring about that. "You could redistribute the food you found," I suggest. "Share what remains with everyone. Go back to the way things used to be inside the Wall."

"Oh, to have the clarity of a child," he says sadly.

"Screw you," I spit back, shocked at my words and then, almost immediately after, angry I didn't say worse.

He holds up his hands. "I didn't mean it as an insult. There's things you don't know, that's all."

"Like the fact that the Vex is a mass poisoning? Which I assume *you* know, too, since I saw your tracks by the quarantined well."

His shoulders slump. "How did you figure it out? About the Vex?"

"Lucky guess," I say. That's all the man deserves. I can't believe how much I'd still respected him, even five minutes earlier. All because he was a Record Keeper. "What's its purpose?"

"That, I don't know," he says, his expression morose. "I'd been hoping to find out, but I didn't uncover anything when I went to look that day. Did you?" He sounds hopeful.

I shake my head, furious. The herbicide was found in the vault. David must know more than he's letting on. I decide to try a new approach. "So how long has Jarek been the one really in charge?"

David's bearing changes, his face hardening. I've gone too far. "You will not tell anyone about the food you saw here," he commands.

I wonder how and when Jarek wrested such power from the Record Keeper House. How long he waited for his turn on the Council of Elders. Is that what Jonas had seen in the vault? Definitive proof of Jarek's control?

Those of us inside the Wall. We're not what you think.

"I need to get to work on the census," I say, by way of a response. "I have a lot of houses to visit today."

I move to collect my paperwork. David follows me, though instinctively I know the interrogation is over. I gained nothing of value, only further disappointment in my leaders.

"I'm sorry about Marina," he says, clearly trying to make himself feel better with a meaningless, unrelated apology. "I know she can be a bit much."

I don't even give him the courtesy of a nod. A person in power choosing to do nothing in the face of injustice is a million times worse than a teenager misbehaving.

46

Throughout my census duties, heavy emotions drag at me: my worry for Jonas, fresh grief over my father's death, fear of the control Jarek's accumulated. It's all I can do to stay inside my own skin until early afternoon.

Everyone makes it to training today, even Oscar, who's supposed to be working on my dress. Reatha greets us but seems distracted, returning to the cave almost immediately. Marie settles in to watch us from the sidelines, her grin so wide it nearly splits her face open when I produce the three potato rolls I snuck from last night's dinner.

"One for each Chemist!" she exclaims.

"That's right." When she runs inside to share them with her mother, I wonder aloud where Albert is.

Oscar shrugs. "He wasn't here when I showed up. I didn't see him inside, either, when I went in for a drink of water."

"You his mom now?" Sal asks me.

"No." I rub the back of my head. I've got a bad feeling, but I can't explain it, even to myself. "Where does he go when he isn't here?"

"Where do *you* go when you're not here?" Sal shoots back.

"It's not the same. I have duties. Places I'm allowed to visit, places I'm not. Just like the rest of you. The Chemists aren't supposed to be *anywhere*, though. Not within the Wall, at least. I assumed he'd stick close to the caves."

"I think Albert gets bored," Meryl says. "I know I would."

"Pair up," Gryphon says, putting an end to the conversation.

We begin by reviewing everything we've learned the past two days. Close combat, staffs, basic nerve and wrist locks. I'm with Eero, and he makes me feel so comfortable that I start telling him Apothecary stories as we practice. The time my dad misdiagnosed a food allergy as measles, how Gran came to be the one everyone called for childbirth, how excited Jonas was when he discovered a book called *Food Is Medicine* inside the library. I get in a good sweep and am helping Eero back to his feet when he tells me he doesn't like what the Carpenter House is working on.

I've been chattering so much that he's caught me off guard. "What is it?"

He glances over at the others. Gryphon has Oscar in a chokehold and is instructing him on how to break free. Meryl has Sal's arm twisted up and behind her back, disabling her. She leans in to whisper, and Sal flushes, smiling.

"That's just it," he says, worry lines creasing his mouth. "I'm not sure. I mean, I know what it looks like, just not what it'll be used for. Jarek worked with my dad on the blueprint, but neither of them would tell me more. It's double-layered wood reinforced with iron bands that crisscross between the layers, like the ribs of a beast. It's big, Rose. It looks like some kind of twisted cage, but the walls curve outward at the top, like they're meant to keep something out, rather than in."

I ask the question I fear I already know the answer to. "When does it need to be done by?"

"Friday." He stares off into the distance. "I hated when we were ordered to build the whipping posts, but what we're making now feels even worse. We're almost done with it. All that's left is to assemble it in the square."

"Have you told your parents how you feel?"

"Yeah." He chews on his lip. "They're scared of the Guardians."

We're both still for a moment. The Guardians are meant to protect us, to *guard* us. Surely the villagers shouldn't have to fear them. And yet…

"I wanted to tell you something else," Eero continues. "I had a dream about Jonas." He talks fast, his brow furrowing. "He was hiding. Cold. Weeping. I could hear him, but I couldn't find him. You don't think he could still be alive, do you?"

My eyes burn. "I don't know, Eero."

"I miss him."

I rub my arms. "Me too."

We resume our sparring, but my heart's no longer in it, and the Carpenter boy gets in one good hit after another. By the time Gryphon calls an end to our training, my bruises have bruises.

"We'll each return to the village by different routes," Gryphon says. "And arrive here separately tomorrow. Stay watchful. The Guardians are on high alert this week. None of us wants to be caught breaking the rules."

Everyone nods. Sal says she's going to hang back to let Marie braid her hair, like the child has been begging to do. Eero, Oscar, Meryl, and I take off in different directions. I'm about a hundred meters from the caves, following the creek, when I hear the crack of a branch behind me. I spin.

It's Gryphon.

"What was wrong with you back there?" he asks. "You let Eero cream you." His face looks weird in the shadows. Warped.

I shrug to hide the thrill that shivers across my skin. *He followed me.* "Off day."

He steps forward, the weirdness I thought I'd seen gone. "Guardians don't have off days."

"Good thing I'm not one, then."

He's studying me, something like a smile playing across his lips. "Yeah. Good thing. Next time, I recommend you don't let Eero throw you as much."

I roll my eyes, but I'm smiling myself. "Fight better." I tap my head. "Why didn't I think of that?"

Gryphon steps closer, sending a lick of flame down my spine. I'd swear by the Soil beneath my feet that he was about to ask to kiss me again, when the tree behind him rustles and Leonidas drops from its branches, his face twisted with glee.

My throat closes like a fist. Gryphon whips around to angle himself between us. Had Leo seen us training? But I barely have time to worry about that before a scream of pure agony rips through the forest. Confrontation taking a backseat, the three of us sprint toward the terrible sound. My lungs burn as I try to keep pace with the Guardians. I think we're heading toward the abandoned industrial district where Peter's body was found. The closer we get, the louder the sounds of battle grow. Metal striking metal, shouts of pain, and an eerie cacophony of rustling that makes my skin crawl.

Finally, we burst into the clearing.

I stumble to a halt, unable to process what I'm seeing.

The ancient, enormous vines that have always clung faithfully to our Wall are…moving.

No, I realize, my mouth going dry. They're not moving. They're *attacking*. They writhe like serpents, the fleshy rustle of their thick cords sounding grotesquely human as they seize Nebula of the Guardian House and lift her off the ground. Jarek and Misia Tzu are there, too, plus a fourth Guardian whose name I don't know. They slash at the vegetation with gleaming blades, their expressions fierce as they try to free Nebula.

A vine whips past my face, leaving a stinging welt. I duck, watching in horror as the thick, green-purple cord trapping Nebula begins to squeeze. She makes a terrible choking scream. Her feet kick the air, her struggles growing weaker as the vine pulses and throbs and her skin tightens around her bones, taking on a horrifying grayish tint.

She's being sucked dry. *Just like Peter.*

"Behind you!" I shout as a thick vine snakes toward Jarek's throat. He spins, his blade flashing in a perfect arc that severs it. Deep violet juices spray from the cut, but three more tendrils take its place.

Gryphon launches himself into the fray, his movements fluid. He fights in perfect synchronicity with his parents, their blades flying in a deadly dance of steel and precision. Leonidas follows suit, but there are too many vines, too many angles of attack. Every cut births two more cords and then the vine seizes a Guardian anew, dragging them back as the others rush in vain to save them.

The vines lash out like whips, jagged barbs glinting in the holy Sun. I watch, horrified, as one wraps around the neck of the second Guardian, lifting him into the air. He severs the vine strangling him, but another surges forward as soon as he hits the ground, grabbing his leg and dragging him across the clearing. He claws at the earth, fingers raking the dirt, screaming as the barbs tear into his flesh.

Blood splatters, painting the ground red.

His cry is cut short as the vine rears back and plunges itself into his stomach, his body jerking violently before it goes limp, flesh sagging as the vine drinks him. His corpse crumples, his eyes wide and empty. The plant releases him with a wet, sickening hiss, turning its hungry tendrils toward Misia.

It's all happening so fast.

Misia fights with the grace of a panther, her short, dark hair gleaming with blood as she ducks beneath a swinging vine, slicing through it in one elegant motion. The severed piece writhes on the ground, twitching. I feel nauseous. The vines are relentless, surging forward, coming at her from every direction. Misia spins, her blade cutting through the air, but a vine catches her from behind, wrapping around her waist, dragging her off her feet.

"MOM!" Gryphon yells, his body a blur as he charges. He leaps, sword flashing, cutting through the vine encircling her in a single stroke. Misia crashes to the ground, rolling to her feet without a flicker of fear in her eyes. Her gaze meets mine across the clearing, and for one dizzying moment, I see a flash of something raw, desperate.

A vine snaps toward me, and I stumble back, heart hammering, my mind blank with terror. I have no weapon. No sword. No way to defend myself. What good are Gryphon's lessons against a thing like *this*? The rustling, humming creature—if you can call it that—lashes out again, this time aiming for my stomach, barbs glinting. I throw myself to the ground at the last possible moment, dirt grinding into my palms as the vine whips overhead. It curls back, ready to strike again. I scramble to my feet, my brain white with panic.

"No!" Gryphon's eyes are wild as he fights his way toward me, but he's surrounded, vines coiling around his blade and pulling him back. I see his muscles strain, his body shaking with effort, but he's unable to reach me.

I can't breathe. Can't move. This is a nightmare. It's not real. *It can't be real.*

"Rose!" Misia's voice, sharp, commanding, cuts through the chaos. I jerk my head toward her, meeting her savage gaze. She's covered in dirt and blood, her hair matted with gore, eyes blazing. "The can!"

I blink, disoriented. What is she talking about? But then I see it, lying on its side a few feet away from me: one of the large metal canisters I'd seen in the Guardians' weapons barn. It has a trigger, like a greenhouse sprayer. I lunge for it, fingers closing around the cool metal. It's heavier than I expected.

When the vine launches its strike, I pull the trigger, a stream of pale mist shooting out, enveloping it. The vine contorts, thrashing against the ground, its flesh bubbling and blistering before it pulls back, retreating like a cornered beast.

It actually worked. Hope flares in my chest.

But before I can release more spray, another tendril lunges, its barb slicing across my side. I remember the thorns I saw growing near Eden's Gate—these are much larger. Pain explodes white-hot behind my eyes, acid spreading through my veins. I drop to my knees, clutching the wound. The vine rears back, ready to strike again. I fumble with the can, vision blurring from the pain. I squeeze the trigger, a cloud of mist shooting forward to meet the vine. It halts mid-strike, shuddering, then recoils with a furious snapping noise. Its barbs curl inward like a fiddlehead fern as it retreats.

The rest of the vines follow then, a purple-tinged green army crawling back up the Wall.

And just like that, we're no longer under attack.

Two Guardians dead. Jarek, Misia, Gryphon, and Leonidas covered in blood and plant gore, their swords limp in their hands. Me on the ground, bleeding, still holding the sprayer.

Jarek opens his mouth to roar at the sky.

"What. Was. That?" Gryphon demands when his father quiets.

Leo limps over to whisper something to Jarek. Is he reporting us for training? It's hard to care about that right now.

Jarek brushes Leonidas off. "Yes, yes," he tells him. His gaze lingers on the two desiccated corpses before he steels himself. "It was a terrible attack by an animal of the Valley," he tells his son. "We must tighten the curfew further."

It's the middle of the day, but I don't say that.

"What in the Yellow Sun are you talking about?" Gryphon demands incredulously. "That wasn't an animal! It was a man-eating vine. Why are you lying to our faces?"

Jarek steps forward and strikes his son with such force that it echoes off the trees.

I launch myself at Jarek, ignoring the pain at my side. Gryphon recovers from his father's blow quickly enough to pluck me from the air.

Jarek is chuckling. "She's got some fight in her, your betrothed. She needs to learn control, though. As I was saying, there has been another terrible animal attack, which means we must cordon off more farmland. Less food requires another Harvest." His tone brokers no disagreement. "We'll add the blessed sacrifice to Friday's celebrations. Won't that be lovely, Rose? Another wedding, another Harvest. All for you."

My throat's burning to scream at him, but I swallow my rage. There's only one explanation for Jarek's blasé reaction to the killer vines. *He already knew.* Misia and Leo, too, by the looks of it. *Oh, poor Gryphon. They've hidden this from him.*

And now he's trying to get us to deny the proof of our own eyes, already planning to use this attack to get people to agree to another Harvest so soon after Jonas, and won't Gryphon and I look like fools if we try to convince the villagers that *plants* are killing us? How long has Jarek known about it, and why hasn't he told anyone outside of the Guardian House, or even his own son?

"You're hurt!" Gryphon cries out, rushing to my side.

I glance down at the blood dripping off the hem of my shirt. *Huh, guess I am.*

It's the last thing I think before everything goes dark.

47

"There, there, that's it now," Aunt Florence is saying. "Just a few more stitches and we'll have you as good as new."

"It's taking you long enough." Leo sounds disgusted.

My eyes flutter open. I'm lying in the Apothecary cottage, on the surgical table. I've seen this room a thousand times, but never from this angle. Aunt Florence is peering at my stomach, her suturing kit nearby. She's squinting through her thick glasses. Leo stands impatiently behind her, trying to see over her shoulder.

I gently explore the edges of the cut left by the vine. It was a bleeder, but it isn't exceptionally deep. Seven stitches should do the trick.

Aunt Florence holds my gaze, her mouth rigid. "You're awake," she says. "Apparently you were attacked by a wild animal."

"Two Guardians died saving her," Leo interjects, shooting me a warning glance.

Aunt Florence's eyes narrow, but she keeps talking to me. "It wasn't as bad as it looked," she says. "You should be back on your feet in no time."

"Where's Gryphon?" I ask.

Leo begins to fiddle with a row of jars holding bandaging materials.

"Leave those alone," Aunt Florence scolds. "They're sterilized."

Leo turns back, rolling his eyes. "Gryphon's patrolling the perimeter, which is what he should've been doing all along rather than sneaking off with you lot. Jarek ordered me to keep an eye on you. You were cut up pretty bad."

"I'm okay," I say, starting to sit up.

Aunt Florence gently pushes me back down. "I need to keep her under observation," she tells Leo.

"She'll be fine," Leo says dismissively. "Her gran's here. Jarek said he wanted a report from you as soon as you were done stitching her up."

Aunt Florence sighs. She cleans my wound, which hurts worse than the sutures she puts in. When she's done, she stretches her back and goes to the sink to wash her hands, her movements slow, measured. It's how she carries herself when she's upset. *Really* upset. She dries her hands on her apron before switching it out for a clean one.

"You take it easy, Rosie. I'll clean up when I return." She gives me the same stern look I used to level on patients I suspected would break their bedrest. "After you," she says to Leo.

They disappear out the door. Alone in the surgery room, I ease myself off the table, wincing at the raw tug of new stitches, and teeter into the main cottage. I expect to see Gran in front of the fire.

Instead, it's Augustus.

"You must be wondering why we kept so much from you," he says as I enter, his voice hoarse.

48

"Lilian is upstairs resting," he says. "I told her I'd talk with you. Will you have a seat, please?"

I carefully lower myself into Gran's favorite chair.

"Jarek's father was Harvested within weeks of his birth," Augustus says, choosing the last subject on earth I expected. "His mother sank into the blues after, though none of us noticed until it was too late. She fed Jarek just enough to keep him alive." His facial lines seem to deepen. "There's a good chance she never touched him except to change his diapers and carry him to chapel. She raised him alone until he was five and started school. That's when she started making her own pruno, drinking every day."

I gasp. A community failure of that magnitude is difficult to imagine. I think of all the people who would've had to look away, starting with her own family and the other Guardian Houses.

Augustus seems to read my mind. "We'll never forgive ourselves. The method she used to make the pruno wasn't safe. She accidentally poisoned herself. Jarek was cared for by his uncle and aunt after that, but he never found his place. When he was fourteen and caught spying through someone's bedroom window, we offered to support him through a traditional Circling, reminding him why we loved him, but the boy refused. He'd broken no law, so the choice was his. I wish we'd insisted. That's about when he began focusing on your mother. He loved her an unhealthy amount."

I shift my weight, wincing as the stitches pull.

"It was the vines that attacked you?" he asks.

I gasp, my hand flying to my side. Of all the secrets inside the Wall, this is the betrayal that hurts the worst. "You *knew* we're being hunted by a plant?"

He drags in a deep breath. "Not for long. I saw it come alive in the quarantined area the day before your wedding. Scooped a bird from the air and sucked it dry." He shudders at the memory. "I told Henrietta, but she asked me to sit on the information until she spoke with Jarek." He spreads his hands. "The next day, she was dead."

A cold, searing shock floods my veins. "You think this is your secret to keep? Then what makes you better than Jarek? Two more citizens died today, Augustus." I spit his name like a curse.

His face sags. "I know you're upset, girl, and it's fair, but don't let your temper get the better of you. After your mother's death, I shared what I knew with some others. We kept it quiet to protect everyone—including you—until we had a plan. And for all their faults, Jarek and his Guardians *are* trying to deal with the green beast. Sure you're right, maybe we should've brought it to the whole village." He sighs, turning his palms upward. "That's the trouble with this Valley. We spend our lives avoiding the ugly truths and calling it kindness. It's a tragedy."

"A *tragedy*," I say, trembling with barely contained rage, "is continuing as we have, supporting a system that favors the few and removes choice from all. We have to tear this rot out by the root, and we need to start by Harvesting Jarek." I blink, shocked by my own words.

He straightens abruptly. "Two wrongs don't make a right."

I stand too quickly, my stitches tugging, and wince. How dare he try to parent me. "I don't want to make a right! I want to save Jonas." I realize I'm shaking. "I want to protect my gran and aunt and uncle." *I want revenge for my mother and brother.*

"I, I, I," he growls. "Do you hear yourself?" I feel heat rise to my cheeks as he continues. "I don't mean to shame you, Rose. Your passion is in the right place, and you're right—I wish I'd spoken up earlier. Before Peter"—his voice hitches on the boy's name, but he continues—"but you're forgetting something important: Noah's Valley is a community. We only work when we work together."

"Jarek wants to harm us! There's no time to waste changing people's minds."

"Says who?"

I twist my lips in frustration. He hasn't seen the plant devour people, hasn't heard Jarek deny it while the corpses of his comrades lie at his feet.

Augustus tsks. "You think I'm a foolish old man, but if there's one thing I've learned in my life, it's this: If you want to go fast, go alone. If you want to go far, go together." He steps forward, walking toward me more softly than his bulky frame should allow. "Consult with your friends, then gather evidence of the killer vines that cannot be denied. And remember: never fight only for yourself, not when others are waging the same battle."

He's so close that I can see the few white hairs in his black eyebrows. I don't know how I'd have responded if not for the Crier outside the door.

"Feast in an hour! The Guardians have meat to share! Gather your families for a feast in an hour!"

My throat tightens as I think of the pink flesh served last night. Is it more of that? And if so, where is it coming from? I'm surprised by the sudden desire I feel to find Gryphon and curl into his arms. He's the only other person who'd understand.

"I need to go. Tell Gran I'll bring her food."

Augustus stares at me as I slip out the door, his expression worried.

If you want to go fast, go alone. If you want to go far, go together. Sounds like something my dad would've said. But he's no longer here, is he? I shake my head and hurry toward the Tzu cottage, intending to clean myself up. As I go, I catalog what I now believe to be true:

At some point, Jarek discovered the plant was hunting us. He evacuated the area where it killed those first Guardians, telling us we were under attack by wild animals. He must have discovered the roots in the industrial area near Eden's Gate and tried to fight back with an herbicide left by our ancestors in the Record Keepers' secret room. In poisoning the plant, though, he accidentally poisoned villagers. Rather than confess, he let us believe it was a mystery illness and allowed the quarantine of that area.

When my mother found out the truth, Jarek had her murdered with a weapon only his loyal Guardians would recognize. He got that from the Record Keeper, too, having manipulated the pathetic David Seingalt to his whims. Though that still doesn't explain why the Harvest basket was down on my wedding day. Did Jarek always intend to frame my brother, and if so, why?

I squint up at the sky. Judging by the pale light, I was unconscious for one, maybe two hours. The village is bustling with news of the feast. As I near the square, I catch the scent of roasting animal flesh. It's different from the too-sweet, fatty smell of the meat cooked in the Tzu kitchen last night, and I thank the Wall for that. I think of Gryphon, tenderly carrying Gran home after dinner, and it makes me wonder what it would feel like to have someone by my side during these terrible times—a partner I could really trust.

I turn down a lane, and there he is, as if my thoughts have led me to him. My heart soars. Gryphon stands in front of the Record Keeper cottage, his back to me, his hands pressed against the wall like he's holding it up. I realize that despite my best efforts, I'm falling for those hands. Imagining them threaded through my hair, pulling me close. I shake my head. *Stop it, Rose. There isn't time for that now. The world's on fire, and anyhow, you're leaving Noah's Valley soon.*

"Gryphon?"

He steps away from the wall and turns, revealing...Marina Seingalt.

She opens her eyes slowly, her expression blissful. When she spots me, a devilish grin curls her mouth. "Guess we got you twice."

It's the betrothal ceremony day all over again.

He begged me to kiss him, you know, Marina had said. It explains why she was so desperate to know how my first night with Gryphon had gone. And Eero's joke from the other day, too. It had rung true. I stumble backward, choking on humiliation. My heart is scorched. I fall against the Minstrel cottage.

"Rose?" Angus, the Minstrel husband, comes to the doorway. He's holding a lyre. "Are you all right?"

Gryphon steps toward me, his expression tight—guilt? It better be—but I'm already racing to the village center.

The size of the cooking fire in front of the stage disorients me, as does the crowd gathered around it. I press my hand to the stitches at my side. Why is everyone so early? The people, the sounds, the smoke, all of it makes me lightheaded. That's why it takes me a moment to notice who is standing on the stage.

Meryl, Sal, Oscar, and Eero.

They look terrified.

49

"Make a path so she can get through!" Jarek bellows, striding to the front of the stage and pointing at me across the village square.

People step aside, just as they had for my wedding.

"Rose Allgood," he croons, "come join your friends."

I find myself stumbling forward. Agitated whispers slice through me, so by the time I reach the stage, I feel like I'm bleeding from a thousand tiny cuts. What's happening?

"That's it," Jarek says, offering me a hand.

I refuse to touch him. I walk to the stairs, stitches tight at my side. I feel the heat from the fire, the throbbing ache of my wound. The smoking pit had been dug and started long ago enough that the great strips of meat are nearly cooked through, the creature's skinned flesh—I'm relieved to see it looks like normal venison—brown and crackling. Were they hunting for this meal too close to the Wall when the beast attacked?

I step onto the stage, wondering what Jarek's endgame could possibly be.

He glares at me for refusing his hand, then turns back to the crowd. He's cleaned himself up. It's only because I'm close that I spot the bruises and scrapes from today's battle. I stare out into the crowd. Most of the villagers' expressions are expectant. They're hungry, and they're being offered an unexpected meal. Like me, they have no idea what Jarek has in store.

"Before we begin the feast, I'm afraid I have some tragic news," Jarek tells the village, his voice carrying.

A frantic buzz runs through the crowd.

He raises his hands. "We have a traitor among us!"

The buzzing turns to a roar. It takes several moments before Jarek gets the audience back under his control.

"That's right," he says. "One or more of your neighbors—or possibly even a member of your own House—has discovered a stash of food inside the Wall, left by our Founders. They've been keeping it for themselves while the rest of us go hungry! We don't know where they found it, but this selfish, unholy behavior undermines our blessed Valley. We need everyone's help in rooting out the evil in our midst."

Shock travels like wildfire through the crowd. I cannot believe Jarek's audacity. He's trying to pin his crimes on an innocent! But then I recognize the genius of it. The accuser is the last one you suspect of the crime.

"How do you know?" yells a voice from the back. "What proof do you have that someone has food hidden by the Founders?"

A contingent of Guardians immediately shoves their way through the throng to locate the challenger, but Jarek stops them with a wave. "It's a fair question," he calls out. He reaches inside his cloak and withdraws two tins, each the size of a deck of cards.

"Behold, smoked fish! A delicacy from the Before Times."

He holds up the tins. The blood-red and gold of the cans glitters in the firelight. The rare food must look like salvation to our hungry villagers.

"We discovered these cans on a patrol of the interior perimeter, this and more, many of them empty because the traitor has been eating them. We're keeping the contraband locked away for everyone's safety. However," he says, pausing for effect, "the

Council has agreed to offer these two tins as a reward to whoever turns in the traitor."

A surge presses those nearest the stage into the wood, squeezing the breath from them as the crowd clambers forward for a closer look.

"Stand back!" I yell. "You're hurting those up front!"

But the villagers don't still until Jarek tucks the food back inside his cloak. "Our discovery of a traitor—along with another wild animal attack just today that cost us two Guardian lives—comes with a necessary rule change."

The crowd collectively gasps at this terrible pronouncement. *Two Guardians dead.*

"Between increased attacks and a traitor among us, the curfew will be pushed up for obvious reasons," Jarek continues. "After tonight's feast, no one is allowed outside of their home after the sun is set, except to attend duties approved by the Guardians. The sooner the traitor is rooted out, the sooner we can begin to return to our normal lives." He gives the side of his cloak holding the tins a shake. Those of us nearby can hear them clink together.

We're weak if we're divided. Jarek knows this. He's created hunger and inequality, and now he's playing on them to turn us against each other rather than question him. I glance in desperation at my friends. They're clinging tight to one another, Oscar on one end and Sal on the other, Eero and Meryl in the middle. Sal holds out her hand for me. I hurry over to grip it, feeling a surge of warmth as she squeezes me back.

"Why are we up here?" I whisper.

She shakes her head. "They dragged us from our homes."

I'm surprised to feel Salvatora shaking, but then I look down and realize it's Eero, on her other side, who's trembling, his shudders so strong that they're being passed down the line.

"But we have more than one problem in our midst," Jarek calls, directing the crowd's attention to the five of us at last. "Feast your eyes upon these criminals."

I hear a shout of anger from the crowd. Jarek's use of the slur has pierced at least one villager's stupor. We don't have "criminals" in Noah's Valley. We have *people*, even when they've done something wrong.

Jarek shakes his head and makes a mollifying gesture. "Now, now, I know it's a harsh term, but these five have been stealing time from the Valley, as well as thieving knowledge from a House not their own!"

The crowd shifts. I scan them, looking for friendly eyes. I mostly spy an unsettling hunger. I've been eating my fill at the Tzu cottage; these people clearly have not.

"You've heard correctly!" Jarek declares. "They've been learning to fight!"

"No!" someone yells from the back of the mob, for that's what he's turning them into, their fear and anxiety finding a focal point in us. They're hungry from a diet of porridge, anxious from the uncertainty of rolling Harvests, and scared because he's telling them wild animals are picking us off.

Oscar grimaces, and I can tell he and I have come to the same conclusion: Jarek is giving the village a common enemy. Us.

"Yes," Jarek says, dropping his voice like he can hardly bear to utter the travesty. "*Fighting*. You'll want to ask yourself what they intended to do with their new skill. Nothing honest, I can promise you that."

"Beat them!" someone yells.

Eero's legs buckle, but Meryl props him up on one side and Sal the other. He's nearly a full head shorter than the girls, still waiting on his teenage growth spurt.

Jarek shakes his head, as if the five of us breaking the law pains him so deeply that he's only able to speak at great personal expense. "That may be the answer, but I cannot make a decision without consulting the Record Keeper and my Council. We are a people of rules, remember. A fair people. They will be kept in the chapel undercroft until we decide on a fitting punishment. Guardians, take them away."

Eero makes a squeaking noise before diving off the stage. Seeking the comfort of his family? I often forget his age on account of his friendship with my brother, but at just fourteen, Eero's little more than a boy. Jarek rolls his eyes at the fruitless escape attempt and flicks his wrist at Leonidas, indicating he should retrieve him. The crowd's roar is reaching a crescendo. I can't tell if they're calling for our blood or arguing with Jarek. Possibly both.

He doesn't seem concerned, his smile placid.

Where's Gryphon? Shouldn't he be on stage with us? Does he care so little for me that he stayed behind with Marina? *That weed-hearted sneak.*

"Silence!" Jarek calls, but the villagers aren't listening. They're talking excitedly among themselves, crowding the stage, making it shift and creak. Jarek's face finally tightens.

I scan the mob, searching for Eero. He'll be trampled in this madness. I spot him as he darts behind the stage, running toward Eden's Gate. He's easy to pick out, skirting the edge of the square in a desperate bid for escape. Leonidas trails him, going too near the Wall if his anxious glances at it are any indication.

Holy Sun and Soil, I realize. Keeping twenty feet from the Wall was never about deference, was it? *That norm exists so none of us trigger the beast.*

That means the herbicide wasn't hypothetical, either. Whoever gave us our religion knew about the threat. It must be what sent our Founders into the Valley to begin with: a beast the likes of which our stories do not tell. *Oh, Jonas.* I picture him up there, surrounded by hungry green vines.

I shove the distraction into my ever-growing cabinet of betrayals, forcing my attention back to the present, waiting for Leonidas to bring Eero back. He's gaining on him, though Eero must not notice because his pace never changes. I spot the other

Carpenters on the opposite side of the stage. How difficult it will be for them to witness their son punished. But we must take our beating. There's no escaping it.

Leo has nearly caught up now. Rather than grab Eero, though, Leonidas raises his weapon, a bo staff just like the one we've been training with. *Oh no!* He means to strike the boy down. I step toward the edge of the stage, a cry on my lips.

Leonidas brings down the staff, not on Eero's head, like I expected, but between his ankles. A minor twist of the staff, and Eero's off his feet. With one quick jab, Leo sends him flying.

Toward the Wall.

The vines above rustle. *The monster.*

I launch myself off the stage, charging around the edge of the crowd and screaming a warning. I move fast, the pain of my new stitches a distant memory. I don't know if Leonidas attacking Eero was an accident, or spite, or something else, but I have to stop him so Eero has a chance to get away.

I hit Leo like a brick arrow, knocking him off his feet. He fights back, even on the ground, moving to sweep my legs out from underneath me, but I'm ready. I jump to avoid his sweep, and when I come down, I manage to tug his knife from his belt. I'd never have been able to best him if he wasn't worn from fighting the vines today.

I stand over Leonidas, one foot on each side of his chest, clutching the knife over his heart. I'm searching for Eero—praying his absence means escape, rather than capture by the leafy beast—when a blade whistles through the air, slicing my shoulder.

Leonidas's knife falls harmlessly to the ground.

I look up to see who's attacked me.

Gryphon.

50

Guardians descend on me before I can react. Blood trickles from my shoulder, and at least one of my stitches has ripped. My only relief is that Eero is hauled past me, unharmed except for whatever bruises spiteful Leonidas gave him. No one speaks out—not that I can hear—as Eero, Sal, Meryl, and Oscar are cinched to the whipping posts rather than brought to the chapel undercroft. Eero's escape attempt must be the reason.

I'm led toward them, the *snap crack* of fresh leather ringing out across the square. Did the Leatherworkers craft new ones alongside the sashes and suspenders they lovingly make for every villager who turns sixteen? My friends cry out in pain, and I fall down a well of shock, disconnecting from the outside world. It barely registers as I'm suddenly led away from the posts, to what fate I do not know.

Throughout, I have only one thought: Gryphon betrayed me. *Twice.*

What have I done, tipping my hand to him? He is and always has been loyal to Jarek, even while hating the man. A Guardian to the bone, not to mention madly in love with my childhood bully. I've been an idiot. He must have planted those sketches to soften me, kissed me to amplify the devastation when I realized who really owned his heart. All his kindness has been a ruse. And it's worked, hasn't it? I was starting to trust him, opening up so he had a chance to...what? Humiliate me?

He and Marina are probably laughing about it now. Amazed someone can be as gullible—as desperate for companionship—as Rose Allgood.

A part of me tries to argue that Gryphon is neither so callous nor does he have the free time to waste rehashing tired, schoolyard bullying at our age. I desperately want to believe this was all some gut-wrenching but ultimately benign misunderstanding. But the only information I can count on is what I see with my own eyes.

My chest tightens. On top of everything else, my existence has gotten my friends in trouble. They'd been training without incident until I joined.

But why had Gryphon started training them at all, if he was only interested in serving his parents? I chew at the inside of my cheek as the Guardians drag me into the chapel undercroft. Nothing makes sense. Everything feels slippery, the complete picture just out of reach. I don't know what to do with the anger and confusion flowing like glass shards in my bloodstream.

I'm dumped on the cellar floor. The usual tables and chairs are stacked to the side, the space looking vast without them. Then the door scrapes closed—I didn't even know it *could* close—and the room falls to darkness.

All alone, I begin to weep.

A half an hour or so later, the door reopens, and my four bloody friends are shoved inside.

Meryl sees me in a corner and immediately hobbles over. "How's the shoulder?" she asks. She was just whipped, but it's my dagger wound she's worried about.

I try to scramble backward, but the wall is right behind me. Tender, true Meryl doesn't understand yet that I'm the reason they're all in trouble. That *I'm* the one Leonidas caught. I can't bear witnessing the birth of her hatred toward me.

"Let us look at you," Sal says, shuffling to stand beside her. Oscar and Eero follow. All four of them are hunched in pain, dried tear tracks muddying their faces, blood dripping down their backs.

"No!" Panic squats on my throat. "This is all my fault!"

Meryl shakes her head, the movement slow and wretched. "No, it's not. It's Jarek's."

My chest is heaving with a familiar guilt, one I inherited from my mother. "None of us would be in trouble if I hadn't started training with you! You were fine until then." I'm beginning to hyperventilate, my breath coming in great whoops.

Sal bends at the knees and slaps me, *hard*, across the cheek. Then she stands, wincing. "Been waiting years to do that," she says. "Didn't think I could get away with it in front of your betrothed, though." Smiling darkly, she continues, "We were never *fine*. We were always taking a risk by training. Don't borrow blame that's not yours. It'll only slow us down."

My cheek stings, but I'm no longer at risk of passing out. "Gryphon. He threw a knife at me."

"And it's a good thing he did," Oscar says. "Or the other Guardians would've killed you a hundred times over. They'd be justified, too. The whole village saw you about to stick Leonidas like a bug."

Meryl's voice is softer. "He couldn't just let you stab his friend, Rose. No matter how he feels about you."

"He did keep you from being whipped," Eero says, something like admiration in his voice. "Took four Guardians to hold him back when he saw you being dragged toward the posts. His dad musta thought whipping you would be more trouble than it was worth, and he waved you on to chapel."

"Gryphon's dead to me," I spit out. "I saw him kissing Marina right before I came to the square."

No one responds to that, though a look of pity crosses Salvatora's face. It stings, coming from her. "Never mind," I say, wishing the floor would open up and swallow me.

There's a commotion outside the basement door. We all tense. What's coming for us next? A few moments later, the door opens and Uncle Richard steps inside, agitated, his ginger hair floating like spun sugar around his head. Leo follows, pawing through my uncle's medical pack.

"You can have this," Leo says, pulling out a suture kit. "Nothing else."

"No painkillers?" Uncle Richard protests. "No ointment for their lashes?"

Leo glares at me. "She wasn't going to offer me a painkiller before plunging my knife into my chest, was she?" he barks. "You have ten minutes."

He slams the door closed behind himself.

Sweet, always-flustered Uncle Richard takes stock of the scene—me crouched in a corner, Sal, Oscar, Eero, and Meryl standing nearby, the backs of their tunics shredded and bloody—and rushes over.

He comes to me first to examine my throbbing shoulder, or so I think. Instead he whispers, "We've waited too long. We must get you all out of here."

51

I'm speechless. Fortunately, Salvatora is not. "What do you mean, get us out of here?"

Uncle Richard glances toward the door, then back at me. "Jarek has forced our hand." He smooths my hair, keeping his voice low. "We haven't got much time. Rosie, I need you to pay attention."

"Shouldn't you stitch her up first?" Meryl asks.

He pulls aside my tunic, revealing the injury. It's crusted with blood, but it's clear the wound isn't deep. The dagger only skimmed the surface. Either Gryphon was very good or I was very lucky. "She doesn't need it." He cleans the edges of the cut with a small cloth as he speaks. "Rose, listen," he says. "Augustus told us you saw the killer vines. Florence and I never would have kept it a secret if we'd known what it would unleash, but it's too late for anything but regret." Tears brim in his pale brown eyes.

Meryl sucks in a breath. "Did you say killer…vines?"

He nods. "You know the ones. Clinging to the Wall, rooted in the evacuated industrial district. The vines are carnivorous."

Eero gasps, and I wonder how terrified the even younger Peter Martinez must have felt, seeing them come to life for the first and last time.

"It seems to feed on mammals. You notice how purple the leaves have looked lately?"

I had, in passing.

"Henrietta believed the color change coincided with the increase in attacks. We think it signals maturation." Uncle Richard looks around the dark basement, lingering on each of the battered captives before turning his attention back to me. "We were hoping to have a few more days to plan how to fight it, but clearly that isn't an option."

We hear noises beyond the cellar door, like an argument. Uncle Richard talks faster. "No more secrets, Rosie. We believe Jarek has known about the monster for months and that he's been trying to poison it. We also believe Henrietta confronted Jarek about the poison the morning of your wedding." He touches my cheek. "And that he had her killed for it. How, we still don't know."

I'm running through the hunches that Uncle Richard has just confirmed when I feel my eyes bulge. Now that I know the Guardians and Peter died by different means than my mother, it's so obvious: it wasn't just a weapon from the vault that had killed Mom—it was *the* weapon, charging on the Tzu roof. And Jarek had commanded one of the only three villagers who wasn't expected at my wedding to shoot her with it.

Albert.

How had Jarek found out the boy was still inside the Wall? And more importantly, if Jarek knows I'm onto him, why hasn't he killed me yet?

"Why am I still alive?" I ask.

Uncle Richard's laugh is humorless. "Personally? I think you look too much like your mother. He killed her once, from afar. Perhaps he couldn't bear to do it again."

Fury tears through me. I live not because I'm a boon to the Valley, not because I matter, but because Jarek can't face his own guilt. I want to scream.

"So what do we do?" Sal asks.

The wave of gratitude I feel at the "we" makes me weak.

"We get you kids out of here. That's first. Then we figure out what's next."

I'm about to ask who my uncle's "we" is when there is a jostling outside the basement door. "Quick, Uncle," I say. "Anansi requires his insulin, and Beate the Potter won't make it if she doesn't get her nitroglycerin today. Hephaestus should be all right for a few more days without his willow bark."

I barely have the last word out of my mouth when the basement door flies open. "Time to go," Leo commands.

"I promise I will, Rosie," Uncle Richard whispers. He pulls a small pot out of his waistband and shoves it into my hand as Leo approaches, then he holds up the needle he hasn't used. "But I haven't finished my sutures," he tells Leo.

"Should've worked quicker." Leo touches his sword's hilt in case his words weren't clear.

Uncle Richard sighs and stands. "You know what to do for a wound, Rose," he tells me. "Trust the process."

The inflection in his voice is soft, but I catch it. *Trust the process.* What process? Being confined to a basement? But Leo is leading him out. I glance at the tin of arnica and echinacea balm he's snuck me, and then into the astounded faces of my friends.

"Do I want to hear more about this killer...thing?" Oscar asks.

"You don't, but I'm going to tell you anyway." When I describe the attack I witnessed, they have outrage, then questions, and finally, acceptance.

"It's got us trapped in here," Eero says, his voice laced with fear. "How do we kill it?"

"I don't know," I say grimly. "It's strong, or Jarek would have simply hacked it up by now." I take as deep a breath as my wounds allow. "But I think I finally know what Jarek and Misia plan to do on Friday."

52

Everything I've learned since Jonas's cruel Harvest has coalesced into a single, awful vision. Jarek's worship of the Founders' items, the food and the newfangled weapons and that pile of explosives that Gryphon said is his father's passion. How Jarek is having his Guardians train with noise makers so they learn to fight without being thrown off by loud explosions. The cage-like structure Eero had said the Carpenter House was being forced to build to keep something *out*.

"I think Jarek wants to blow open the Wall." My whole body is shaking. "He craves power. And wants things he cannot have. I'll bet he imagines both lie Beyond."

I expect gasps, argument. Instead, all four go as still as stone.

"Gryphon also suspects that," Meryl finally says.

The ground seems to drop out from beneath me.

Meryl looks at the others. "It's time we tell her everything. No more secrets. They're hungry and they bite everyone, especially the ones keeping them."

"None of us knew if we could trust you," Oscar says matter-of-factly. "Even after you started training."

I'm flabbergasted. "But you trust Gryphon!"

"We do." They nod, practically in unison.

"And it'd save us a lot of time if you did, too," Meryl says. "He suspects his dad, and he wants to stop him."

"How?" I ask. I don't bother responding about Gryphon. She can't seriously expect me to trust him while admitting he's kept a secret this huge from me.

"We don't know yet."

A stone apron of exhaustion drops onto my shoulders. So many secrets have led us to waste so much time. I hold up the balm. "The sooner we get this on, the better you'll feel."

They hesitate, and then Oscar turns, lifting his shirt. I try not to weep at the sight of his swollen, bloody back. I apply the ointment as gently as possible. He flinches at my touch and then sighs. I made the balm myself. It draws out pain, reduces swelling, and speeds up healing.

"Did Gryphon know about the vines?" I ask. I think not. He seemed genuinely stunned by the earlier attack.

Eero shakes his head, glancing enviously at Oscar. "No. None of us did, until today."

I carefully pull Oscar's shirt down—the balm will keep it from fusing to his flesh—and move on to Eero. When I finish with him, I indicate Sal is next, but she gestures toward Meryl instead.

"The poison Uncle Richard referred to," I say, "the one my mother confronted Jarek about? It does repel the plant. I saw it with my own eyes when it attacked in the quarantined area. But it's poisonous to humans, too."

Meryl's head whips around, causing her to grimace at the pain. "The quarantined area? Holy Wall...it's the Vex, isn't it? They were trying to destroy the plant and killed villagers instead."

I nod, impressed with her quick thinking. These four deserve to know as much as I do. Should I also share my plan to save Jonas? Even despite what we've been through, it's hard for me to trust them. I remember what Augustus said, though.

If you want to go fast, go alone. If you want to go far, go together.

"I'm going up the Wall on Friday." The words start out tentative and then pour out in a rush. "To save Jonas. When I come back down—*if* I come back down—I want Jarek Harvested. With him out of the way, we can figure out as a village how to move forward."

"You want to get Jarek Harvested..." Sal trails off, incredulous. "And how exactly do you plan to do that? Bat your mom's eyelashes and ask him nicely to get in the basket?"

Meryl lightly smacks Salvatora on the arm, but Sal's right. It does sound unlikely, when she puts it like that. "I figure he'll have no choice if everyone learns what he's been hiding from them," I offer weakly.

"They won't believe you. Not over the man whose orders they've been following for so long," Sal says. She watches me finish applying balm to Meryl and then sighs with relief as I begin treating her back.

"Sal's right," Meryl says apologetically. "Maybe if we'd stood up to Jarek right away, we'd have had a fighting chance. But he's trained us to lose a little bit of freedom, day by day. People are ready to follow him to the death now. It's that, or admit what they've allowed him to get away with."

"We're losing sight of the real issue," Oscar chimes in.

"Which is?" I ask.

Oscar glances at the floor before drawing a circle in the dust that's accumulated in the corner. "This is Noah's Valley," he says, pointing at it. "We've lived here peacefully for what, over a hundred years?"

I bite my tongue to keep from saying the exact number: 120. We all nod.

"Sure, the Valley needs improvements. But we didn't have problems like *this*"—he gestures to his own swollen back—"until Jarek got a taste for power. And items from Beyond, it sounds like."

I blink at his circle, feeling stupid. "What're you saying?"

"I'm saying we wreck the Harvest basket, the tablet, and whatever explosives he plans to use to break open the Wall,"

Oscar says, dropping back on his heels. "Ensure there *is* no going Beyond, *ever*. With the temptation gone, Jarek should be easier to get back in line."

Eero shakes his head. "The Engineer House will just make more explosives."

"No," I say, finally hopeful. "Gryphon was clear we don't have the materials inside the Wall to recreate them." I add the next part slowly. It's *so* important they understand. "I think it's a great idea to get rid of Jarek's stash. But if we destroy the tablet and the basket, Jonas will be trapped atop the Wall forever."

Oscar's expression tells me everything he won't say. The same knowledge is reflected in Sal, Eero, and Meryl's faces. They believe my twin is dead.

"I'm sorry," Meryl says, her expression miserable. "But I think Oscar's spot-on. We can't risk Jarek ever having access to the outside world. We don't know what horrors might follow him back in. And it's not like we can continue with the Harvests, now that there might be something up there...attacking those who are honored. The only way to guarantee our safety is to destroy the weapons *and* the tablet. Once those are gone, we can tell the villagers about the poison and show them the threat at Eden's Gate. Together, we can figure out how to fight it. Right?"

She holds out a hand. Sal slides hers on top, then Oscar, then Eero, and lastly, reluctantly, me.

I make the deal because I know they're right. The Founders' stash in the vault started all of this, simple greed eroding decades of community. If it's not Jarek trying to blow a hole in the Wall, now that those inside have a taste for the Beyond, it'll be someone else. We must permanently destroy their access to such dangers.

My friends don't need to know that I'll be up the Wall with my brother by the time they do.

53

I manage to scrape out a few hours of sleep on the chilly basement floor, all of it threaded with nightmares. Jonas screaming for help, his face contorted with terror. Gran being ferried up in the basket and abandoned like a sacrifice for the green monster. Gryphon and Marina kissing, stopping only long enough to laugh and point at me. Every one of my teeth falling out.

I wake in a start after each, squeeze Lucky Bunny, whisper to him that everything's going to be all right. The new plan is not so very different from the previous one, I let him know. I never believed I could sneak back down the Wall with Jonas, not really. Heaven is a one-way trip—I know that.

I also know that if there's even the slimmest possibility that my twin is alive up there, huddled and hiding, I can't go on living without trying to save him. If I can manage it, I'll take some explosives to drop down on the vine monster—the Beast, as I've come to think of it—so even if I don't make it back, I can protect those within.

Finally, a plan lets me sleep soundly.

The only window in the basement leaks in gray, ghostly light when morning comes. Today's Thursday, and there's no sun in sight. If the Astronomer House was correct, and they almost always are, tomorrow will be lousy with it.

Tomorrow night, the celebration.

The end of my life inside the Wall. I plan to go as soon as the tablet is charged.

Eero stirs next to me, groaning as he rises. "Nothing like sleeping on a stone floor with a bloody back." He starts to stretch and then thinks better of it. "At least it's cold."

I check everyone's wounds before examining the stitches on my belly and the cut at my shoulder. We're all sore but not showing signs of infection. There'd been enough ointment for all of us. We're going to heal.

"At least you got some sleep," Sal grumbles.

She and Meryl are lying near the door, Sal's arm thrown gently over the Entertainer. She is dropping a soft kiss on Meryl's head when footsteps clomp down the stairs. Sal helps Meryl up and away from the door as quickly as she can, both of them growing pale with the pain of sudden movement.

The door opens.

Gryphon and Leonidas stride in. Gryphon has a black eye and a split lip. Leo looks like he slept on a bed of feathers. I'm surprised Jarek didn't punish him for almost showing the whole village the green beast in action.

"Gryphon!" Meryl cries, stepping toward him.

His jaw cuts a hard edge. "We're here for Rose. The rest of you await judgment."

See? I want to tell the others. *You're finally witnessing his true colors.* Instead, I steel my nerves. No way am I walking out that door with the Betrayer. "Why am I being taken away?"

"The Record Keeper believes you—and more specifically, our wedding—are important to preserving village unity. *In light of recent events.* So you must prepare."

My chest burns. He has *got* to be kidding. "I'm not leaving the others down here. Certainly not to marry *you.*"

"You have no choice." Leo smirks.

Gryphon's eyes pierce me. "Guardians are stationed at the

Apothecary cottage. There's a concern that your aunt, uncle, and gran are supporting your rebellion. Any further...disrespect on your part will be considered proof of their participation."

They're holding my family hostage. Why am I not surprised?

"Go," Sal tells me. "We'd rather be down here than doing our chores, anyhow. Isn't that right, Oscar? Eero? Mer?"

They nod, their eyes shining.

Still, I can't imagine leaving them behind.

"Please," Gryphon says, his gaze weighted.

His earnest tone might have worked, if he hadn't recently sliced my shoulder open after, oh, kissing the girl who'd made my school years torment. Not to mention that he apparently suspected Jarek's plan all along and never said a thing to me. Suddenly, I feel small and foolish, but a heartbeat later I'm furious again, burning mad that I allowed myself to confide in him over Jonas and the vault.

I loathe Gryphon Tzu more than ever before.

But I don't see that I have any choice but to go with him. I turn to the others. Fierce Sal, talented Oscar, innocent Eero, and clever, optimistic Meryl. It's her that I entrust Lucky Bunny to, hoping his charm comforts them as it has me. I shove the tiny carving into her hands as a promise.

"I won't forget about you down here," I tell them all.

"Remember the plan," Oscar says, tipping his head. "And trust the process."

"What's he mean?" Leo barks. "What plan?"

"To atone for our mistakes, of course," I say with false piety. I push past Leo and am halfway up the stairs when I hear him tell Gryphon he's going to stay back and teach the others a lesson. I'm not positive what the response is, but when Leo appears rubbing his rapidly swelling cheek, I have a good guess.

"Bring them food, water, and a bucket," Gryphon snarls at the Guardian at the top of the stairs. "Leo, my father will want a report on their condition immediately."

Leo glares at Gryphon and then storms off. I wonder what would happen if I did the same, just walked through the chapel's front door and didn't look back. I decide to test it. I make it nearly to the entrance before Gryphon grips my arm with viselike strength.

"You'll not want to leave yet," he says.

I turn as quickly as my wounds allow and get in his face. "And why's that?" I ask.

"You're needed in here."

I stick out my chin. "Did Marina tell you to say that?" Almost immediately I regret my words, what they reveal about the state of my heart.

"No," he says, gently leaning me against the nearest wall in an exact recreation of the move he'd used on Marina last night. *How dare he!* I hate the way it makes my stomach flip.

"But she did allow me close enough to retrieve this." He holds up the white-ribboned key to the Record Keeper vault.

Relief verging on euphoria courses through me.

Gryphon's body molds to mine, ensuring that the Guardians behind cannot see him hand me the key. He studies the thing with distaste until I slip the tied-off ribbon over my head, hiding the key beneath my clothing.

"You owe me," he says. "Her lips were greasy."

My heartbeat echoes off his chest and returns to me, stronger than it left. "Why?" I ask. I mean why did he take the risk of stealing the key, why is he helping me, why did he make everything so confusing?

Why???

He places his finger under my chin, continuing the ruse that we're lovers reuniting after an awful night apart. "You said Jonas saw something in the vault, something you think caused his Harvest. It could be connected to whatever is going on with my father and the other Guardians. In any case, you wanted the key, so I got it for you."

Folded in the warmth of his body, I weaken, tears pricking my eyes at the surge of emotions his explanation brings. Emotions I ought not feel, given my plans for tomorrow night. I'm going to abandon our sacred union, and yet, for one selfish moment, I want to stay here with Gryphon forever. "Thank you," I say.

His mouth tightens. He glances over his shoulder. One Guardian has exited through the chapel's rear door, presumably to get supplies for the prisoners. The other is watching Gryphon and me suspiciously. He breaks away from his station and begins striding toward us.

I speak quickly. "Did you know it was a plant attacking us?"

He shudders. "No, that's the first time I've seen it." His glance flicks to my shoulder. "And I'm sorry I threw a knife at you. I couldn't...I couldn't let you kill him. I wish there'd been another way."

I nod. He's telling the truth. The approaching Guardian is nearly upon us now, his hand on his sword. Sojourner Confucius steps out, her expression severe.

"Rose," she says loudly. "I'm ready for you."

The Guardian who'd been approaching stops, confused.

I look to Gryphon. He steps aside and holds out an arm, the picture of graciousness. "My mother has requested pre-wedding counseling for each of us, given the situation. I've already completed mine."

54

I follow Sojourner into her office, running through all the excuses I can think of to get out of this. I cannot possibly listen to homilies and marriage advice for a union I have no intention of honoring, especially not while Noah's Valley is under attack from within.

Sojourner closes the door behind me. The chamber is hushed, soothing, the walls lined with dark wood and bookshelves, a desk in the center. I've landed on what I consider my best bet—telling her I'm ill—when she holds up a hand to silence me. She presses her ear to the door. Listens. Then reaches for one of the red cloaks of her House and hands it to me.

"It won't pass close inspection, but if you keep the hood up and stay off the main streets, you should be all right."

I'm stunned. "What are you doing?"

"Gryphon said you need to get inside the Record Keeper cottage," she says, guiding me toward the rear exit.

I stop so abruptly that my feet skid. "No, I mean *what are you doing*? Lying about my duty is illegal."

She takes the cloak from my hand and wraps it gently around my shoulders, clasping it at my neck. "Rose, a good heart always breaks a bad law." She pulls up the hood, the simple blue cross tattooed below her ear exposed when she glances again toward the door to the chapel. "You have until the bells ring. I hope you find what you're looking for."

And then she shoves me through the exit, which I'm surprised to find leads directly outside. I hear the distant sound of voices, Leo and someone else. I flatten against the back of the chapel. Brown grass scratches my ankles. Outside of the chapel's shadow, there's a broad open stretch of cobblestone I must cross to get anywhere else in the village.

"...Only for another night," Leo says, his voice low. "Then he's sending the four of them out first, after we kill the Beast and blow open the Wall. Let them draw the worst of whatever's out there."

My body freezes mid-step as Tomris of the Cynane Guardian house—protectors of the village's north quadrant—comes into view, Leo at her side. It's only because of their nearness that I'm able to hear the details of their hushed conversation. I press farther into the wall, my shoulder and side screaming and my pulse pounding so loud I'm certain it will give me away as they station themselves mere feet from my location.

Tomris whispers her response. "Do you think Jarek's right? That our Founders were...tricked? That it's not that bad beyond the Wall? He seems so certain, but why found this place if not?"

Is that what he's telling the Guardians?

"I do not presume to question my leaders," Leo growls, silencing her. "But like I said, that's why it's good he's sending them out first. If he's wrong, they'll take the brunt of it."

They don't even glance my way as I slowly, silently inch farther down the building, until I'm on the opposite side from them. I take measured breaths to calm myself. Is it better to race across the exposed stretch or to walk at a leisurely pace, a simple Priest out doing my duty? I settle somewhere in between, my nerves grinding too hard to measure my steps. If anyone glances my way, they'll think I'm struggling with some sort of full-body cramp, but luck must be on my side because no one calls out before I reach the nearest alley's protection.

I make it another fifty feet before a second pair of patrolling Guardians forces me to dive between barrels stacked in front of the Coopers' relocated cottage. My heartbeat clobbers my ears, sweat gathering at my back.

The Guardians pass.

I stand, look both ways.

It's clear.

I sprint the remaining distance, diving into the library. I have no plan should I encounter someone. Fortunately, the room is—as usual—empty during working hours. I nudge the door closed behind me and scurry across the open floor, thanking my good luck too soon.

"Marina?" Simon calls out. "Bring me a sandwich from last night's meat if you're making yourself one."

My throat tightens. I glide across to the cellar door, pull out the key with shaking hands, and slide it into the keyhole. I twist, fully expecting it not to work. Instead, a delicate series of clicks floats like music by my ears. I turn the metal ring and pull. The door swings open. I manage to palm the key, step into the basement, and swing it nearly closed just as Simon Seingalt enters the library.

"Marina? Did you hear me?"

He's just visible through the crack. I'm too afraid to close it and draw his attention, so I hold my breath. He glances around the library, makes a frustrated huff, and disappears. I ease the door fully shut and drop onto the top stair. Time isn't on my side, but my pulse is racing too fast. I force it to calm, massaging my temples. My hand is halfway to my pocket before I remember that I gave Lucky Bunny to Meryl.

It's a good reminder of my mission's urgency. My friends are still trapped in the chapel basement, and according to Leo, they're going to be sent out as bait tomorrow. The villagers will be told blowing open the Wall is for our greater good, and they'll believe it, once Jarek shows them the carnivorous plant. Of course, he'll say he just discovered the thing. I stand, reaching for the switch I saw just before I closed the door. I flick it on, illuminating a row of bulbs leading deeper into the Seingalts' cellar. I pray the light isn't visible from outside.

I hear no footsteps and take that as a good sign.

"Here goes nothing," I whisper, heading down the wooden stairs.

I shake the cloak as I descend, releasing the chill of the morning and the perfume of chapel incense. The steps creak beneath my feet. I count seventeen of them, and then I'm standing on the basement floor.

It's made of stone like what's found in the chapel undercroft: one great unbroken slab. The vault sits across the room, the walls between choked with books and scrolls, carelessly jammed on shelves. A contraption of metal and tubes takes up the nearest corner. I sniff in its direction. Pruno. That's the smell always lingering around David. Next to it is another machine blowing out warm air.

The vault's metal door is slightly ajar. Rather than a knob, it has a plate-sized wheel on its face. Before going to it, I still, straining my ears for sounds of life. *Nothing.*

The door looks heavy. It's possible the Record Keeper simply chooses not to close it. The norms protecting this place—not to mention the lock at the top of the stairs—should be more than sufficient to keep out meddlers. Or maybe David's drinking has made him lazy. Whatever the reason the door has been left open, I'm grateful.

I creep forward, nearly silent in my soft goatskin shoes. I'm surprised by the lack of damp down here. Last night under the chapel, I'd grown used to the feel and smell of it. I decide that must be the purpose of the machine spitting out warm air beside the pruno still: to remove humidity from the air and preserve our sacred records. I pull on the wheel, needing to plant my feet to move the massive metal door.

I look inside. Squeeze my eyes shut and then open them. Do

it again. The vault is empty except for two items in its center: a pedestal as large as a kitchen table, an enormous, closed book resting on its surface. If it were stood upright on the ground, it would reach as high as my waist. Open, it must be longer than both my arms stretched wide.

A rope dangles over the center of the massive book, leading to a bare bulb. I pull on it, surprised to feel it's cool and smooth. The bulb glares to life, so bright that I must shield my eyes until they adjust. I see then that the "rope" is a string of tiny, metal balls of impressive uniformity, clearly from the Before Times. I return my attention to the book, running my hands across the leather binding, over letters etched so deeply I could have read them with my fingertips alone.

"Noah's Valley Correctional Institute" is stamped across its cover.

We are not what we seem.

55

The world tilts off its axis as I open the cover. The first page is as thin as lace, every word on it handwritten.

By agreement of the original prisoners, the information contained herein will become the private property of Noah's Valley Correctional Institute warden Helen Hayes, heretofore to be known as the Record Keeper. The Record Keeper will ensure that no one in the Valley can access this information unless deemed necessary for the community's survival. The true history of our origin dies with the first generation.

So sayeth we all.

Disbelief stipples my skin, icy pinpricks of unease.

Below that declaration are hundreds of signatures, curved and crammed all over the page, written in different-colored inks. Blue, black, even purple, all of them faded by time. Several are no clearer than chicken scratch, but others I can read.

Linda DuPree
JOLLY HENDRIX
Allen Johnson

I turn to the next page, scaring up the scent of dust and decay. This paper feels different than the previous page. It's thick and smooth, like an oak leaf. Whatever the material is, it's preserved the black ink so well that the words look like they are newly written.

Part I: The History of Noah's Valley

Panic scrapes at my tender edges. It's becoming difficult to breathe. An essay is pasted below the title, originally written for something called *The New York Times*. It's dated August 15th, 120 years ago.

Thanks to generous funding from TechnoSphere founder Arrow Korr, the Behavioral Realignment and Inheritance Study (BRAINS) is ready to accept its first 400 volunteers. This unique project in southeastern Minnesota, dubbed "Noah's Valley" by its founders, is the first in a planned series of experimental settlements designed to separate violent offenders from the general population.

Footsteps overhead reveal someone is moving through the Record Keeper cottage—Marina? Simon?—but I can't stop reading long enough to care. My heart beats a sick, thudding rhythm in my chest.

All 400 volunteers are serving multiple life sentences without the possibility of parole. Should the experiment succeed, however, Korr envisions similar facilities will be built to house lesser criminals, indigents, and migrants "more humanely" going forward.

The footsteps sound like they've entered the library.

To give the volunteers the best chance of rehabilitation, Korr's experts have constructed a walled agrarian society that minimizes prisoner stress. Basic burdens have been eliminated: each volunteer will be assigned a name, a spouse, a house, and a profession. Positive behaviors will be modeled and rewarded, with the Valley's legal, religious, and educational systems designed to promote radical equality, conformity, unity, and acceptance. Volunteers will be delivered inside the settlement with the requisite supplies and resources to survive in perpetuity. Then the insurmountable wall surrounding Noah's Valley will be sealed.

Korr opened up in an interview, admitting that it's bittersweet to begin a project he will never see completed, but that he is honored to offer "[his] fellow man a path to redemption." The biotech mogul was referring to the study's ultimate goal: that law enforcement officials will eventually declare the volunteers' descendants reformed, inviting them to return to our law-abiding society after five generations.

According to Korr, multigenerational confinement provides an ethical alternative to capital punishment that "ensures the offenders' worst tendencies are eradicated and the harm they caused fully repaired" before any descendants have their freedom.

The footsteps overhead stop.

While many support its mission, certain human rights advocates oppose the Valley initiative. One concern nearly halted the project in its infancy: who will free the fifth generation?

Korr amended the Valley's blueprint in response, adding "a concealed exit set to automatically open 120 years *from the official day of founding."* He hopes others will see the compromise as a gesture of good faith but is *"willing to bet our volunteers won't want to leave anyway. They'll have it better in there than most of us do out here."*

Other concerns raised include the risk of inter-prisoner violence, particularly given the severity of some qualifying offenses. When asked about the protocol should a volunteer need to be removed from the sealed experiment before the fifth generation, TechnoSphere's public relations director responded as follows:

"Safety is the most important thing to Mr. Korr. That's why Noah's Valley has guard stations positioned at even intervals throughout the community. Their warden—Dr. Helen Hayes—will be given an electronic tablet that enables outside communication, in addition to controlling a basket that removes volunteers, if necessary, to shelter atop the wall until they can be safely collected and returned to traditional incarceration."

The TechnoSphere PR team also had an answer for critics who raised alarms about the safety of southern Minnesotans. "For the security of the nearby environs (and in addition to the Valley's great wall), Arrow will be donating a multi-million-dollar Verdant Beast™ to guard the settlement."

The implementation of TechnoSphere's latest biodefense system was instrumental in fast-tracking DOC approval for this project, particularly given CEO Arrow Korr's newly appointed position as Secretary of Defense.

Korr assured the public of the experiment's safety, citing successful trials of the Verdant Beast™ in their corporate-owned testing facilities as proof of concept.

I feel as though I'm made of dust, one second from blowing away.
"A real kick in the pants, isn't it?"
I whip around to face the voice behind me.

56

David Seingalt bows as if the weight of the world rests on his shoulders.

"Our ancestors being criminals, that is." He stumbles over the word that Jarek had so comfortably levied against my friends and me. "All of them. Well, all of them but mine. As I'm sure you read, the Record Keeper was our warden."

My words sound far away. "Originally. We've all mixed since."

He leans toward me, his tone almost pleading. "You understand why I don't stand up to Jarek now, don't you?" His eyes drop. "It's in our blood to be evil. It's our destiny."

I'm spinning inside out, a meaningless Möbius strip of agony. The Valley wasn't built to shield us from the chaos of the outside world. It was founded to protect the outside world from *us*. But there's something more—another important truth the essay revealed. I can feel it, like something sharp lodged in my throat.

"If you keep turning pages," David says, rubbing his caterpillar mustache, "you'll find one devoted to each of the original prisoners. Name. Age. Crimes. There's some pretty gruesome stuff in there. A handful who tortured their victims, some mass murderers, and can you believe they recruited a cannibal to the Leatherworker House?" He laughs at that, though it's utterly humorless.

No, no, no, this cannot be. Lillian Allgood, the descendant of a cold-blooded killer? Sweet Jonas, sharing DNA with a monster?

"Helen Hayes wasn't the only warden. She was assisted by a second, someone called Rodriquez. They took notes for the first couple of years together," David continues. "It was rough. For the volunteers, that is. Adjusting. A few had to be removed, but most did not. Against all odds, they managed to foster a healthy community.

"Then communication with the outside world stopped suddenly. Rodriquez took the basket up the Wall to investigate." He blinks, frowning. "He never returned."

I think of our chapel. Our place of spiritual refuge. Was its bell tower designed as a lookout, a vantage point from which to guard our ancestors? The sharp, slippery truth contained in the essay starts to surface again, but I still can't grip it. The second I think I have it, it spins away.

David keeps talking. "Hayes thought something terrible must have happened beyond the Wall. Figured they'd forgotten about everyone inside. How scary must that have been? Trapped here with a village full of murderers, the world outside gone dark." He shakes his head at the horror of it. "She decided their best chance at survival was to form a new society for real. No wardens and guards versus criminals, no 'us' separate from 'them.' Just people." He sings the last word. "As you surely read, they agreed the truth of their crimes would die with that first generation." He chuckles. It sounds like bone dice clicking. "Honestly, they were probably happy to do it. After the original prisoners died off, only the Record Keeper House would hold the truth of who they'd been."

I groan as I finally recall what was missing from the text. "The Harvest wasn't mentioned."

David reads my mind, his voice going hoarse. "Blood was always the price of the Verdant Beast's protection. That thing's a carnivore, plain and simple. Perhaps it would have been unpopular to mention at the time." He shrugs. "But Hayes knew it needed monthly feedings. She writes about it in her private record, says that's why we have to Harvest."

The Verdant Beast hunting us wasn't an accident. *It was a feature*. The cruelty is staggering. "Did the volunteers know?"

He doesn't break eye contact. "A few may have guessed, but I have no evidence of them being told."

"But *you* knew," I hiss.

He holds up his hands. "Since only very recently. Not even a year."

"You knew, and you allowed villagers to be sent up there to be eaten alive." The image of my twin, body mangled and drained of blood, forces me to my knees on the cold stone floor. I barely register the pain. "Oh, Jackrabbit," I whisper, aching deep in my soul.

"It's better to lose a few than the many. Their sacrifices protect us all," he tries to reassure me.

I lunge for him, forcing the old drunkard back and out of the vault. He barely catches himself on the rough-hewn wall, the weight of his body lacerating his hand against it. David's blood drips from the wound.

And I feel no desire to treat it.

"Protect?" I bark. I'm thinking back to the two Guardians we lost eight months ago, the ones killed before my eyes just yesterday. Jonas's face morphs to Peter's in my head. "That monster is *hunting* us."

David studies his hand. The bare light makes his eyes glitter. "It's too hungry," he acknowledges. "Hayes was worried that might happen. That's why she brought herbicide in here, one that Arrow Korr didn't know about. Apparently, he was very protective of the Verdant Beasts. I discovered it by accident when I found her panic room. She housed all sorts of things she'd need if things went south—food stores, weapons, even vanity items like a full-length mirror." David rubs his nose. "After the first unplanned death, I decided to use her herbicide. It worked, too, for a while."

That means David, not Jarek, was behind the poisoning of our water. It takes all my willpower not to punch him in the throat. Sure, I saw his footprints at the well, but the senseless, trusting girl in me had assumed good faith. *To be betrayed by your own Record Keeper...*

"Six lives lost to the Vex." I spit. "And you're responsible for each and every one of them."

"You're right, I'm afraid." David shudders, obvious guilt twisting his features. "I told Jarek the truth about everything—the Verdant Beast, the panic room, and the poison I'd discovered inside it—after the Beast killed those first two Guardians eight months ago, which I regret. Jarek really believed an animal had killed his comrades, and he never would have poured the herbicide at its roots if I hadn't told him the truth. He believed in the poison longer than me, forcing our Chemists to recreate it. I'm certain that's the reason for their self-Harvest. I gave him the last of Reatha's brew the other day, so I suppose we'll see soon enough who was right."

"But he plans to open the Wall whether or not the last of the poison kills the Verdant Beast." I phrase it like fact, though really I'm still guessing.

"He plans to try," David says, confirming the terrible truth. "He's become obsessed with the hidden chamber, all the Before Times treasures and weapons inside. He wants more."

Gryphon was right. His father means to go Beyond.

"And it's only a matter of time until he succeeds," David continues. "In the meantime, we're trapped in here like livestock." He's watching me process what I've learned. "It's not a prison until you need to escape, is it?" he asks.

Words rattle around my skull, down my throat and back, but they can't find my mouth. I think I might be sick.

"I see you burning to fix this, Rose. Your mother was the same way. You'll soon realize, as I have, that it's best to go quietly. We all end up in the same place, just some of us with fewer bruises." He pulls a flask from his pocket and drinks, wiping his mouth on the back of his sleeve. "Jarek has too much power and a taste for rare delights. He'll not go back to hardworking days and cricket stew, not now that he believes there's a better way to live."

I step closer, into the sour smell of pruno radiating off him. We have a lot of problems here, but one's more urgent than the rest. "Jarek is mad with power, David. If he blows a hole in the Wall, we have no idea what might come through. You say the world went dark a hundred years ago and that the Wardens never found out why. If that's true, the Verdant Beast is the least of our worries." *I mean, holy Wall, it might even be protecting us from something worse.* I take a deep breath, collecting all my scant confidence, and add, "We have to stop him. For the Valley."

David's face sharpens at that. "Stop Jarek? The two of us?"

Thoughts are crashing into each other. "It's not just the two of us. There are others. With you on our side, we stand a chance. You're still the Record Keeper. You're still in charge of our rules."

He shakes his head sadly, gesturing toward his disheveled state, his foot still cast in plaster. It satisfies me now to realize it probably wasn't an animal trap that got him, that his limb was more likely crushed by the Verdant Beast.

"Look at me, Rose," he says. "Who's going to follow this man?"

I grab his shirt. "If we tell them the truth about Jarek, *everyone*! With him gone, we can have a clean start within. We'll avoid Eden's Gate until we find a way to destroy the Beast, and once we're safe again, we'll review all the Valley's laws, hang on to the ones that work and reconsider the rest. Without the Guardians in your way, you could make it happen!"

I'm talking too fast. I think I may have lost him when suddenly his face lights up. "You really think we can stop Jarek?"

I nod.

To my surprise, David chuckles. "He's not too smart, you know? Strong, certainly, good at forming an army. Clever, even."

He indicates a stack of books, their covers garish and unfamiliar. "According to one of these, it's the sneaky leader you have to watch out for. The show-off, obvious brute who has nothing but strength on his side?" The Record Keeper grins, having made up his mind. "He can be defeated."

I match his smile, feeling instantly lighter. With the Record Keeper of all people on our side, we may be able to defeat Jarek without destroying the tablet and basket, meaning I could return to the Valley with Jonas. Even if he's no longer alive, I can bring his body back down.

The Verdant Beast cannot have my brother.

Suddenly, I remember something David glossed over. "The secret room. The vault with the new weapons." I speak with a voice that brooks no argument, one I wouldn't dare have used against him just a week ago. "Show it to me."

Annoyance flashes across David's face, but he must sense that I won't be backing down today. He slides his thumb into a nearly invisible indent inside the closest bookcase. "I tripped the mechanism by accident," he says. "Hayes hid it well. That woman thought of everything." He says the last bit with a puff of pride.

I'm about to remind him that he may not even be a blood relative to Hayes, given our marrying rules, when the case swings open, revealing a room nearly as large as the full cottage above.

My jaw drops. *Sun and Soil, just how big is this place?*

Before he can stop me, I step inside. The walls are lined with shelves, overflowing with tools I don't understand and more types of food than I recognize. I walk over to them, marveling at the sheer volume of stuff left over, even with David and the Guardians pillaging the Warden's supply. I spy an enormous metallic container labelled "canned ham." I do not know what ham is, but the unnervingly realistic painting on its face looks just like the loaf of pink meat the Tzus served us the other night.

"It has everything but an exit," David says. "Nearly a hundred twenty years to the day since the Valley's founding, and Korr said that we'd open to the world by then. But if there's a door, I haven't seen it." His voice grows heavy. "I'm sorry, Rose. But I think it's one more lie he told the public."

My eyes scour the shelves. *I'm looking for what, exactly?* Weapons I can use to save my brother. Plus any herbicide Jarek hasn't already taken. Unfortunately for me, the combat items are picked clean. I see only food and tools and a singular patch of goblin's gold on the floor on the far side of the room. The luminous moss is typically found in caves—Mom had the Stonemasons collect it from the quarry sometimes for its microbial properties.

I turn toward David. "It doesn't change anything," I say.

"What?"

"This secret room." I indicate the stores lining the walls. "It doesn't matter that it's here, or even that there is no exit. What matters is that we stop Jarek and kill the Verdant Beast." With a sinking feeling, I see I've already lost him. In the last couple minutes, the fire that'd momentarily sprung into his eyes has been snuffed out. "David?"

He takes another swig of pruno. "I need some time alone. To think."

"But—"

"Give me time," he barks, clearly ready for me to leave.

I've used up all my goodwill. Now I can only pray that I've convinced him. I follow David's lead as he weaves back to the main chamber, toward his pruno contraption, and fills up his flask. I worry he's going to drink himself into a stupor, but short of tying him up and destroying the still, I don't know what I can do but hope he comes through for us. I consider seeking out the other two Councilmembers—Alexandra and Nero—but think better of it. They were fine covering up Peter's cause of death and have been accomplices to Jarek's sudden and oppressive changes to Valley law. The only person I can truly trust is myself.

Or maybe not. After all, we're descended from monsters here. *Cannibals. Murderers.*

I'm halfway up the stairs when David calls out to me, his voice unbearably weary. "You'll be hungry to tell the others what you discovered down here," he says. "How we're the spawn of evildoers, doomed to wither on the tendrils of a vine. You'll burn to share this heaviness with someone, *anyone*. Learn from me, Rose. Don't tell anyone. It'll only make them as miserable as you are right now."

57

So sing me a story, dear, I'm down on my knees,
Praying to Heaven, bring me back, please.

So sleep, my darling, don't you be scared,
The Wall made us whole, love, and so we were spared.

The village's childhood lullaby, passed down from grandparents to grandbabies, is not a sweet family song, but rather the prison lament of those serving a multi-generational life sentence.

This place is not perfection, it's a prison.

My ancestors weren't brave settlers. They weren't even Founders. They were depraved killers, exiled from society. And we, their descendants, are dying at the hands of the very Beast designed to guard them. My world is shattered. A sticky bleakness crawls in through my mouth, my nostrils, my pores, gagging me. I don't have the presence of mind to avoid Guardians, so it's good I don't encounter any as I blunder toward the only comfort I know: the Apothecary cottage.

Gran is seated in her chair by the fire when I spill inside. I stagger over, dropping at her feet, and spew everything I've learned. I considered David's warning about inflicting this burden on others, but I won't keep his secret. Gran wouldn't want me to. She pats my head as I talk, letting me choke it out. She doesn't speak until I have no more words or tears.

"Is that all, Rosie?"

I lift my head from her lap, swiping at my nose. "What do you mean, is that all? Our ancestors were *monsters*!" Poor Jonas. This is what he'd seen in the vault, it must be, and he'd had to shoulder it alone.

Gran's face creases with pity. I don't understand. But then I do.

"You knew?" I ask.

"Yes." She rubs my head one last time before reaching for her mug of tea. "A handful of my generation know. Or did, before Jarek or old age took us. We had a Record Keeper in our day not much smarter than Simon." Her mouth twitches. "She told someone she wanted to impress that the Valley was started as a prison colony, and it wasn't long until a handful of us found out."

I can't believe how calm she is. "It didn't bother you?"

"Shush," she says, pursing her lips. "We are what *we* do, not what our ancestors did."

I blink. This is not going at all how I expected. "But they were murderers. They tortured people!"

She grimaces. "I'll grant you the original settlers did dreadful things, based on what I've heard." She tips my chin back, so I'm forced to look her in the eye. "But within the Wall, they couldn't avoid one another. They had to figure out how to work together. They had Circling, and dinner swaps, and barn buildings, and Story Time, and all the other wonderful ways we know to live in community. Many would have considered them impossible to rehabilitate—maybe I would have, too, if I hadn't seen this place—but they managed to do it for themselves. Isn't the fact that we haven't had a single murder inside the Wall, not by the original prisoners *or* their descendants, until your mother was killed, proof that we are not our history?"

"Killed by Jarek."

"Maybe so, but it's because we failed him first," she says, echoing what Augustus told me. "If he broke the social contract, he'll need to atone for it. But we broke it, too, especially my generation, who looked away when he was young and needing."

My skepticism must be written on my face, because she cups my cheek and continues. "Dear Rosie, I know it's so much to take in. I've had a lifetime to reason with this knowledge, but I was just as scared as you when I first found out. I want you to come to your own conclusions, my love. I mean that. But if you'll spare an old woman her pulpit for just a moment longer, I'll tell you how I came to see it. I've never been able to talk so freely before."

Because I cannot bring myself to quash the spark in her voice, I nod.

Gran smiles, the creases around her mouth deepening. "I believe we're at a turning point in the Valley. Everything we've worked so hard to build for the past five generations is in peril. We have a lot to own up to, but there are more people than you know on the side of good. True good. They just need someone to organize, to rally around in this moment." Her eyes soften. "If you choose it, I believe that someone could be you."

My laugh surprises me. "Who would follow me? I don't exactly have a reputation for rebellion around here."

Gran shakes her head, and the small effort clearly drains her. "Not follow you. *Trust you.* And your loyalty is exactly why they would!" I hear in her voice that she truly believes it, though I can't bring myself to share her faith. But she's not done.

"Within the Wall, we don't have rulers," she says. "Or at least, we didn't use to. Everything worth doing, we did in community. Tell me, Rose." Her voice is growing thin, reedy. I know her energy is almost up. "How'd you get here? To the Apothecary cottage, right now, when you're meant to be locked and guarded beneath the chapel?"

I rub my temples, trying to keep a throbbing headache at bay. Gryphon came for me. Oscar, Meryl, Eero, and Sal made me go, even though I wanted to stay with them. Then Sojourner lent me her cloak and helped me slip out through the back door of her office. It is a lot of people, when I lay it out like that, but what do they expect of me?

"My friends helped," I finally answer. It's true. Moreover, it's what Gran hoped to hear.

Her resulting smile is interrupted, body suddenly racked with coughs. I jump to my feet, making sure her throat is clear before gently rubbing her back. When she's able to breathe again, I rush to get her water. She takes a few sips, but she's so weak. She's unable to talk anymore.

I prop her up with a pillow, making sure the fire is fed and her pain tonic in reach. When I ask her if she wants me to stay, she waves me away. I fear she's hanging on just for me. I can't let her down, but I have no idea what it looks like to succeed.

I pull Gran's blanket up around her neck, kiss her forehead, and step outside. Voices to my right startle me, so I tug up my red hood and hurry back the way I came.

I reach the chapel just as the bells start to ring.

58

Sojourner is waiting at her private exit door. She tugs me in, grabs her cloak, and ushers me back to the main chapel, where Gryphon is pacing.

"Welcome back," he says loudly. "I missed you."

The Guardian monitoring the basement stairs has been joined by another. They're engaged in a heated game of dice, all but ignoring us.

It's good because I can't play along, can't act like we're two kids in love, can't pretend that anything is all right or ever will be again. Gryphon dips his chin to the Head Priest, then takes me in his charge, leading us outside.

"Are you okay?" he asks, his voice low and concerned.

Our whole world is a lie.

"I'm fine." It's all I can manage.

"What did you see in the vault?"

I shake my head once, abruptly. I can't bring myself to tell him.

Rather than pressure me, he rubs my back in a surprisingly tender move before drawing himself upright. The village is going about its regular business—deliveries being made, people working in their cottages—but it feels like everyone's spying on us. Narrowed gazes, whispering lips. Gryphon leans close and throws an arm around my waist, careful to keep it just below my stitches.

We'll look affectionate to anyone watching. They won't know he's holding me upright.

"I'm bringing you back to our cottage," he says, pitching his voice low so only I can hear, "but I have to tell you something first. About my father." Gryphon takes a deep breath before admitting, "Rose, he intends to go beyond the Wall."

If I look surprised, it's only because I'm still reeling from what I learned inside the Record Keeper vault. "Oh?"

"I know," Gryphon soothes. Solemn, misinterpreting. I don't correct him. "But there's no need to worry. I know how to stop him without anyone else getting hurt."

"By destroying the explosives, tablet, and Harvest basket before Jarek can use them?"

He falters mid-stride, mouth dropping open like a pitcher plant. I feel a sudden and unexpected loss, knowing I'll never view my own carnivorous rootlings the same way again.

"Yeah, Rose." Gryphon blinks several times. "That's actually weirdly…"

I glance at my old friend sideways, feeling an unexpected burst of pleasure amidst all the traumas. Gryphon always seems so serious, so carefully in control. I've grieved these normal, human moments between us. "Thanks," I say. "I just came up with it."

I can practically hear his gears turning. I decide to put the Guardian out of his misery. "I'm pulling your leg," I admit, touching his arm lightly. "I already knew about your dad. And Oscar and I discussed that plan earlier."

To my surprise, he starts chuckling, and then so do I. For a precious moment, we're kids again.

"I missed your laugh, Rosie."

My mouth snaps closed, my heartbeat hammering. He hasn't called me by the familiar version of my name since before the betrothal ceremony. I want to keep the connection going between us. I'm not ready to tell him about our ancestors, but I can share this: "I think David Seingalt's on our side."

Gryphon's eyes flash, sharp again. "I don't trust a man who is more interested in collecting cans of beans than he is in fulfilling duties, but I won't get in his way if he wants to help." His jaw tightens. "My father must be stopped. Removing his access to the outside world is the way."

I feel another surge of tenderness toward Gryphon. He's in an untenable position. As much as he hates Jarek, he obviously still craves the man's respect, if not his love. In this way, our parents brand themselves on our skin, for good or ill. We've almost reached the Tzu house. "I agree. And we put an end to Harvests."

A boy from the Beekeeping House watches us from his cottage door. Is he eavesdropping? Looking for someone to turn in so he can claim his two tins of fish?

This is how Jarek continues to poison us.

Gryphon nods. "Agreed. The tablet will be easy enough for us to get to, and without it, the basket is useless. Our focus has to be destroying the explosives in the training barn."

Something occurs to me. "We need the Record Keeper to testify to the other villagers that there *were* weapons in the first place." I think back to David's sad face in the basement, his shame at the choices he's made. I have to believe he'll do the right thing when given the chance. "But we can't wait to destroy them. If we're going to do it, we need to get to them tonight. I—"

My sentence is cut short by Jarek charging out of his house, his face purple with rage. Instantly, Gryphon steps in front of me.

"You KNOW you're not allowed to guard her!" Jarek grabs his son by the shirt and pins him against the cottage wall, his forearm pressed against Gryphon's neck. It's the exact move Gryphon recently taught us all how to escape, yet he doesn't execute the maneuver that would free him. If Jarek had any trust left in his son, it's gone, and still, Gryphon will not fight him.

Misia rushes out of the house at the commotion. She appears for a moment like she wants to pull Jarek off her son, but ultimately, she just stands by. Jarek has them both under his thumb, though Misia is no innocent.

"Practicing family togetherness, I see," I say, channeling Salvatora. "Shall I go inside and make us lunch, or do none of you trust me with a knife?"

Jarek glances over, his expression making clear he wouldn't mind trading out Gryphon for me against that wall. Instead, he grinds his forearm into his son's neck a little harder—enough that Gryphon's face drains of blood—before he releases him. Then he strides over to me, fury radiating. I can't believe he's leaving his back open. Then again, I suppose he knows his son poses no threat. I wonder what it will take for Gryphon to finally stand up to his father.

"Misia will be watching you," Jarek snarls into my face, so near that flecks of spittle land on my cheeks. When I make no response, he spins on his heel. "Gryphon, you and Leonidas are on perimeter patrol. We have traitors in our midst. We must flush them out."

Another snipe hunt for Gryphon. I'm almost impressed at how completely his father is committing to the traitor story, keeping it up behind the scenes when he knows we know the lie of it. I suppose, in a way, Jarek truly believes what he's saying. Not that anyone besides him is hoarding food and weapons, but I bet anyone who doesn't enthusiastically follow him looks like a traitor from where he's sitting.

To those who choose darkness, light is the enemy.

"See you later," I tell Gryphon. I suddenly feel drunk with terrible knowledge, high on hopelessness.

"You will not," Misia says, bristling. "You'll be confined to your room, alone. It's only proper the night before your wedding."

"Little late for that," I snort.

I don't know where my impudence is coming from, but I don't hate it, either. They've already lied to me and imprisoned me. Whipped my friends and killed my mother and Harvested my brother. The least I deserve is a bit of rebellion. My boldness seems to alarm Gryphon, though. He glides around his father and steps up to me, his hand soft on my cheek. He leans toward my ear, breath sweet and sizzling.

"Trust," he says, "and don't do anything reckless." He lingers a moment longer than etiquette allows, breathing in the scent of me. Then he walks away with his father, leaving me weak-kneed. I'm not sure who or what I'm meant to trust, but I'll give him this: his delivery is excellent.

"Inside," Misia orders.

"I need to use the bathroom." It's the truth. I can't remember the last time I went.

Misia appears ready to argue but instead leads us both to the rear of the cottage, electing to wait outside the door like she's worried I'll bolt. Two Guardians are stationed at the base of the ladder leading to the rooftop charging station. Are they protecting it from my friends, locked up in the chapel basement? Seems unlikely. I recall what Gran said about more people being on the side of right than I know, think of Uncle Richard's "we" breaking us out of jail.

Well, I wish those folks would show themselves.

I use the toilet, then wash my face and hands. I also strip the dirty bandages off my stitches and the cut on my shoulder and gently wash the tender flesh. They're both still free of the heat of infection. I dig through the assortment of shampoos, soaps, and scents I'd prepared just days earlier—though it feels like a lifetime—until I find the little pot of balm I'd tucked away. Past Rose gets a star for her foresight, though at the time I assumed I'd need it for Gryphon's injuries, not my own. I slather my wounds with fresh salve and manage to apply clean bandages before Misia starts pounding on the door and telling me that either I'm coming out or she's coming in.

I choose the former.

Back inside the cottage, I'm allowed a quick meal of cold porridge and then it's straight to the bedroom, where I'm left alone with my thoughts. They all lead to the same place: Jonas might be alive, waiting for me, and I must get to him. He might be dead, prey to our supposed protector, and still I must get to him. We also have to find a way to stop Jarek *and* the Verdant Beast. Maybe now that I finally know everything we're up against, Mom's journal will reveal clues I couldn't have seen before. I reach under the mattress for it, but my fingertips brush empty air. My heart plummets. I check again.

It's gone.

Heart thudding, I walk to the wardrobe.

Gryphon's sketches are also no longer here.

They've stripped us of what gives us hope.

After I change into clean clothes and rebind my hair into its buns, all that's left to do is pace the room: door, cupboard, bed, desk. Door, cupboard, bed, desk. My thoughts are black. Occasionally, noises draw me to the window. Guardians hassling someone to get back to their duties. Carpenters putting the final touches on an enormous construction just beyond my line of sight. Popping sounds that remind me of the flash bangs—more training for blowing up the Wall?

Jarek will doom us all.

Forty some-odd Guardians against the unknowable force that brought down our Founders' world? It'll be carnage. How time has flipped our roles—it's us inside who now need protection from what's out there, rather than the other way around. In that way, we aren't too different than I always thought...and I guess that's what Gran meant.

Door, cupboard, bed, desk. Door, cupboard, bed, desk.

The confinement is making my skin crawl. I wonder who has

my mother's journal. I refuse to believe it's Jarek, because Mom would hate that. Perhaps one of his lackeys, then. Maybe even the one who searched our greenhouse the day I found it. *Good luck decoding it*, I huff.

Hours of pacing crescendos into something like a hypnotic trance. With it come memories of my father braiding my hair, images so clear that I reach out for him. Jonas trying to tell me a joke, pealing with laughter before he ever reaches the punchline. My mother singing, her voice lavender honey.

Eventually, I collapse on the bed. I think I don't sleep, but when I startle awake, it's pitch-black out. I blink, my wounds throbbing and my legs tight. I massage my calves, oddly furious with myself. I've been waiting for a sign to spur my destiny.

There has only ever been me.

Steal Jarek's explosives. Ascend the Wall. Find my brother.

Destroy the Verdant Beast.

It starts now.

59

I'm halfway down the stairs when Misia calls out from the kitchen. "That better not be you showing your face."

"I'd like some tea," I say, not slowing. "I can't sleep."

She's seated at the kitchen table, cleaning her fingernails with a dagger. Again, I think how lonely she must be. She doesn't even have the comfort of books.

"If you drink tea, you'll just need to use the bathroom," she says.

"I'll pee in a bucket."

She doesn't stop me because I don't give her a chance to. I stride to the stove and move the teapot to the front before bustling to the cupboard, reaching for the jar of dried peppermint leaves and a tea ball. I stuff the aromatic mint into the ball and then drop it into a mug. It feels like a million ants crawling beneath my clothes to behave normally, but I can't rush out the door past her. She wouldn't hesitate to plunge that knife into some part of me that would be invisible beneath a wedding dress.

"I can make tea for you, too," I say, aiming for nonchalance.

She chuckles. "I don't trust you, little cook, not since your porridge sentenced Jarek and me to the shitter."

Good. It did get Jarek. I hadn't been sure.

"Suit yourself," I say. "Have you seen the honey?"

She huffs. "You're the one who rearranged my kitchen."

I make a show of rustling through all the cupboards, finally locating the honeypot exactly where I'd put it. "Here it is!" I hold it up. "You sure you don't want any?"

She's gone back to cleaning her fingernails. "Positive."

This is as good a chance as I'll get. My back to her, I open the jar of Veronal crystals—the sleep aid provided by the Chemist—that I'd found when I first cleaned the kitchen. I've only ever injected the drug as an anesthetic, one all Apothecaries keep primed in their kits in case of emergencies. Too much can stop a heart, but I don't know what an overdose looks like in crystal form. I tip a small spoonful into the mug—a dose I'm reasonably confident won't kill her—followed by a healthy measure of honey.

The teapot screams, making me jump. I nearly drop the Veronal jar but manage to keep my grip on it. I reach for the hot water and pour it over the crystals and honey, dissolving both. I use a spoon to stir the drink, the green-brown of the mint already seeping out of the ball. Screwing the cap back on the remaining crystals, I tuck them and the honeypot into their cupboard.

"Is that mint?" Misia asks.

"Yep," I say, turning to lean against the counter. I hold the steaming cup to my nose and close my eyes in pleasure. I silently thank the Sun, Soil, and Water that Veronal has no medicinal odor. Then I feel a jolt as I wonder if we were taught to worship those things because they—along with our bodies—feed the Verdant Beast. "Too hot to drink, though."

"Add some cool water," Misia suggests.

The tenderness in her voice unsettles me, but I command myself to act normal. I turn away from her and top off the mug.

"My mom used to brew me mint tea with honey when I had a bellyache," Misia says, her voice lighter than I've ever heard it. "Sometimes I pretended my stomach hurt just to get some."

Misia, as a little girl. With a mother who surely loved her. Is her mom still alive in the village, I wonder? What House would produce a Misia? I turn back to face her. Lean against the counter again. Take a sip of the drugged tea.

Misia watches me, something like affection softening her cheeks. "I always wanted a daughter, you know. It's probably best I didn't get one. She'd have been a piece of work, just like you."

Piece of work. I poisoned the woman with slippery elm. I'm surprised with a burst of something that feels like fondness for her.

"Here," Misia says, holding out her hand. "Give me some of that."

I offer her the mug. She downs half of it before handing it back.

"That's delicious," she says. "The perfect temperature, just the right amount of honey. Exactly like my mother used to make. You're excellent in a kitchen, Rose. It's a shame about your nasty habit of poiso—" Her face hits the table before she can get the last bit out, but I think I know where she was headed.

I pivot to the sink and spit out the Veronal-laced tea I'd been holding and then rinse my mouth with water. I check Misia's pulse. It's steady, but the drug has only started to hit her bloodstream. I don't have the luxury of monitoring her, though.

I grab my cloak and slip into the night.

60

"Took you long enough," Oscar says, separating from the shadows.

My stomach somersaults as four others emerge.

Sal, Meryl, Eero, and...Lozen?

My fists fly up, ready to fight, but Sal steps in front of me. "She's with us," she says. Then she hugs me as fiercely as our wounds allow. It takes me a moment to recover from my surprise, and then I'm returning the embrace. I try to pull away, but she holds me for a moment longer.

"We need to get out of here," Lozen whispers. Her hand is hovering over her sword hilt, and she's glancing uneasily toward the square.

"We're following *her* now?" I ask the others.

"Have to," Oscar says. "She broke us out. Plus, she brought the bombs."

Meryl holds up a canvas sack that looks like it's full of potatoes. A tiny grin plays across her lips. "Gryphon said he could buy us an hour, maybe more. We do this in two stages. Step one, we destroy all the stockpiled weapons inside the training barn and get back to where we're expected to be—you to Gryphon's, us to the chapel basement—before they notice we're missing."

"And step two?" I ask, wondering what barely camouflaged

torment Misia is going to inflict on me once she wakes up and realizes I've poisoned her twice.

"Step two is tomorrow night." Sal's eyes spark in the moonlight. "Augustus says he's gathering the villagers he trusts to overwhelm Jarek. Once they do, we can fight the green beast. All of us. Together."

"Noah's Valley, united again!" Oscar whoops quietly.

I blink rapidly, ordering the tears to stay in my eyes, but it's no use. I've finally found my fellowship. Too bad I've got less than a day left with them.

"If you don't mind weeping later," Lozen says, her tone unimpressed, "this is sorta time sensitive."

I swipe at my face. "Sorry."

"Here," Meryl says, slipping Lucky Bunny into my hand. "Maybe this'll help."

I don't want to admit how happy I am to see the wooden toy, but my fresh wave of tears tells on me.

"He helped me out of that awful basement," Meryl says, "but he was very clear he wants to return to you."

As long as you're exchanging gifts"—Lozen peers around a corner, watching for Guardians—"someone give her a cloak."

"I've got one," I say, tucking Lucky Bunny into my pocket.

"Not like this, you don't." Oscar yanks his hood over his head. The cloth is sewn to look so much like night and stone that if I hadn't been staring straight at him, I would have thought he disappeared. He tugs his hood back down and grins, handing me my own. "I sewed these months ago, back when we started training. Thought they might come in handy. Of course, if I'd known they'd be lying across our bloody shoulders, I might have gone for a lighter fabric."

"Quit bragging," Lozen hisses, leading us away from the Tzu house as I don the cloak. She's got an uncanny eye for keeping to the dark spots. "So, who knows where the Guardian training grounds are?"

"Me," I say, keeping my voice low to match hers. I call up a rough image of the route Gryphon took me on. "Mostly. But aren't we just following you?"

"With luck," she whispers, holding up a fist indicating we should stop. Leo crosses in front, a few feet away. If not for Oscar's smartly crafted cloaks, I'd bet the greenhouse he would've noticed us. Lozen counts to five fingers, starting with her thumb. When her pinkie pops up, we begin moving again. "But if we get separated, someone still needs to reach the barn and destroy the rest of the explosives. This mission is too important."

She leads us to the edge of the village unseen. A broad expanse separates us from the cover of the woods. If we make it to the forest, we're home free. *It's dark enough that we can do this*, I think. A split second later, a pregnant moon bursts through the clouds, illuminating the ground.

It's all I can do not to groan.

"When I say go," Lozen says in a low voice, "you go. Be as noiseless as you can, but don't sacrifice quick for quiet. Got that?"

We nod, but she isn't looking at us. She's staring at the open field. Her shoulders bunch up, like she's about to take off.

Then, "Who goes there?"

All five of us glue ourselves to the side of the building. I can't be the only one whose knees have suddenly turned to water.

"I said, who is that?" Tomris appears to our left, about thirty feet away. She's shining a torch down the alleyways, working her way toward us. "Identify yourself!"

We're done for. If we move a single inch, she'll grab that whistle around her neck and blow. We'll have a half-dozen Guardians surrounding us in under a minute. If we stay put, we're only seconds away from her exposing us with her torchlight.

"Over here!" Leonidas calls out from behind her.

"You find them?" Tomris hollers back.

"Yeah," he says, his voice sounding weird, like he's being strangled.

I turn to Meryl, intending to hug her in relief, but her face is screwed up.

"Hurry!" Leonidas says. Except it's not Leonidas. It's Meryl throwing her voice in a near-perfect imitation of him.

Her Entertainer House training has saved us.

When Tomris marches in the opposite direction, we dash across the open field, loamy grass perfuming the crisp night air. Stumps of harvested hay swallow our footfalls, and in no time, we're safe inside the forest.

Lozen counts heads, then, "Good. Here's where we split up."

"No way!" Oscar protests.

"Yes way," Lozen says, firmly. "We need a failsafe. The only option is to make two teams. Meryl and Oscar, you're with me. Sal and Eero, you go with Rose. We'll divide the explosives." She tugs two objects out of Meryl's bag and holds them up in the shadowy moonlight. The first is a ball of metal the size of an apple. "These explosives are deadly and effective, so don't take risks with your safety. Thankfully, even you nerds would struggle to set one off on accident. Pay attention." She points at a depression in the metal orb's side. "Two people touch the bomb here to activate it. Once it's planted, you *both* have to press the thumbprint detonator"—here she holds up a black square with a red button at its center—"for it to go off."

I shake my head in wonder. Brown-nose Rose, learning how to set a bomb.

Lozen drops the explosive and detonator back into Meryl's bag. "Whichever team reaches the training barn first places their bombs. Get at *least* three hundred feet away before you set them off. That's about a minute's walk. But don't walk it."

"I still don't understand why we have to separate." Oscar sounds worried, and who can blame him?

But Lozen only rolls her eyes. "If both teams end up at the barn safe and sound, I'll apologize, okay?"

"It's fine," Meryl says. "She's just being cautious, and she's right. This is our only chance to get rid of Jarek's stockpile."

Lozen nods grimly. "Oscar, Meryl, and I will follow the west path to the training grounds. Rose, Eero, and Sal take the east. First group to reach the barn and lay their explosives, whistle like this." She blows out three quick chirps. "If you're answered with the same, that means the other team is too close. Count to twenty before you set off your explosives. If you hear nothing, you're in the clear. Blow that building sky-high and return to this spot. Got it?" She smiles, holding out her fist.

We put our hands on top of hers, pushing down, then up.

"Got it," we whisper.

Lozen offers me four explosives plus a detonator. I stuff them into the deep pockets lining the cloak's interior. Oscar's really created a marvel.

We're about to break into two groups when Eero whispers, "This one's for Jonas."

We all hear him. My heart squeezes.

"For Jonas," we solemnly confirm.

61

Sal, Eero, and I hurry through the forest. Without needing to speak, the three of us pause at the lip of the training field, staying to our cover. The woods are eerily quiet. All the Guardians must be in the village, maintaining martial law for Jarek. Even so, the empty training field drenched in moonlight makes the hair along my arms stand up.

I squeeze Eero and Sal's hands. They twitch, then nod. I touch my chest and point at the west side of the barn, Sal and the east side, then Eero and the lookout hill fifty feet ahead. Next, I twirl two fingers and point at the ground, indicating we should meet back here. They nod again. I hand Sal two of the explosive devices and keep the other two for myself; together, we press a finger into the depression of each to activate them. Sticking to our cover, we dash around the perimeter of the training ground until we reach the storage barn.

She drops an explosive at the southeast corner. I run in the opposite direction and do the same at the building's southwest edge. I glance back at the lookout hill and tell myself I can see Eero's outline. Then I nestle my second explosive in the northwest corner.

I can't see Sal, but I trust she's completed her job. I'm immensely grateful she cannot discharge the bombs without me.

That means it's safe for me to run inside the barn and grab a few explosives to use on the Verdant Beast before we destroy Jarek's stash.

I'm relieved to find the two-panel door is unlocked. I slip inside, allowing myself half a breath to get my bearings.

I hear a scratching sound.

I gulp, cold skittering down my spine.

My gaze travels to the animal pens that line the opposite side of the building. Ugly-looking hooks hang from the ceiling, but the stalls are empty.

Where did the noise come from?

"Hello?" I whisper. I wait a beat. When I hear nothing in response, I decide I imagined it. I've already wasted precious seconds. I drop to my knees before the weapons horde, shoveling a handful of explosives into the gap of my cloak's inner lining. It's weighted as I rise, a leaden mantle. I race toward the exit and back into the silvery moonlight, closing the door behind me. Now I only have to hurry to the rendezvous spot, and Sal, Eero, and I can destroy Jarek's stockpile once and for all.

"Took you long enough."

I whip around. Marina Seingalt is staring at me, wearing an expression somewhere between disgust and curiosity. She stands next to Misia, Jarek, and four fully armed Guardians, including Leo and his father. Nero Carter, Farmer and Council member, is also there, appearing unsettled. Oscar, Eero, and Meryl are off to the side, on their knees.

My hand flies to my mouth to cover an involuntary cry.

Lozen stands behind them, her sword drawn, poised in line with their necks.

"It looks like we've captured our traitor," Jarek says. "I can't wait to tell the villagers."

"How stupid do you think they are?" I demand, pulse thudding. "No one'll believe I've been sneaking weapons into Noah's Valley and storing them in the Guardians' training barn!"

"We'll work out the details later." Jarek's eyes are gleaming.

"Why are *you* here?" I look at Marina, for the first time not even trying to mask the revulsion I feel. "And where's your father?" I can't tell if Oscar, Eero, and Meryl are injured, not with the shadows from the moonlight playing tricks on me. I refuse to look at Lozen.

"Sleeping off a bender, I assume," Jarek says, answering for her. "He won't be happy to hear what you've been up to. I can soften the blow if you tell me where Salvatora is."

Far away, I hope. *Run, Sal.* "Last I saw, she was in the chapel's undercroft."

"Enough," Jarek says. "Lozen, bring those three to the stocks. I've got something special in mind for Rose."

My heart plummets. This is my fault. I chose to deviate from the plan, and now I'm the reason it failed. Meryl, Eero, and Oscar won't make eye contact with me. I imagine how furious they must be, and I can't blame them. Our one chance, and I blew it. I should save everyone some time and run through Lozen's sword myself.

She tries to catch my eye, and when she does, she shakes her head. *I have to go along with this. Trust me*, her expression says.

Too bad I'm done trusting people. I wish I could kill her with my eyes.

Marina laughs shrilly, pulling me from my thoughts. "Something special in mind for Rose? Why don't you call it what it is? We're going to Harvest her, right?" There's a sick glint in her eye.

Even amidst these dire circumstances, I enjoy the burst of satisfaction her words bring me. Marina doesn't know Jarek means to keep me because I remind him of my mother. He's been manipulating all of us, even those who think they're on his side.

"How nice for you to be able to join your brother in Heaven, Rose," Marina continues. She's taunting, her beautiful face twisted like a rope of fabric. "Since you're not going to be with us much longer, I should probably confess something." She bats her eyelashes. "I'm afraid that I'm the reason Jonas was Harvested. I couldn't marry a clown like him. Always laughing and joking, like he was better than the rest of us. And the *toymaking*? Gross." Her grin turns ugly. "When I caught him in the vault, I went straight to Jarek. Someone had to take the fall for your mom's murder once she found out about the Beast, so..." She waves in the direction of Eden's Gate. "Bye-bye, Jonas."

I lunge at her. Leo is on me, but he underestimates my fury. I twist beneath him and jab upward, finding the gap just beneath his deltoid. With a great growl of rage, I wrench his arm back and up. The wet popping sound as it dislocates is music to my ears. My dark pleasure lasts until the other Guardians pounce on me, holding me down until Jarek's strong, cold fingers can slide beneath the cloak at my neck and press into my nerve points.

I drop to the ground, temporarily paralyzed. A Guardian steps forward and shackles my arms and legs. When did the Blacksmith House construct these restraints?

Jarek wipes his hands on his pants, like it disgusted him to touch me. "Rose isn't going to be Harvested, you fool," he tells Marina in a cool voice. "We'll keep her somewhere private. Her skills are needed."

Marina has no response. She's staring at me, unblinking, her eyes consuming her face. Whatever she saw in me just now terrified her.

Jarek prods me with his foot. "I would have preferred you join us willingly. Unfortunately, you've been fighting me the whole way. That's fine. I'm patient." He smiles, revealing two sharp canines. "You're precious to me, Rose."

The rage that had overtaken me is ebbing, along with the effects of Jarek's double nerve lock. I can wiggle my fingers and toes, and I can speak. "You can't expose our people to the world Beyond. It's too dangerous."

"You are not privy to the same information I am," Jarek says, looking at something past me. "Albert, would you mind joining us?"

My mouth goes chalky when Albert glides out of the woods, rolling down the horse path in his wheelchair. He glances toward Marina, his expression nakedly hopeful. She ignores him.

"Apparently, poor Albert has been hiding out ever since his mother tried to self-Harvest him," Jarek says. "But he was able to sneak away just before Reatha and Marie went up in the basket. He's offered to help us reconstruct the poison so we have a defense against this Beast and any more. With your help, of course, as concoctions aren't his specialty. He's a true hero of the Valley."

Albert looks to me, clearly worried I'll contradict his lie and reveal that in fact, all three Chemists have been living inside the Wall this whole time. But I won't sentence Reatha and Marie to death.

"Albert wasn't sure who to trust after he escaped Reatha," Jarek continues, "so he went to the Record Keeper."

Poor, lovesick Albert must have been trying to catch a glimpse of Marina. His foolishness will be the death of us all.

"David had the good sense to bring him to me. Albert is ready to rejoin the village now, help usher in a new era. His service will be his punishment for a crime." Jarek's sharp canines make another appearance, but it's a look of true pain this time. "He confessed that he was the one who Harvested your mother. It happened in a most unusual way, with a weapon from a time before the Wall."

"Noooo," I moan. Jarek appears genuinely upset, just as he was when he first saw my mother's body, but I don't care because I'm overcome with a horrible awareness. I'd guessed, but I hadn't known. Of course it was Albert, whose then-hovering wheelchair I'd seen a flash of right before my wedding. I start panic-coughing, choking on my own saliva. I try to sit up, but my extremities are still weak from the nerve locks.

"It's a good thing we caught you red-handed with the weapons you've been hoarding," Jarek says, flicking his wrist at the nearest Guardian, who removes my cloak. The explosives inside clink against each other. "It'll make it more palatable when we marry you in shackles and then tell the villagers—sorrowfully—that they won't be seeing much of you for a while. That it could take years to rehabilitate our Rose."

"Sit her up!" Albert says, hurrying over to where I'm drowning in my spit. "She can't marry anyone if she's dead."

The Guardian who threw on my shackles maneuvers me into an upright position, facing Jarek. My cuffed wrists rest on my lap, my legs out in front.

"You'll probably want to prepare for tomorrow's ceremony," Jarek says. "I know Misia will be excited to do your hair and makeup. *Girl time*, I think it's called. Guardians, take Rose back to her house."

62

"Naturally curly, just as I suspected," Misia says.

This morning—Friday—broke liquid with sunshine, just as the Astronomer House predicted, and it stayed golden all day. Misia confined me to my room through all of it. When the afternoon came, she half-carried, half-dragged me downstairs to wash my hair at the kitchen sink, my hands and feet still shackled. Next, she cut away my clothes and sponge bathed me after joining me in the bathroom to watch while I peed. She brought in two female Guardians, one to stand sentry at the door and the other to hold a blade at my neck, as she removed the wrist shackles to drag on my wedding dress. The skin beneath the restraints was tender, bright red braceleting both wrists.

None of the precautions are necessary.

I've lost my anger. My fight. Jarek has the weapons and the explosives. I don't care that I'm bathed like an infant, that these Guardians have seen me naked. My brother is lost forever. Soon the Wall that has protected us for over a century will be breached, allowing unknown horrors to enter while we're left to battle the Verdant Beast. The best I can hope for is that Jarek manages to kill it when he blows open the Wall.

"I'm glad I started with your hair," Misia says. "So it had time to dry."

I'm seated in a chair in front of the ornate mirror inside the Tzu kitchen, wearing a red wedding gown, exactly as I was seven days ago.

But I'm not the same person I was then.

I know the mirror I'm looking at came from original prison warden Helen Hayes's secret stash. I know Jarek has stockpiled her weapons, has hidden the Verdant Beast from us, has used fear and greed to turn the villagers against one another. I know that my mother was killed because she uncovered Jarek's plans, and my brother was illegally Harvested because Marina didn't want to marry him and they needed someone to pin with Mom's murder. I know that I'm powerless.

I'm only a girl in a blood-red wedding dress.

"Stop fidgeting," Misia says, tugging so hard at my hair that my neck jerks back. I've been motionless, but she's claimed every opportunity to hurt me since my capture. Cracking my skull with a mug as she washed my hair. Pinching my skin between two buttons as she yanked on my dress. I drugged her and left her husband to find her unconscious at her post, so none of it surprises me.

"There," she says, setting down a wide-toothed comb. "Look at how striking you are."

Everything I care about has or will be stolen from me. My mother and father. Jonas. Gran, Aunt Florence, and Uncle Richard, who will certainly be punished until I agree to help Albert craft the herbicide that will kill us if monsters Beyond don't first. Meryl, Oscar, Eero, and Sal, if they're even still alive. It feels as though my very soul is draining into the earth.

A single question—a single unexplained fact—is scratching at me, but I brush it away.

"I said look." Misia jerks my chin and forces me to stare at my reflection. "Even more arresting than your mother. Neither of you was ever beautiful, but there's something interesting there."

I don't recognize the girl staring back at me. Her dark brown hair cascades in curls threaded with currant-colored ribbons and tiny, polished stones that glitter like captured stars. Her eyes have been lined with a pencil, her lids dusted with pink. The colors make them appear impossibly large, her lashes lush. The artificial rosiness of her cheeks complements her broad nose and strong chin. Her lips are plump and cherry kissed. She wears the most beautiful crimson gown, a delicate pattern of beads accenting her chest and waist, leading to a full skirt.

Only her shackled hands disturb the picture.

"Do you like it?" Misia asks.

The creature in the mirror nods. What does it matter? This isn't matrimony; it's propaganda. I wonder how many people will recognize that. I wonder how many more will hate me for violating everything our collective is supposed to be, once they hear Jarek's accusations against me.

That irritating question tries knocking at my consciousness again. It's related to last night, to the weapons barn.

Again, I push it away.

"We're ready," Misia calls to the Guardians who've been waiting outside the door.

I'm helped to my feet and led into the dying lavender light of late afternoon. The tablet must be fully charged, not that it'll be needed any longer, not once there's an enormous hole in the Wall. What lie will Jarek spin for the villagers to allow him to destroy our protection and send my friends out as bait?

The Guardians guide me to the square. In front of Eden's Gate sits the structure Eero and the other Carpenters have been building. It's nearly fifty feet tall and twice as wide. It does indeed look like a mix between a wall and a cage.

It won't keep out whatever lies in wait Beyond.

The trills and drums of the wedding march begin as soon as I step into view of the Minstrels. Every villager is in attendance and wearing red, as required.

I'm not nervous. I'm not scared.

I'm *numb*.

The crowd parts for me, a few glancing at my shackles. Most keep their eyes trained on my face. The marriage lane ends at the stage. Gryphon is positioned on it, wearing his matrimonial reds. He's breathtaking, just as he was at our first ceremony. He's a Guardian carved of stone, caught between his family and his conscience, unable to fully serve either. Maybe today he'll finally commit to the winning team.

Jarek's.

I want to follow Gran's advice to trust, but it's impossible after everything I've experienced. Sojourner also stands on the stage, keeping separate from Jarek. Misia hurries to join her husband, inserting herself between him and Gryphon.

I continue my shuffling walk down the path, shackles biting at my skin. If I close my eyes, their metal clang almost sounds like the bells I wore last time I made this march. As I near the stage, I can see Meryl, Eero, and Oscar tied to the whipping posts beside it, facing away from the crowd. I suck air through my teeth. The backs of their shirts are shredded, the exposed skin swollen, black with blood and gore. Lozen guards them. Her face is puffy, her eyes shiny, like she's been crying. I'm surprised they allow her this expression of emotion. Albert sits in his wheelchair on the opposite side of the stage, a sullen Marina standing beside him.

Sal's nowhere to be seen. That, at least, is something.

My eyes rip back to Lozen, the question that's been nagging at me suddenly at the forefront, impossible to avoid: who told Albert to shoot my mother? Because it wasn't Jarek. He may have killed my father, but he loved my mother too much to hurt her. And murder isn't something Albert would have done on his own. He was born a follower, his worship of Marina proof of that.

Was it Marina who commanded him? Possibly. She said she orchestrated my brother's Harvest, after all. But I still feel something just out of reach, a trail I can't muster the energy to follow. I stumble climbing the stairs. Jarek rushes forward to help, acting the solicitous father-in-law. I let him. What does it matter anymore? He guides me to stand next to Gryphon. Gryphon slips his arm around my waist—one of the few places I'm not cut, bruised, or stitched—but the touch barely registers.

"Thank you all for gathering to celebrate the union of my son, Gryphon Tzu of the Guardian House, and Rose Allgood, formerly of the Apothecaries," Jarek intones. "Before we begin, I have some disturbing news to share. Nero Carter of the Farmer House?"

Nero strides onto the stage. He turns to address the villagers. He lacks Jarek's ability to charm a crowd and launches clumsily into his message. "Rose Allgood is the traitor we've been searching for. We caught the girl last night with a massive cache of weapons that she must have discovered while trespassing after curfew. We believe our ancestors left them here for us to protect ourselves, and she was hoarding 'em."

Ah, so that's why they brought Nero to the ambush last night. Someone outside of the Guardian House to testify against me, and a Council Elder to boot. I don't think they'll need it. No one in the crowd moves, except a few whose eyes flash with something like venom. They've let themselves be led by a madman, allowed him to manufacture a tool out of their fear, one he uses against them right now, right under their noses. They're in deep.

One by one, I hold their gazes until they look away.

I'll be damned if I'll let them forget that they know better.

"It was a disappointment," Jarek says, reclaiming the stage from Nero. "But not a surprise. It's in her blood." He pauses long enough for the villagers to wonder what he means, then draws in a noisy breath. "We've recently discovered that Rose's mother had been poisoning us."

Gasps of disbelief and outrage burn through the crowd.

"Yes, that's right!" he says. "Henrietta Allgood was the original traitor. We believe she may have even been the one who first discovered the weapons, later getting her children involved.

That would explain why her own son murdered her, driven as he must have been to madness by her selfish crimes." He shakes his head sadly. "The Record Keeper has much deliberating to do about how to proceed with the weapons that Rose's family has collected. In the meanwhile, you must understand that I don't believe it's Rose's fault that she strayed. She was born to it, after all. And she will soon be family." He shoots me a magnanimous smile. "Which is why Misia and I will take over her behavioral correction. She'll be invisible to the community for some time. Know that she's in good hands."

I risk a glance at Sojourner. She's staring at the sky, her jawbone rigid.

"Now let us conduct the wedding we've all come here to witness, followed by a very special surprise."

"Not without the Record Keeper." It's Gryphon standing next to me speaking. He's staring at the crowd rather than his father.

"What did you say?" Jarek asks, his tone icy.

Gryphon keeps his arm around me as he raises his voice. "The Record Keeper must be present at every wedding. It's the law."

My heart skips. It's true. But will Jarek care? Apparently he does.

Jarek flicks his hand at Leonidas. "Find David."

We hold our collective breath. The pain of my stitches and shackles, even the rawness of my broken heart is suspended. Our society teeters on the brink. If we fall over the edge, there's no coming back, but the habit of listening to the Record Keeper is ingrained so deeply in us that maybe, *maybe*, if David can find his courage, we can rebuild.

It's our last chance.

Leo leads David into the square. He drags his injured foot but otherwise appears surprisingly bright-eyed, his hair combed, red clothes immaculate. I feel a bubble of hope that I'm too afraid to trust as David limps up the stairs, his eyes trained on me.

"Please," I cry. "Tell them the truth."

He nods encouragingly as he limps over to me, the picture of vulnerability. When he reaches my side, he puts his face so close to my ear that even Gryphon cannot hear. "The truth?" His caterpillar mustache brushes my flesh. "The truth is that it's the sneaky leader that you have to watch out for."

His chuckle makes my blood run cold.

63

With David at his appointed place, Jarek has gone back to addressing the crowd, roaring at them to get them fired up for the ceremony, talking about how blessed our village is, how wonderful our system.

David continues to whisper in my ear. "You can't possibly believe Jarek had the vision to pull this off on his own?" My brain has locked up, but David keeps talking. "I'm sorry about Henrietta, but she stood in the way of our advancement. When I caught Albert spying on Marina after his family supposedly self-Harvested, he was easy enough to convince to take care of my problem. All it took was a piece of the hover panel, plus Marina's hand in marriage, and the boy was mine. We all have our price."

"How could you?" I spit. I suppose I should stop being surprised. The leadership of this place is rotten at its core.

One of David's shoulders lifts as his eyes travel to the center of the stage. The people of Noah's Valley are staring up at Jarek as if he's a god, hanging onto his every word.

"How could I not?" David asks. "Mealworm porridge is only fine until you know better. The future is coming, Rose, and it'll be so much nicer than what we have now. Canned food, books on every subject—gold, even."

We've learned of gold in our books. It has no value, not really. You can't eat it, can't create tools from it. His mention of it scratches something in my memories, though. I don't pursue it, because nothing matters anymore. I am a shell, light as a leaf, empty as a pocket. "Everything you said to me was a lie."

Gryphon glances over at me, gives my waist a gentle squeeze, then returns his attention to his father. To the outside world, it must look like David is sharing some knowledge from his House with me, a standard wedding day gift. They don't know he's pouring poison into my ear.

David shakes his head dismissively. "On the contrary. I *do* regret telling Jarek the truth of our founding, and he really isn't very smart. He runs everything by me and still manages to think he's the one in charge. Fortunately, that works for me. Less risk, more reward." He's speaking low but conversationally, like we're neighbors enjoying midday tea. "Do you know what else? Korr was telling the truth in that article about there being a door inside the Valley that'll open tonight." He coughs into his hand. "I found Hayes's journal confirming it, though she writes that it's small, an afterthought, really. The descendants of the prisoners were never meant to escape. I don't think Korr would have bothered building it at all if not for a required safety inspection before prisoners could be transferred inside."

"You're going to lead Jarek and the Guardians out through the tunnel?" I ask, my voice flat. "So he doesn't have to blow up the Wall?" That, at least, is something.

David's making a wheezing sound, and I realize he's chuckling. "I've already shared more than enough with Jarek. He doesn't even know there *is* a tunnel. Whatever is beyond it is mine, including a rapid exit should one be necessary." His chuckling stops. "Unfortunately, Hayes was too paranoid to write down its exact location for fear the prisoners would find it, but where else could it be but in the basement of what was her home? And when it pops open tonight—a hundred and twenty years to the day from our official founding—I'll be the only one there to see it. Can you imagine the riches on the other side, given what we've seen in her stash?" He sweeps his hand, indicating the entire village gathered for my wedding. "Which is why your ceremony had to be this evening. I don't want anyone stumbling in while I'm taking inventory."

I'd strangle him if my hands weren't shackled. "Jarek blowing open the Wall will put everyone in danger, even you."

"That, or it'll kill the Verdant Beast and clear the path to more wealth. You haven't seen what some of the weapons we discovered can do, Rose."

He's as evil as Jarek. Worse. Jarek might be the blade, but David is the hand that guides it. "I'll tell Jarek that you're manipulating him."

David pets his mustache with the side of his pointer finger. "Does he seem like a man who could be convinced he's not running the show?"

I follow David's gaze. Jarek appears completely in his element as he tells the villagers that he and the Record Keeper have an exciting plan to care for everyone, that tonight is going to be a night they'll never forget, beginning with the wedding.

Gryphon glances down at me again, this time flicking his glance to David.

David steps away from me.

"But I almost forgot," Jarek finishes, his booming voice reaching the far corners of the square, "that first we have three criminals on the whipping post to deal with."

"No!" The scream cuts through the crisp air, coming from the rear of the crowd, near the chapel. The village parts to reveal Reatha. Her face is gaunt, gray, her hair wild. She looks like she hasn't slept since I last saw her. She stumbles toward the stage. Her hand flies to her mouth when she spots Oscar, Eero, and Meryl tied up. She runs to them, making it all the way to their whipping posts.

The Guardians stand frozen in surprise. To them, she's risen from the dead.

She yells at the crowd. "How can you all stand there like sheep? These are our children!"

She's turning back to untie my friends, but the Guardians finally wake up and pull her away, looking to Jarek for guidance. He holds up a hand but says nothing, his birdlike face studying Reatha as the Guardians release her.

The crowd shuffles uncomfortably, and Reatha approaches the stage. She talks as she walks, her voice as loud as she can make it. "I took my family into hiding after Jarek had me create the poison we call the Vex." Gasps ring out from the villagers. "That's right! The Vex isn't an illness but an herbicide. Jarek used it against you. And he bewitched my own son into helping him!"

I glance back to David, who's staring at the ground, looking for all the world like a harmless, bookish man. Only I am close enough to see the smirk beneath his mustache. He really is a puppeteer.

"I believe he means to explore the Beyond," Reatha is saying, "opening us up to untold dangers." The throng glances from her to Jarek and then David, uneasy. A baby's cry splits the air. Still, Jarek remains quiet. I can't believe it. Why is he letting her rouse the people against him? Even Misia appears shocked by his silence.

Reatha has reached the stage. She peers up, her eyes beseeching me. "I'm so sorry, Rose. Your mother warned me about how dangerous Jarek is. He made terrible threats against your father, and shortly after, Kirby was dead. I believe Jarek killed him. That's why I agreed to make the poison, until I learned what it was being used for. That's when I took my two children and hid. I told myself I was doing it to protect the village, but really, I was scared Jarek would Harvest Albert or Marie, just like he Harvests the family of anyone who stands up to him."

She turns back to the audience. "It's true," she screams. "Look around! You let him take others in the hope that he won't take you. You know Jarek is culling our herd, but you don't object. You've forgotten yourself. You've forgotten your community." She points toward the Wall. "And now, he's going to breach our only protection. He intends to let the outside in. Raiders, creatures, the Sun and Water knows what else. And for what?"

"For evolution," Jarek declares. His voice is loud but unnervingly calm. Have he and David planned for this, too? "That's the only reason to open the Wall."

His announcement is so shocking that the entire village goes quiet.

Jarek continues. "The Record Keepers and the Guardians have seen the Before Times items Rose and her mother discovered. You'll understand when you see them, too. Tools that will make your life easier. Carpenter House, would you not like a sun-powered drill? Blacksmiths, what about a handheld welding torch? There is food, too, entire shelves of delicacies that melt on your tongue and fill your bellies. Weapons that can protect us from the wildest beast. And there is surely all of that and more waiting for us Beyond, if we can just go outside and take it." He pauses, breathes for emphasis. "We must allow the future in."

So that's their game. They mean to pass blame to me, to act like now that I've discovered goods from Beyond, there's no turning back. This is the natural order of things, so we may as well make the best of it. Based on the way the crowd is nodding, vacant eyes reflecting the setting sun, it's working. Jarek and David are going to win. They're going to get everything they want. Greed has replaced community.

"Guardians," Jarek says, "pass out the rancher candy we discovered in Rose's stash."

Some of his troops move through the crowd, offering the sweets to the starved villagers as Jarek goes on. "Rose's mother made a mistake by hiding what she'd found from us and hoarding it, but she did us a favor by discovering it in the first place. Now we know what's possible." He turns to face me, tilting his head in a mockery of compassion. "She loved you, Rose."

"She was murdered!" Reatha yells. "Because she threatened Jarek's master plan." She turns back to the gathered villagers. "People of Noah's Valley, we cannot let him do the same to anyone else! It's time to act. Starting now, we must—"

She drops in mid-sentence, a mother-of-pearl-handled dagger quivering in her spine, buried to its hilt.

"Reatha is also a traitor," Jarek tells the crowd, staring at the knife he's just thrown.

I moan and sag against Gryphon, unable to believe my eyes. David exits the stage. Albert appears, maneuvering his wheelchair through the stunned crowd to his mother's side. He stares down at her, stricken.

"Now!" Lozen yells.

She cuts Meryl, Eero, and Oscar free just as a handful of villagers, led by Augustus and armed with little more than their courage, rush at the nearest Guardians. Eero's parents, Zaha and Aldo of the Carpenter House, are fighting with their bare hands, their years of hard work and labor paying off in the form of powerful swipes and kicks. Near them, Oscar's father, Dale, of the Tailor House leaps on the back of a Guardian, surprising her with his ferocity. Augustus is cutting through a swath of them, swinging a metal pipe. The Guardians are caught unawares, and many of them seem reluctant to fight their fellow citizens, some of whom used to be family.

Jarek moves to the edge of the stage to watch it all coolly, Misia by his side. The battle below is chaotic and brutal, with the thud of fists on flesh and the screams of the wounded filling the air along with the smell of sweat and fear, Guardians against villagers. I think, unwillingly, to our ancestors. *Were we always going to turn out like this?* I dive toward the stairs, but my shackles take me down. I try to right myself. Gryphon is by my side, a key in his hand.

"What's happening?" I ask.

"War." His stricken expression shocks me. "I've been preparing for this my whole life, but I didn't know we'd be battling each other."

He undoes the shackles at my wrists. How did he get the key from his mother? I rub at my bloodied skin as the cuffs fall to the stage, their clank lost in the angry cries of the raging fight. Do we stand a chance? I feel a spark of hope, and it's terrifying. Giving up had been so much easier.

Sal appears out of nowhere, jumping between me and Gryphon.

"It's now or never, Rose," she cries, holding out the detonator.

The explosives! I glance over at Jarek and Misia. They see nothing beyond the fight in front of them. Sal pushes my thumb into the depression at the same time as hers. I have only a millisecond to worry that we're too far away from the weapons barn when a far-off explosion echoes with such force that it knocks me off my feet.

All right, I see why they make those things so hard to set off.

Gryphon helps me up.

I hear a whoop and realize it's Lozen, who's fighting Tomris just in front of the stage. "Guess I was wrong about their range!" she calls out before sliding between the older Guardian's legs. She springs up, knocking her opponent at the base of the neck with her sword hilt. Tomris drops like a sack of beets, and Lozen dives to shove a Guardian off another villager.

She's doing her part, but Jarek's training is paying off. The rest of his Guardians are forming organized pockets, forcing the villagers nearest them to kneel. Anyone who doesn't is knocked unconscious or worse. I think I see a Guardian run his blade through the Blacksmith's son. My earlier burst of hope is replaced by horror. The rebel villagers—those who've already lost too much—are fighting with everything they have, but there simply aren't enough of them. Jarek's army is too well-trained, their blades too sharp.

The uprising, if it had been that, is being quelled. Efficiently.

Jarek must realize it as the same time as me. He turns, his face lit with an ugly, gloating satisfaction that morphs to rage when he sees that Gryphon has knelt to unlock the manacles around my ankles. Gryphon has his back to his father and so doesn't see him approach, and there isn't time to warn him. I rip the dagger from Gryphon's belt and aim it, heart pounding, hand trembling. For a split second, I hesitate—I've never taken a life—but then I fling it. Jarek dives to the side just as the blade leaves my fingers, and it sails wide, clattering uselessly to the ground below.

My ankle shackles freed, Gryphon stands. He doesn't know that I just tried to kill his father. Yet his onyx eyes are full of emotion.

It looks, weirdly, like he's going to kiss me.

"Please forgive me," he whispers.

Then everything goes black.

64

I blink. Sit up. It's evening. My wrists are restrained, but rope has replaced the shackles. My ankles are bound as well. I'm somewhere in the forest, a chubby moon climbing to the ceiling of the sky. I think I hear the creek singing nearby, accompanied by the chirp of crickets.

I'm alone except for Gryphon. He's standing guard, but he glances over when I rouse.

I rub at a sore spot near the base of my neck. He'd used the same nerve lock on me that his father had, only he'd gone deeper, jamming so hard I passed out. *Traitor.* "You'll have to teach me that move," I say. "Either that, or I'm going to start wearing a metal collar."

Gryphon steps closer. He's so tall, outlined by the moon. I can't read his expression.

I hold up my restrained hands. "Like father, like son?" It's a low blow, but he's earned it.

He drops to his haunches. I can finally see his face. His eyes are aching. "If you're free, you'll run back to the village to fight. If you fight, you'll die. The Guardians were regaining control."

"That wasn't your call to make, Gryphon!" Despair sinks its claws deep into my chest. We've left the others behind. *I've* left them, and not for the first time. Meryl, Oscar, Sal, Eero, even

Lozen. Where were Uncle Richard and Aunt Florence in the crowd? Are they still alive? "Whatever happened to letting me make my own choices?"

He doesn't respond to my verbal strike, but I know it registers. "We can still save the Valley, Rose," he says simply.

"Not tied up, I can't." I try to make my voice light, as if I'm willing to concede to him, but the truth is I'm desperate to break free so I can help my friends and family. I have no illusion that I can stop a well-trained Guardian holding a sword, but neither can I hide out in the woods while Jarek kills those I love.

"I know there's no hope for my father," he says. "I accept it."

My heart breaks for him, but now isn't the time. "We have to get back and help our friends, Gryphon."

He shakes his head. "The others are meeting us here, if they're still alive."

I make an angry noise. "You could've said that."

"We regroup," he continues as if I hadn't spoken. "And decide together what to do next."

I hold up my hands. "If we're ambushed, I'm dead."

He narrows his eyes. He wants to argue, but he knows I'm right. With a grunt of frustration, he cuts the rope binding my hands and then my feet. I stand slowly, massaging my wrists. Gryphon stands, too. I'm considering attempting a nerve lock on *him*. I study his neck, stalling to get my bearings. Which way lies the village? I don't want to hurt him, don't think I can, but I can't understand why he's keeping me here. We have to help the others.

"It must be terrible to give up on your father," I say. Do I hear a clash of metal from the east? See a lighter swath of sky? "But I'm glad you chose the Valley."

"I didn't choose the Valley, Rose."

The intensity in his voice draws my gaze. I look into his obsidian eyes. They're full of heat...and something tender. "I chose you," he says simply.

"About time you were honest about that," Lozen says, gliding as quiet as a ghost from between two trees. One of her eyes is swollen shut.

"A little late, if you ask me." This from Augustus, who follows her, the front of his tunic drenched with blood.

"Seconded," Sal says, limping from the other direction.

I run over and hug her. "You're alive!"

"For the moment." She pulls away from my embrace and steps to the side.

Albert appears from behind her. My rage surges and then almost immediately dampens. His face is so warped with grief that he's nearly unrecognizable.

"Update," Gryphon demands of the new arrivals.

"We might have gotten the balance to shift toward our cause," Augustus says. "Until Jarek decided to make an example of the others."

"What others?" I ask. I don't want the answer.

He looks at me mournfully. "He executed Richard."

My knees buckle. Gryphon catches me, holding me tight.

Sweet Uncle Richard with the perennial dusting of carrot-colored hair across his cheek because his razor always missed. I hadn't gone a day in my entire life without seeing him, not until I was moved to the Tzu cottage.

And now he's dead.

Augustus continues. "He tied Meryl, Eero, and Oscar to the whipping posts again." He rubs the back of his head, clearly uncomfortable. "And your grandmother and Florence alongside them. He said they're all traitors, but that it's your fault." His eyes grow flinty. "Because you're the one to blame, he says, he'll trade you for them. Either you surrender, or they're Harvested."

Sal's blinking away tears. "They all knew what they were agreeing to," she says, trying to give me a brave face. "They knew tonight might go this way. It was a risk they chose to take."

I shake my head. *No*. I cannot hide out here while they die.

"Don't turn yourself in, Rose," Gryphon says, reading my mind. "We only need a little more time. My father's weapons are gone. All that's left is to destroy the tablet, the basket, and the Verdant Beast."

"I can destroy the tablet if I can only get my hands on it," I say. I'm thinking as quickly as I can. "I'll tell Jarek I think there's more information on there to kill the Verdant Beast."

"He's already looked at it every which way," Gryphon says. "Him and the Record Keeper. Any information on there, they know of."

My brain is working frantically. "Then I'll tell him I need to talk to him privately, away from the others. That there's something my mother told me that I need to tell him. He'll follow me! And then I can drug him."

"How?" Sal asks.

"Will this help?" Albert rolls over to me. He hands me the medical kit I had to give up when I moved to the Tzu house. I have no idea how he got his hands on it, but I'm deeply moved. I slide the kit's strap over my head, peeking inside at the syringes, salves, tinctures, and medications. I feel the familiar weight of it pressed against my shoulder and exhale. Reclaiming this piece of me is a comfort beyond measure.

"Thank you," I say to him.

"I'm so sorry, Rose." He looks unbearably sad.

"When I followed you through the village that day, when you first led me to the caves. Did you shoot over my head?" I thought it was a stone from the sky at the time. That was before I saw the weapon that tore a hole through Jarek's arm.

He nods. "I was just playing."

"And you told Jarek you'd help him to make more herbicide?"

Albert nods again. "It's not just Jarek, though. He thinks he's the one in charge, but the Record Keeper is the real mastermind. He's been working behind the scenes this whole time."

I look to the others. "It's true. David Seingalt admitted as much onstage." I watch them wrestle with this before turning my attention back to Albert. I go absolutely still. "And the Record Keeper ordered you to use that same weapon you fired over my head to kill my mother?"

I hear the whisper of Gryphon's steel—this is the first he's heard of Albert's treachery—but it's far too late for that.

Albert's voice comes out as a moan. "He said she was poisoning the Valley, and that if I didn't do something, Marina would die. I trusted him because he helped me upgrade my chair. And I just had to pull a trigger. He said it wouldn't even feel real." He swallows a sob. "I made a terrible mistake, Rose. One that cost us both our moms. I'm so sorry."

I have nothing to say to that. It's the truth, and he's going to have to live with it.

"Let me get all this straight." Lozen is tossing her knife in the air, catching it. Tossing it in the air, catching it, never missing even though she only has one functioning eye. "The Record Keeper is the original traitor—he's really the one behind Jarek and the Guardian army he's created, who are—all but me—gathered in the village square right now. And Jarek has the tablet. You're going to do what, Rose? Sashay over to him, flash your eyes, and tell him you need just a private moment of his time to share a secret your mother told you, and he's going to believe you because you resemble the only woman he's ever loved? Gross, by the way. Then, once you have him far enough away, you're going to plunge a syringe in his neck, grab the tablet, and smash it against the nearest rock?"

I nod.

"Easy peasy." Lozen rolls her eyes. "Best plan ever."

"I refuse to allow this," Gryphon says. The moonlight is strong enough to reveal the agony etched on his face.

"What's the alternative?" I say, exasperated. "I hide out in the woods for the rest of my life? There's only two thousand acres against over three dozen Guardians. They'll find me eventually, and in the meantime, they'll torture and kill everyone I love, not to mention people will still be Harvested if not outright killed by the Verdant Beast." I throw my hands in the air. "At least with my plan, our families live another night."

Gryphon's words are measured. Dangerous. "I need a moment alone with Rose."

The others stand their ground.

"Now!" he barks.

When I don't react, everyone shuffles back into the forest, Lozen glaring at Gryphon before she goes. He waits until they're out of sight and then spins on me. "You can stop pretending. I know what you intend to do."

65

I straighten my spine. "Of course you do. I just told everyone. I'm going to lure Jarek away from the others, incapacitate him, and destroy the tablet."

He speaks, low and lethal. "You know that isn't your plan."

I look away. "What makes you say that?"

He stares skyward in frustration, like he can't believe he has to explain it to me. "You sneak out to treat the elderly even though it could get you Harvested." He doesn't give me a chance to respond. "When Oscar was about to get a lashing the other night because of your wedding dress, you protected him without a thought. Same thing when Leonidas was attacking Eero."

My mouth goes dry.

He closes the distance between us. His nearness awakens goosebumps along my flesh. "And weren't you just now begging to run back and throw yourself into a fight you stood no chance of surviving? That's not just Apothecary training." He settles a finger in my open collar, above my heart. It's the lightest of touches, but I shiver as his heat radiates across my skin. "That's you. That's in there."

He's quiet for a moment, his finger still resting on me.

"And that's why I know," he continues, his voice raw, "that

if against all odds you manage to drug my father and take the tablet, after you destroy it, you'll charge the Verdant Beast, revealing the truth about the Valley to its citizens and sacrificing your life for the greater good. Only," he says softly, "I can't let you do that."

My blood runs cold because he's right.

I realized when I saw Guardians attacking the handful of rebel villagers that our only chance at survival lies in fighting together, and we'll only do that if we have a common enemy larger than the one Jarek has created. Leo nearly throwing Eero to the Beast is what gave me the idea. I blink back tears. *I'm so sorry, sweet brother, but I can't come looking for you. There's something I must do instead. We devoted our lives to saving others. Apothecaries to the end.*

But I can't confess this to Gryphon, can't give him a chance to slow me down, so I slap his hand away. "That's completely ridiculous. Besides, who are you to tell me what I can and can't do?"

Hurt blooms on his cheeks, but then something shifts beneath his skin and his jaw hardens. "I'm not asking, Rose." His voice is deep and menacing. "If I have to restrain you, I will."

My mouth curls. "Good luck trying, you big bully. It's only tonight that you even came close to standing up to your father, and what a poor attempt it was." I aim to make him hate me. Surely all the resentment he's banked over the years is still there, simmering just below the surface.

The pulse in his forehead throbs. "Don't forget that I laid you flat dozens of times in training, and I can do it again."

I lean in, close enough to smell his scent of pine and musk. "I don't even like you, Gryphon Tzu. I told the truth after the betrothal ceremony. It was Nikola I loved all along."

He blinks, searching my face with a mixture of fury and desperation that I don't understand. Or maybe I do. Our souls recognized each other when we were children.

Slowly, Gryphon's gaze dips to my lips. Fireflies spark to life beneath my skin.

Before I can stop myself—before I even want to—we crash together, all heat and hunger and impossible need. I grab hold of his neck, clinging to the strength coiled beneath his skin. The kiss isn't soft. It's wildfire, a battlefield, pain braided with pleasure until I can't tell the difference.

And then too soon, it's over. Gryphon releases me.

"Don't ever say that again," he rumbles.

I stare into his beautiful eyes, at his strong nose, at those soft lips that just bruised mine. "Gryphon." It's the only word I can manage.

"I see you, Rose," he says carefully, gently brushing a lock of hair away from the birthmark on my forehead before kissing it lightly. "I've seen you since we were kids and you first stitched me up." He takes my hands to his mouth, brushing my fingertips against his lips. "You were as steady as stone that day. I've loved you every minute of every day since, Rosie."

I almost lose my resolve, my heart thundering in response to his. Desperate to stay focused, I glance upward. The cold air smells like stars. "The northern lights are out tonight."

He shakes his head, unwilling to let me distract him. "I can't let you give up your life for others."

The naked anguish in his eyes is too much. I can't play this out any longer. "Come here," I say, trying to lead him to the shelter of the large rock I'd woken up by. I hold him with one hand. The other dips into my medical kit, years and years of training guiding me to exactly what I need. "I have to tell you something, but you should be sitting down for it."

He won't budge. I look back at him, squeezing his hand for all I'm worth. The moon outlines the strength of him. "Please," I beg.

With a torn expression, he finally lets me guide him to the rock. "You're not going to convince me to let you run into the arms of the Verdant Beast," he says as he drops heavily onto the ground next to me, "so don't even try."

It occurs to me he hasn't slept in at least a day. How's he still going?

"We'll think of an alternative," he says. "There's an answer for every question, I swear."

"There is," I agree, trying to capture every angle of his beautiful face as I lean in for another kiss. He feels the sting of my needle before the touch of my lips, but the liquid Veranol is quick. He barely has time to pull away.

Betrayal etches his features.

It's the last image I'll see of him.

66

The glow from the village outlines the trees in a soft light that grows stronger the nearer I get. Soon, I hear the yell of angry voices, the clash of swords—Guardians fighting Guardians? Am I too late with my plan to unite the village against the Verdant Beast?

I redouble my efforts. I must reach the square before Jarek does more harm. The only way to save my friends and family is to turn myself in, and the only way to save our society is to demonstrate the real danger we're up against right after.

Gryphon will understand in time.

I've loved you every minute of every day since, Rosie.

I toss the stabbing pain into a compartment and lock it tight. I can't think of Gryphon, or even Jonas. I can only think of my community. I've ignored our problems, but Gran was right about our strengths. We're good people. We were born of rough beginnings, and we overcame, together. We take care of each other through thick and thin. That's worth everything.

I break into the square, expecting chaos, heart pounding like a war drum in my ears. The twilight sky is smeared a deep violet. My gaze is drawn immediately to Eden's Gate. A handful of Guardians cluster fifty yards or so in front of it, breathing heavily as if they've just battled.

A pile of bodies rises up behind them. My hand flies to my mouth. Am I too late?

"Rose!" Misia calls out.

I drag my eyes to the right. Across the empty square, she has my eighty-seven-year-old gran tied to a whipping post. Sojourner and Aunt Florence are on one side. On her other are Meryl, Eero, and Oscar. They're still alive! But then I notice Guardians holding their swords out, ready to strike them down if I make a wrong move. Augustus, kneeling in front of an angry-looking Tomris with her blade at his neck, looks like he'll be the first casualty. The rest of Noah's Valley is gathered behind them, a few hundred people, their faces haunted, some of them wearing tunics drenched in blood.

"You came," Jarek says, stepping down from the stage and walking past the whipping posts. He's gripping the tablet in one hand and the back of little Marie's neck in the other. Tears stream down her face.

I hurry forward until I'm close enough to smell the sourness of Jarek's sweat. He's afraid. Of what? Has he finally realized the Record Keeper is pulling his strings?

"It's going to be okay, Marie," I say. I'm lying. Her brother is a murderer and she's lost her mother. But I can't look at her sweet face, her buck teeth biting her trembling lips, and say nothing. "Everything is going to be all right, honey."

I hear Misia's snort.

"You can make that true, Rose," Jarek says, stepping even nearer.

The villagers begin whispering, their eyes blazing when they meet mine. Are they thinking of people we used to be? Now that they've had a front-row seat to Jarek's evil, now that they've seen the bodies of their neighbors stacked like firewood, are there more than a handful willing to rebel?

"You're already dressed for your wedding," Jarek is saying. "We can locate your groom and see it through to the end.

Everything in the Valley can return to normal. Whatever this has been"—he waves his hand to indicate all of me—"can end. We can have our lives back."

I glance down at my dress. Many of the beads have been ripped away, the lovely lace hem is torn and dragging, and the front is darkened with blood—maybe mine, maybe not. My hair has come loose from its elaborate ribbons.

"My friends and family are innocent," I say clearly.

Jarek's mouth twitches. "They are not. They're traitors. They've worked against their community, tearing the fabric of the Valley."

I lean forward, pitching my voice for Jarek's ears only. It takes everything in me not to glance over at the Verdant Beast, gauging the distance between me and it. "My mother wrote about you. In coded notes in her journal. Messages only an Apothecary could decipher. I didn't think you deserved to hear them, but I might be willing to trade."

Jarek blinks, his words stolen from him.

"Let her go." I glance at Marie. "And I'll tell you."

His hope is so naked that I'd pity the man if he hadn't chosen greed and ugliness over his community.

"Tell me now," he says, not releasing Marie. But neither does he raise his voice so any but us three can hear him. He must know I'm bluffing, but isn't that the way of love? The brain kneels to the heart.

"I cannot," I say. I'll show the villagers the Verdant Beast, but I want to destroy the tablet while I'm at it, remove that tool from Jarek's abuse of power. "It's too personal. For your ears only."

Jarek's face is clenched so tightly it's turning in on itself. Then suddenly, it relaxes. "Fine. Marie, go join my wife."

He shoves her away and then smiles, his expression an altar to evil.

My tongue turns to cloth. It's clear from his expression that he's figured out I'm lying. But what can I do? I've talked myself into a corner. I begin to walk toward Eden's Gate, my hand sliding into my medical kit. It takes a moment to find the syringe I seek, because my fingers are numb with terror. Will I be able to use the needle? It seems unlikely. In fact, I feel a terrible, cold certainty that Jarek is going to plunge a knife in my back, just as he did to Reatha. There are so many things I wish I'd said, so many truths. I try to line them up, looking for comfort in the order, at least, but they evade me. I hear a terrible groaning shush, followed by a bloodcurdling scream.

Forty feet to my left, the Verdant Beast has come to life without me, drawn to the pile of villagers' corpses.

67

Its gnarled tendrils twist and writhe in the dim light as it plucks the first body from the pile, Pierre of the Dentist House. It squeezes him tight before plunging needled vines into his soft belly. The greedy Beast doesn't even finish with him before going back for another, and then a third. I can't bear to watch as the bodies of people I knew and cared for—Meeman of the Fisher House, Augustus's father Hephaestus—are consumed, don't want to hear the wet, sucking sound of its feeding, don't want to notice the pulsating purple veins growing engorged.

Those who watch are frozen in a mixture of disbelief and terror. "Everyone, get back!" Jarek yells, his face contorted. "It will leave us alone once it's taken its fill."

But somehow I doubt that's true. The Verdant Beast, kept sated for over a century on our monthly bodies, has developed an appetite, reaching a maturity its creators couldn't have envisioned. A scream pierces the air as Nero of the Farmer House is grabbed, then constricted. Leonidas leaps to his aid, but his sword barely nicks it.

The vines near Eden's Gate are thicker, but they also look like they're slower than the ones we encountered on the edge of the quarantine zone. Easier to dodge, but hard to cut through. I'm trying to decide what presents the most danger in the moment—the

Beast behind me or Jarek in front of me—when he points at me.

"Take her," he commands the nearest Guardians.

They surge forward, weapons glinting, but before they can reach me, a war cry splits the air, followed by Lozen vaulting over an overturned cart, her fists already bloodied. Augustus takes advantage of the distraction to throw Tomris to the ground. When Sal shoots out of the shadows of an alley, racing to free the prisoners with quick, precise movements, my heart soars.

Their presence, coupled with the Verdant Beast's horror, finally jolts the village into action. While some scream and flee, many more grab nearby items to use as weapons—wood beams, torches, pitchforks—and advance on the Beast. The strong save the bodies of our fallen, pulling them from the monster's hungry grasp. We are finally battling as one! I cheer on those who've joined the fight as I duck under a Guardian who tries to grab me. Beside me, Augustus takes down another with a sweep of his pipe. Even more villagers join the fray, now fighting the Guardians as well as the Verdant Beast, their desperate fury making up for their lack of training.

We might actually have a chance this time—

"Enough!" Jarek's voice cracks like a whip above the pandemonium. He draws his sword, the blade catching the moonlight as he moves like lightning toward Augustus. Suddenly the Plumber is on the ground, blood streaming from a gash in his arm. Sal tries to intervene but takes a kick to the ribs that sends her sprawling. Even Lozen with all her training can barely hold her own against Jarek in full battle rage. His blade slices the air in clean, merciless arcs as he holds off several villagers at once.

Now that I see the true extent of his skill, it terrifies me.

I'm searching for a weapon when a new fighter stumbles onto the scene, his movements sluggish but determined. *Gryphon*. The drugs I gave him have left him disoriented, but his eyes burn with purpose as he barrels toward his father.

"Stand down, boy," Jarek snarls. "You're in no condition to fight."

Gryphon answers with a wild swing that Jarek easily deflects, but it forces him to step back.

"You taught me to never stand down," Gryphon says, slurring his words, pushing farther forward. "To never show weakness." Another swing, this one better coordinated. The words that follow are a little clearer. "Guess the lesson stuck."

I try to circle Jarek while he's distracted, looking for something I can use as a bo staff, but one of his remaining Guardians blocks my path. Behind us, I can hear the chilling, leathery *shush* of the Verdant Beast's vines creeping closer.

"You disappoint me," Jarek tells his son, parrying another attack as Gryphon drives him closer to Eden's Gate. "I thought you were stronger than this. Thought you understood what needed to be done to survive."

"Survival isn't enough!" Gryphon shouts. His next strike draws blood, a thin line across Jarek's cheek. "You taught me that, too. You taught me to conquer, to dominate. But you never taught me to *live*."

I think Gryphon might stand a chance if he had all his faculties, but he overplays his hand. His next swing goes wide, and Jarek raises his blade for the killing strike.

"No!" I scream.

A flash of movement catches my eye. Misia had been fighting off the Verdant Beast but she turns at her son's need, a knife gleaming in her hand. She moves with the silent grace of someone who's spent years making herself invisible, reaching Jarek's side before he senses her presence. Her blade slides between his ribs, not deep enough to kill but enough to make him howl in fury.

"My wife," he growls, whipping around to face her. "Finally showing your true colors."

"My true colors?" Misia's laugh is as bitter as winter wind. "You never saw my colors *at all*. You only saw what you wanted to see. A vessel for your own ambition."

If she'd hoped that would slow him, she banked wrong. Jarek attacks with renewed fury, driving both Misia and Gryphon back. The two of them fight together beautifully, mother and son moving in tandem, but it's not enough. Jarek is too skilled, too strong. And despite it all, they don't *want* to hurt him. I see the moment it starts to go wrong. Gryphon stumbles, the drugs still clouding his reflexes. Misia moves to protect him, leaving herself open. Jarek's blade arcs through the air—

I don't think. I just move, launching myself at Jarek. I feel the slap of steel against my side as his blade comes down at an angle, sparing my life. Still, the pain is immediate and intense, and I instinctively roll away. Lozen appears beside me, helping me to my feet while Sal and Augustus move to protect me. Oscar, Meryl, and Eero soon follow. The nearest villagers form a half circle around us, armed with tools and makeshift weapons. Gryphon and Misia move to stand alongside them.

Jarek is suddenly outnumbered, his back to the Beast.

He swipes at the blood running down his side from Misia's wound, his face twisted with rage. He holds up his bloody fist. "ENOUGH!" he screams, voice echoing through the Valley, reverberating up the Wall. "I'll kill you all myself if I must. I'm the only one strong enough to—"

He never finishes the sentence.

A vine as thick as a tree trunk unfurls toward him, its barbs reaching like fingertips. It comes from behind, wrapping around Jarek's neck and lifting him off his feet. He slashes at it with his sword, but it only coils more of itself, cocooning him in a bristling, violet-green embrace.

"No!" he screams. "I am strong! I am—"

The vines contract.

There's a wet, popping sound. Jarek's blood rains down.

68

Perez charges toward us, his son, Leo, by his side. "Converge on the traitors!" Perez yells. "Strike them down!"

The standing Guardians, all but Misia, follow his command. They've been training for exactly this. Those of us he means to kill instinctually tighten our circle, our backs to one another. Sal to my left, Meryl beside him, then Lozen, Gryphon, Oscar, Augustus, and Eero. Eight of us against twice as many.

We begin moving as one toward the chapel.

I hear Boudicca trying to rally the remaining villagers in the square, perhaps vying for Jarek's position. "David Seingalt believes there are treasures beyond our wildest dreams outside the Wall—feasts and gold and splendor the likes of which we've only heard about in stories! And who would know, if not our Record Keeper?"

How ludicrous that must sound with the Verdant Beast actively consuming the corpses of their neighbors. But I feel another jolt at the mention of gold, even as we're fighting for our lives. I don't have time to linger on it. The three of us with weapons—Lozen, Gryphon, and Augustus—are swinging them, but we're being attacked from all sides.

"Retreat!" Gryphon commands.

We're following his order when a sword flashes. Meryl is

struck. I see her fall to the ground.

"Mer!" Sal screams. She lunges to protect her love, but she's weaponless. Lozen intercepts the blade poised for Sal and, in the same breath, anchors herself to defend Meryl. That leaves no choice for the rest of us—Sal included—but to stumble back into the narrow cobblestone alley.

The screech of Guardian steel cuts through the air. The acrid stench of blood and sweat burns my nostrils, and I can feel the rough stone scraping my shoulder as we press back, the tight space the only thing choking off their attempts to flank us. Gryphon and Augustus hold the line like twin wolves, all muscle and instinct, but I can see them both growing weary under the weight of so many. They can't keep fighting for much longer. Oscar's breath rasps, and Sal swears as Eero and I drag her away from the flashing swords.

"Stop fighting us," I hiss. "Meryl needs you alive, not dead on the street."

My palm burns where I've scraped it raw against the brick, steadying myself as we're herded like cattle down the narrowing alley. We're trapped. Where can you run to when you live in a prison, all the golden promises of harmony nothing but lies? I nearly gasp as it comes to me, clear this time, the thought that was scraping at me when Boudicca spoke back in the square.

The secret room in the Record Keeper vault. There's *goblin's gold* inside. And I think I know why.

"Retreat to the Record Keeper cottage!" I scream. "Through the library and into the vault!"

"The chapel is a more defensible location," Gryphon yells. "We should double back to it."

"The Record Keeper cottage!" I insist.

"We go, and we die," Gryphon hollers. "I need room to fight. I can protect you inside the chapel."

I put my hand on his back, which is soaked with sweat. "The Record Keeper cottage," I say. "You have to trust me."

Even from behind, I can see him tense. The others will follow him if he doesn't back down, and if they do, we're dead. Will he let me make this choice for us? Time seems to stand still, and then finally, he shouts. "To the Record Keeper cottage!"

Our friends react instantly. Eero, guiding a shell-shocked Salvatora, takes point. Oscar and I follow, and Gryphon and Augustus guard our retreat. The thunder of our footsteps blends with the clash of weapons. Still, we push forward until the Record Keeper cottage looms ahead. We slam into the door and shove it open, breathless and desperate. The six of us burst inside and wrench the door closed behind us just as the Guardians crash against it. Eero cleverly jams it with a chair. It'll buy us seconds.

Books blur past as we race through the library and toward the open basement door. Somewhere along the line I've ripped my stitches, and I'm leaving a trail of blood on the polished floor. I hope to the Wall and the Sun and the Water that my guess is right. Because if it's not, I'm leading my friends to certain death. We scramble through the doorway, our footbeats echoing on the seventeen steps as we descend.

Behind us, the library door splinters open with a violent crack. "They're inside!" Augustus shouts, racing back up the basement stairs, metal pipe raised. "Go! I'll hold them off!"

"Augustus, no—" I yell. I see it happen as if in slow motion. Beautiful, fierce Augustus, wielding his length of pipe like a scythe. The first two Guardians to breach the top of the stairs fall, but there are more right behind them. Leo's blade catches the light, then comes down.

Blood sprays across the stone walls.

My scream echoes. Strong arms drag me back—Gryphon, pulling me away as the Plumber's body crumples. I think of Wendy, knowing too well the grief that's soon to follow. I turn to see Sal looking wildly in every direction, searching the scroll-filled room for an exit, a weapon, any reason I would have led us down here to die like trapped rats.

"I hope you know what you're doing," she says. There's no anger in her tone, only fear.

"Through here," I say, finding the same indentation I saw David press to reveal the warden's panic room. Boots hammer the stairs, Guardians leaping past Augustus. The bookcase flies open, and we rush into the huge secret room behind it. It's gutted of goods. Either Jarek or the Record Keeper moved them, but it doesn't matter. That's not what we're here for.

And we're not alone.

69

Sal and Oscar succeed in shutting the bookcase behind us, but it's only a matter of time until the Guardians break through it.

But I have eyes only for David.

He leans against the far wall, wearing a funny little smile.

"You figured out where the exit is, too?" He raps the stone behind him with his knuckles. "I heard it starting to shift, or I fear I never would have located it. I'll share the treasure on the other side. You can have half—Suns, more. Just let me come with you."

The Guardians snarl and pound at the bookshelf, hunting for a way to get to us.

"You're a fool," I say to David. "It's not going to open to treasure."

His face twitches. "You don't know that."

My eyes catch on the goblin's gold near his feet. It needs a damp environment to grow, but this basement has a dehumidifying machine. It must be getting moisture through cracks in the wall invisible to the naked eye. I should have realized that when I first noticed the moss, but I'd been too deep in grief and shock and overwhelm.

"This isn't an extension of her secret vault," I say, stepping closer, eyes on the moss. Greed has blinded David to the obvious. "Why would she put treasure beyond her own reach? It's the exit

Korr was required to build, nothing more."

His mask slips, revealing the rot beneath. "Whatever it is, it's mine," he hisses, pulling a knife from his belt.

Before I can react, Gryphon leaps forward and pinches David's neck. The Record Keeper crashes to the floor, just as a tremor nearly knocks us all off our feet. Cracks splinter across the ceiling tiles.

Holy Sun.

"It's opening!" Eero yells.

My heart pounds my ribs hard enough to bruise. The seemingly unbroken wall hisses, then begins to slide open with a deep, mechanical exhale. A smell washes over us, alien and indescribable. Not good, not bad, but...different.

The bookcase explodes as David's pruno still flies through it. The Guardians have used it as a battering ram. We're out of time.

"Come on!" I shout.

I yank Eero into the darkness with me, noting a lever just inside the entrance. Oscar grabs Sal's arm, pulling them both through. Gryphon is the last to enter, backing toward us with his sword raised to fend off the Guardians surging through the breach. Steel screams when his blade meets the first attacker. He's almost inside the chamber—just two more steps and I can slam the lever down—when Leo launches himself out of the blur of bodies and drives his foot into Gryphon's gut. Gryphon stumbles, his guard dropping for a heartbeat.

"Gryphon!" I scream, but Leo is already raising his sword for a killing blow.

Oscar and Eero move before I can, flying at Leo as one, their small frames crashing into the man. All three tumble together, Eero and Oscar's fists flying wildly. But they're no match for a trained Guardian. Leo shoves Eero away and rolls on top of Oscar, pinning the boy's shoulders to the stone floor. Leo's sword gleams as he lifts it high above Oscar's chest at the same time as a mechanical whirring fills the air, growing louder, closer.

Albert's wheelchair shoots through the shattered bookshelf, tears streaming down his face as he screams wordlessly. He slams into Leonidas with a thud, sending him sprawling. Without slowing, he spins and rockets toward a second Guardian locked in combat with Gryphon, catching the Guardian square in the back. The impact ricochets Albert and Gryphon into the chamber alongside Sal and me, Albert's chair catching and releasing the lever.

With a screech that cuts through the chaos, the door begins to slide closed. Leo scrambles to his feet, his eyes catching mine in a flash of hate and shock. He surges forward just as the passage seals shut, his outstretched blade scraping against the stone.

There is a moment of darkness, then a single, dim light flicks on at our feet.

I throw myself at the door, digging into the crack until my fingernails peel back. *Oscar and Eero are on the other side. There must be a way to save them.* I find the lever and tug on it. I'm answered by a bone-deep scraping noise, low and threatening. I stumble back, expecting the door to open, but instead, the walls shake, the stone trembling beneath our feet. With a grinding roar, the ceiling begins to drop.

"Get away from the door!" I yell, grabbing the nearest hand. "Now!"

We dive into blackness, the tunnel behind us shrieking as it collapses. A fist-sized chunk of ceiling glances off my shoulder. I bite down a cry and taste blood. Gryphon's hand is in mine, or maybe it's Sal's—I can't see. My lungs burn with each breath of debris-thick air, and somewhere behind me, Albert is shouting for us to move faster, but my legs feel like water and the ground keeps shifting. I don't know if we're escaping or being buried alive.

Almost as soon as it starts, it stops.

Light blooms.

Weak, flickering points sputter to life along the walls, just like the one at the entrance. They're unlike any illumination I've ever seen, neither flame nor bulb, casting shadows that dance across stone. They provide enough light to show that the direction we came from is now an impassable pile of rock. Blinding dust hangs thick in the air, making my throat tight.

"Is anyone hurt?" I ask. It's a ridiculous question. Each one of us is shattered. Albert is grieving his mother, Gryphon his father, even if he might deny it. We had to leave Meryl, Eero, Lozen, and Oscar behind.

"I don't see a ventilation system," Albert says, anxiety tightening his voice. "This area wasn't made for lingering."

The four of us look at one another, then to the only path available to us—the one leading into the unknown. I'm overcome with both dread and sadness. We've been confined to Noah's Valley for generations, and now, we have no choice but to leave. Our eyes meet again, and we exchange a look of silent agreement.

Then we turn our backs on everything we've ever called home.

70

Sal and Albert lead the way. Gryphon steadies me, and I start moving, my chest tight with unshed tears. Eero and Oscar might still be alive. Same with Lozen, Meryl, my gran, Aunt Florence, and Marie. I didn't see any of them die. We may all meet again. I have to believe it.

We walk. And walk. And walk.

The tunnel stretches before us like a wound in the earth. Wooden support beams line the walls at regular intervals, ancient timber groaning beneath their weight. Our footsteps echo on rails that run along the ground, metal like the mining tracks in the history books, gleaming dully in the strange illumination. Those odd lights continue their steady progression along the walls, coming to life just ahead of us and dying behind us, as if the tunnel itself is guiding us forward. The air grows colder, carries new smells. Mossy, sharp.

The only sounds are the hollow thud of our footsteps and our labored breathing. The tunnel seems endless, stretching to infinity. Eventually time loses meaning. We could have been walking for hours or days.

And then, without warning, it ends.

The final lights flick on to reveal a door rising before us, a monolith of gleaming metal. No handle, no hinges, just a smooth silver-gray surface marked with strange symbols that seem to shift when I look at them directly. A red light pulses near its center like a dying heart.

"What's on the other side?" Sal whispers.

None of us, not even Albert, has a guess.

At our approach, the door hisses open.

All our lives spent inside the Wall, and suddenly there's an exit. Sal puts one hand on Albert's shoulder and offers the other to me. I take it, grabbing Gryphon with my free hand. We enter the new world side by side.

71

Overhead are more stars than we've ever seen. They wheel above us in an endless black sea, breathtaking and overwhelming.

"By the Soil," Sal whispers beside me, her fierce composure cracking as she takes in the vastness. No Wall. No boundaries. Just sky forever.

We stand at the edge of a clearing. It's ringed by thick, dry underbrush, and beyond that, trees. They resemble our hardwoods but a click off, wide where they should be tall, their branches misshapen in the moonlight. The way their skeleton fingers reach skyward, I can't tell if they're dead or alive. The grass underfoot is wild, untamed, growing in defiant clumps between crumbling sheets of what look like stone roads.

Our footsteps sound liquid out here, both muffled and overloud. Or maybe that's just the blood pounding in my eardrums. I take a trembling breath. I'm not sure what to feel. Shock? Grief? Hope?

I force myself to turn around, to face the Wall that's defined my entire existence. In the moonlight, it's both more and less impressive, a massive curve of stone that stretches up into the starlit sky. And clinging to the surface, its body pulsing with an obscene, sickening rhythm, is the Verdant Beast.

On this side of the Wall, the monster is tinted completely violet. I can see straight through parts of its translucent flesh, to where dark shapes move within its digestive chambers, their forms still recognizably human. A hand presses against the membrane, fingers splayed like a final plea. My body lurches forward, but Sal's arm snaps out, stopping me cold. She shakes her head once, her eyes two pools of sorrow. The Beast is too large, too hungry.

Something cracks open inside me then—not grief, but rage. Cold and sharp and absolute. The Verdant Beast has been built to consume. It will go on feeding, swallowing my friends and family one by one. But I will find a way to destroy it. I will save those trapped inside the Wall.

That's when a light reflecting off the clouds catches my eye.

The others see it, too. We make our way through the ruins, following the cracked pathway up a hill. We pass rusted hulks of ancient machines half-buried in the earth, being slowly devoured by time and creeping vines. This greenery looks blessedly normal compared to what we've left behind, but still I have no love for it.

We reach a high ridge. Everything appears flat and gray under a bruised-black sky. For a second, I think there's nothing out there, just foggy emptiness, like the land itself gave up.

Then, the wind shifts, clearing the fog.

72

A massive vineyard stretches below.

The crop reminds me of the hops I grew in my greenhouse, only monstrous, stretched across soaring trellises that march beneath the moon in cold, geometric lines. Something about the image makes my skin crawl, and I suppress a shudder.

The wind picks up again, curling around us like a breath, and more of the truth comes into view.

By the Sun and the Water. The massive plants aren't hops—they're writhing Verdant Beasts, their vines seeking sky and soil. Tens of them, maybe hundreds, are arranged in orderly rows like crops in a field. Each one's swollen to enormous size, their corpulent bodies shaded purple.

A walled settlement lies at the base of each. From this distance, they look about half the size of Noah's Valley, some of them so close their walls are nearly touching.

Bile burns my throat as the horrible truth crashes over me: It's a farm for the Verdant Beasts.

My mouth tastes of metal. I want to scream, to tear the sky open with my rage at the layers of lies I've been forced to accept, when I notice that the light that drew us up this hill is coming from the center of the field of Beasts. It's glowing white, an unblinking beacon.

Gryphon's hand finds mine. Solid. Warm. Real.

"Rose," he says quietly, pointing down. "Look."

I pull my gaze to the ground. Just ahead, arranged in weathered stones, an arrow points toward the white light. At its tip sits a tiny wooden rabbit carved by a boy who would have been a wonderful toymaker, if only the Valley had allowed it.

Jonas.

THE HOUSES OF NOAH'S VALLEY

ARTIST
House name: Bingen
Name source: Hildegard of Bingen
Symbol: tattoo gun crossed with paintbrush

ANIMAL FARMER (TWO HOUSES)

HOUSE ONE
House name: Grandin
Name source: Temple Grandin

HOUSE TWO
House name: Cavendish
Name source: Margaret Cavendish
Symbol: crossed shepherd's crooks

APOTHECARY
House name: Allgood
Name source: A functional name reflecting the House's purpose, i.e., to return the body to balance, to make "all good."
Symbol: Rod of Asclepius

ASTRONOMER
House name: Sagan
Name source: Carl Sagan
Symbol: star

BAKER
House name: Beard
Name source: James Beard
Symbol: pretzel

BEEKEEPER
House name: Crane
Name source: Eva Crane
Symbol: honeycomb cell

BLACKSMITH
House name: Brim
Name source: Elizabeth Brim
Symbol: anvil

BUTCHER
House name: Hemings
Name source: Simon Hemings
Symbol: cleaver

CANDLEMAKER
House name: Lumen
Name source: Latin word for light
Symbol: candle

CARPENTER
House name: Nakashima
Name source: George Nakashima
Symbol: hammer

CHEMIST
House name: Franklin
Name source: Rosalind Franklin
Symbol: the alchemical symbol for mercury

COBBLER
House name: Brogan
Name source: brogan (n.), a heavy shoe
Symbol: winged sandal

COOPER
House name: Hoop
Name source: a reference to the metal bands used to shape barrels
Symbol: barrel

CRIER
House name: Revere
Name source: Paul Revere
Symbol: bell

CROP FARMER (THREE HOUSES)

HOUSE ONE
House name: Huerta
Name source: Dolores Huerta

HOUSE TWO
House name: Carter
Name source: Jimmy Carter

HOUSE THREE
House name: LaDuke
Name source: Winona LaDuke
Symbol: wheat stalk

DENTIST
House name: Taylor
Name source: Lucy Hobbs Taylor
Symbol: tooth

ENGINEER
House name: Bell
Name source: Alexander Graham Bell
Symbol: single gear

ENTERTAINER
House name: Redgrave
Name source: the Redgrave family, a British acting dynasty spanning five generations
Symbol: comedy and tragedy masks

FERMENTER
House name: Koji
Name source: Japanese origin; a substance to promote fermentation
Symbol: three bubbles

FISHER
House name: Cousteau
Name source: Jacques Cousteau
Symbol: fish

FORESTER
House name: Wangari
Name source: Wangari Maathai
Symbol: fir tree

Glassworker
House name: Chihuly
Name source: Dale Chihuly
Symbol: bottle

Guardian (five Houses)

House One
House name: Tzu
Name source: Sun Tzu

House Two
House name: Zenobia
Name source: Septimia Zenobia

House Three
House name: Cynane
Name source: Cynane of Macedon

House Four
House name: Caesar
Name source: Julius Caesar

House Five
House name: Khan
Name source: Kublai Khan
Symbol: three short lines below the left eye

Insect Farmer
House name: Merian
Name source: Maria Sibylla Merian
Symbol: ant

Leatherworker
House name: New
Name source: Lloyd Kiva New
Symbol: awl

Mason
House name: Yevele
Name source: Henry Yevele
Symbol: mason's trowel

Miller
House name: Bedstone
Name source: the lower, stationary millstone in a grain mill
Symbol: fer-de-moline

Minstrel
House name: Turner
Name source: Tina Turner
Symbol: musical note

Plumber
House name: Auger
Name source: a tool for clearing blocked pipes
Symbol: pipe wrench

Potter
House name: Martinez
Name source: Maria Poveka Montoya Martinez
Symbol: ribbon tool

Priest
House name: Confucius
Name source: Confucius
Symbol: cross

Record Keeper
House name: Seingalt
Name source: Giacomo Chevalier De Seingalt Casanova
Symbol: quill pen

Roofer
House name: Sinan
Name source: Mimar Sinan
Symbol: inverted v (a roof)

Ropemaker
House name: Burfield
Name source: Thomas Burfield
Symbol: figure 8

Tailor
House name: Dior
Name source: Christian Dior
Symbol: needle and thread

Teacher
House name: Washington
Name source: Booker T. Washington
Symbol: abc

Waste Manager
House name: Bazalgette
Name source: Joseph Bazalgette
Symbol: recycle symbol

Weaver
House name: Chel
Name source: Ix Chel
Symbol: hanging textile

Acknowledgments

The Verdant Cage would not have been possible without The Pelletier Women™. When I first came to Liz with the idea for the book, she spent hours helping me to expand on and refine it and has offered me boundless insight since. After I'd drafted the novel and was assigned Madison as an editor, I thought, "Well, there's no way they're *both* creative geniuses." Dear reader, you don't know the half of it. Madison took my worldbuilding and writing to the next level and was an absolute joy to work with (and to talk foster kittens and birds with). Eternal gratitude to both Liz and Madison for sharing their vision, warmth, and unparalleled eye for story.

Thank you also to the people working behind the scenes to make this book possible: Deon for keeping it all on track; Heather for being the glue; Victoria, Melanie, Meredith, Cai, Lindsey, and Hannah at Entangled and Grace and Rylee at BookSparks for being the best publicity and marketing team I could ask for; Curtis for production; Britt for formatting; Elizabeth and Bree for doing such a wonderful job with the book layout and those gorgeous inner pages; Becca, Jessica, and Hannah for their editing; and all the early readers for their helpful feedback. A special thanks to Liz Wayant for creating the absolutely stunning cover art.

Jill Marsal, your support throughout this project has been crucial, starting with negotiating the deal and then all the emotional shoring up since. Speaking of emotional shoring, Erica Ruth Neubauer, Shannon Baker, Carolyn Crooke, Kristi Belcamino, Sarah Stonich, Rachel Howzell Hall, and Matt Goldman, your therapy payment is coming your way. I treasure the time we write together, but even more, I treasure our download sessions. And big love to Christine Hollermann, a magnificent travel partner and person.

I'd be remiss not to thank the libraries and bookstores that make my career possible and that have provided me thousands of hours of escape, connection, and joy. If you're lucky enough to have either a bookstore or a library nearby, please visit it when you can. They're the cornerstones of our communities.

And finally, to my beautiful babies, Zoë and Xander: thank you for magnifying all the good in the world. Your momma loves you to the moon and back.